A Far Country

Winston Churchill

Sheba Blake Publishing Corp.

Contents

Part One

Chapter One

My name is Hugh Paret. I was a corporation lawyer, but by no means a typical one, the choice of my profession being merely incidental, and due, as will be seen, to the accident of environment. The book I am about to write might aptly be called The Autobiography of a Romanticist. In that sense, if in no other, I have been a typical American, regarding my country as the happy hunting-ground of enlightened self-interest, as a function of my desires. Whether or not I have completely got rid of this romantic virus I must leave to those the aim of whose existence is to eradicate it from our literature and our life. A somewhat Augean task!

I have been impelled therefore to make an attempt at setting forth, with what frankness and sincerity I may, with those powers of selection of which I am capable, the life I have lived in this modern America; the passions I have known, the evils I have done. I endeavour to write a biography of the inner life; but in order to do this I shall have to relate those causal experiences of the outer existence that take place in the world of space and time, in the four walls of the home, in the school and university, in the noisy streets, in the realm of business and politics. I shall try to set down, impartially, the motives that have impelled my actions, to reveal in some degree the amazing mixture of good and evil which has made me what I am to-day: to avoid the tricks of memory and resist the inherent desire to present myself other and better than I am. Your American romanticist is a sentimental spoiled child who believes in miracles, whose needs are mostly baubles, whose desires are dreams. Expediency is his motto. Innocent of a knowledge of the principles of the universe, he lives in a state of ceaseless activity, admitting no limitations, impatient of all restrictions.

What he wants, he wants very badly indeed. This wanting things was the corner-stone of my character, and I believe that the science of the future will bear me out when I say that it might have been differently built upon. Certain it is that the system of education in vogue in the 70's and 80's never contemplated the search for natural corner-stones.

At all events, when I look back upon the boy I was, I see the beginnings of a real person who fades little by little as manhood arrives and advances, until suddenly I am aware that a stranger has taken his place....

I lived in a city which is now some twelve hours distant from the Atlantic seaboard. A very different city, too, it was in youth, in my grandfather's day and my father's, even in my own boyhood, from what it has since become in this most material of ages.

There is a book of my photographs, preserved by my mother, which I have been looking over lately. First is presented a plump child of two, gazing in smiling trustfulness upon a world of sunshine; later on a lean boy in plaided kilts, whose wavy, chestnut-brown hair has been most carefully parted on the side by Norah, his nurse. The face is still childish. Then appears a youth of fourteen or thereabout in long trousers and the queerest of short jackets, standing beside a marble table against a classic background; he is smiling still in undiminished hope and trust, despite increasing vexations and crossings, meaningless lessons which had to be learned, disciplines to rack an aspiring soul, and long, uncomfortable hours in the stiff pew of the First Presbyterian Church. Associated with this torture is a peculiar Sunday smell and the faint rustling of silk dresses. I can see the stern black figure of Dr. Pound, who made interminable statements to the Lord.

"Oh, Lord," I can hear him say, "thou knowest..."

These pictures, though yellowed and faded, suggest vividly the being I once was, the feelings that possessed and animated me, love for my playmates, vague impulses struggling for expression in a world forever thwarting them. I recall, too, innocent dreams of a future unidentified, dreams from which I emerged vibrating with an energy that was lost for lack of a definite objective: yet it was constantly being renewed. I often wonder what I might have become if it could have been harnessed, directed! Speculations are vain. Calvinism, though it had begun to make compromises, was still a force in those days, inimical to spontaneity and human instincts. And when I think of Calvinism I see, not Dr. Pound, who preached it, but my father, who practised and embodied it. I loved him, but he made of righteousness a stern and terrible thing implying not joy, but punishment, the, suppression rather than the expansion of aspirations. His religion seemed woven all of austerity, contained no shining threads to catch my eye. Dreams, to him, were matters for suspicion and distrust.

I sometimes ask myself, as I gaze upon his portrait now, the duplicate of the one painted for the Bar Association, whether he ever could have felt the secret, hot thrills I knew and did not identify with religion. His religion was real to him, though he failed utterly to make it comprehensible to me. The apparent calmness, evenness of his life awed me. A successful lawyer, a respected and trusted citizen, was he lacking somewhat in virility, vitality? I cannot judge him, even to-day. I never knew him. There were times in my youth when the curtain of his unfamiliar spirit was withdrawn a little: and once, after I had passed the crisis of some childhood disease, I awoke to find him bending over my bed with a tender expression that surprised and puzzled me.

He was well educated, and from his portrait a shrewd observer might divine in him a genteel taste for literature. The fine features bear witness to the influence of an American environment, yet suggest the intellectual Englishman of Matthew Arnold's time. The face is distinguished, ascetic, the chestnut hair lighter and thinner than my own; the side whiskers are not too obtrusive, the eyes blue-grey. There is a large black cravat crossed and held by a cameo pin, and the coat has odd, narrow lapels. His habits of mind were English, although he harmonized well enough with the manners and traditions of a city whose inheritance was Scotch-Irish; and he invariably drank tea for breakfast. One of my earliest recollections is of the silver breakfast service and egg-cups which my great-grandfather brought with him from Sheffield to Philadelphia shortly after the Revolution. His son, Dr. Hugh Moreton Paret, after whom I was named, was the best known physician of the city in the decorous, Second Bank days.

My mother was Sarah Breck. Hers was my Scotch-Irish side. Old Benjamin Breck, her grandfather, undaunted by sea or wilderness, had come straight from Belfast to the little log settlement by the great river that mirrored then the mantle of primeval forest on the hills. So much for chance. He kept a store with a side porch and square-paned windows, where hams and sides of bacon and sugar loaves in blue glazed paper hung beside ploughs and calico prints, barrels of flour, of molasses and rum, all of which had been somehow marvellously transported over the passes of those forbidding mountains,—passes we blithely thread to-day in dining cars and compartment sleepers. Behind the store were moored the barges that floated down on the swift current to the Ohio, carrying goods to even remoter settlements in the western wilderness.

Benjamin, in addition to his emigrant's leather box, brought with him some of that pigment that was to dye the locality for generations a deep blue. I refer, of course, to his Presbyterianism. And in order the better to ensure to his progeny the fastness of this dye, he married the granddaughter of a famous divine, celebrated in the annals of New England,—no doubt with some injustice,—as a staunch advocate on the doctrine of infant damnation. My cousin Robert Breck had old Benjamin's portrait, which has since gone to the Kinley's. Heaven knows who painted it, though no great art were needed to suggest on canvas the tough fabric of that sitter, who was more Irish than Scotch. The heavy stick he holds might, with a slight stretch of the imagination, be a blackthorn; his head looks capable of withstanding many blows; his hand of giving many. And, as I gazed the other day at this picture hanging in the shabby suburban parlour, I could only contrast him with his anaemic descendants who possessed the likeness. Between the children of poor Mary Kinley,— Cousin Robert's daughter, and the hardy stock of the old country there is a gap indeed!

Benjamin Breck made the foundation of a fortune. It was his son who built on the Second Bank the wide, corniced mansion in which to house comfortably his eight children. There, two tiers above the river, lived my paternal grandfather, Dr. Paret, the Breck's physician and friend; the Durretts and the Hambletons, iron-masters; the Hollisters, Sherwins, the McAlerys and Ewanses,—Breck connections,—the Willetts and Ogilvys; in short, everyone of importance in the days between the 'thirties and the Civil War. Theirs were generous houses surrounded by shade trees, with glorious back yards—I have been told—where apricots and pears and peaches and even nectarines grew.

The business of Breck and Company, wholesale grocers, descended to my mother's first cousin, Robert Breck, who lived at Claremore. The very sound of that word once sufficed to give me a shiver of delight; but the Claremore I knew has disappeared as completely as Atlantis, and the place is now a suburb (hateful word!) cut up into building lots and connected with Boyne Street and the business section of the city by trolley lines. Then it was "the country," and fairly saturated with romance. Cousin Robert, when he came into town to spend his days at the store, brought with him some of this romance, I had almost said of this aroma. He was no suburbanite, but rural to the backbone, professing a most proper contempt for dwellers in towns.

Every summer day that dawned held Claremore as a possibility. And such was my capacity for joy that my appetite would depart completely when I heard my mother say, questioningly and with proper wifely respect

"If you're really going off on a business trip for a day or two, Mr. Paret" (she generally addressed my father thus formally), "I think I'll go to Robert's and take Hugh."

"Shall I tell Norah to pack, mother," I would exclaim, starting up.

"We'll see what your father thinks, my dear."

"Remain at the table until you are excused, Hugh," he would say.

Released at length, I would rush to Norah, who always rejoiced with me, and then to the wire fence which marked the boundary of the Peters domain next door, eager, with the refreshing lack of consideration characteristic of youth, to announce to the Peterses—who were to remain at home the news of my good fortune. There would be Tom and Alfred and Russell and Julia and little Myra with her grass-stained knees, faring forth to seek the adventures of a new day in the shady western yard. Myra was too young not to look wistful at my news, but the others pretended indifference, seeking to lessen my triumph. And it was Julia who invariably retorted "We can go out to Uncle Jake's farm whenever we want to. Can't we, Tom?"...

No journey ever taken since has equalled in ecstasy that leisurely trip of thirteen miles in the narrow-gauge railroad that wound through hot fields of nodding corn tassels and between delicious, acrid-smelling woods to Claremore. No silent palace "sleeping in the sun," no edifice decreed by Kubla Khan could have worn more glamour than the house of Cousin Robert Breck.

It stood half a mile from the drowsy village, deep in its own grounds amidst lawns splashed with shadows, with gravel paths edged—in barbarous fashion, if you please with shells. There were flower beds of equally barbarous design; and two iron deer, which, like the figures on Keats's Grecian urn, were ever ready poised to flee,—and yet never fled. For Cousin Robert was rich, as riches went in those days: not only rich, but comfortable. Stretching behind the house were sweet meadows of hay and red clover basking in the heat, orchards where the cows cropped beneath the trees, arbours where purple clusters of Concords hung beneath warm leaves: there were woods beyond, into which, under the guidance of Willie Breck, I made adventurous excursions, and in the autumn gathered hickories and walnuts. The house was a rambling, wooden mansion painted grey, with red scroll-work on its porches and horsehair furniture inside. Oh, the smell of its darkened interior on a midsummer day! Like the flavour of that choicest of tropical fruits, the mangosteen, it baffles analysis, and the nearest I can come to it is a mixture of matting and corn-bread, with another element too subtle to define.

The hospitality of that house! One would have thought we had arrived, my mother and I, from the ends of the earth, such was the welcome we got from Cousin Jenny, Cousin Robert's wife, from Mary and Helen with the flaxen pig-tails, from Willie, whom I recall as permanently without shoes or stockings. Met and embraced by Cousin Jenny at the station and driven to the house in the squeaky surrey, the moment we arrived she and my mother would put on the dressing-sacks I associated with hot weather, and sit sewing all day long in rocking-chairs at the coolest end of the piazza. The women of that day scorned lying down, except at night, and as evening came on they donned starched dresses; I recall in particular one my mother wore, with little vertical stripes of black and white, and a full skirt. And how they talked, from the beginning of the visit until the end! I have often since wondered where the topics came from.

It was not until nearly seven o'clock that the train arrived which brought home my Cousin Robert. He was a big man; his features and even his ample moustache gave a disconcerting impression of rugged integrity, and I remember him chiefly in an alpaca or seersucker coat. Though much less formal, more democratic—in a word—than my father, I stood in awe of him for a different reason, and this I know now was because he possessed the penetration to discern the flaws in my youthful character, —flaws that persisted in manhood. None so quick as Cousin Robert to detect deceptions which were hidden from my mother.

His hobby was carpentering, and he had a little shop beside the stable filled with shining tools which Willie and I, in spite of their attractions, were forbidden to touch. Willie, by dire experience, had learned to keep the law; but on one occasion I stole in alone, and promptly cut my finger with a chisel. My mother and Cousin Jenny accepted the fiction that the injury had been done with a flint arrowhead that Willie had given me, but when Cousin Robert came home and saw my bound hand and heard the story, he gave me a certain look which sticks in my mind.

"Wonderful people, those Indians were!" he observed. "They could make arrowheads as sharp as chisels."

I was most uncomfortable....

He had a strong voice, and spoke with a rising inflection and a marked accent that still remains peculiar to our locality, although it was much modified in my mother and not at all noticeable in my father; with an odd nasal alteration of the burr our Scotch-Irish ancestors had brought with them across the seas. For instance, he always called my father Mr. Par- r-ret. He had an admiration and respect for him that seemed to forbid the informality of "Matthew." It was shared by others of my father's friends and relations.

"Sarah," Cousin Robert would say to my mother, "you're coddling that boy, you ought to lam him oftener. Hand him over to me for a couple of months—I'll put him through his paces.... So you're going to send him to college, are you? He's too good for old Benjamin's grocery business."

He was very fond of my mother, though he lectured her soundly for her weakness in indulging me. I can see him as he sat at the head of the supper table, carving liberal helpings which Mary and Helen and Willie devoured with country appetites, watching our plates.

"What's the matter, Hugh? You haven't eaten all your lamb."

"He doesn't like fat, Robert," my mother explained.

"I'd teach him to like it if he were my boy."

"Well, Robert, he isn't your boy," Cousin Jenny would remind him.... His bark was worse than his bite. Like many kind people he made use of brusqueness to hide an inner tenderness, and on the train he was hail fellow well met with every Tom, Dick and Harry that commuted,—although the word was not invented in those days,—and the conductor and brakeman too. But he had his standards, and held to them....

Mine was not a questioning childhood, and I was willing to accept the scheme of things as presented to me entire. In my tenderer years, when I had broken one of the commandments on my father's tablet (there were more than ten), and had, on his home-coming, been sent to bed, my mother would come softly upstairs after supper with a book in her hand; a book of selected Bible stories on which Dr. Pound had set the seal of his approval, with a glazed picture cover, representing Daniel in the lions' den and an angel standing beside him. On the somewhat specious plea that Holy Writ might have a chastening effect, she was permitted to minister to me in my shame. The amazing adventure of Shadrach, Meshach and Abednego particularly appealed to an imagination needing little stimulation. It never occurred to me to doubt that these gentlemen had triumphed over caloric laws. But out of my window, at the back of the second storey, I often saw a sudden, crimson glow in the sky to the southward, as though that part of the city had caught fire.

There were the big steel-works, my mother told me, belonging to Mr. Durrett and Mr. Hambleton, the father of Ralph Hambleton and the grandfather of Hambleton Durrett, my schoolmates at Miss Caroline's. I invariably connected the glow, not with Hambleton and Ralph, but with Shadrach, Meshach and Abednego! Later on, when my father took me to the steel-works, and I beheld with awe a huge pot filled with molten metal that ran out of it like water, I asked him—if I leaped into that stream, could God save me? He was shocked. Miracles, he told me, didn't happen any more.

"When did they stop?" I demanded.

"About two thousand years ago, my son," he replied gravely.

"Then," said I, "no matter how much I believed in God, he wouldn't save me if I jumped into the big kettle for his sake?"

For this I was properly rebuked and silenced.

My boyhood was filled with obsessing desires. If God, for example, had cast down, out of his abundant store, manna and quail in the desert, why couldn't he fling me a little pocket money? A paltry quarter of a dollar, let us say, which to me represented wealth. To avoid the reproach of the Pharisees, I went into the closet of my bed-chamber to pray, requesting that the quarter should be dropped on the north side of Lyme Street, between Stamford and Tryon; in short, as conveniently near home as possible. Then I issued forth, not feeling overconfident, but hoping. Tom Peters, leaning over the ornamental cast-iron fence which separated his front yard from the street, presently spied me scanning the sidewalk.

"What are you looking for, Hugh?" he demanded with interest.

"Oh, something I dropped," I answered uneasily.

"What?"

Naturally, I refused to tell. It was a broiling, midsummer day; Julia and Russell, who had been warned to stay in the shade, but who were engaged in the experiment of throwing the yellow cat from the top of the lattice fence to see if she would alight on her feet, were presently attracted, and joined in the search. The mystery which I threw around it added to its interest, and I was not inconsiderably annoyed. Suppose one of them were to find the quarter which God had intended for me? Would that be justice?

"It's nothing," I said, and pretended to abandon the quest—to be renewed later. But this ruse failed; they continued obstinately to search; and after a few minutes Tom, with a shout, picked out of a hot crevice between the bricks—a nickel!

"It's mine!" I cried fiercely.

"Did you lose it?" demanded Julia, the canny one, as Tom was about to give it up.

My lying was generally reserved for my elders.

"N-no," I said hesitatingly, "but it's mine all the same. It was—sent to me."

"Sent to you!" they exclaimed, in a chorus of protest and derision. And how, indeed, was I to make good my claim? The Peterses, when assembled, were a clan, led by Julia and in matters of controversy, moved as one. How was I to tell them that in answer to my prayers for twenty-five cents, God had deemed five all that was good for me?

"Some—somebody dropped it there for me."

"Who?" demanded the chorus. "Say, that's a good one!"

Tears suddenly blinded me. Overcome by chagrin, I turned and flew into the house and upstairs into my room, locking the door behind me. An interval ensued, during which I nursed my sense of wrong, and it pleased me to think that the money would bring a curse on the Peters family. At length there came a knock on the door, and a voice calling my name.

"Hugh! Hugh!"

It was Tom.

"Hughie, won't you let me in? I want to give you the nickel."

"Keep it!" I shouted back. "You found it."

Another interval, and then more knocking.

"Open up," he said coaxingly. "I—I want to talk to you."

I relented, and let him in. He pressed the coin into my hand. I refused; he pleaded.

"You found it," I said, "it's yours."

"But—but you were looking for it."

"That makes no difference," I declared magnanimously.

Curiosity overcame him.

"Say, Hughie, if you didn't drop it, who on earth did?"

"Nobody on earth," I replied cryptically....

Naturally, I declined to reveal the secret. Nor was this by any means the only secret I held over the Peters family, who never quite knew what to make of me. They were not troubled with imaginations. Julia was a little older than Tom and had a sharp tongue, but over him I exercised a distinct fascination, and I knew it. Literal himself, good-natured and warm-hearted, the gift I had of tingeing life with romance (to put the thing optimistically), of creating kingdoms out of back yards—at which Julia and Russell sniffed—held his allegiance firm.

Chapter Two

I must have been about twelve years of age when I realized that I was possessed of the bard's inheritance. A momentous journey I made with my parents to Boston about this time not only stimulated this gift, but gave me the advantage of which other travellers before me have likewise availed themselves—of being able to take certain poetic liberties with a distant land that my friends at home had never seen. Often during the heat of summer noons when we were assembled under the big maple beside the lattice fence in the Peters' yard, the spirit would move me to relate the most amazing of adventures. Our train, for instance, had been held up in the night by a band of robbers in black masks, and rescued by a traveller who bore a striking resemblance to my Cousin Robert Breck. He had shot two of the robbers. These fabrications, once started, flowed from me with ridiculous ease. I experienced an unwonted exhilaration, exaltation; I began to believe that they had actually occurred. In vain the astute Julia asserted that there were no train robbers in the east. What had my father done? Well, he had been very brave, but he had had no pistol. Had I been frightened? No, not at all; I, too, had wished for a pistol. Why hadn't I spoken of this before? Well, so many things had happened to me I couldn't tell them all at once. It was plain that Julia, though often fascinated against her will, deemed this sort of thing distinctly immoral.

I was a boy divided in two. One part of me dwelt in a fanciful realm of his own weaving, and the other part was a commonplace and protesting inhabitant of a world of lessons, disappointments and discipline. My instincts were not vicious. Ideas bubbled up within me continually from an apparently inexhaustible spring, and the very strength of the longings they set in motion puzzled and troubled my parents: what I seem to see most distinctly now is a young mind engaged in a ceaseless struggle for self-expression, for self-development, against the inertia of a tradition of which my father was the embodiment. He was an enigma to me then. He sincerely loved me, he cherished ambitions concerning me, yet thwarted every natural, budding growth, until I grew unconsciously to regard him as my enemy, although I had an affection for him and a pride in him that flared up at times. Instead of confiding to him my aspirations, vague though they were, I became more and more secretive as I grew older. I knew instinctively that he regarded these aspirations as evidences in my character of serious moral flaws. And I would sooner have suffered many afternoons of his favourite punishment—solitary confinement in my room— than reveal to him those occasional fits of creative fancy which caused me to neglect my lessons in order to put them on paper. Loving literature, in his way, he was characteristically incapable of recognizing the literary instinct, and the symptoms of its early stages he mistook for inherent frivolity, for lack of respect for the truth; in brief, for original sin. At the age of fourteen I had begun secretly (alas, how many things I did secretly!) to write stories of a sort, stories that never were finished.

He regarded reading as duty, not pleasure. He laid out books for me, which I neglected. He was part and parcel of that American environment in which literary ambition was regarded as sheer madness. And no one who has not experienced that environment can have any conception of the pressure it exerted to stifle originality, to thrust the new generation into its religious and commercial moulds. Shall we ever, I wonder, develop the enlightened education that will know how to take advantage of such initiative as was mine? that will be on the watch for it, sympathize with it and guide it to fruition?

I was conscious of still another creative need, that of dramatizing my ideas, of converting them into action. And this need was to lead me farther than ever afield from the path of righteousness. The concrete realization of ideas, as many geniuses will testify, is an expensive undertaking, requiring a little pocket money; and I have already touched upon that subject. My father did not believe in pocket money. A sea story that my Cousin Donald Ewan gave me at Christmas inspired me to compose one of a somewhat different nature; incidentally, I deemed it a vast improvement on Cousin Donald's book. Now, if I only had a boat, with the assistance of Ham Durrett and Tom Peters, Gene Hollister and Perry Blackwood and other friends, this story of mine might be staged. There were, however, as usual, certain seemingly insuperable difficulties: in the first place, it was winter time; in the second, no facilities existed in the city for operations of a nautical character; and, lastly, my Christmas money amounted only to five dollars. It was my father who pointed out these and other objections. For, after a careful perusal of the price lists I had sent for, I had been forced to appeal to him to supply additional funds with which to purchase a row- boat. Incidentally, he read me a lecture on extravagance, referred to my last month's report at the Academy, and finished by declaring that he would not permit me to have a boat even in the highly improbable case of somebody's presenting me with one. Let it not be imagined that my ardour or my determination were extinguished. Shortly after I had retired from his presence it occurred to me that he had said nothing to forbid my making a boat, and the first thing I did after school that day was to procure, for twenty-five cents, a second-hand book on boat construction. The woodshed was chosen as a shipbuilding establishment. It was convenient—and my father never went into the back yard in cold weather. Inquiries of lumber-yards developing the disconcerting fact that four dollars and seventy-five cents was inadequate to buy the material itself, to say nothing of the cost of steaming and bending the ribs, I reluctantly abandoned the ideal of the graceful craft I had sketched, and compromised on a flat bottom. Observe how the ways of deception lead to transgression: I recalled the cast-off lumber pile of Jarvis, the carpenter, a good-natured Englishman, coarse and fat: in our neighbourhood his reputation for obscenity was so well known to mothers that I had been forbidden to go near him or his shop. Grits Jarvis, his son, who had inherited the talent, was also contraband. I can see now the huge bulk of the elder Jarvis as he stood in the melting, soot- powdered snow in front of his shop, and hear his comments on my pertinacity.

"If you ever wants another man's missus when you grows up, my lad, Gawd 'elp 'im!"

"Why should I want another man's wife when I don't want one of my own?" I demanded, indignant.

He laughed with his customary lack of moderation.

"You mind what old Jarvis says," he cried. "What you wants, you gets."

I did get his boards, by sheer insistence. No doubt they were not very valuable, and without question he more than made up for them in my mother's bill. I also got something else of equal value to me at the moment,—the assistance of Grits, the contraband; daily, after school, I smuggled him into the shed through the alley, acquiring likewise the services of Tom Peters, which was more of a triumph than it would seem. Tom always had to be "worked up" to participation in my ideas, but in the end he almost invariably succumbed. The notion of building a boat in the dead of winter, and so far from her native element, naturally struck him at first as ridiculous. Where in Jehoshaphat was I going to sail it if I ever got it made? He much preferred to throw snowballs at innocent wagon drivers.

All that Tom saw, at first, was a dirty, coal-spattered shed with dim recesses, for it was lighted on one side only, and its temperature was somewhere below freezing. Surely he could not be blamed for a tempered enthusiasm! But for me, all the dirt and cold and discomfort were blotted out, and I beheld a gallant craft manned by sturdy seamen forging her way across blue water in the South Seas. Treasure Island, alas, was as yet unwritten; but among my father's books were two old volumes in which I had hitherto taken no interest, with crude engravings of palms and coral reefs, of naked savages and tropical mountains covered with jungle, the adventures, in brief, of one Captain Cook. I also discovered a book by a later traveller. Spurred on by a mysterious motive power, and to the great neglect of the pons asinorum and the staple products of the Southern States, I gathered an amazing amount of information concerning a remote portion of the globe, of head-hunters and poisoned stakes, of typhoons, of queer war-craft that crept up on you while you were dismantling galleons, when desperate hand-to-hand encounters ensued. Little by little as I wove all this into personal adventures soon to be realized, Tom forgot the snowballs and the maddened grocery-men who chased him around the block; while Grits would occasionally stop sawing and cry out:—

"Ah, s'y!" frequently adding that he would be G—d—d.

The cold woodshed became a chantry on the New England coast, the alley the wintry sea soon to embrace our ship, the saw-horses—which stood between a coal-bin on one side and unused stalls filled with rubbish and kindling on the other—the ways; the yard behind the lattice fence became a backwater, the flapping clothes the sails of ships that took refuge there—on Mondays and Tuesdays. Even my father was symbolized with unparalleled audacity as a watchful government which had, up to the present, no inkling of our semi-piratical intentions! The cook and the housemaid, though remonstrating against the presence of Grits, were friendly confederates; likewise old Cephas, the darkey who, from my earliest memory, carried coal and wood and blacked the shoes, washed the windows and scrubbed the steps.

One afternoon Tom went to work....

The history of the building of the good ship Petrel is similar to that of all created things, a story of trial and error and waste. At last, one March day she stood ready for launching. She had even been caulked; for Grits, from an unknown and unquestionably dubious source, had procured a bucket of tar, which we heated over afire in the alley and smeared into every crack. It was natural that the news of such a feat as we were accomplishing should have leaked out, that the "yard" should have been visited from time to time by interested friends, some of whom came to admire, some to scoff, and all to speculate. Among the scoffers, of course, was Ralph Hambleton, who stood with his hands in his pockets and cheerfully predicted all sorts of dire calamities. Ralph was always a superior boy, tall and a trifle saturnine and cynical, with an amazing self-confidence not wholly due to the wealth of his father, the iron- master. He was older than I.

"She won't float five minutes, if you ever get her to the water," was his comment, and in this he was supported on general principles by Julia and Russell Peters. Ralph would have none of the Petrel, or of the South Seas either; but he wanted,—so he said,—"to be in at the death." The Hambletons were one of the few families who at that time went to the sea for the summer, and from a practical knowledge of craft in general Ralph was not slow to point out the defects of ours. Tom and I defended her passionately.

Ralph was not a romanticist. He was a born leader, excelling at organized games, exercising over boys the sort of fascination that comes from doing everything better and more easily than others. It was only during the progress of such enterprises as this affair of the Petrel that I succeeded in winning their allegiance; bit by bit, as Tom's had been won, fanning their enthusiasm by impersonating at once Achilles and Homer, recruiting while relating the Odyssey of the expedition in glowing colours. Ralph always scoffed, and when I had no scheme on foot they went back to him. Having surveyed the boat and predicted calamity, he departed, leaving a circle of quaint and youthful figures around the Petrel in the shed: Gene Hollister, romantically inclined, yet somewhat hampered by a strict parental supervision; Ralph's cousin Ham Durrett, who was even then a rather fat boy, good-natured but selfish; Don and Harry Ewan, my second cousins; Mac and Nancy Willett and Sam and Sophy McAlery. Nancy was a tomboy, not to be denied, and Sophy her shadow. We held a council, the all-important question of which was how to get the Petrel to the water, and what water to get her to. The river was not to be thought of, and Blackstone Lake some six miles from town. Finally, Logan's mill-pond was decided on,—a muddy sheet on the outskirts of the city. But how to get her to Logan's mill-pond?

Cephas was at length consulted. It turned out that he had a coloured friend who went by the impressive name of Thomas Jefferson Taliaferro (pronounced Tolliver), who was in the express business; and who, after surveying the boat with some misgivings,—for she was ten feet long,—finally consented to transport her to "tide-water" for the sum of two dollars. But it proved that our combined resources only amounted to a dollar and seventy-five cents. Ham Durrett never contributed to anything. On this sum Thomas Jefferson compromised.

Saturday dawned clear, with a stiff March wind catching up the dust into eddies and whirling it down the street. No sooner was my father safely on his way to his office than Thomas Jefferson was reported to be in the alley, where we assembled, surveying with some misgivings Thomas Jefferson's steed, whose ability to haul the Petrel two miles seemed somewhat doubtful. Other difficulties developed; the door in the back of the shed proved to be too narrow for our ship's beam. But men embarked on a desperate enterprise are not to be stopped by such trifles, and the problem was solved by sawing out two adjoining boards. These were afterwards replaced with skill by the ship's carpenter, Able Seaman Grits Jarvis. Then the Petrel by heroic efforts was got into the wagon, the seat of which had been removed, old Thomas Jefferson perched himself precariously in the bow and protestingly gathered up his rope-patched reins.

"Folks'll 'low I'se plum crazy, drivin' dis yere boat," he declared, observing with concern that some four feet of the stern projected over the tail-board. "Ef she topples, I'll git to heaven quicker'n a bullet."

When one is shanghaied, however,—in the hands of buccaneers,—it is too late to withdraw. Six shoulders upheld the rear end of the Petrel, others shoved, and Thomas Jefferson's rickety horse began to move forward in spite of himself. An expression of sheer terror might have been observed on the old negro's crinkled face, but his voice was drowned, and we swept out of the alley. Scarcely had we travelled a block before we began to be joined by all the boys along the line of march; marbles, tops, and even incipient baseball games were abandoned that Saturday morning; people ran out of their houses, teamsters halted their carts. The breathless excitement, the exaltation I had felt on leaving the alley were now tinged with other feelings, unanticipated, but not wholly lacking in delectable quality,—concern and awe at these unforeseen forces I had raised, at this ever growing and enthusiastic body of volunteers springing up like dragon's teeth in our path. After all, was not I the hero of this triumphal procession? The thought was consoling, exhilarating. And here was Nancy marching at my side, a little subdued, perhaps, but unquestionably admiring and realizing that it was I who had created all this. Nancy, who was the aptest of pupils, the most loyal of followers, though I did not yet value her devotion at its real worth, because she was a girl. Her imagination kindled at my touch. And on this eventful occasion she carried in her arms a parcel, the contents of which were unknown to all but ourselves. At length we reached the muddy shores of Logan's pond, where two score eager hands volunteered to assist the Petrel into her native element.

Alas! that the reality never attains to the vision. I had beheld, in my dreams, the Petrel about to take the water, and Nancy Willett standing very straight making a little speech and crashing a bottle of wine across the bows. This was the content of the mysterious parcel; she had stolen it from her father's cellar. But the number of uninvited spectators, which had not been foreseen, considerably modified the programme,—as the newspapers would have said. They pushed and crowded around the ship, and made frank and even brutal remarks as to her seaworthiness; even Nancy, inured though she was to the masculine sex, had fled to the heights, and it looked at this supreme moment as though we should have to fight for the Petrel. An attempt to muster her doughty buccaneers failed; the gunner too had fled,—Gene Hollister; Ham Durrett and the Ewanses were nowhere to be seen, and a muster revealed only Tom, the fidus Achates, and Grits Jarvis.

"Ah, s'y!" he exclaimed in the teeth of the menacing hordes. "Stand back, carn't yer? I'll bash yer face in, Johnny. Whose boat is this?"

Shall it be whispered that I regretted his belligerency? Here, in truth, was the drama staged,—my drama, had I only been able to realize it. The good ship beached, the head-hunters hemming us in on all sides, the scene prepared for one of those struggles against frightful odds which I had so graphically related as an essential part of our adventures.

"Let's roll the cuss in the fancy collar," proposed one of the head- hunters,—meaning me.

"I'll stove yer slats if yer touch him," said Grits, and then resorted to appeal. "I s'y, carn't yer stand back and let a chap 'ave a charnst?"

The head-hunters only jeered. And what shall be said of the Captain in this moment of peril? Shall it be told that his heart was beating wildly?—bumping were a better word. He was trying to remember that he was the Captain. Otherwise, he must admit with shame that he, too, should have fled. So much for romance when the test comes. Will he remain to fall fighting for his ship? Like Horatius, he glanced up at the hill, where, instead of the porch of the home where he would fain have been, he beheld a wisp of a girl standing alone, her hat on the back of her head, her hair flying in the wind, gazing intently down at him in his danger. The renegade crew was nowhere to be seen. There are those who demand the presence of a woman in order to be heroes....

"Give us a chance, can't you?" he cried, repeating Grits's appeal in not quite such a stentorian tone as he would have liked, while his hand trembled on the gunwale. Tom Peters, it must be acknowledged, was much more of a buccaneer when it was a question of deeds, for he planted himself in the way of the belligerent chief of the head-hunters (who spoke with a decided brogue).

"Get out of the way!" said Tom, with a little squeak in his voice. Yet there he was, and he deserves a tribute.

An unlooked-for diversion saved us from annihilation, in the shape of one who had a talent for creating them. We were bewilderingly aware of a girlish figure amongst us.

"You cowards!" she cried. "You cowards!"

Lithe, and fairly quivering with passion, it was Nancy who showed us how to face the head-hunters. They gave back. They would have been brave indeed if they had not retreated before such an intense little nucleus of energy and indignation!...

"Ah, give 'em a chanst," said their chief, after a moment.... He even helped to push the boat towards the water. But he did not volunteer to be one of those to man the Petrel on her maiden voyage. Nor did Logan's pond, that wild March day, greatly resemble the South Seas. Nevertheless, my eye on Nancy, I stepped proudly aboard and seized an "oar." Grits and Tom followed,—when suddenly the Petrel sank considerably below the water-line as her builders had estimated it. Ere we fully realized this, the now friendly head-hunters had given us a shove, and we were off! The Captain, who should have been waving good- bye to his lady love from the poop, sat down abruptly,—the crew likewise; not, however, before she had heeled to the scuppers, and a half-bucket of iced water had run it. Head-hunters were mere daily episodes in Grits's existence, but water... He muttered something in cockney that sounded like a prayer.... The wind was rapidly driving us toward the middle of the pond, and something cold and ticklish was seeping through the seats of our trousers. We sat like statues....

The bright scene etched itself in my memory—the bare brown slopes with which the pond was bordered, the Irish shanties, the clothes-lines with red flannel shirts snapping in the biting wind; Nancy motionless on the bank; the group behind her, silent now, impressed in spite of itself at the sight of our intrepidity.

The Petrel was sailing stern first.... Would any of us, indeed, ever see home again? I thought of my father's wrath turned to sorrow because he had refused to gratify a son's natural wish and present him with a real rowboat.... Out of the corners of our eyes we watched the water creeping around the gunwale, and the very muddiness of it seemed to enhance its coldness, to make the horrors of its depths more mysterious and hideous. The voice of Grits startled us.

"O Gawd," he was saying, "we're a-going to sink, and I carn't swim! The blarsted tar's give way back here."

"Is she leaking?" I cried.

"She's a-filling up like a bath tub," he lamented.

Slowly but perceptibly, in truth, the bow was rising, and above the whistling of the wind I could hear his chattering as she settled.... Then several things happened simultaneously: an agonized cry behind me, distant shouts from the shore, a sudden upward lunge of the bow, and the torture of being submerged, inch by inch, in the icy, yellow water. Despite the splashing behind me, I sat as though paralyzed until I was waist deep and the boards turned under me, and then, with a spasmodic contraction of my whole being I struck out—only to find my feet on the muddy bottom. Such was the inglorious end of the good ship Petrel! For she went down, with all hands, in little more than half a fathom of water.... It was not until then I realized that we had been blown clear across the pond!

Figures were running along the shore. And as Tom and I emerged dragging Grits between us,—for he might have been drowned there abjectly in the shallows,—we were met by a stout and bare-armed Irishwoman whose scanty hair, I remember, was drawn into a tight knot behind her head; and who seized us, all three, as though we were a bunch of carrots.

"Come along wid ye!" she cried.

Shivering, we followed her up the hill, the spectators of the tragedy, who by this time had come around the pond, trailing after. Nancy was not among them. Inside the shanty into which we were thrust were two small children crawling about the floor, and the place was filled with steam from a wash-tub against the wall and a boiler on the stove. With a vigorous injunction to make themselves scarce, the Irishwoman slammed the door in the faces of the curious and ordered us to remove our clothes. Grits was put to bed in a corner, while Tom and I, provided with various garments, huddled over the stove. There fell to my lot the red flannel shirt which I had seen on the clothes-line. She gave us hot coffee, and was back at her wash-tub in no time at all, her entire comment on a proceeding that seemed to Tom and me to have certain elements of gravity being, "By's will be by's!" The final ironical touch was given the anti- climax when our rescuer turned out to be the mother of the chief of the head-hunters himself! He had lingered perforce with his brothers and sister outside the cabin until dinner time, and when he came in he was meek as Moses.

Thus the ready hospitality of the poor, which passed over the heads of Tom and me as we ate bread and onions and potatoes with a ravenous hunger. It must have been about two o'clock in the afternoon when we bade good-bye to our preserver and departed for home....

At first we went at a dog-trot, but presently slowed down to discuss the future looming portentously ahead of us. Since entire concealment was now impossible, the question was,—how complete a confession would be necessary? Our cases, indeed, were dissimilar, and Tom's incentive to hold back the facts was not nearly so great as mine. It sometimes seemed to me in those days unjust that the Peterses were able on the whole to keep out of criminal difficulties, in which I was more or less continuously involved: for it did not strike me that their sins were not those of the imagination. The method of Tom's father was the slipper. He and Tom understood each other, while between my father and myself was a great gulf fixed. Not that Tom yearned for the slipper; but he regarded its occasional applications as being as inevitable as changes in the weather; lying did not come easily to him, and left to himself he much preferred to confess and have the matter over with. I have already suggested that I had cultivated lying, that weapon of the weaker party, in some degree, at least, in self-defence.

Tom was loyal. Moreover, my conviction would probably deprive him for six whole afternoons of my company, on which he was more or less dependent. But the defence of this case presented unusual difficulties, and we stopped several times to thrash them out. We had been absent from dinner, and doubtless by this time Julia had informed Tom's mother of the expedition, and anyone could see that our clothing had been wet. So I lingered in no little anxiety behind the Peters stable while he made the investigation. Our spirits rose considerably when he returned to report that Julia had unexpectedly been a trump, having quieted his mother by the surmise that he was spending the day with his Aunt Fanny. So far, so good. The problem now was to decide upon what to admit. For we must both tell the same story.

It was agreed that we had fallen into Logan's Pond from a raft: my suggestion. Well, said Tom, the Petrel hadn't proved much better than a raft, after all. I was in no mood to defend her.

This designation of the Petrel as a "raft" was my first legal quibble. The question to be decided by the court was, What is a raft? just as the supreme tribunal of the land has been required, in later years, to decide, What is whiskey? The thing to be concealed if possible was the building of the "raft," although this information was already in the possession of a number of persons, whose fathers might at any moment see fit to congratulate my own on being the parent of a genius. It was a risk, however, that had to be run. And, secondly, since Grits Jarvis was contraband, nothing was to be said about him.

I have not said much about my mother, who might have been likened on such occasions to a grand jury compelled to indict, yet torn between loyalty to an oath and sympathy with the defendant. I went through the Peters yard, climbed the wire fence, my object being to discover first from Ella, the housemaid, or Hannah, the cook, how much was known in high quarters. It was Hannah who, as I opened the kitchen door, turned at the sound, and set down the saucepan she was scouring.

"Is it home ye are? Mercy to goodness!" (this on beholding my shrunken costume) "Glory be to God you're not drownded! and your mother worritin' her heart out! So it's into the wather ye were?"

I admitted it.

"Hannah?" I said softly.

"What then?"

"Does mother know—about the boat?"

"Now don't ye be wheedlin'."

I managed to discover, however, that my mother did not know, and surmised that the best reason why she had not been told had to do with Hannah's criminal acquiescence concerning the operations in the shed. I ran into the front hall and up the stairs, and my mother heard me coming and met me on the landing.

"Hugh, where have you been?"

As I emerged from the semi-darkness of the stairway she caught sight of my dwindled garments, of the trousers well above my ankles. Suddenly she had me in her arms and was kissing me passionately. As she stood before me in her grey, belted skirt, the familiar red-and-white cameo at her throat, her heavy hair parted in the middle, in her eyes was an odd, appealing look which I know now was a sign of mother love struggling with a Presbyterian conscience. Though she inherited that conscience, I have often thought she might have succeeded in casting it off—or at least some of it—had it not been for the fact that in spite of herself she worshipped its incarnation in the shape of my father. Her voice trembled a little as she drew me to the sofa beside the window.

"Tell me about what happened, my son," she said.

It was a terrible moment for me. For my affections were still quiveringly alive in those days, and I loved her. I had for an instant an instinctive impulse to tell her the whole story,—South Sea Islands and all! And I could have done it had I not beheld looming behind her another figure which represented a stern and unsympathetic Authority, and somehow made her, suddenly, of small account. Not that she would have understood the romance, but she would have comprehended me. I knew that she was powerless to save me from the wrath to come. I wept. It was because I hated to lie to her,—yet I did so. Fear gripped me, and—like some respectable criminals I have since known—I understood that any confession I made would inexorably be used against me.... I wonder whether she knew I was lying? At any rate, the case appeared to be a grave one, and I was presently remanded to my room to be held over for trial....

Vividly, as I write, I recall the misery of the hours I have spent, while awaiting sentence, in the little chamber with the honeysuckle wall-paper and steel engravings of happy but dumpy children romping in the fields and groves. On this particular March afternoon the weather had become morne, as the French say; and I looked down sadly into the grey back yard which the wind of the morning had strewn with chips from the Petrel. At last, when shadows were gathering in the corners of the room, I heard footsteps. Ella appeared, prim and virtuous, yet a little commiserating. My father wished to see me, downstairs. It was not the first time she had brought that summons, and always her manner was the same!

The scene of my trials was always the sitting room, lined with grim books in their walnut cases. And my father sat, like a judge, behind the big desk where he did his work when at home. Oh, the distance between us at such an hour! I entered as delicately as Agag, and the expression in his eye seemed to convict me before I could open my mouth.

"Hugh," he said, "your mother tells me that you have confessed to going, without permission, to Logan's Pond, where you embarked on a raft and fell into the water."

The slight emphasis he contrived to put on the word raft sent a colder shiver down my spine than the iced water had done. What did he know? or was this mere suspicion? Too late, now, at any rate, to plead guilty.

"It was a sort of a raft, sir," I stammered.

"A sort of a raft," repeated my father. "Where, may I ask, did you find it?"

"I—I didn't exactly find it, sir."

"Ah!" said my father. (It was the moment to glance meaningly at the jury.) The prisoner gulped. "You didn't exactly find it, then. Will you kindly explain how you came by it?"

"Well, sir, we—I—put it together."

"Have you any objection to stating, Hugh, in plain English, that you made it?"

"No, sir, I suppose you might say that I made it."

"Or that it was intended for a row-boat?"

Here was the time to appeal, to force a decision as to what constituted a row-boat.

"Perhaps it might be called a row-boat, sir," I said abjectly.

"Or that, in direct opposition to my wishes and commands in forbidding you to have a boat, to spend your money foolishly and wickedly on a whim, you constructed one secretly in the woodshed, took out a part of the back partition, thus destroying property that did, not belong to you, and had the boat carted this morning to Logan's Pond?"

I was silent, utterly undone. Evidently he had specific information.... There are certain expressions that are, at times, more than mere figures of speech, and now my father's wrath seemed literally towering. It added visibly to his stature.

"Hugh," he said, in a voice that penetrated to the very corners of my soul, "I utterly fail to understand you. I cannot imagine how a son of mine, a son of your mother who is the very soul of truthfulness and honour—can be a liar." (Oh, the terrible emphasis he put on that word!) "Nor is it as if this were a new tendency—I have punished you for it before. Your mother and I have tried to do our duty by you, to instil into you Christian teaching. But it seems wholly useless. I confess that I am at a less how to proceed. You seem to have no conscience whatever, no conception of what you owe to your parents and your God. You not only persistently disregard my wishes and commands, but you have, for many months, been leading a double life, facing me every day, while you were secretly and continually disobeying me. I shudder to think where this determination of yours to have what you desire at any price will lead you in the future. It is just such a desire that distinguishes wicked men from good."

I will not linger upon a scene the very remembrance of which is painful to this day.... I went from my father's presence in disgrace, in an agony of spirit that was overwhelming, to lock the door of my room and drop face downward on the bed, to sob until my muscles twitched. For he had, indeed, put into me an awful fear. The greatest horror of my boyish imagination was a wicked man. Was I, as he had declared, utterly depraved and doomed in spite of myself to be one?

There came a knock at my door—Ella with my supper. I refused to open, and sent her away, to fall on my knees in the darkness and pray wildly to a God whose attributes and character were sufficiently confused in my mind. On the one hand was the stern, despotic Monarch of the Westminster Catechism, whom I addressed out of habit, the Father who condemned a portion of his children from the cradle. Was I one of those who he had decreed before I was born must suffer the tortures of the flames of hell? Putting two and two together, what I had learned in Sunday school and gathered from parts of Dr. Pound's sermons, and the intimation of my father that wickedness was within me, like an incurable disease,—was not mine the logical conclusion? What, then, was the use of praying?... My supplications ceased abruptly. And my ever ready imagination, stirred to its depths, beheld that awful scene of the last day: the darkness, such as sometimes creeps over the city in winter, when the jaundiced smoke falls down and we read at noonday by gas-light. I beheld the tortured faces of the wicked gathered on the one side, and my mother on the other amongst the blessed, gazing across the gulf at me with yearning and compassion. Strange that it did not strike me that the sight of the condemned whom they had loved in life would have marred if not destroyed the happiness of the chosen, about to receive their crowns and harps! What a theology—that made the Creator and Preserver of all mankind thus illogical!

Chapter Three

Although I was imaginative, I was not morbidly introspective, and by the end of the first day of my incarceration my interest in that solution had waned. At times, however, I actually yearned for someone in whom I could confide, who could suggest a solution. I repeat, I would not for worlds have asked my father or my mother or Dr. Pound, of whom I had a wholesome fear, or perhaps an unwholesome one. Except at morning Bible reading and at church my parents never mentioned the name of the Deity, save to instruct me formally. Intended or no, the effect of my religious training was to make me ashamed of discussing spiritual matters, and naturally I failed to perceive that this was because it laid its emphasis on personal salvation.... I did not, however, become an unbeliever, for I was not of a nature to contemplate with equanimity a godless universe....

My sufferings during these series of afternoon confinements did not come from remorse, but were the result of a vague sense of injury; and their effect was to generate within me a strange motive power, a desire to do something that would astound my father and eventually wring from him the confession that he had misjudged me. To be sure, I should have to wait until early manhood, at least, for the accomplishment of such a coup. Might it not be that I was an embryonic literary genius? Many were the books I began in this ecstasy of self-vindication, only to abandon them when my confinement came to an end.

It was about this time, I think, that I experienced one of those shocks which have a permanent effect upon character. It was then the custom for ladies to spend the day with one another, bringing their sewing; and sometimes, when I unexpectedly entered the sitting-room, the voices of my mother's visitors would drop to a whisper. One afternoon

I returned from school to pause at the head of the stairs. Cousin Bertha Ewan and Mrs. McAlery were discussing with my mother an affair that I judged from the awed tone in which they spoke might prove interesting.

"Poor Grace," Mrs. McAlery was saying, "I imagine she's paid a heavy penalty. No man alive will be faithful under those circumstances."

I stopped at the head of the stairs, with a delicious, guilty feeling.

"Have they ever heard of her?" Cousin Bertha asked.

"It is thought they went to Spain," replied Mrs. McAlery, solemnly, yet not without a certain zest. "Mr. Jules Hollister will not have her name mentioned in his presence, you know. And Whitcomb chased them as far as New York with a horse-pistol in his pocket. The report is that he got to the dock just as the ship sailed. And then, you know, he went to live somewhere out West,—in Iowa, I believe."

"Did he ever get a divorce?" Cousin Bertha inquired.

"He was too good a church member, my dear," my mother reminded her.

"Well, I'd have got one quick enough, church member or no church member," declared Cousin Bertha, who had in her elements of daring.

"Not that I mean for a moment to excuse her," Mrs. McAlery put in, "but Edward Whitcomb did have a frightful temper, and he was awfully strict with her, and he was old enough, anyhow, to be her father. Grace Hollister was the last woman in the world I should have suspected of doing so hideous a thing. She was so sweet and simple."

"Jennings was very attractive," said my Cousin Bertha. "I don't think I ever saw a handsomer man. Now, if he had looked at me—"

The sentence was never finished, for at this crucial moment I dropped a grammar....

I had heard enough, however, to excite my curiosity to the highest pitch. And that evening, when I came in at five o'clock to study, I asked my mother what had become of Gene Hollister's aunt.

"She went away, Hugh," replied my mother, looking greatly troubled.

"Why?" I persisted.

"It is something you are too young to understand."

Of course I started an investigation, and the next day at school I asked the question of Gene Hollister himself, only to discover that he believed his aunt to be dead! And that night he asked his mother if his Aunt Grace were really alive, after all? Whereupon complications and explanations ensued between our parents, of which we saw only the surface signs.... My father accused me of eavesdropping (which I denied), and sentenced me to an afternoon of solitary confinement for repeating something which I had heard in private. I have reason to believe that my mother was also reprimanded.

It must not be supposed that I permitted the matter to rest. In addition to Grits Jarvis, there was another contraband among my acquaintances, namely, Alec Pound, the scrape-grace son of the Reverend Doctor Pound. Alec had an encyclopaedic mind, especially well stocked with the kind of knowledge I now desired; first and last he taught me much, which I would better have got in another way. To him I appealed and got the story, my worst suspicions being confirmed. Mrs. Whitcomb's house had been across the alley from that of Mr. Jennings, but no one knew that anything was "going on," though there had been signals from the windows—the neighbours afterwards remembered....

I listened shudderingly.

"But," I cried, "they were both married!"

"What difference does that make when you love a woman?" Alec replied grandly. "I could tell you much worse things than that."

This he proceeded to do. Fascinated, I listened with a sickening sensation. It was a mild afternoon in spring, and we stood in the deep limestone gutter in front of the parsonage, a little Gothic wooden house set in a gloomy yard.

"I thought," said I, "that people couldn't love any more after they were married, except each other."

Alec looked at me pityingly.

"You'll get over that notion," he assured me.

Thus another ingredient entered my character. Denied its food at home, good food, my soul eagerly consumed and made part of itself the fermenting stuff that Alec Pound so willing distributed. And it was fermenting stuff. Let us see what it did to me. Working slowly but surely, it changed for me the dawning mystery of sex into an evil instead of a holy one. The knowledge of the tragedy of Grace Hollister started me to seeking restlessly, on bookshelves and elsewhere, for a secret that forever eluded me, and forever led me on. The word fermenting aptly describes the process begun, suggesting as it does something closed up, away from air and sunlight, continually working in secret, engendering forces that fascinated, yet inspired me with fear. Undoubtedly this secretiveness of our elders was due to the pernicious dualism of their orthodox Christianity, in which love was carnal and therefore evil, and the flesh not the gracious soil of the spirit, but something to be deplored and condemned, exorcised and transformed by the miracle of grace. Now love had become a terrible power (gripping me) whose enchantment drove men and women from home and friends and kindred to the uttermost parts of the earth....

It was long before I got to sleep that night after my talk with Alec Pound. I alternated between the horror and the romance of the story I had heard, supplying for myself the details he had omitted: I beheld the signals from the windows, the clandestine meetings, the sudden and desperate flight. And to think that all this could have happened in our city not five blocks from where I lay!

My consternation and horror were concentrated on the man,—and yet I recall a curious bifurcation. Instead of experiencing that automatic righteous indignation which my father and mother had felt, which had animated old Mr. Jules Hollister when he had sternly forbidden his daughter's name to be mentioned in his presence, which had made these people outcasts, there welled up within me an intense sympathy and pity. By an instinctive process somehow linked with other experiences, I seemed to be able to enter into the feelings of these two outcasts, to understand the fearful yet fascinating nature of the impulse that had led them to elude the vigilance and probity of a world with which I myself was at odds. I pictured them in a remote land, shunned by mankind. Was there something within me that might eventually draw me to do likewise? The desire in me to which my father had referred, which would brook no opposition, which twisted and squirmed until it found its way to its object? I recalled the words of Jarvis, the carpenter, that if I ever set my heart on another man's wife, God help him. God help me!

A wicked man! I had never beheld the handsome and fascinating Mr. Jennings, but I visualised him now; dark, like all villains, with a black moustache and snapping black eyes. He carried a cane. I always associated canes with villains. Whereupon I arose, groped for the matches, lighted the gas, and gazing at myself in the mirror was a little reassured to find nothing sinister in my countenance....

Next to my father's faith in a Moral Governor of the Universe was his belief in the Tariff and the Republican Party. And this belief, among others, he handed on to me. On the cinder playground of the Academy we Republicans used to wage, during campaigns, pitched battles for the Tariff. It did not take a great deal of courage to be a Republican in our city, and I was brought up to believe that Democrats were irrational, inferior, and—with certain exceptions like the Hollisters—dirty beings. There was only one degree lower, and that was to be a mugwump. It was no wonder that the Hollisters were Democrats, for they had a queer streak in them; owing, no doubt, to the fact that old Mr. Jules Hollister's mother had been a Frenchwoman. He looked like a Frenchman, by the way, and always wore a skullcap.

I remember one autumn afternoon having a violent quarrel with Gene Hollister that bade fair to end in blows, when he suddenly demanded:—

"I'll bet you anything you don't know why you're a Republican."

"It's because I'm for the Tariff," I replied triumphantly.

But his next question floored me. What, for example, was the Tariff? I tried to bluster it out, but with no success.

"Do you know?" I cried finally, with sudden inspiration.

It turned out that he did not.

"Aren't we darned idiots," he asked, "to get fighting over something we don't know anything about?"

That was Gene's French blood, of course. But his question rankled. And how was I to know that he would have got as little satisfaction if he had hurled it into the marching ranks of those imposing torch-light processions which sometimes passed our house at night, with drums beating and fifes screaming and torches waving,—thousands of citizens who were for the Tariff for the same reason as I: to wit, because they were Republicans.

Yet my father lived and died in the firm belief that the United States of America was a democracy!

Resolved not to be caught a second time in such a humiliating position by a Democrat, I asked my father that night what the Tariff was. But I was too young to understand it, he said. I was to take his word for it that the country would go to the dogs if the Democrats got in and the Tariff were taken away. Here, in a nutshell, though neither he nor I realized it, was the political instruction of the marching hordes. Theirs not to reason why. I was too young, they too ignorant. Such is the method of Authority!

The steel-mills of Mr. Durrett and Mr. Hambleton, he continued, would be forced to shut down, and thousands of workmen would starve. This was just a sample of what would happen. Prosperity would cease, he declared. That word, Prosperity, made a deep impression on me, and I recall the certain reverential emphasis he laid on it. And while my solicitude for the workmen was not so great as his and Mr. Durrett's, I was concerned as to what would happen to us if those twin gods, the Tariff and Prosperity, should take their departure from the land. Knowing my love for the good things of the table, my father intimated, with a rare humour I failed to appreciate, that we should have to live henceforth in spartan simplicity. After that, like the intelligent workman, I was firmer than ever for the Tariff.

Such was the idealistic plane on which—and from a good man—I received my first political instruction! And for a long time I connected the dominance of the Republican Party with the continuation of manna and quails, in other words, with nothing that had to do with the spiritual welfare of any citizen, but with clothing and food and material comforts. My education was progressing....

Though my father revered Plato and Aristotle, he did not, apparently, take very seriously the contention that that government alone is good "which seeks to attain the permanent interests of the governed by evolving the character of its citizens." To put the matter brutally, politics, despite the lofty sentiments on the transparencies in torchlight processions, had only to do with the belly, not the soul.

Politics and government, one perceives, had nothing to do with religion, nor education with any of these. A secularized and disjointed world! Our leading citizens, learned in the classics though some of them might be, paid no heed to the dictum of the Greek idealist, who was more practical than they would have supposed. "The man who does not carry his city within his heart is a spiritual starveling."

One evening, a year or two after that tariff campaign, I was pretending to study my lessons under the student lamp in the sitting-room while my mother sewed and my father wrote at his desk, when there was a ring at the door-bell. I welcomed any interruption, even though the visitor proved to be only the druggist's boy; and there was always the possibility of a telegram announcing, for instance, the death of a relative. Such had once been the case when my Uncle Avery Paret had died in New York, and I was taken out of school for a blissful four days for the funeral.

I went tiptoeing into the hall and peeped over the banisters while Ella opened the door. I heard a voice which I recognized as that of Perry Blackwood's father asking for Mr. Paret; and then to my astonishment, I saw filing after him into the parlour some ten or twelve persons. With the exception of Mr. Ogilvy, who belonged to one of our old families, and Mr. Watling, a lawyer who had married the youngest of Gene Hollister's aunts, the visitors entered stealthily, after the manner of burglars; some of these were heavy-jowled, and all had an air of mystery that raised my curiosity and excitement to the highest pitch. I caught hold of Ella as she came up the stairs, but she tore herself free, and announced to my father that Mr. Josiah Blackwood and other gentlemen had asked to see him. My father seemed puzzled as he went downstairs.... A long interval elapsed, during which I did not make even a pretence of looking at my arithmetic. At times the low hum of voices rose to what was almost an uproar, and on occasions I distinguished a marked Irish brogue.

"I wonder what they want?" said my mother, nervously.

At last we heard the front door shut behind them, and my father came upstairs, his usually serene face wearing a disturbed expression.

"Who in the world was it, Mr. Paret?" asked my mother.

My father sat down in the arm-chair. He was clearly making an effort for self-control.

"Blackwood and Ogilvy and Watling and some city politicians," he exclaimed.

"Politicians!" she repeated. "What did they want? That is, if it's anything you can tell me," she added apologetically.

"They wished me to be the Republican candidate for the mayor of this city."

This tremendous news took me off my feet. My father mayor!

"Of course you didn't consider it, Mr. Paret," my mother was saying.

"Consider it!" he echoed reprovingly. "I can't imagine what Ogilvy and Watling and Josiah Blackwood were thinking of! They are out of their heads. I as much as told them so."

This was more than I could bear, for I had already pictured myself telling the news to envious schoolmates.

"Oh, father, why didn't you take it?" I cried.

By this time, when he turned to me, he had regained his usual expression.

"You don't know what you're talking about, Hugh," he said. "Accept a political office! That sort of thing is left to politicians."

The tone in which he spoke warned me that a continuation of the conversation would be unwise, and my mother also understood that the discussion was closed. He went back to his desk, and began writing again as though nothing had happened.

As for me, I was left in a palpitating state of excitement which my father's self-control or sang-froid only served to irritate and enhance, and my head was fairly spinning as, covertly, I watched his pen steadily covering the paper.

How could he—how could any man of flesh and blood sit down calmly after having been offered the highest honour in the gift of his community! And he had spurned it as if Mr. Blackwood and the others had gratuitously insulted him! And how was it, if my father so revered the Republican Party that he would not suffer it to be mentioned slightingly in his presence, that he had refused contemptuously to be its mayor?...

The next day at school, however, I managed to let it be known that the offer had been made and declined. After all, this seemed to make my father a bigger man than if he had accepted it. Naturally I was asked why he had declined it.

"He wouldn't take it," I replied scornfully. "Office-holding should be left to politicians."

Ralph Hambleton, with his precocious and cynical knowledge of the world, minimized my triumph by declaring that he would rather be his grandfather, Nathaniel Durrett, than the mayor of the biggest city in the country. Politicians, he said, were bloodsuckers and thieves, and the only reason for holding office was that it enabled one to steal the taxpayers' money....

As I have intimated, my vision of a future literary career waxed and waned, but a belief that I was going to be Somebody rarely deserted me. If not a literary lion, what was that Somebody to be? Such an environment as mine was woefully lacking in heroic figures to satisfy the romantic soul. In view of the experience I have just related, it is not surprising that the notion of becoming a statesman did not appeal to me; nor is it to be wondered at, despite the somewhat exaggerated respect and awe in which Ralph's grandfather was held by my father and other influential persons, that I failed to be stirred by the elements of greatness in the grim personality of our first citizen, the iron-master. For he possessed such elements. He lived alone in Ingrain Street in an uncompromising mansion I always associated with the Sabbath, not only because I used to be taken there on decorous Sunday visits by my father, but because it was the very quintessence of Presbyterianism. The moment I entered its "portals"—as Mr. Hawthorne appropriately would have called them—my spirit was overwhelmed and suffocated by its formality and orderliness. Within its stern walls Nathaniel Durrett had made a model universe of his own, such as the Deity of the Westminster Confession had no doubt meant his greater one to be if man had not rebelled and foiled him.... It was a world from which I was determined to escape at any cost.

My father and I were always ushered into the gloomy library, with its high ceiling, with its long windows that reached almost to the rococo cornice, with its cold marble mantelpiece that reminded me of a tombstone, with its interminable book shelves filled with yellow bindings. On the centre table, in addition to a ponderous Bible, was one of those old-fashioned carafes of red glass tipped with blue surmounted by a tumbler of blue tipped with red. Behind this table Mr. Durrett sat reading a volume of sermons, a really handsome old man in his black tie and pleated shirt; tall and spare, straight as a ramrod, with a finely moulded head and straight nose and sinewy hands the colour of mulberry stain. He called my father by his first name, an immense compliment, considering how few dared to do so.

"Well, Matthew," the old man would remark, after they had discussed Dr. Pound's latest flight on the nature of the Trinity or the depravity of man, or horticulture, or the Republican Party, "do you have any better news of Hugh at school?"

"I regret to say, Mr. Durrett," my father would reply, "that he does not yet seem to be aroused to a sense of his opportunities."

Whereupon Mr. Durrett would gimble me with a blue eye that lurked beneath grizzled brows, quite as painful a proceeding as if he used an iron tool. I almost pity myself when I think of what a forlorn stranger I was in their company. They two, indeed, were of one kind, and I of another sort who could never understand them,—nor they me. To what depths of despair they reduced me they never knew, and yet they were doing it all for my good! They only managed to convince me that my love of folly was ineradicable, and that I was on my way head first for perdition. I always looked, during these excruciating and personal moments, at the coloured glass bottle.

"It grieves me to hear it, Hugh," Mr. Durrett invariably declared. "You'll never come to any good without study. Now when I was your age..."

I knew his history by heart, a common one in this country, although he made an honourable name instead of a dishonourable one. And when I contrast him with those of his successors whom I was to know later...! But I shall not anticipate. American genius had not then evolved the false entry method of overcapitalization. A thrilling history, Mr. Durrett's, could I but have entered into it. I did not reflect then that this stern old man must have throbbed once; nay, fire and energy still remained in his bowels, else he could not have continued to dominate a city. Nor did it occur to me that the great steel-works that lighted the southern sky were the result of a passion, of dreams similar to those possessing me, but which I could not express. He had founded a family whose position was virtually hereditary, gained riches which for those days were great, compelled men to speak his name with a certain awe. But of what use were such riches as his when his religion and morality compelled him to banish from him all the joys in the power of riches to bring?

No, I didn't want to be an iron-master. But it may have been about this time that I began to be impressed with the power of wealth, the adulation and reverence it commanded, the importance in which it clothed all who shared in it....

The private school I attended in the company of other boys with whom I was brought up was called Densmore Academy, a large, square building of a then hideous modernity, built of smooth, orange-red bricks with threads of black mortar between them. One reads of happy school days, yet I fail to recall any really happy hours spent there, even in the yard, which was covered with black cinders that cut you when you fell. I think of it as a penitentiary, and the memory of the barred lower windows gives substance to this impression.

I suppose I learned something during the seven years of my incarceration. All of value, had its teachers known anything of youthful psychology, of natural bent, could have been put into me in three. At least four criminally wasted years, to say nothing of the benumbing and desiccating effect of that old system of education! Chalk and chalk-dust! The Mediterranean a tinted portion of the map, Italy a man's boot which I drew painfully, with many yawns; history no glorious epic revealing as it unrolls the Meaning of Things, no revelation of that wondrous distillation of the Spirit of man, but an endless marching and counter- marching up and down the map, weary columns of figures to be learned by rote instantly to be forgotten again. "On June the 7th General So-and-so proceeded with his whole army—" where? What does it matter? One little chapter of Carlyle, illuminated by a teacher of understanding, were worth a million such text-books. Alas, for the hatred of Virgil! "Paret" (a shiver), "begin at the one hundred and thirtieth line and translate!" I can hear myself droning out in detestable English a meaningless portion of that endless journey of the pious AEneas; can see Gene Hollister, with heart-rending glances of despair, stumbling through Cornelius Nepos in an unventilated room with chalk-rubbed blackboards and heavy odours of ink and stale lunch. And I graduated from Densmore Academy, the best school in our city, in the 80's, without having been taught even the rudiments of citizenship.

Knowledge was presented to us as a corpse, which bit by bit we painfully dissected. We never glimpsed the living, growing thing, never experienced the Spirit, the same spirit that was able magically to waft me from a wintry Lyme Street to the South Seas, the energizing, electrifying Spirit of true achievement, of life, of God himself. Little by little its flames were smothered until in manhood there seemed no spark of it left alive. Many years were to pass ere it was to revive again, as by a miracle. I travelled. Awakening at dawn, I saw, framed in a port-hole, rose-red Seriphos set in a living blue that paled the sapphire; the seas Ulysses had sailed, and the company of the Argonauts. My soul was steeped in unimagined colour, and in the memory of one rapturous instant is gathered what I was soon to see of Greece, is focussed the meaning of history, poetry and art. I was to stand one evening in spring on the mound where heroes sleep and gaze upon the plain of Marathon between darkening mountains and the blue thread of the strait peaceful now, flushed with pink and white blossoms of fruit and almond trees; to sit on the cliff-throne whence a Persian King had looked down upon a Salamis fought and lost.... In that port-hole glimpse a Themistocles was revealed, a Socrates, a Homer and a Phidias, an AEschylus, and a Pericles; yes, and a John brooding Revelations on his sea-girt rock as twilight falls over the waters....

I saw the Roman Empire, that Scarlet Woman whose sands were dyed crimson with blood to appease her harlotry, whose ships were laden with treasures from the immutable East, grain from the valley of the Nile, spices from Arabia, precious purple stuffs from Tyre, tribute and spoil, slaves and jewels from conquered nations she absorbed; and yet whose very emperors were the unconscious instruments of a Progress they wot not of, preserved to the West by Marathon and Salamis. With Caesar's legions its message went forth across Hispania to the cliffs of the wild western ocean, through Hercynian forests to tribes that dwelt where great rivers roll up their bars by misty, northern seas, and even to Celtic fastnesses beyond the Wall....

Chapter Four

In and out of my early memories like a dancing ray of sunlight flits the spirit of Nancy. I was always fond of her, but in extreme youth I accepted her incense with masculine complacency and took her allegiance for granted, never seeking to fathom the nature of the spell I exercised over her. Naturally other children teased me about her; but what was worse, with that charming lack of self-consciousness and consideration for what in after life are called the finer feelings, they teased her about me before me, my presence deterring them not at all. I can see them hopping around her in the Peters yard crying out:—

"Nancy's in love with Hugh! Nancy's in love with Hugh!"

A sufficiently thrilling pastime, this, for Nancy could take care of herself. I was a bungler beside her when it came to retaliation, and not the least of her attractions for me was her capacity for anger: fury would be a better term. She would fly at them—even as she flew at the head-hunters when the Petrel was menaced; and she could run like a deer. Woe to the unfortunate victim she overtook! Masculine strength, exercised apologetically, availed but little, and I have seen Russell Peters and Gene Hollister retire from such encounters humiliated and weeping. She never caught Ralph; his methods of torture were more intelligent and subtle than Gene's and Russell's, but she was his equal when it came to a question of tongues.

"I know what's the matter with you, Ralph Hambleton," she would say. "You're jealous." An accusation that invariably put him on the defensive. "You think all the girls are in love with you, don't you?"

These scenes I found somewhat embarrassing. Not so Nancy. After discomfiting her tormenters, or wounding and scattering them, she would return to my side.... In spite of her frankly expressed preference for me she had an elusiveness that made a continual appeal to my imagination. She was never obvious or commonplace, and long before I began to experience the discomforts and sufferings of youthful love I was fascinated by a nature eloquent with contradictions and inconsistencies. She was a tomboy, yet her own sex was enhanced rather than overwhelmed by contact with the other: and no matter how many trees she climbed she never seemed to lose her daintiness. It was innate.

She could, at times, be surprisingly demure. These impressions of her daintiness and demureness are particularly vivid in a picture my memory has retained of our walking together, unattended, to Susan Blackwood's birthday party. She must have been about twelve years old. It was the first time I had escorted her or any other girl to a party; Mrs. Willett had smiled over the proceeding, but Nancy and I took it most seriously, as symbolic of things to come. I can see Powell Street, where Nancy lived, at four o'clock on a mild and cloudy December afternoon, the decorous, retiring houses, Nancy on one side of the pavement by the iron fences and I on the other by the tree boxes. I can't remember her dress, only the exquisite sense of her slimness and daintiness comes back to me, of her dark hair in a long braid tied with a red ribbon, of her slender legs clad in black stockings of shining silk. We felt the occasion to be somehow too significant, too eloquent for words....

In silence we climbed the flight of stone steps that led up to the Blackwood mansion, when suddenly the door was opened, letting out sounds of music and revelry. Mr. Blackwood's coloured butler, Ned, beamed at us hospitably, inviting us to enter the brightness within. The shades were drawn, the carpets were covered with festal canvas, the folding doors between the square rooms were flung back, the prisms of the big chandeliers flung their light over animated groups of matrons and children. Mrs. Watling, the mother of the Watling twins—too young to be present was directing with vivacity the game of "King William was King James's son," and Mrs. McAlery was playing the piano.

"Now choose you East, now choose you West, Now choose the one you love the best!"

Tom Peters, in a velvet suit and consequently very miserable, refused to embrace Ethel Hollister; while the scornful Julia lurked in a corner: nothing would induce her to enter such a foolish game. I experienced a novel discomfiture when Ralph kissed Nancy.... Afterwards came the feast, from which Ham Durrett, in a pink paper cap with streamers, was at length forcibly removed by his mother. Thus early did he betray his love for the flesh pots....

It was not until I was sixteen that a player came and touched the keys of my soul, and it awoke, bewildered, at these first tender notes. The music quickened, tripping in ecstasy, to change by subtle phrases into themes of exquisite suffering hitherto unexperienced. I knew that I loved Nancy.

With the advent of longer dresses that reached to her shoe tops a change had come over her. The tomboy, the willing camp-follower who loved me and was unashamed, were gone forever, and a mysterious, transfigured being, neither girl nor woman, had magically been evolved. Could it be possible that she loved me still? My complacency had vanished; suddenly I had become the aggressor, if only I had known how to "aggress"; but in her presence I was seized by an accursed shyness that paralyzed my tongue, and the things I had planned to say were left unuttered. It was something—though I did not realize it—to be able to feel like that.

The time came when I could no longer keep this thing to myself. The need of an outlet, of a confidant, became imperative, and I sought out Tom Peters. It was in February; I remember because I had ventured—with incredible daring—to send Nancy an elaborate, rosy Valentine; written on the back of it in a handwriting all too thinly disguised was the following verse, the triumphant result of much hard thinking in school hours:—

Should you of this the sender guess Without another sign, Would you repent, and rest content To be his Valentine

I grew hot and cold by turns when I thought of its possible effects on my chances.

One of those useless, slushy afternoons, I took Tom for a walk that led us, as dusk came on, past Nancy's house. Only by painful degrees did I succeed in overcoming my bashfulness; but Tom, when at last I had blurted out the secret, was most sympathetic, although the ailment from which I suffered was as yet outside of the realm of his experience. I have used the word "ailment" advisedly, since he evidently put my trouble in the same category with diphtheria or scarlet fever, remarking that it was "darned hard luck." In vain I sought to explain that I did not regard it as such in the least; there was suffering, I admitted, but a degree of bliss none could comprehend who had not felt it. He refused to be envious, or at least to betray envy; yet he was curious, asking many questions, and I had reason to think before we parted that his admiration for me was increased. Was it possible that he, too, didn't love Nancy? No, it was funny, but he didn't. He failed to see much in girls: his tone remained commiserating, yet he began to take an interest in the progress of my suit.

For a time I had no progress to report. Out of consideration for those members of our weekly dancing class whose parents were Episcopalians the meetings were discontinued during Lent, and to call would have demanded a courage not in me; I should have become an object of ridicule among my friends and I would have died rather than face Nancy's mother and the members of her household. I set about making ingenious plans with a view to encounters that might appear casual. Nancy's school was dismissed at two, so was mine. By walking fast I could reach Salisbury Street, near St. Mary's Seminary for Young Ladies, in time to catch her, but even then for many days I was doomed to disappointment. She was either in company with other girls, or else she had taken another route; this I surmised led past Sophy McAlery's house, and I enlisted Tom as a confederate. He was to make straight for the McAlery's on Elm while I followed Powell, two short blocks away, and if Nancy went to Sophy's and left there alone he was to announce the fact by a preconcerted signal. Through long and persistent practice he had acquired a whistle shrill enough to wake the dead, accomplished by placing a finger of each hand between his teeth;—a gift that was the envy of his acquaintances, and the subject of much discussion as to whether his teeth were peculiar. Tom insisted that they were; it was an added distinction.

On this occasion he came up behind Nancy as she was leaving Sophy's gate and immediately sounded the alarm. She leaped in the air, dropped her school-books and whirled on him.

"Tom Peters! How dare you frighten me so!" she cried.

Tom regarded her in sudden dismay.

"I—I didn't mean to," he said. "I didn't think you were so near."

"But you must have seen me."

"I wasn't paying much attention," he equivocated,—a remark not calculated to appease her anger.

"Why were you doing it?"

"I was just practising," said Tom.

"Practising!" exclaimed Nancy, scornfully. "I shouldn't think you needed to practise that any more."

"Oh, I've done it louder," he declared, "Listen!"

She seized his hands, snatching them away from his lips. At this critical moment I appeared around the corner considerably out of breath, my heart beating like a watchman's rattle. I tried to feign nonchalance.

"Hello, Tom," I said. "Hello, Nancy. What's the matter?"

"It's Tom—he frightened me out of my senses." Dropping his wrists, she gave me a most disconcerting look; there was in it the suspicion of a smile. "What are you doing here, Hugh?"

"I heard Tom," I explained.

"I should think you might have. Where were you?"

"Over in another street," I answered, with deliberate vagueness. Nancy had suddenly become demure. I did not dare look at her, but I had a most uncomfortable notion that she suspected the plot. Meanwhile we had begun to walk along, all three of us, Tom, obviously ill at ease and discomfited, lagging a little behind. Just before we reached the corner I managed to kick him. His departure was by no means graceful.

"I've got to go;" he announced abruptly, and turned down the side street. We watched his sturdy figure as it receded.

"Well, of all queer boys!" said Nancy, and we walked on again.

"He's my best friend," I replied warmly.

"He doesn't seem to care much for your company," said Nancy.

"Oh, they have dinner at half past two," I explained.

"Aren't you afraid of missing yours, Hugh?" she asked wickedly.

"I've got time. I'd—I'd rather be with you." After making which audacious remark I was seized by a spasm of apprehension. But nothing happened. Nancy remained demure. She didn't remind me that I had reflected upon Tom.

"That's nice of you, Hugh."

"Oh, I'm not saying it because it's nice," I faltered. "I'd rather be with you than—with anybody."

This was indeed the acme of daring. I couldn't believe I had actually said it. But again I received no rebuke; instead came a remark that set me palpitating, that I treasured for many weeks to come.

"I got a very nice valentine," she informed me.

"What was it like?" I asked thickly.

"Oh, beautiful! All pink lace and—and Cupids, and the picture of a young man and a young woman in a garden."

"Was that all?"

"Oh, no, there was a verse, in the oddest handwriting. I wonder who sent it?"

"Perhaps Ralph," I hazarded ecstatically.

"Ralph couldn't write poetry," she replied disdainfully. "Besides, it was very good poetry."

I suggested other possible authors and admirers. She rejected them all. We reached her gate, and I lingered. As she looked down at me from the stone steps her eyes shone with a soft light that filled me with radiance, and into her voice had come a questioning, shy note that thrilled the more because it revealed a new Nancy of whom I had not dreamed.

"Perhaps I'll meet you again—coming from school," I said.

"Perhaps," she answered. "You'll be late to dinner, Hugh, if you don't go...."

I was late, and unable to eat much dinner, somewhat to my mother's alarm. Love had taken away my appetite.... After dinner, when I was wandering aimlessly about the yard, Tom appeared on the other side of the fence.

"Don't ever ask me to do that again," he said gloomily.

I did meet Nancy again coming from school, not every day, but nearly every day. At first we pretended that there was no arrangement in this, and we both feigned surprise when we encountered one another. It was Nancy who possessed the courage that I lacked. One afternoon she said:—

"I think I'd better walk with the girls to-morrow, Hugh."

I protested, but she was firm. And after that it was an understood thing that on certain days I should go directly home, feeling like an exile. Sophy McAlery had begun to complain: and I gathered that Sophy was Nancy's confidante. The other girls had begun to gossip. It was Nancy who conceived the brilliant idea—the more delightful because she said nothing about it to me—of making use of Sophy. She would leave school with Sophy, and I waited on the corner near the McAlery house. Poor Sophy! She was always of those who piped while others danced. In those days she had two straw-coloured pigtails, and her plain, faithful face is before me as I write. She never betrayed to me the excitement that filled her at being the accomplice of our romance.

Gossip raged, of course. Far from being disturbed, we used it, so to speak, as a handle for our love-making, which was carried on in an inferential rather than a direct fashion. Were they saying that we were lovers? Delightful! We laughed at one another in the sunshine.... At last we achieved the great adventure of a clandestine meeting and went for a walk in the afternoon, avoiding the houses of our friends. I've forgotten which of us had the boldness to propose it. The crocuses and tulips had broken the black mould, the flower beds in the front yards were beginning to blaze with scarlet and yellow, the lawns had turned a living green. What did we talk about? The substance has vanished, only the flavour remains.

One awoke of a morning to the twittering of birds, to walk to school amidst delicate, lace-like shadows of great trees acloud with old gold: the buds lay curled like tiny feathers on the pavements. Suddenly the shade was dense, the sunlight white and glaring, the odour of lilacs heavy in the air, spring in all its fulness had come,—spring and Nancy. Just so subtly, yet with the same seeming suddenness had budded and come to leaf and flower a perfect understanding, which nevertheless remained undefined. This, I had no doubt, was my fault, and due to the incomprehensible shyness her presence continued to inspire. Although we did not altogether abandon our secret trysts, we began to meet in more natural ways; there were garden parties and picnics where we strayed together through the woods and fields, pausing to tear off, one by one, the petals of a daisy, "She loves me, she loves me not." I never ventured to kiss her; I always thought afterwards I might have done so, she had seemed so willing, her eyes had shone so expectantly as I sat beside her on the grass; nor can I tell why I desired to kiss her save that this was the traditional thing to do to the lady one loved. To be sure, the very touch of her hand was galvanic. Paradoxically, I saw the human side of her, the yielding gentleness that always amazed me, yet I never overcame my awe of the divine; she was a being sacrosanct. Whether this idealism were innate or the result of such romances as I had read I cannot say.... I got, indeed, an avowal of a sort. The weekly dancing classes having begun again, on one occasion when she had waltzed twice with Gene Hollister I protested.

"Don't be silly, Hugh," she whispered. "Of course I like you better than anyone else—you ought to know that."

We never got to the word "love," but we knew the feeling.

One cloud alone flung its shadow across these idyllic days. Before I was fully aware of it I had drawn very near to the first great junction-point of my life, my graduation from Densmore Academy. We were to "change cars," in the language of Principal Haime. Well enough for the fortunate ones who were to continue the academic journey, which implied a postponement of the serious business of life; but month after month of the last term had passed without a hint from my father that I was to change cars. Again and again I almost succeeded in screwing up my courage to the point of mentioning college to him,—never quite; his manner, though kind and calm, somehow strengthened my suspicion that I had been judged and found wanting, and doomed to "business": galley slavery, I deemed it, humdrum, prosaic, degrading! When I thought of it at night I experienced almost a frenzy of self-pity. My father couldn't intend to do that, just because my monthly reports hadn't always been what he thought they ought to be! Gene Hollister's were no better, if as good, and he was going to Princeton. Was I, Hugh Paret, to be denied the distinction of being a college man, the delights of university existence, cruelly separated and set apart from my friends whom I loved! held up to the world and especially to Nancy Willett as good for nothing else! The thought was unbearable. Characteristically, I hoped against hope.

I have mentioned garden parties. One of our annual institutions was Mrs. Willett's children's party in May; for the Willett house had a garden that covered almost a quarter of a block. Mrs. Willett loved children, the greatest regret of her life being that providence had denied her a large family. As far back as my memory goes she had been something of an invalid; she had a sweet, sad face, and delicate hands so thin as to seem almost transparent; and she always sat in a chair under the great tree on the lawn, smiling at us as we soared to dizzy heights in the swing, or played croquet, or scurried through the paths, and in and out of the latticed summer-house with shrieks of laughter and terror. It all ended with a feast at a long table made of sawhorses and boards covered with a white cloth, and when the cake was cut there was wild excitement as to who would get the ring and who the thimble.

We were more decorous, or rather more awkward now, and the party began with a formal period when the boys gathered in a group and pretended indifference to the girls. The girls were cleverer at it, and actually achieved the impression that they were indifferent. We kept an eye on them, uneasily, while we talked. To be in Nancy's presence and not alone with Nancy was agonizing, and I wondered at a sang-froid beyond my power to achieve, accused her of coldness, my sufferings being the greater because she seemed more beautiful, daintier, more irreproachable than I had ever seen her. Even at that early age she gave evidence of the social gift, and it was due to her efforts that we forgot our best clothes and our newly born self-consciousness. When I begged her to slip away with me among the currant bushes she whispered:— "I can't, Hugh. I'm the hostess, you know."

I had gone there in a flutter of anticipation, but nothing went right that day. There was dancing in the big rooms that looked out on the garden; the only girl with whom I cared to dance was Nancy, and she was busy finding partners for the backward members of both sexes; though she was my partner, to be sure, when it all wound up with a Virginia reel on the lawn. Then, at supper, to cap the climax of untoward incidents, an animated discussion was begun as to the relative merits of the various colleges, the girls, too, taking sides. Mac Willett, Nancy's cousin, was going to Yale, Gene Hollister to Princeton, the Ewan boys to our State University, while Perry Blackwood and Ralph Hambleton and Ham Durrett were destined for Harvard; Tom Peters, also, though he was not to graduate from the Academy for another year. I might have known that Ralph would have suspected my misery. He sat triumphantly next to Nancy herself, while I had been told off to entertain the faithful Sophy. Noticing my silence, he demanded wickedly:—

"Where are you going, Hugh?"

"Harvard, I think," I answered with as bold a front as I could muster. "I haven't talked it over with my father yet." It was intolerable to admit that I of them all was to be left behind.

Nancy looked at me in surprise. She was always downright.

"Oh, Hugh, doesn't your father mean to put you in business?" she exclaimed.

A hot flush spread over my face. Even to her I had not betrayed my apprehensions on this painful subject. Perhaps it was because of this very reason, knowing me as she did, that she had divined my fate. Could my father have spoken of it to anyone?

"Not that I know of," I said angrily. I wondered if she knew how deeply she had hurt me. The others laughed. The colour rose in Nancy's cheeks, and she gave me an appealing, almost tearful look, but my heart had hardened. As soon as supper was over I left the table to wander, nursing my wrongs, in a far corner of the garden, gay shouts and laughter still echoing in my ears. I was negligible, even my pathetic subterfuge had been detected and cruelly ridiculed by these friends whom I had always loved and sought out, and who now were so absorbed in their own prospects and happiness that they cared nothing for mine. And Nancy! I had been betrayed by Nancy!... Twilight was coming on. I remember glancing down miserably at the new blue suit I had put on so hopefully for the first time that afternoon.

Separating the garden from the street was a high, smooth board fence with a little gate in it, and I had my hand on the latch when I heard the sound of hurrying steps on the gravel path and a familiar voice calling my name.

"Hugh! Hugh!"

I turned. Nancy stood before me.

"Hugh, you're not going!"

"Yes, I am."

"Why?"

"If you don't know, there's no use telling you."

"Just because I said your father intended to put you in business! Oh, Hugh, why are you so foolish and so proud? Do you suppose that anyone— that I—think any the worse of you?"

Yes, she had read me, she alone had entered into the source of that prevarication, the complex feelings from which it sprang. But at that moment I could not forgive her for humiliating me. I hugged my grievance.

"It was true, what I said," I declared hotly. "My father has not spoken. It is true that I'm going to college, because I'll make it true. I may not go this year."

She stood staring in sheer surprise at sight of my sudden, quivering passion. I think the very intensity of it frightened her. And then, without more ado, I opened the gate and was gone....

That night, though I did not realize it, my journey into a Far Country was begun.

The misery that followed this incident had one compensating factor. Although too late to electrify Densmore and Principal Haime with my scholarship, I was determined to go to college now, somehow, sometime. I would show my father, these companions of mine, and above all Nancy herself the stuff of which I was made, compel them sooner or later to admit that they had misjudged me. I had been possessed by similar resolutions before, though none so strong, and they had a way of sinking below the surface of my consciousness, only to rise again and again until by sheer pressure they achieved realization.

Yet I might have returned to Nancy if something had not occurred which I would have thought unbelievable: she began to show a marked preference for Ralph Hambleton. At first I regarded this affair as the most obvious of retaliations. She, likewise, had pride. Gradually, however, a feeling of uneasiness crept over me: as pretence, her performance was altogether too realistic; she threw her whole soul into it, danced with Ralph as often as she had ever danced with me, took walks with him, deferred to his opinions until, in spite of myself, I became convinced that the preference was genuine. I was a curious mixture of self- confidence and self-depreciation, and never had his superiority seemed more patent than now. His air of satisfaction was maddening.

How well I remember his triumph on that hot, June morning of our graduation from Densmore, a triumph he had apparently achieved without labour, and which he seemed to despise. A fitful breeze blew through the chapel at the top of the building; we, the graduates, sat in two rows next to the platform, and behind us the wooden benches nicked by many knives—were filled with sisters and mothers and fathers, some anxious, some proud and some sad. So brief a span, like that summer's day, and youth was gone! Would the time come when we, too, should sit by the waters of Babylon and sigh for it? The world was upside down.

We read the one hundred and third psalm. Then Principal Haime, in his long "Prince Albert" and a ridiculously inadequate collar that emphasized his scrawny neck, reminded us of the sacred associations we had formed, of the peculiar responsibilities that rested on us, who were the privileged of the city. "We had crossed to-day," he said, "an invisible threshold. Some were to go on to higher institutions of learning. Others..." I gulped. Quoting the Scriptures, he complimented those who had made the most of their opportunities. And it was then that he called out, impressively, the name of Ralph Forrester Hambleton. Summa cum laude! Suddenly I was seized with passionate, vehement regrets at the sound of the applause. I might have been the prize scholar, instead of Ralph, if I had only worked, if I had only realized what this focussing day of graduation meant! I might have been a marked individual, with people murmuring words of admiration, of speculation concerning the brilliancy of my future!... When at last my name was called and I rose to receive my diploma it seemed as though my incompetency had been proclaimed to the world...

That evening I stood in the narrow gallery of the flag-decked gymnasium and watched Nancy dancing with Ralph.

I let her go without protest or reproach. A mysterious lesion seemed to have taken place, I felt astonished and relieved, yet I was heavy with sadness. My emancipation had been bought at a price. Something hitherto spontaneous, warm and living was withering within me.

Chapter Five

It was true to my father's character that he should have waited until the day after graduation to discuss my future, if discussion be the proper word. The next evening at supper he informed me that he wished to talk to me in the sitting-room, whither I followed him with a sinking heart. He seated himself at his desk, and sat for a moment gazing at me with a curious and benumbing expression, and then the blow fell.

"Hugh, I have spoken to your Cousin Robert Breck about you, and he has kindly consented to give you a trial."

"To give me a trial, sir!" I exclaimed.

"To employ you at a small but reasonable salary."

I could find no words to express my dismay. My dreams had come to this, that I was to be made a clerk in a grocery store! The fact that it was a wholesale grocery store was little consolation.

"But father," I faltered, "I don't want to go into business."

"Ah!" The sharpness of the exclamation might have betrayed to me the pain in which he was, but he recovered himself instantly. And I could see nothing but an inexorable justice closing in on me mechanically; a blind justice, in its inability to read my soul. "The time to have decided that," he declared, "was some years ago, my son. I have given you the best schooling a boy can have, and you have not shown the least appreciation of your advantages. I do not enjoy saying this, Hugh, but in spite of all my efforts and of those of your mother, you have remained undeveloped and irresponsible. My hope, as you know, was to have made you a professional man, a lawyer, and to take you into my office. My father and grandfather were professional men before me. But you are wholly lacking in ambition."

And I had burned with it all my life!

"I have ambition," I cried, the tears forcing themselves to my eyes.

"Ambition—for what, my son?"

I hesitated. How could I tell him that my longings to do something, to be somebody in the world were never more keen than at that moment? Matthew Arnold had not then written his definition of God as the stream of tendency by which we fulfil the laws of our being; and my father, at any rate, would not have acquiesced in the definition. Dimly but passionately I felt then, as I had always felt, that I had a mission to perform, a service to do which ultimately would be revealed to me. But the hopelessness of explaining this took on, now, the proportions of a tragedy. And I could only gaze at him.

"What kind of ambition, Hugh?" he repeated sadly.

"I—I have sometimes thought I could write, sir, if I had a chance. I like it better than anything else. I—I have tried it. And if I could only go to college—"

"Literature!" There was in his voice a scandalized note.

"Why not, father?" I asked weakly.

And now it was he who, for the first time, seemed to be at a loss to express himself. He turned in his chair, and with a sweep of the hand indicated the long rows of musty-backed volumes. "Here," he said, "you have had at your disposal as well-assorted a small library as the city contains, and you have not availed yourself of it. Yet you talk to me of literature as a profession. I am afraid, Hugh, that this is merely another indication of your desire to shun hard work, and I must tell you frankly that I fail to see in you the least qualification for such a career. You have not even inherited my taste for books. I venture to say, for instance, that you have never even read a paragraph of Plutarch, and yet when I was your age I was completely familiar with the Lives. You will not read Scott or Dickens."

The impeachment was not to be denied, for the classics were hateful to me. Naturally I was afraid to make such a damning admission. My father had succeeded in presenting my ambition as the height of absurdity and presumption, and with something of the despair of a shipwrecked mariner my eyes rested on the green expanses of those book-backs, Bohn's Standard Library! Nor did it occur to him or to me that one might be great in literature without having read so much as a gritty page of them....

He finished his argument by reminding me that worthless persons sought to enter the arts in the search for a fool's paradise, and in order to satisfy a reprehensible craving for notoriety. The implication was clear, that imaginative production could not be classed as hard work. And he assured me that literature was a profession in which no one could afford to be second class. A Longfellow, a Harriet Beecher Stowe, or nothing. This was a practical age and a practical country. We had indeed produced Irvings and Hawthornes, but the future of American letters was, to say the least, problematical. We were a utilitarian people who would never create a great literature, and he reminded me that the days of the romantic and the picturesque had passed. He gathered that I desired to be a novelist. Well, novelists, with certain exceptions, were fantastic fellows who blew iridescent soap-bubbles and who had no morals. In the face of such a philosophy as his I was mute. The world appeared a dreary place of musty offices and smoky steel-works, of coal dust, of labour without a spark of inspiration. And that other, the world of my dreams, simply did not exist.

Incidentally my father had condemned Cousin Robert's wholesale grocery business as a refuge of the lesser of intellect that could not achieve the professions,—an inference not calculated to stir my ambition and liking for it at the start.

I began my business career on the following Monday morning. At breakfast, held earlier than usual on my account, my mother's sympathy was the more eloquent for being unspoken, while my father wore an air of unwonted cheerfulness; charging me, when I departed, to give his kindest remembrances to my Cousin Robert Breck. With a sense of martyrdom somehow deepened by this attitude of my parents I boarded a horse-car and went down town. Early though it was, the narrow streets of the wholesale district reverberated with the rattle of trucks and echoed with the shouts of drivers. The day promised to be scorching. At the door of the warehouse of Breck and Company I was greeted by the ineffable smell of groceries in which the suggestion of parched coffee prevailed. This is the sharpest remembrance of all, and even to-day that odour affects me somewhat in the manner that the interior of a ship affects a person prone to seasickness. My Cousin Robert, in his well-worn alpaca coat, was already seated at his desk behind the clouded glass partition next the alley at the back of the store, and as I entered he gazed at me over his steel-rimmed spectacles with that same disturbing look of clairvoyance I have already mentioned as one of his characteristics. The grey eyes were quizzical, and yet seemed to express a little commiseration.

"Well, Hugh, you've decided to honour us, have you?" he asked.

"I'm much obliged for giving me the place, Cousin Robert," I replied.

But he had no use for that sort of politeness, and he saw through me, as always.

"So you're not too tony for the grocery business, eh?"

"Oh, no, sir."

"It was good enough for old Benjamin Breck," he said. "Well, I'll give you a fair trial, my boy, and no favouritism on account of relationship, any more than to Willie."

His strong voice resounded through the store, and presently my cousin Willie appeared in answer to his summons, the same Willie who used to lead me, on mischief bent, through the barns and woods and fields of Claremore. He was barefoot no longer, though freckled still, grown lanky and tall; he wore a coarse blue apron that fell below his knees, and a pencil was stuck behind his ear.

"Get an apron for Hugh," said his father.

Willie's grin grew wider.

"I'll fit him out," he said.

"Start him in the shipping department," directed Cousin Robert, and turned to his letters.

I was forthwith provided with an apron, and introduced to the slim and anaemic but cheerful Johnny Hedges, the shipping clerk, hard at work in the alley. Secretly I looked down on my fellow-clerks, as one destined for a higher mission, made out of better stuff,—finer stuff. Despite my attempt to hide this sense of superiority they were swift to discover it; and perhaps it is to my credit as well as theirs that they did not resent it. Curiously enough, they seemed to acknowledge it. Before the week was out I had earned the nickname of Beau Brummel.

"Say, Beau," Johnny Hedges would ask, when I appeared of a morning, "what happened in the great world last night?"

I had an affection for them, these fellow-clerks, and I often wondered at their contentment with the drab lives they led, at their self- congratulation for "having a job" at Breck and Company's.

"You don't mean to say you like this kind of work?" I exclaimed one day to Johnny Hedges, as we sat on barrels of XXXX flour looking out at the hot sunlight in the alley.

"It ain't a question of liking it, Beau," he rebuked me. "It's all very well for you to talk, since your father's a millionaire" (a fiction so firmly embedded in their heads that no amount of denial affected it), "but what do you think would happen to me if I was fired? I couldn't go home and take it easy—you bet not. I just want to shake hands with myself when I think that I've got a home, and a job like this. I know a feller—a hard worker he was, too who walked the pavements for three months when the Colvers failed, and couldn't get nothing, and took to drink, and the last I heard of him he was sleeping in police stations and walking the ties, and his wife's a waitress at a cheap hotel. Don't you think it's easy to get a job."

I was momentarily sobered by the earnestness with which he brought home to me the relentlessness of our civilization. It seemed incredible. I should have learned a lesson in that store. Barring a few discordant days when the orders came in too fast or when we were short handed because of sickness, it was a veritable hive of happiness; morning after morning clerks and porters arrived, pale, yet smiling, and laboured with cheerfulness from eight o'clock until six, and departed as cheerfully for modest homes in obscure neighbourhoods that seemed to me areas of exile. They were troubled with no visions of better things. When the travelling men came in from the "road" there was great hilarity. Important personages, these, looked up to by the city clerks; jolly, reckless, Elizabethan-like rovers, who had tasted of the wine of liberty—and of other wines with the ineradicable lust for the road in their blood. No more routine for Jimmy Bowles, who was king of them all. I shudder to think how much of my knowledge of life I owe to this Jimmy, whose stories would have filled a quarto volume, but could on no account have been published; for a self-respecting post-office would not have allowed them to pass through the mails. As it was, Jimmy gave them circulation enough. I can still see his round face, with the nose just indicated, his wicked, twinkling little eyes, and I can hear his husky voice fall to a whisper when "the boss" passed through the store. Jimmy, when visiting us, always had a group around him. His audacity with women amazed me, for he never passed one of the "lady clerks" without some form of caress, which they resented but invariably laughed at. One day he imparted to me his code of morality: he never made love to another man's wife, so he assured me, if he knew the man! The secret of life he had discovered in laughter, and by laughter he sold quantities of Cousin Robert's groceries.

Mr. Bowles boasted of a catholic acquaintance in all the cities of his district, but before venturing forth to conquer these he had learned his own city by heart. My Cousin Robert was not aware of the fact that Mr. Bowles "showed" the town to certain customers. He even desired to show it to me, but an epicurean strain in my nature held me back. Johnny

Hedges went with him occasionally, and Henry Schneider, the bill clerk, and I listened eagerly to their experiences, afterwards confiding them to Tom....

There were times when, driven by an overwhelming curiosity, I ventured into certain strange streets, alone, shivering with cold and excitement, gripped by a fascination I did not comprehend, my eyes now averted, now irresistibly raised toward the white streaks of light that outlined the windows of dark houses....

One winter evening as I was going home, I encountered at the mail-box a young woman who shot at me a queer, twisted smile. I stood still, as though stunned, looking after her, and when halfway across the slushy street she turned and smiled again. Prodigiously excited, I followed her, fearful that I might be seen by someone who knew me, nor was it until she reached an unfamiliar street that I ventured to overtake her. She confounded me by facing me.

"Get out!" she cried fiercely.

I halted in my tracks, overwhelmed with shame. But she continued to regard me by the light of the street lamp.

"You didn't want to be seen with me on Second Street, did you? You're one of those sneaking swells."

The shock of this sudden onslaught was tremendous. I stood frozen to the spot, trembling, convicted, for I knew that her accusation was just; I had wounded her, and I had a desire to make amends.

"I'm sorry," I faltered. "I didn't mean—to offend you. And you smiled—" I got no farther. She began to laugh, and so loudly that I glanced anxiously about. I would have fled, but something still held me, something that belied the harshness of her laugh.

"You're just a kid," she told me. "Say, you get along home, and tell your mamma I sent you."

Whereupon I departed in a state of humiliation and self-reproach I had never before known, wandering about aimlessly for a long time. When at length I arrived at home, late for supper, my mother's solicitude only served to deepen my pain. She went to the kitchen herself to see if my mince-pie were hot, and served me with her own hands. My father remained at his place at the head of the table while I tried to eat, smiling indulgently at her ministrations.

"Oh, a little hard work won't hurt him, Sarah," he said. "When I was his age I often worked until eleven o'clock and never felt the worse for it. Business must be pretty good, eh, Hugh?"

I had never seen him in a more relaxing mood, a more approving one. My mother sat down beside me.... Words seem useless to express the complicated nature of my suffering at that moment,—my remorse, my sense of deception, of hypocrisy,—yes, and my terror. I tried to talk naturally, to answer my father's questions about affairs at the store, while all the time my eyes rested upon the objects of the room, familiar since childhood. Here were warmth, love, and safety. Why could I not be content with them, thankful for them? What was it in me that drove me from these sheltering walls out into the dark places? I glanced at my father. Had he ever known these wild, destroying desires? Oh, if I only could have confided in him! The very idea of it was preposterous. Such placidity as theirs would never understand the nature of my temptations, and I pictured to myself their horror and despair at my revelation. In imagination I beheld their figures receding while I drifted out to sea, alone. Would the tide—which was somehow within me—carry me out and out, in spite of all I could do?

"Give me that man That is not passion's slave, and I will wear him In my heart's core...."

I did not shirk my tasks at the store, although I never got over the feeling that a fine instrument was being employed where a coarser one would have done equally well. There were moments when I was almost overcome by surges of self-commiseration and of impotent anger: for instance, I was once driven out of a shop by an incensed German grocer whom I had asked to settle a long-standing account. Yet the days passed, the daily grind absorbed my energies, and when I was not collecting, or tediously going over the stock in the dim recesses of the store, I was running errands in the wholesale district, treading the burning brick of the pavements, dodging heavy trucks and drays and perspiring clerks who flew about with memorandum pads in their hands, or awaiting the pleasure of bank tellers. Save Harvey, the venerable porter, I was the last to leave the store in the evening, and I always came away with the taste on my palate of Breck and Company's mail, it being my final duty to "lick" the whole of it and deposit it in the box at the corner. The gum on the envelopes tasted of winter-green.

My Cousin Robert was somewhat astonished at my application.

"We'll make a man of you yet, Hugh," he said to me once, when I had performed a commission with unexpected despatch....

Business was his all-in-all, and he had an undisguised contempt for higher education. To send a boy to college was, in his opinion, to run no inconsiderable risk of ruining him. What did they amount to when they came home, strutting like peacocks, full of fads and fancies, and much too good to associate with decent, hard-working citizens? Nevertheless when autumn came and my friends departed with eclat for the East, I was desperate indeed! Even the contemplation of Robert Breck did not console me, and yet here, in truth, was a life which might have served me as a model. His store was his castle; and his reputation for integrity and square dealing as wide as the city. Often I used to watch him with a certain envy as he stood in the doorway, his hands in his pockets, and greeted fellow-merchant and banker with his genuine and dignified directness. This man was his own master. They all called him "Robert," and they made it clear by their manner that they knew they were addressing one who fulfilled his obligations and asked no favours.

Crusty old Nathaniel Durrett once declared that when you bought a bill of goods from Robert Breck you did not have to check up the invoice or employ a chemist. Here was a character to mould upon. If my ambition could but have been bounded by Breck and Company, I, too, might have come to stand in that doorway content with a tribute that was greater than Caesar's.

I had been dreading the Christmas holidays, which were indeed to be no holidays for me. And when at length they arrived they brought with them from the East certain heroes fashionably clad, citizens now of a larger world than mine. These former companions had become superior beings, they could not help showing it, and their presence destroyed the Balance of Things. For alas, I had not wholly abjured the feminine sex after all! And from being a somewhat important factor in the lives of Ruth Hollister and other young women I suddenly became of no account. New interests, new rivalries and loyalties had arisen in which I had no share; I must perforce busy myself with invoices of flour and coffee and canned fruits while sleigh rides and coasting and skating expeditions to Blackstone Lake followed one another day after day,—for the irony of circumstances had decreed a winter uncommonly cold. There were evening parties, too, where I felt like an alien, though my friends were guilty of no conscious neglect; and had I been able to accept the situation simply, I should not have suffered.

The principal event of those holidays was a play given in the old Hambleton house (which later became the Boyne Club), under the direction of the lively and talented Mrs. Watling. I was invited, indeed, to participate; but even if I had had the desire I could not have done so, since the rehearsals were carried on in the daytime. Nancy was the leading lady. I have neglected to mention that she too had been away almost continuously since our misunderstanding, for the summer in the mountains,—a sojourn recommended for her mother's health; and in the autumn she had somewhat abruptly decided to go East to boarding-school at Farmington. During the brief months of her absence she had marvellously acquired maturity and aplomb, a worldliness of manner and a certain frivolity that seemed to put those who surrounded her on a lower plane. She was only seventeen, yet she seemed the woman of thirty whose role she played. First there were murmurs, then sustained applause. I scarcely recognized her: she had taken wings and soared far above me, suggesting a sphere of power and luxury hitherto unimagined and beyond the scope of the world to which I belonged.

Her triumph was genuine. When the play was over she was immediately surrounded by enthusiastic admirers eager to congratulate her, to dance with her. I too would have gone forward, but a sense of inadequacy, of unimportance, of an inability to cope with her, held me back, and from a corner I watched her sweeping around the room, holding up her train, and leaning on the arm of Bob Lansing, a classmate whom Ralph had brought home from Harvard. Then it was Ralph's turn: that affair seemed still to be going on. My feelings were a strange medley of despondency and stimulation....

Our eyes met. Her partner now was Ham Durrett. Capriciously releasing him, she stood before me,

"Hugh, you haven't asked me to dance, or even told me what you thought of the play."

"I thought it was splendid," I said lamely.

Because she refrained from replying I was farther than ever from understanding her. How was I to divine what she felt? or whether any longer she felt at all? Here, in this costume of a woman of the world, with the string of pearls at her neck to give her the final touch of brilliancy, was a strange, new creature who baffled and silenced me.... We had not gone halfway across the room when she halted abruptly.

"I'm tired," she exclaimed. "I don't feel like dancing just now," and led the way to the big, rose punch-bowl, one of the Durretts' most cherished possessions. Glancing up at me over the glass of lemonade I had given her she went on: "Why haven't you been to see me since I came home? I've wanted to talk to you, to hear how you are getting along."

Was she trying to make amends, or reminding me in this subtle way of the cause of our quarrel? What I was aware of as I looked at her was an attitude, a vantage point apparently gained by contact with that mysterious outer world which thus vicariously had laid its spell on me; I was tremendously struck by the thought that to achieve this attitude meant emancipation, invulnerability against the aches and pains which otherwise our fellow-beings had the power to give us; mastery over life, —the ability to choose calmly, as from a height, what were best for one's self, untroubled by loves and hates. Untroubled by loves and hates! At that very moment, paradoxically, I loved her madly, but with a love not of the old quality, a love that demanded a vantage point of its own. Even though she had made an advance—and some elusiveness in her manner led me to doubt it I could not go to her now. I must go as a conqueror, —a conqueror in the lists she herself had chosen, where the prize is power.

"Oh, I'm getting along pretty well," I said. "At any rate, they don't complain of me."

"Somehow," she ventured, "somehow it's hard to think of you as a business man."

I took this for a reference to the boast I had made that I would go to college.

"Business isn't so bad as it might be," I assured her.

"I think a man ought to go away to college," she declared, in what seemed another tone. "He makes friends, learns certain things,—it gives him finish. We are very provincial here."

Provincial! I did not stop to reflect how recently she must have acquired the word; it summed up precisely the self-estimate at which I had arrived. The sting went deep. Before I could think of an effective reply Nancy was being carried off by the young man from the East, who was clearly infatuated. He was not provincial. She smiled back at me brightly over his shoulder.... In that instant were fused in one resolution all the discordant elements within me of aspiration and discontent. It was not so much that I would show Nancy what I intended to do—I would show myself; and I felt a sudden elation, and accession of power that enabled me momentarily to despise the puppets with whom she danced.... From this mood I was awakened with a start to feel a hand on my shoulder, and I turned to confront her father, McAlery Willett; a gregarious, easygoing, pleasure-loving gentleman who made only a pretence of business, having inherited an ample fortune from his father, unique among his generation in our city in that he paid some attention to fashion in his dress; good living was already beginning to affect his figure. His mellow voice had a way of breaking an octave.

"Don't worry, my boy," he said. "You stick to business. These college fellows are cocks of the walk just now, but some day you'll be able to snap your fingers at all of 'em."

The next day was dark, overcast, smoky, damp-the soft, unwholesome dampness that follows a spell of hard frost. I spent the morning and afternoon on the gloomy third floor of Breck and Company, making a list of the stock. I remember the place as though I had just stepped out of it, the freight elevator at the back, the dusty, iron columns, the continuous piles of cases and bags and barrels with narrow aisles between them; the dirty windows, spotted and soot-streaked, that looked down on Second Street. I was determined now to escape from all this, and I had my plan in mind.

No sooner had I swallowed my supper that evening than I set out at a swift pace for a modest residence district ten blocks away, coming to a little frame house set back in a yard,—one of those houses in which the ringing of the front door-bell produces the greatest commotion; children's voices were excitedly raised and then hushed. After a brief silence the door was opened by a pleasant-faced, brown-bearded man, who stood staring at me in surprise. His hair was rumpled, he wore an old house coat with a hole in the elbow, and with one finger he kept his place in the book which he held in his hand.

"Hugh Paret!" he exclaimed.

He ushered me into a little parlour lighted by two lamps, that bore every evidence of having been recently vacated. Its features somehow bespoke a struggle for existence; as though its occupants had worried much and loved much. It was a room best described by the word "home"—home made more precious by a certain precariousness. Toys and school-books strewed the floor, a sewing-bag and apron lay across the sofa, and in one corner was a roll-topped desk of varnished oak. The seats of the chairs were comfortably depressed.

So this was where Mr. Wood lived! Mr. Wood, instructor in Latin and Greek at Densmore Academy. It was now borne in on me for the first time that he did live and have his ties like any other human being, instead of just appearing magically from nowhere on a platform in a chalky room at nine every morning, to vanish again in the afternoon. I had formerly stood in awe of his presence. But now I was suddenly possessed by an embarrassment, and (shall I say it?) by a commiseration bordering on contempt for a man who would consent to live thus for the sake of being a schoolteacher. How strange that civilization should set such a high value on education and treat its functionaries with such neglect!

Mr. Wood's surprise at seeing me was genuine. For I had never shown a particular interest in him, nor in the knowledge which he strove to impart.

"I thought you had forgotten me, Hugh," he said, and added whimsically: "most boys do, when they graduate."

I felt the reproach, which made it the more difficult for me to state my errand.

"I knew you sometimes took pupils in the evening, Mr. Wood."

"Pupils,—yes," he replied, still eyeing me. Suddenly his eyes twinkled. He had indeed no reason to suspect me of thirsting for learning. "But I was under the impression that you had gone into business, Hugh."

"The fact is, sir," I explained somewhat painfully, "that I am not satisfied with business. I feel—as if I ought to know more. And I came to see if you would give me lessons about three nights a week, because I want to take the Harvard examinations next summer."

Thus I made it appear, and so persuaded myself, that my ambition had been prompted by a craving for knowledge. As soon as he could recover himself he reminded me that he had on many occasions declared I had a brain.

"Your father must be very happy over this decision of yours," he said.

That was the point, I told him. It was to be a surprise for my father; I was to take the examinations first, and inform him afterwards.

To my intense relief, Mr. Wood found the scheme wholly laudable, and entered into it with zest. He produced examinations of preceding years from a pigeonhole in his desk, and inside of half an hour the arrangement was made, the price of the lessons settled. They were well within my salary, which recently had been raised....

When I went down town, or collecting bills for Breck and Company, I took a text-book along with me in the street-cars. Now at last I had behind my studies a driving force. Algebra, Latin, Greek and history became worth while, means to an end. I astonished Mr. Wood; and sometimes he would tilt back his chair, take off his spectacles and pull his beard.

"Why in the name of all the sages," he would demand, "couldn't you have done this well at school? You might have led your class, instead of Ralph Hambleton."

I grew very fond of Mr. Wood, and even of his thin little wife, who occasionally flitted into the room after we had finished. I fully intended to keep up with them in after life, but I never did. I forgot them completely....

My parents were not wholly easy in their minds concerning me; they were bewildered by the new aspect I presented. For my lately acquired motive was strong enough to compel me to restrict myself socially, and the evenings I spent at home were given to study, usually in my own room. Once I was caught with a Latin grammar: I was just "looking over it," I said. My mother sighed. I knew what was in her mind; she had always been secretly disappointed that I had not been sent to college. And presently, when my father went out to attend a trustee's meeting, the impulse to confide in her almost overcame me; I loved her with that affection which goes out to those whom we feel understand us, but I was learning to restrain my feelings. She looked at me wistfully.... I knew that she would insist on telling my father, and thus possibly frustrate my plans. That I was not discovered was due to a certain quixotic twist in my father's character. I was working now, and though not actually earning my own living, he no longer felt justified in prying into my affairs.

When June arrived, however, my tutor began to show signs that his conscience was troubling him, and one night he delivered his ultimatum. The joke had gone far enough, he implied. My intentions, indeed, he found praiseworthy, but in his opinion it was high time that my father were informed of them; he was determined to call at my father's office.

The next morning was blue with the presage of showers; blue, too, with the presage of fate. An interminable morning. My tasks had become utterly distasteful. And in the afternoon, so when I sat down to make out invoices, I wrote automatically the names of the familiar customers, my mind now exalted by hope, now depressed by anxiety. The result of an interview perhaps even now going on would determine whether or no I should be immediately released from a slavery I detested. Would Mr. Wood persuade my father? If not, I was prepared to take more desperate measures; remain in the grocery business I would not. In the evening, as I hurried homeward from the corner where the Boyne Street car had dropped me, I halted suddenly in front of the Peters house, absorbing the scene where my childhood had been spent: each of these spreading maples was an old friend, and in these yards I had played and dreamed. An unaccountable sadness passed over me as I walked on toward our gate; I entered it, gained the doorway of the house and went upstairs, glancing into the sitting room. My mother sat by the window, sewing. She looked up at me with an ineffable expression, in which I read a trace of tears.

"Hugh!" she exclaimed.

I felt very uncomfortable, and stood looking down at her.

"Why didn't you tell us, my son?" In her voice was in truth reproach; yet mingled with that was another note, which I think was pride.

"What has father said?" I asked.

"Oh, my dear, he will tell you himself. I—I don't know—he will talk to you."

Suddenly she seized my hands and drew me down to her, and then held me away, gazing into my face with a passionate questioning, her lips smiling, her eyes wet. What did she see? Was there a subtler relationship between our natures than I guessed? Did she understand by some instinctive power the riddle within me? divine through love the force that was driving me on she knew not whither, nor I? At the sound of my father's step in the hall she released me. He came in as though nothing had happened.

"Well, Hugh, are you home?" he said....

Never had I been more impressed, more bewildered by his self-command than at that time. Save for the fact that my mother talked less than usual, supper passed as though nothing had happened. Whether I had shaken him, disappointed him, or gained his reluctant approval I could not tell. Gradually his outward calmness turned my suspense to irritation....

But when at length we were alone together, I gained a certain reassurance. His manner was not severe. He hesitated a little before beginning.

"I must confess, Hugh; that I scarcely know what to say about this proceeding of yours. The thing that strikes me most forcibly is that you might have confided in your mother and myself."

Hope flashed up within me, like an explosion.

"I—I wanted to surprise you, father. And then, you see, I thought it would be wiser to find out first how well I was likely to do at the examinations."

My father looked at me. Unfortunately he possessed neither a sense of humour nor a sense of tragedy sufficient to meet such a situation. For the first time in my life I beheld him at a disadvantage; for I had, somehow, managed at length to force him out of position, and he was puzzled. I was quick to play my trump card.

"I have been thinking it over carefully," I told him, "and I have made up my mind that I want to go into the law."

"The law!" he exclaimed sharply.

"Why, yes, sir. I know that you were disappointed because I did not do sufficiently well at school to go to college and study for the bar."

I felt indeed a momentary pang, but I remembered that I was fighting for my freedom.

"You seemed satisfied where you were," he said in a puzzled voice, "and your Cousin Robert gives a good account of you."

"I've tried to do the work as well as I could, sir," I replied. "But I don't like the grocery business, or any other business. I have a feeling that I'm not made for it."

"And you think, now, that you are made for the law?" he asked, with the faint hint of a smile.

"Yes, sir, I believe I could succeed at it. I'd like to try," I replied modestly.

"You've given up the idiotic notion of wishing to be an author?"

I implied that he himself had convinced me of the futility of such a wish. I listened to his next words as in a dream.

"I must confess to you, Hugh, that there are times when I fail to understand you. I hope it is as you say, that you have arrived at a settled conviction as to your future, and that this is not another of those caprices to which you have been subject, nor a desire to shirk honest work. Mr. Wood has made out a strong case for you, and I have therefore determined to give you a trial. If you pass the examinations with credit, you may go to college, but if at any time you fail to make good progress, you come home, and go into business again. Is that thoroughly understood?"

I said it was, and thanked him effusively.... I had escaped,—the prison doors had flown open. But it is written that every happiness has its sting; and my joy, intense though it was, had in it a core of remorse....

I went downstairs to my mother, who was sitting in the hall by the open door.

"Father says I may go!" I said.

She got up and took me in her arms.

"My dear, I am so glad, although we shall miss you dreadfully.... Hugh?"

"Yes, mother."

"Oh, Hugh, I so want you to be a good man!"

Her cry was a little incoherent, but fraught with a meaning that came home to me, in spite of myself....

A while later I ran over to announce to the amazed Tom Peters that I was actually going to Harvard with him. He stood in the half-lighted hallway, his hands in his pockets, blinking at me.

"Hugh, you're a wonder!" he cried. "How in Jehoshaphat did you work it?"...

I lay long awake that night thinking over the momentous change so soon to come into my life, wondering exultantly what Nancy Willett would say now. I was not one, at any rate, to be despised or neglected.

Chapter Six

The following September Tom Peters and I went East together. In the early morning Boston broke on us like a Mecca as we rolled out of the old Albany station, joint lords of a "herdic." How sharply the smell of the salt-laden east wind and its penetrating coolness come back to me! I seek in vain for words to express the exhilarating effect of that briny coolness on my imagination, and of the visions it summoned up of the newer, larger life into which I had marvellously been transported. We alighted at the Parker House, full-fledged men of the world, and tried to act as though the breakfast of which we partook were merely an incident, not an Event; as though we were Seniors, and not freshmen, assuming an indifference to the beings by whom we were surrounded and who were breakfasting, too,—although the nice-looking ones with fresh faces and trim clothes were all undoubtedly Olympians. The better to proclaim our nonchalance, we seated ourselves on a lounge of the marble-paved lobby and smoked cigarettes. This was liberty indeed! At length we departed for Cambridge, in another herdic.

Boston! Could it be possible? Everything was so different here as to give the place the aspect of a dream: the Bulfinch State House, the decorous shops, the still more decorous dwellings with the purple-paned windows facing the Common; Back Bay, still boarded up, ivy-spread, suggestive of a mysterious and delectable existence. We crossed the Charles River, blue-grey and still that morning; traversed a nondescript district, and at last found ourselves gazing out of the windows at the mellowed, plum-coloured bricks of the University buildings.... All at once our exhilaration evaporated as the herdic rumbled into a side street and backed up before the door of a not-too-inviting, three-storied house with a queer extension on top. Its steps and vestibule were, however, immaculate. The bell was answered by a plainly overworked servant girl, of whom we inquired for Mrs. Bolton, our landlady. There followed a period of waiting in a parlour from which the light had been almost wholly banished, with slippery horsehair furniture and a marble-topped table; and Mrs. Bolton, when she appeared, dressed in rusty black, harmonized perfectly with the funereal gloom. She was a tall, rawboned, severe lady with a peculiar red-mottled complexion that somehow reminded one of the outcropping rocks of her native New England soil.

"You want to see your rooms, I suppose," she remarked impassively when we had introduced ourselves, and as we mounted the stairs behind her Tom, in a whisper, nicknamed her "Granite Face." Presently she left us.

"Hospitable soul!" said Tom, who, with his hands in his pockets, was gazing at the bare walls of our sitting-room. "We'll have to go into the house-furnishing business, Hughie. I vote we don't linger here to-day— we'll get melancholia."

Outside, however, the sun was shining brightly, and we departed immediately to explore Cambridge and announce our important presences to the proper authorities.... We went into Boston to dine.... It was not until nine o'clock in the evening that we returned and the bottom suddenly dropped out of things. He who has tasted that first, acute homesickness of college will know what I mean. It usually comes at the opening of one's trunk. The sight of the top tray gave me a pang I shall never forget. I would not have believed that I loved my mother so much! These articles had been packed by her hands; and in one corner, among the underclothes on which she had neatly sewed my initials, lay the new Bible she had bought. "Hugh Moreton Paret, from his Mother. September, 1881." I took it up (Tom was not looking) and tried to read a passage, but my eyes were blurred. What was it within me that pressed and pressed until I thought I could bear the pain of it no longer? I pictured the sitting- room at home, and my father and mother there, thinking of me. Yes, I must acknowledge it; in the bitterness of that moment I longed to be back once more in the railed-off space on the floor of Breck and Company, writing invoices....

Presently, as we went on silently with our unpacking, we became aware of someone in the doorway.

"Hello, you fellows!" he cried. "We're classmates, I guess."

We turned to behold an ungainly young man in an ill-fitting blue suit. His face was pimply, his eyes a Teutonic blue, his yellow hair rumpled, his naturally large mouth was made larger by a friendly grin.

"I'm Hermann Krebs," he announced simply. "Who are you?"

We replied, I regret to say, with a distinct coolness that did not seem to bother him in the least. He advanced into the room, holding out a large, red, and serviceable hand, evidently it had never dawned on him that there was such a thing in the world as snobbery. But Tom and I had been "coached" by Ralph Hambleton and Perry Blackwood, warned to be careful of our friendships. There was a Reason! In any case Mr. Krebs would not have appealed to us. In answer to a second question he was informed what city we hailed from, and he proclaimed himself likewise a native of our state.

"Why, I'm from Elkington!" he exclaimed, as though the fact sealed our future relationships. He seated himself on Tom's trunk and added: "Welcome to old Harvard!"

We felt that he was scarcely qualified to speak for "old Harvard," but we did not say so.

"You look as if you'd been pall-bearers for somebody," was his next observation.

To this there seemed no possible reply.

"You fellows are pretty well fixed here," he went on, undismayed, gazing about a room which had seemed to us the abomination of desolation. "Your folks must be rich. I'm up under the skylight."

Even this failed to touch us. His father—he told us with undiminished candour—had been a German emigrant who had come over in '49, after the cause of liberty had been lost in the old country, and made eye-glasses and opera glasses. There hadn't been a fortune in it. He, Hermann, had worked at various occupations in the summer time, from peddling to farming, until he had saved enough to start him at Harvard. Tom, who had been bending over his bureau drawer, straightened up.

"What did you want to come here for?" he demanded.

"Say, what did you?" Mr. Krebs retorted genially. "To get an education, of course."

"An education!" echoed Tom.

"Isn't Harvard the oldest and best seat of learning in America?" There was an exaltation in Krebs's voice that arrested my attention, and made me look at him again. A troubled chord had been struck within me.

"Sure," said Tom.

"What did you come for?" Mr. Krebs persisted.

"To sow my wild oats," said Tom. "I expect to have something of a crop, too."

For some reason I could not fathom, it suddenly seemed to dawn on Mr. Krebs, as a result of this statement, that he wasn't wanted.

"Well, so long," he said, with a new dignity that curiously belied the informality of his farewell.

An interval of silence followed his departure.

"Well, he's got a crust!" said Tom, at last.

My own feeling about Mr. Krebs had become more complicated; but I took my cue from Tom, who dealt with situations simply.

"He'll come in for a few knockouts," he declared. "Here's to old Harvard, the greatest institution of learning in America! Oh, gee!"

Our visitor, at least, made us temporarily forget our homesickness, but it returned with redoubled intensity when we had put out the lights and gone to bed.

Before we had left home it had been mildly hinted to us by Ralph and Perry Blackwood that scholarly eminence was not absolutely necessary to one's welfare and happiness at Cambridge. The hint had been somewhat superfluous; but the question remained, what was necessary? With a view of getting some light on this delicate subject we paid a visit the next evening to our former friends and schoolmates, whose advice was conveyed with a masterly circumlocution that impressed us both. There are some things that may not be discussed directly, and the conduct of life at a modern university—which is a reflection of life in the greater world—is one of these. Perry Blackwood and Ham did most of the talking, while Ralph, characteristically, lay at full length on the window-seat, interrupting with an occasional terse and cynical remark very much to the point. As a sophomore, he in particular seemed lifted immeasurably above us, for he was—as might have been expected already a marked man in his class. The rooms which he shared with his cousin made a tremendous impression on Tom and me, and seemed palatial in comparison to our quarters at Mrs. Bolton's, eloquent of the freedom and luxury of undergraduate existence; their note, perhaps, was struck by the profusion of gay sofa pillows, then something of an innovation. The heavy, expensive furniture was of a pattern new to me; and on the mantel were three or four photographs of ladies in the alluring costume of the musical stage, in which Tom evinced a particular interest.

"Did grandfather send 'em?" he inquired.

"They're Ham's," said Ralph, and he contrived somehow to get into those two words an epitome of his cousin's character. Ham was stouter, and his clothes were more striking, more obviously expensive than ever.... On our way homeward, after we had walked a block or two in silence, Tom exclaimed:—

"Don't make friends with the friendless!—eh, Hughie? We knew enough to begin all right, didn't we?"...

Have I made us out a pair of deliberate, calculating snobs? Well, after all it must be remembered that our bringing up had not been of sufficient liberality to include the Krebses of this world. We did not, indeed, spend much time in choosing and weighing those whom we should know and those whom we should avoid; and before the first term of that Freshman year was over Tom had become a favourite. He had the gift of making men feel that he delighted in their society, that he wished for nothing better than to sit for hours in their company, content to listen to the arguments that raged about him. Once in a while he would make a droll observation that was greeted with fits of laughter. He was always referred to as "old Tom," or "good old Tom"; presently, when he began to pick out chords on the banjo, it was discovered that he had a good tenor voice, though he could not always be induced to sing.... Somewhat to the jeopardy of the academic standard that my father expected me to sustain, our rooms became a rendezvous for many clubable souls whose maudlin, midnight attempts at harmony often set the cocks crowing.

"Free from care and despair, What care we? 'Tis wine, 'tis wine That makes the jollity."

As a matter of truth, on these occasions it was more often beer; beer transported thither in Tom's new valise,—given him by his mother,—and stuffed with snow to keep the bottles cold. Sometimes Granite Face, adorned in a sky-blue wrapper, would suddenly appear in the doorway to declare that we were a disgrace to her respectable house: the university authorities should be informed, etc., etc. Poor woman, we were outrageously inconsiderate of her.... One evening as we came through the hall we caught a glimpse in the dimly lighted parlour of a young man holding a shy and pale little girl on his lap, Annie, Mrs. Bolton's daughter: on the face of our landlady was an expression I had never seen there, like a light. I should scarcely have known her. Tom and I paused at the foot of the stairs. He clutched my arm.

"Darned if it wasn't our friend Krebs!" he whispered.

While I was by no means so popular as Tom, I got along fairly well. I had escaped from provincialism, from the obscure purgatory of the wholesale grocery business; new vistas, exciting and stimulating, had been opened up; nor did I offend the sensibilities and prejudices of the new friends I made, but gave a hearty consent to a code I found congenial. I recognized in the social system of undergraduate life at Harvard a reflection of that of a greater world where I hoped some day to shine; yet my ambition did not prey upon me. Mere conformity, however, would not have taken me very far in a sphere from which I, in common with many others, desired not to be excluded.... One day, in an idle but inspired moment, I paraphrased a song from "Pinafore," applying it to a college embroglio, and the brief and lively vogue it enjoyed was sufficient to indicate a future usefulness. I had "found myself." This was in the last part of the freshman year, and later on I became a sort of amateur, class poet-laureate. Many were the skits I composed, and Tom sang them....

During that freshman year we often encountered Hermann Krebs, whistling merrily, on the stairs.

"Got your themes done?" he would inquire cheerfully.

And Tom would always mutter, when he was out of earshot: "He has got a crust!"

When I thought about Krebs at all,—and this was seldom indeed,—his manifest happiness puzzled me. Our cool politeness did not seem to bother him in the least; on the contrary, I got the impression that it amused him. He seemed to have made no friends. And after that first evening, memorable for its homesickness, he never ventured to repeat his visit to us.

One windy November day I spied his somewhat ludicrous figure striding ahead of me, his trousers above his ankles. I was bundled up in a new ulster,—of which I was secretly quite proud,—but he wore no overcoat at all.

"Well, how are you getting along?" I asked, as I overtook him.

He made clear, as he turned, his surprise that I should have addressed him at all, but immediately recovered himself.

"Oh, fine," he responded. "I've had better luck than I expected. I'm correspondent for two or three newspapers. I began by washing windows, and doing odd jobs for the professors' wives." He laughed. "I guess that doesn't strike you as good luck."

He showed no resentment at my patronage, but a self-sufficiency that made my sympathy seem superfluous, giving the impression of an inner harmony and content that surprised me.

"I needn't ask how you're getting along," he said....

At the end of the freshman year we abandoned Mrs. Bolton's for more desirable quarters.

I shall not go deeply into my college career, recalling only such incidents as, seen in the retrospect, appear to have had significance. I have mentioned my knack for song-writing; but it was not, I think, until my junior year there was startlingly renewed in me my youthful desire to write, to create something worth while, that had so long been dormant.

The inspiration came from Alonzo Cheyne, instructor in English; a remarkable teacher, in spite of the finicky mannerisms which Tom imitated. And when, in reading aloud certain magnificent passages, he forgot his affectations, he managed to arouse cravings I thought to have deserted me forever. Was it possible, after all, that I had been right and my father wrong? that I might yet be great in literature?

A mere hint from Alonzo Cheyne was more highly prized by the grinds than fulsome praise from another teacher. And to his credit it should be recorded that the grinds were the only ones he treated with any seriousness; he took pains to answer their questions; but towards the rest of us, the Chosen, he showed a thinly veiled contempt. None so quick as he to detect a simulated interest, or a wily effort to make him ridiculous; and few tried this a second time, for he had a rapier-like gift of repartee that transfixed the offender like a moth on a pin. He had a way of eyeing me at times, his glasses in his hand, a queer smile on his lips, as much as to imply that there was one at least among the lost who was made for better things. Not that my work was poor, but I knew that it might have been better. Out of his classes, however, beyond the immediate, disturbing influence of his personality I would relapse into indifference....

Returning one evening to our quarters, which were now in the "Yard," I found Tom seated with a blank sheet before him, thrusting his hand through his hair and biting the end of his penholder to a pulp. In his muttering, which was mixed with the curious, stingless profanity of which he was master, I caught the name of Cheyne, and I knew that he was facing the crisis of a fortnightly theme. The subject assigned was a narrative of some personal experience, and it was to be handed in on the morrow. My own theme was already, written.

"I've been holding down this chair for an hour, and I can't seem to think of a thing." He rose to fling himself down on the lounge. "I wish I was in Canada."

"Why Canada?"

"Trout fishing with Uncle Jake at that club of his where he took me last summer." Tom gazed dreamily at the ceiling. "Whenever I have some darned foolish theme like this to write I want to go fishing, and I want to go like the devil. I'll get Uncle Jake to take you, too, next summer."

"I wish you would."

"Say, that's living all right, Hughie, up there among the tamaracks and balsams!" And he began, for something like the thirtieth time, to relate the adventures of the trip.

As he talked, the idea presented itself to me with sudden fascination to use this incident as the subject of Tom's theme; to write it for him, from his point of view, imitating the droll style he would have had if he had been able to write; for, when he was interested in any matter, his oral narrative did not lack vividness. I began to ask him questions: what were the trees like, for instance? How did the French-Canadian guides talk? He had the gift of mimicry: aided by a partial knowledge of French I wrote down a few sentences as they sounded. The canoe had upset and he had come near drowning. I made him describe his sensations.

"I'll write your theme for you," I exclaimed, when he had finished.

"Gee, not about that!"

"Why not? It's a personal experience."

His gratitude was pathetic.... By this time I was so full of the subject that it fairly clamoured for expression, and as I wrote the hours flew. Once in a while I paused to ask him a question as he sat with his chair tilted back and his feet on the table, reading a detective story. I sketched in the scene with bold strokes; the desolate bois brule on the mountain side, the polished crystal surface of the pool broken here and there with the circles left by rising fish; I pictured Armand, the guide, his pipe between his teeth, holding the canoe against the current; and I seemed to smell the sharp tang of the balsams, to hear the roar of the rapids below. Then came the sudden hooking of the big trout, habitant oaths from Armand, bouleversement, wetness, darkness, confusion; a half- strangled feeling, a brief glimpse of green things and sunlight, and then strangulation, or what seemed like it; strangulation, the sense of being picked up and hurled by a terrific force whither? a blinding whiteness, in which it was impossible to breathe, one sharp, almost unbearable pain, then another, then oblivion.... Finally, awakening, to be confronted by a much worried Uncle Jake.

By this time the detective story had fallen to the floor, and Tom was huddled up in his chair, asleep. He arose obediently and wrapped a wet towel around his head, and began to write. Once he paused long enough to mutter:—

"Yes, that's about it,—that's the way I felt!" and set to work again, mechanically,—all the praise I got for what I deemed a literary achievement of the highest order! At three o'clock, a.m., he finished, pulled off his clothes automatically and tumbled into bed. I had no desire for sleep. My brain was racing madly, like an engine without a governor. I could write! I could write! I repeated the words over and over to myself. All the complexities of my present life were blotted out, and I beheld only the long, sweet vista of the career for which I was now convinced that nature had intended me. My immediate fortunes became unimportant, immaterial. No juice of the grape I had ever tasted made me half so drunk.... With the morning, of course, came the reaction, and I suffered the after sensations of an orgie, awaking to a world of necessity, cold and grey and slushy, and necessity alone made me rise from my bed. My experience of the night before might have taught me that happiness lies in the trick of transforming necessity, but it did not. The vision had faded,—temporarily, at least; and such was the distraction of the succeeding days that the subject of the theme passed from my mind....

One morning Tom was later than usual in getting home. I was writing a letter when he came in, and did not notice him, yet I was vaguely aware of his standing over me. When at last I looked up I gathered from his expression that something serious had happened, so mournful was his face, and yet so utterly ludicrous.

"Say, Hugh, I'm in the deuce of a mess," he announced.

"What's the matter?" I inquired.

He sank down on the table with a groan.

"It's Alonzo," he said.

Then I remembered the theme.

"What—what's he done?" I demanded.

"He says I must become a writer. Think of it, me a writer! He says I'm a young Shakespeare, that I've been lazy and hid my light under a bushel! He says he knows now what I can do, and if I don't keep up the quality, he'll know the reason why, and write a personal letter to my father. Oh, hell!"

In spite of his evident anguish, I was seized with a convulsive laughter. Tom stood staring at me moodily.

"You think it's funny,—don't you? I guess it is, but what's going to become of me? That's what I want to know. I've been in trouble before, but never in any like this. And who got me into it? You!"

Here was gratitude!

"You've got to go on writing 'em, now." His voice became desperately pleading. "Say, Hugh, old man, you can temper 'em down—temper 'em down gradually. And by the end of the year, let's say, they'll be about normal again."

He seemed actually shivering.

"The end of the year!" I cried, the predicament striking me for the first time in its fulness. "Say, you've got a crust!"

"You'll do it, if I have to hold a gun over you," he announced grimly.

Mingled with my anxiety, which was real, was an exultation that would not down. Nevertheless, the idea of developing Tom into a Shakespeare,—Tom, who had not the slightest desire to be one I was appalling, besides having in it an element of useless self-sacrifice from which I recoiled. On the other hand, if Alonzo should discover that I had written his theme, there were penalties I did not care to dwell upon .... With such a cloud hanging over me I passed a restless night.

As luck would have it the very next evening in the level light under the elms of the Square I beheld sauntering towards me a dapper figure which I recognized as that of Mr. Cheyne himself. As I saluted him he gave me an amused and most disconcerting glance; and when I was congratulating myself that he had passed me he stopped.

"Fine weather for March, Paret," he observed.

"Yes, sir," I agreed in a strange voice.

"By the way," he remarked, contemplating the bare branches above our heads, "that was an excellent theme your roommate handed in. I had no idea that he possessed such—such genius. Did you, by any chance, happen to read it?"

"Yes, sir,—I read it."

"Weren't you surprised?" inquired Mr. Cheyne.

"Well, yes, sir—that is—I mean to say he talks just like that, sometimes—that is, when it's anything he cares about."

"Indeed!" said Mr. Cheyne. "That's interesting, most interesting. In all my experience, I do not remember a case in which a gift has been developed so rapidly. I don't want to give the impression—ah that there is no room for improvement, but the thing was very well done, for an undergraduate. I must confess I never should have suspected it in Peters, and it's most interesting what you say about his cleverness in conversation." He twirled the head of his stick, apparently lost in reflection. "I may be wrong," he went on presently, "I have an idea it is you—" I must literally have jumped away from him. He paused a moment, without apparently noticing my panic, "that it is you who have influenced Peters."

"Sir?"

"I am wrong, then. Or is this merely commendable modesty on your part?"

"Oh, no, sir."

"Then my hypothesis falls to the ground. I had greatly hoped," he added meaningly, "that you might be able to throw some light on this mystery."

I was dumb.

"Paret," he asked, "have you time to come over to my rooms for a few minutes this evening?"

"Certainly, sir."

He gave me his number in Brattle Street....

Like one running in a nightmare and making no progress I made my way home, only to learn from Hallam,—who lived on the same floor,—that Tom had inconsiderately gone to Boston for the evening, with four other weary spirits in search of relaxation! Avoiding our club table, I took what little nourishment I could at a modest restaurant, and restlessly paced the moonlit streets until eight o'clock, when I found myself in front of one of those low-gabled colonial houses which, on less soul-shaking occasions, had exercised a great charm on my imagination. My hand hung for an instant over the bell.... I must have rung it violently, for there appeared almost immediately an old lady in a lace cap, who greeted me with gentle courtesy, and knocked at a little door with glistening panels. The latch was lifted by Mr. Cheyne himself.

"Come in, Paret," he said, in a tone that was unexpectedly hospitable.

I have rarely seen a more inviting room. A wood fire burned brightly on the brass andirons, flinging its glare on the big, white beam that crossed the ceiling, and reddening the square panes of the windows in their panelled recesses. Between these were rows of books,—attractive books in chased bindings, red and blue; books that appealed to be taken down and read. There was a table covered with reviews and magazines in neat piles, and a lamp so shaded as to throw its light only on the white blotter of the pad. Two easy chairs, covered with flowered chintz, were ranged before the fire, in one of which I sank, much bewildered, upon being urged to do so.

I utterly failed to recognize "Alonzo" in this new atmosphere. And he had, moreover, dropped the subtly sarcastic manner I was wont to associate with him.

"Jolly old house, isn't it?" he observed, as though I had casually dropped in on him for a chat; and he stood, with his hands behind him stretched to the blaze, looking down at me. "It was built by a certain Colonel Draper, who fought at Louisburg, and afterwards fled to England at the time of the Revolution. He couldn't stand the patriots, I'm not so sure that I blame him, either. Are you interested in colonial things, Mr. Paret?"

I said I was. If the question had concerned Aztec relics my answer would undoubtedly have been the same. And I watched him, dazedly, while he took down a silver porringer from the shallow mantel shelf.

"It's not a Revere," he said, in a slightly apologetic tone as though to forestall a comment, "but it's rather good, I think. I picked it up at a sale in Dorchester. But I have never been able to identify the coat of arms."

He showed me a ladle, with the names of "Patience and William Simpson" engraved quaintly thereon, and took down other articles in which I managed to feign an interest. Finally he seated himself in the chair opposite, crossed his feet, putting the tips of his fingers together and gazing into the fire.

"So you thought you could fool me," he said, at length.

I became aware of the ticking of a great clock in the corner. My mouth was dry.

"I am going to forgive you," he went on, more gravely, "for several reasons. I don't flatter, as you know. It's because you carried out the thing so perfectly that I am led to think you have a gift that may be cultivated, Paret. You wrote that theme in the way Peters would have written it if he had not been—what shall I say?—scripturally inarticulate. And I trust it may do you some good if I say it was something of a literary achievement, if not a moral one."

"Thank you, sir," I faltered.

"Have you ever," he inquired, lapsing a little into his lecture-room manner, "seriously thought of literature as a career? Have you ever thought of any career seriously?"

"I once wished to be a writer, sir," I replied tremulously, but refrained from telling him of my father's opinion of the profession. Ambition—a purer ambition than I had known for years—leaped within me at his words. He, Alonzo Cheyne, had detected in me the Promethean fire!

I sat there until ten o'clock talking to the real Mr. Cheyne, a human Mr. Cheyne unknown in the lecture-room. Nor had I suspected one in whom cynicism and distrust of undergraduates (of my sort) seemed so ingrained, of such idealism. He did not pour it out in preaching; delicately, unobtrusively and on the whole rather humorously he managed to present to me in a most disillusionizing light that conception of the university held by me and my intimate associates. After I had left him I walked the quiet streets to behold as through dissolving mists another Harvard, and there trembled in my soul like the birth-struggle of a flame something of the vision later to be immortalized by St. Gaudens, the spirit of Harvard responding to the spirit of the Republic—to the call of Lincoln, who voiced it. The place of that bronze at the corner of Boston Common was as yet empty, but I have since stood before it to gaze in wonder at the light shining in darkness on mute, uplifted faces, black faces! at Harvard's son leading them on that the light might live and prevail.

I, too, longed for a Cause into which I might fling myself, in which I might lose myself... I halted on the sidewalk to find myself staring from the opposite side of the street at a familiar house, my old landlady's, Mrs. Bolton's, and summoned up before me was the tired, smiling face of Hermann Krebs. Was it because when he had once spoken so crudely of the University I had seen the reflection of her spirit in his eyes? A light still burned in the extension roof—Krebs's light; another shone dimly through the ground glass of the front door. Obeying a sudden impulse, I crossed the street.

Mrs. Bolton, in the sky-blue wrapper, and looking more forbidding than ever, answered the bell. Life had taught her to be indifferent to surprises, and it was I who became abruptly embarrassed.

"Oh, it's you, Mr. Paret," she said, as though I had been a frequent caller. I had never once darkened her threshold since I had left her house.

"Yes," I answered, and hesitated.... "Is Mr. Krebs in?"

"Well," she replied in a lifeless tone, which nevertheless had in it a touch of bitterness, "I guess there's no reason why you and your friends should have known he was sick."

"Sick!" I repeated. "Is he very sick?"

"I calculate he'll pull through," she said. "Sunday the doctor gave him up. And no wonder! He hasn't had any proper food since he's be'n here!" She paused, eyeing me. "If you'll excuse me, Mr. Paret, I was just going up to him when you rang."

"Certainly," I replied awkwardly. "Would you be so kind as to tell him— when he's well enough—that I came to see him, and that I'm sorry?"

There was another pause, and she stood with a hand defensively clutching the knob.

"Yes, I'll tell him," she said.

With a sense of having been baffled, I turned away.

Walking back toward the Yard my attention was attracted by a slowly approaching cab whose occupants were disturbing the quiet of the night with song.

"Shollity—'tis wine, 'tis wine, that makesh—shollity."

The vehicle drew up in front of a new and commodious building,—I believe the first of those designed to house undergraduates who were willing to pay for private bathrooms and other modern luxuries; out of one window of the cab protruded a pair of shoeless feet, out of the other a hatless head I recognized as belonging to Tom Peters; hence I surmised that the feet were his also. The driver got down from the box, and a lively argument was begun inside—for there were other occupants—as to how Mr. Peters was to be disembarked; and I gathered from his frequent references to the "Shgyptian obelisk" that the engineering problem presented struck him as similar to the unloading of Cleopatra's Needle.

"Careful, careful!" he cautioned, as certain expelling movements began from within, "Easy, Ham, you jam-fool, keep the door shut, y'll break me."

"Now, Jerry, all heave sh'gether!" exclaimed a voice from the blackness of the interior.

"Will ye wait a minute, Mr. Durrett, sir?" implored the cabdriver. "You'll be after ruining me cab entirely." (Loud roars and vigorous resistance from the obelisk, the cab rocking violently.) "This gintleman" (meaning me) "will have him by the head, and I'll get hold of his feet, sir." Which he did, after a severe kick in the stomach.

"Head'sh all right, Martin."

"To be sure it is, Mr. Peters. Now will ye rest aisy awhile, sir?"

"I'm axphyxiated," cried another voice from the darkness, the mined voice of Jerome Kyme, our classmate.

"Get the tackles under him!" came forth in commanding tones from Conybear.

In the meantime many windows had been raised and much gratuitous advice was being given. The three occupants of the cab's seat who had previously clamoured for Mr. Peters' removal, now inconsistently resisted it; suddenly he came out with a jerk, and we had him fairly upright on the pavement minus a collar and tie and the buttons of his evening waistcoat. Those who remained in the cab engaged in a riotous game of hunt the slipper, while Tom peered into the dark interior, observing gravely the progress of the sport. First flew out an overcoat and a much-battered hat, finally the pumps, all of which in due time were adjusted to his person, and I started home with him, with much parting counsel from the other three.

"Whereinell were you, Hughie?" he inquired. "Hunted all over for you. Had a sousin' good time. Went to Babcock's—had champagne—then to see Babesh in—th'—Woods. Ham knows one of the Babesh had supper with four of 'em. Nice Babesh!"

"For heaven's sake don't step on me again!" I cried.

"Sh'poloshize, old man. But y'know I'm William Shakespheare. C'n do what I damplease." He halted in the middle of the street and recited dramatically:—

"'Not marble, nor th' gilded monuments Of prinches sh'll outlive m' powerful rhym e.'"

"How's that, Alonzho, b'gosh?"

"Where did you learn it?" I demanded, momentarily forgetting his condition.

"Fr'm Ralph," he replied, "says I wrote it. Can't remember...."

After I had got him to bed,—a service I had learned to perform with more or less proficiency,—I sat down to consider the events of the evening, to attempt to get a proportional view. The intensity of my disgust was not hypocritical as I gazed through the open door into the bedroom and recalled the times when I, too, had been in that condition. Tom Peters drunk, and sleeping it off, was deplorable, without doubt; but Hugh Paret drunk was detestable, and had no excuse whatever. Nor did I mean by this to set myself on a higher ethical plane, for I felt nothing but despair and humility. In my state of clairvoyance I perceived that he was a better man, than I, and that his lapses proceeded from a love of liquor and the transcendent sense of good-fellowship that liquor brings.

Chapter Seven

The crisis through which I passed at Cambridge, inaugurated by the events I have just related, I find very difficult to portray. It was a religious crisis, of course, and my most pathetic memory concerning it is of the vain attempts to connect my yearnings and discontents with the theology I had been taught; I began in secret to read my Bible, yet nothing I hit upon seemed to point a way out of my present predicament, to give any definite clew to the solution of my life. I was not mature enough to reflect that orthodoxy was a Sunday religion unrelated to a world whose wheels were turned by the motives of self-interest; that it consisted of ideals not deemed practical, since no attempt was made to put them into practice in the only logical manner,—by reorganizing civilization to conform with them. The implication was that the Christ who had preached these ideals was not practical.... There were undoubtedly men in the faculty of the University who might have helped me had I known of them; who might have given me, even at that time, a clew to the modern, logical explanation of the Bible as an immortal record of the thoughts and acts of men who had sought to do just what I was seeking to do,—connect the religious impulse to life and make it fruitful in life: an explanation, by the way, a thousand-fold more spiritual than the old. But I was hopelessly entangled in the meshes of the mystic, the miraculous and supernatural. If I had analyzed my yearnings, I might have realized that I wanted to renounce the life I had been leading, not because it was sinful, but because it was aimless. I had not learned that the Greek word for sin is "a missing of the mark." Just aimlessness! I had been stirred with the desire to perform some service for which the world would be grateful: to write great literature, perchance. But it had never been suggested to me that such swellings of the soul are religious, that religion is that kind of feeling, of motive power that drives the writer and the scientist, the statesman and the sculptor as well as the priest and the Prophet to serve mankind for the joy of serving: that religion is creative, or it is nothing: not mechanical, not a force imposed from without, but a driving power within. The "religion" I had learned was salvation from sin by miracle: sin a deliberate rebellion, not a pathetic missing of the mark of life; useful service of man, not the wandering of untutored souls who had not been shown the way. I felt religious. I wanted to go to church, I wanted to maintain, when it was on me, that exaltation I dimly felt as communion with a higher power, with God, and which also was identical with my desire to write, to create....

I bought books, sets of Wordsworth and Keats, of Milton and Shelley and Shakespeare, and hid them away in my bureau drawers lest Tom and my friends should see them. These too I read secretly, making excuses for not joining in the usual amusements. Once I walked to Mrs. Bolton's and inquired rather shamefacedly for Hermann Krebs, only to be informed that he had gone out.... There were lapses, of course, when I went off on the old excursions,—for the most part the usual undergraduate follies, though some were of a more serious nature; on these I do not care to dwell. Sex was still a mystery.... Always I awoke afterwards to bitter self-hatred and despair.... But my work in English improved, and I earned the commendation and friendship of Mr. Cheyne. With a wisdom for which I was grateful he was careful not to give much sign of it in classes, but the fact that he was "getting soft on me" was evident enough to be regarded with suspicion. Indeed the state into which I had fallen became a matter of increasing concern to my companions, who tried every means from ridicule to sympathy, to discover its cause and shake me out of it. The theory most accepted was that I was in love.

"Come on now, Hughie—tell me who she is. I won't give you away," Tom would beg. Once or twice, indeed, I had imagined I was in love with the sisters of Boston classmates whose dances I attended; to these parties Tom, not having overcome his diffidence in respect to what he called "social life," never could be induced to go.

It was Ralph who detected the true cause of my discontent. Typical as no other man I can recall of the code to which we had dedicated ourselves, the code that moulded the important part of the undergraduate world and defied authority, he regarded any defection from it in the light of treason. An instructor, in a fit of impatience, had once referred to him as the Mephistopheles of his class; he had fatal attractions, and a remarkable influence.

His favourite pastime was the capricious exercise of his will on weaker characters, such as his cousin, Ham Durrett; if they "swore off," Ralph made it his business to get them drunk again, and having accomplished this would proceed himself to administer a new oath and see that it was kept. Alcohol seemed to have no effect whatever on him. Though he was in the class above me, I met him frequently at a club to which I had the honour to belong, then a suite of rooms over a shop furnished with a pool and a billiard table, easy-chairs and a bar. It has since achieved the dignity of a house of its own.

We were having, one evening, a "religious" argument, Cinibar, Laurens and myself and some others. I can't recall how it began; I think Cinibar had attacked the institution of compulsory chapel, which nobody defended; there was something inherently wrong, he maintained, with a religion to which men had to be driven against their wills. Somewhat to my surprise I found myself defending a Christianity out of which I had been able to extract but little comfort and solace. Neither Laurens nor Conybear, however, were for annihilating it: although they took the other side of the discussion of a subject of which none of us knew anything, their attacks were but half-hearted; like me, they were still under the spell exerted by a youthful training.

We were all of us aware of Ralph, who sat at some distance looking over the pages of an English sporting weekly. Presently he flung it down.

"Haven't you found out yet that man created God, Hughie?" he inquired. "And even if there were a personal God, what reason have you to think that man would be his especial concern, or any concern of his whatever? The discovery of evolution has knocked your Christianity into a cocked hat."

I don't remember how I answered him. In spite of the superficiality of his own arguments, which I was not learned enough to detect, I was ingloriously routed. Darwin had kicked over the bucket, and that was all there was to it.... After we had left the club both Conybear and Laurens admitted they were somewhat disturbed, declaring that Ralph had gone too far. I spent a miserable night, recalling the naturalistic assertions he had made so glibly, asking myself again and again how it was that the religion to which I so vainly clung had no greater effect on my actions and on my will, had not prevented me from lapses into degradation. And I hated myself for having argued upon a subject that was still sacred. I believed in Christ, which is to say that I believed that in some inscrutable manner he existed, continued to dominate the world and had suffered on my account.

To whom should I go now for a confirmation of my wavering beliefs? One of the results—it will be remembered of religion as I was taught it was a pernicious shyness, and even though I had found a mentor and confessor, I might have hesitated to unburden myself. This would be different from arguing with Ralph Hambleton. In my predicament, as I was wandering through the yard, I came across a notice of an evening talk to students in Holder Chapel, by a clergyman named Phillips Brooks. This was before the time, let me say in passing, when his sermons at Harvard were attended by crowds of undergraduates. Well, I stood staring at the notice, debating whether I should go, trying to screw up my courage; for I recognized clearly that such a step, if it were to be of any value, must mean a distinct departure from my present mode of life; and I recall thinking with a certain revulsion that I should have to "turn good." My presence at the meeting would be known the next day to all my friends, for the idea of attending a religious gathering when one was not forced to do so by the authorities was unheard of in our set. I should be classed with the despised "pious ones" who did such things regularly. I shrank from the ridicule. I had, however, heard of Mr. Brooks from Ned Symonds, who was by no means of the pious type, and whose parents attended Mr. Brooks's church in Boston.... I left my decision in abeyance. But when evening came I stole away from the club table, on the plea of an engagement, and made my way rapidly toward Holder Chapel. I had almost reached it—when I caught a glimpse of Symonds and of some others approaching,—and I went on, to turn again. By this time the meeting, which was in a room on the second floor, had already begun. Palpitating, I climbed the steps; the door of the room was slightly ajar; I looked in; I recall a distinct sensation of surprise,—the atmosphere of that meeting was so different from what I had expected. Not a "pious" atmosphere at all! I saw a very tall and heavy gentleman, dressed in black, who sat, wholly at ease, on the table! One hand was in his pocket, one foot swung clear of the ground; and he was not preaching, but talking in an easy, conversational tone to some forty young men who sat intent on his words. I was too excited to listen to what he was saying, I was making a vain attempt to classify him. But I remember the thought, for it struck me with force,—that if Christianity were so thoroughly discredited by evolution, as Ralph Hambleton and other agnostics would have one believe, why should this remarkably sane and able-looking person be standing up for it as though it were still an established and incontrovertible fact?

He had not, certainly, the air of a dupe or a sentimentalist, but inspired confidence by his very personality. Youthlike, I watched him narrowly for flaws, for oratorical tricks, for all kinds of histrionic symptoms. Again I was near the secret; again it escaped me. The argument for Christianity lay not in assertions about it, but in being it. This man was Christianity.... I must have felt something of this, even though I failed to formulate it. And unconsciously I contrasted his strength, which reinforced the atmosphere of the room, with that of Ralph Hambleton, who was, a greater influence over me than I have recorded, and had come to sway me more and more, as he had swayed others. The strength of each was impressive, yet this Mr. Brooks seemed to me the bodily presentment of a set of values which I would have kept constantly before my eyes.... I felt him drawing me, overcoming my hesitation, belittling my fear of ridicule. I began gently to open the door—when something happened,—one of those little things that may change the course of a life. The door made little noise, yet one of the men sitting in the back of the room chanced to look around, and I recognized Hermann Krebs. His face was still sunken from his recent illness. Into his eyes seemed to leap a sudden appeal, an appeal to which my soul responded yet I hurried down the stairs and into the street. Instantly I regretted my retreat, I would have gone back, but lacked the courage; and I strayed unhappily for hours, now haunted by that look of Krebs, now wondering what the remarkably sane-looking and informal clergyman whose presence dominated the little room had been talking about. I never learned, but I did live to read his biography, to discover what he might have talked about,—for he if any man believed that life and religion are one, and preached consecration to life's task.

Of little use to speculate whether the message, had I learned it then, would have fortified and transformed me!

In spite of the fact that I was unable to relate to a satisfying conception of religion my new-born determination, I made up my mind, at least, to renounce my tortuous ways. I had promised my father to be a lawyer; I would keep my promise, I would give the law a fair trial; later on, perhaps, I might demonstrate an ability to write. All very praiseworthy! The season was Lent, a fitting time for renunciations and resolves. Although I had more than once fallen from grace, I believed myself at last to have settled down on my true course—when something happened. The devil interfered subtly, as usual—now in the person of Jerry Kyme. It should be said in justice to Jerry that he did not look the part. He had sunny-red, curly hair, mischievous blue eyes with long lashes, and he harboured no respect whatever for any individual or institution, sacred or profane; he possessed, however, a shrewd sense of his own value, as many innocent and unsuspecting souls discovered as early as our freshman year, and his method of putting down the presumptuous was both effective and unique. If he liked you, there could be no mistake about it.

One evening when I was engaged in composing a theme for Mr. Cheyne on no less a subject than the interpretation of the work of William Wordsworth, I found myself unexpectedly sprawling on the floor, in my descent kicking the table so vigorously as to send the ink-well a foot or two toward the ceiling. This, be it known, was a typical proof of Jerry's esteem. For he had entered noiselessly, jerking the back of my chair, which chanced to be tilted, and stood with his hands in his pockets, surveying the ruin he had wrought, watching the ink as it trickled on the carpet. Then he picked up the book.

"Poetry, you darned old grind!" he exclaimed disgustedly. "Say, Parry, I don't know what's got into you, but I want you to come home with me for the Easter holidays. It'll do you good. We'll be on the Hudson, you know, and we'll manage to make life bearable somehow."

I forgot my irritation, in sheer surprise.

"Why, that's mighty good of you, Jerry—" I began, struggling to my feet.

"Oh, rot!" he exclaimed. "I shouldn't ask you if I didn't want you."

There was no denying the truth of this, and after he had gone I sat for a long time with my pen in my mouth, reflecting as to whether or not I should go. For I had the instinct that here was another cross-roads, that more depended on my decision than I cared to admit. But even then I knew what I should do. Ridiculous not to—I told myself. How could a week or ten days with Jerry possibly affect my newborn, resolve?

Yet the prospect, now, of a visit to the Kymes' was by no means so glowing as it once would have been. For I had seen visions, I had dreamed dreams, beheld a delectable country of my very own. A year ago— nay, even a month ago—how such an invitation would have glittered!... I returned at length to my theme, over which, before Jerry's arrival, I had been working feverishly. But now the glamour had gone from it.

Presently Tom came in.

"Anyone been here?" he demanded.

"Jerry," I told him.

"What did he want?"

"He wanted me to go home with him at Easter."

"You're going, of course."

"I don't know. I haven't decided."

"You'd be a fool not to," was Tom's comment. It voiced, succinctly, a prevailing opinion.

It was the conclusion I arrived at in my own mind. But just why I had been chosen for the honour, especially at such a time, was a riddle. Jerry's invitations were charily given, and valued accordingly; and more than once, at our table, I had felt a twinge of envy when Conybear or someone else had remarked, with the proper nonchalance, in answer to a question, that they were going to Weathersfield. Such was the name of the Kyme place....

I shall never forget the impression made on me by the decorous luxury of that big house, standing amidst its old trees, halfway up the gentle slope that rose steadily from the historic highway where poor Andre was captured. I can see now the heavy stone pillars of its portico vignetted in a flush of tenderest green, the tulips just beginning to flame forth their Easter colours in the well-kept beds, the stately, well-groomed evergreens, the vivid lawns, the clipped hedges. And like an overwhelming wave of emotion that swept all before it, the impressiveness of wealth took possession of me. For here was a kind of wealth I had never known, that did not exist in the West, nor even in the still Puritan environs of Boston where I had visited. It took itself for granted, proclaimed itself complacently to have solved all problems. By ignoring them, perhaps. But I was too young to guess this. It was order personified, gaining effect at every turn by a multitude of details too trivial to mention were it not for the fact that they entered deeply into my consciousness, until they came to represent, collectively, the very flower of achievement. It was a wealth that accepted tribute calmly, as of inherent right. Law and tradition defended its sanctity more effectively than troops. Literature descended from her high altar to lend it dignity; and the long, silent library displayed row upon row of the masters, appropriately clad in morocco or calf,—Smollett, Macaulay, Gibbon, Richardson, Fielding, Scott, Dickens, Irving and Thackeray, as though each had striven for a tablet here. Art had denied herself that her canvases might be hung on these walls; and even the Church, on that first Sunday of my visit, forgot the blood of her martyrs that she might adorn an appropriate niche in the setting. The clergyman, at one of the dinner parties, gravely asked a blessing as upon an Institution that included and absorbed all other institutions in its being....

The note of that house was a tempered gaiety. Guests arrived from New York, spent the night and departed again without disturbing the even tenor of its ways. Unobtrusive servants ministered to their wants,—and to mine....

Conybear was there, and two classmates from Boston, and we were treated with the amiable tolerance accorded to college youths and intimates of the son of the house. One night there was a dance in our honour. Nor have I forgotten Jerry's sister, Nathalie, whom I had met at Class Days, a slim and willowy, exotic young lady of the Botticelli type, with a crown of burnished hair, yet more suggestive of a hothouse than of spring. She spoke English with a French accent. Capricious, impulsive, she captured my interest because she put a high value on her favour; she drove me over the hills, informing me at length that I was sympathique— different from the rest; in short, she emphasized and intensified what I may call the Weathersfield environment, stirred up in me new and vague aspirations that troubled yet excited me.

Then there was Mrs. Kyme, a pretty, light-hearted lady, still young, who seemed to have no intention of growing older, who romped and played songs for us on the piano. The daughter of an old but now impecunious Westchester family, she had been born to adorn the position she held, she was adapted by nature to wring from it the utmost of the joys it offered. From her, rather than from her husband, both of the children seemed to have inherited. I used to watch Mr. Grosvenor Kyme as he sat at the end of the dinner-table, dark, preoccupied, taciturn, symbolical of a wealth new to my experience, and which had about it a certain fabulous quality. It toiled not, neither did it spin, but grew as if by magic, day and night, until the very conception of it was overpowering. What must it be to have had ancestors who had been clever enough to sit still until a congested and discontented Europe had begun to pour its thousands and hundreds of thousands into the gateway of the western world, until that gateway had become a metropolis? ancestors, of course, possessing what now suddenly appeared to me as the most desirable of gifts—since it reaped so dazzling a harvest-business foresight. From time to time these ancestors had continued to buy desirable corners, which no amount of persuasion had availed to make them relinquish. Lease them, yes; sell them, never! By virtue of such a system wealth was as inevitable as human necessity; and the thought of human necessity did not greatly bother me. Mr. Kyme's problem of life was not one of making money, but of investing it. One became automatically a personage....

It was due to one of those singular coincidences—so interesting a subject for speculation—that the man who revealed to me this golden romance of the Kyme family was none other than a resident of my own city, Mr. Theodore Watling, now become one of our most important and influential citizens; a corporation lawyer, new and stimulating qualification, suggesting as it did, a deus ex machina of great affairs. That he, of all men, should come to Weathersfield astonished me, since I was as yet to make the connection between that finished, decorous, secluded existence and the source of its being. The evening before my departure he arrived in company with two other gentlemen, a Mr. Talbot and a Mr. Saxes, whose names were spoken with respect in a sphere of which I had hitherto taken but little cognizance-Wall Street. Conybear informed me that they were "magnates,"... We were sitting in the drawing-room at tea, when they entered with Mr. Watling, and no sooner had he spoken to Mrs. Kyme than his quick eye singled me out of the group.

"Why, Hugh!" he exclaimed, taking my hand. "I had no idea I should meet you here—I saw your father only last week, the day I left home." And he added, turning to Mrs. Kyme, "Hugh is the son of Mr. Matthew Paret, who has been the leader of our bar for many years."

The recognition and the tribute to my father were so graciously given that I warmed with gratitude and pride, while Mr. Kyme smiled a little, remarking that I was a friend of Jerry's. Theodore Watling, for being here, had suddenly assumed in my eyes a considerable consequence, though the note he struck in that house was a strange one. It was, however, his own note, and had a certain distinction, a ring of independence, of the knowledge of self-worth. Dinner at Weathersfield we youngsters had usually found rather an oppressive ceremony, with its shaded lights and precise ritual over which Mr. Kyme presided like a high priest; conversation had been restrained. That night, as Johnnie Laurens afterwards expressed it, "things loosened up," and Mr. Watling was responsible for the loosening. Taking command of the Kyme dinner table appeared to me to be no mean achievement, but this is just what he did, without being vulgar or noisy or assertive. Suavitar in modo, forbiter in re. If, as I watched him there with a newborn pride and loyalty, I had paused to reconstruct the idea that the mention of his name would formerly have evoked, I suppose I should have found him falling short of my notion of a gentleman; it had been my father's opinion; but Mr. Watling's marriage to Gene Hollister's aunt had given him a standing with us at home. He possessed virility, vitality in a remarkable degree, yet some elusive quality that was neither tact nor delicacy—though related to these differentiated him from the commonplace, self-made man of ability. He was just off the type. To liken him to a clothing store model of a well-built, broad-shouldered man with a firm neck, a handsome, rather square face not lacking in colour and a conventional, drooping moustache would be slanderous; yet he did suggest it. Suggesting it, he redeemed it: and the middle western burr in his voice was rather attractive than otherwise. He had not so much the air of belonging there, as of belonging anywhere—one of those anomalistic American citizens of the world who go abroad and make intimates of princes. Before the meal was over he had inspired me with loyalty and pride, enlisted the admiration of Jerry and Conybear and Johnnie Laurens; we followed him into the smoking-room, sitting down in a row on a leather lounge behind our elders.

Here, now that the gentlemen were alone, there was an inspiring largeness in their talk that fired the imagination. The subject was investments, at first those of coal and iron in my own state, for Mr. Watling, it appeared, was counsel for the Boyne Iron Works.

"It will pay you to keep an eye on that company, Mr. Kyme," he said, knocking the ashes from his cigar. "Now that old Mr. Durrett's gone—"

"You don't mean to say Nathaniel Durrett's dead!" said Mr. Kyme.

The lawyer nodded.

"The old regime passed with him. Adolf Scherer succeeds him, and you may take my word for it, he's a coming man. Mr. Durrett, who was a judge of men, recognized that. Scherer was an emigrant, he had ideas, and rose to be a foreman. For the last few years Mr. Durrett threw everything on his shoulders...."

Little by little the scope of the discussion was enlarged until it ranged over a continent, touching lightly upon lines of railroad, built or projected, across the great west our pioneers had so lately succeeded in wresting from the savages, upon mines of copper and gold hidden away among the mountains, and millions of acres of forest and grazing lands which a complacent government would relinquish provided certain technicalities were met: touching lightly, too, very lightly,—upon senators and congressmen at Washington. And for the first time I learned that not the least of the functions of these representatives of the people was to act as the medium between capital and investment, to facilitate the handing over of the Republic's resources to those in a position to develop them. The emphasis was laid on development, or rather on the resulting prosperity for the country: that was the justification, and it was taken for granted as supreme. Nor was it new to me; this cult of prosperity. I recalled the torch-light processions of the tariff enthusiasts of my childhood days, my father's championship of the Republican Party. He had not idealized politicians, either. For the American, politics and ethics were strangers.

Thus I listened with increasing fascination to these gentlemen in evening clothes calmly treating the United States as a melon patch that existed largely for the purpose of being divided up amongst a limited and favored number of persons. I had a feeling of being among the initiated. Where, it may be asked, were my ideals? Let it not be supposed that I believed myself to have lost them. If so, the impression I have given of myself has been wholly inadequate. No, they had been transmuted, that is all, transmuted by the alchemy of Weathersfield, by the personality of Theodore Watling into brighter visions. My eyes rarely left his face; I hung on his talk, which was interspersed with native humour, though he did not always join in the laughter, sometimes gazing at the fire, as though his keen mind were grappling with a problem suggested. I noted the respect in which his opinions were held, and my imagination was fired by an impression of the power to be achieved by successful men of his profession, by the evidence of their indispensability to capital itself.... At last when the gentlemen rose and were leaving the room, Mr. Watling lingered, with his hand on my arm.

"Of course you're going through the Law School, Hugh," he said.

"Yes, sir," I replied.

"Good!" he exclaimed emphatically. "The law, to-day, is more of a career than ever, especially for a young man with your antecedents and advantages, and I know of no city in the United States where I would rather start practice, if I were a young man, than ours. In the next twenty years we shall see a tremendous growth. Of course you'll be going into your father's office. You couldn't do better. But I'll keep an eye on you, and perhaps I'll be able to help you a little, too."

I thanked him gratefully.

A famous artist, who started out in youth to embrace a military career and who failed to pass an examination at West Point, is said to have remarked that if silicon had been a gas he would have been a soldier. I am afraid I may have given the impression that if I had not gone to Weathersfield and encountered Mr. Watling I might not have been a lawyer. This impression would be misleading. And while it is certain that I have not exaggerated the intensity of the spiritual experience I went through at Cambridge, a somewhat belated consideration for the truth compels me to register my belief that the mood would in any case have been ephemeral. The poison generated by the struggle of my nature with its environment had sunk too deep, and the very education that was supposed to make a practical man of me had turned me into a sentimentalist. I became, as will be seen, anything but a practical man in the true sense, though the world in which I had been brought up and continued to live deemed me such. My father was greatly pleased when I wrote him that I was now more than ever convinced of the wisdom of choosing the law as my profession, and was satisfied that I had come to my senses at last. He had still been prepared to see me "go off at a tangent," as he expressed it. On the other hand, the powerful effect of the appeal made by Weathersfield and Mr. Watling must not be underestimated. Here in one object lesson was emphasized a host of suggestions each of which had made its impression. And when I returned to Cambridge Alonzo Cheyne knew that he had lost me....

I pass over the rest of my college course, and the years I spent at the Harvard Law School, where were instilled into me without difficulty the dictums that the law was the most important of all professions, that those who entered it were a priestly class set aside to guard from profanation that Ark of the Covenant, the Constitution of the United States. In short, I was taught law precisely as I had been taught religion,—scriptural infallibility over again,—a static law and a static theology,—a set of concepts that were supposed to be equal to any problems civilization would have to meet until the millennium. What we are wont to call wisdom is often naively innocent of impending change. It has no barometric properties.

I shall content myself with relating one incident only of this period. In the January of my last year I went with a party of young men and girls to stay over Sunday at Beverly Farms, where Mrs. Fremantle—a young Boston matron had opened her cottage for the occasion. This "cottage," a roomy, gabled structure, stood on a cliff, at the foot of which roared the wintry Atlantic, while we danced and popped corn before the open fires. During the daylight hours we drove about the country in sleighs, or made ridiculous attempts to walk on snow-shoes.

On Sunday afternoon, left temporarily to my own devices, I wandered along the cliff, crossing into the adjoining property. The wind had fallen; the waves, much subdued, broke rhythmically against the rocks; during the night a new mantle of snow had been spread, and the clouds were still low and menacing. As I strolled I became aware of a motionless figure ahead of me,—one that seemed oddly familiar; the set of the shabby overcoat on the stooping shoulders, the unconscious pose contributed to a certain sharpness of individuality; in the act of challenging my memory, I halted. The man was gazing at the seascape, and his very absorption gave me a sudden and unfamiliar thrill. The word absorption precisely expresses my meaning, for he seemed indeed to have become a part of his surroundings,—an harmonious part. Presently he swung about and looked at me as though he had expected to find me there—and greeted me by name.

"Krebs!" I exclaimed.

He smiled, and flung out his arm, indicating the scene. His eyes at that moment seemed to reflect the sea,—they made the gaunt face suddenly beautiful.

"This reminds me of a Japanese print," he said.

The words, or the tone in which he spoke, curiously transformed the picture. It was as if I now beheld it, anew, through his vision: the grey water stretching eastward to melt into the grey sky, the massed, black trees on the hillside, powdered with white, the snow in rounded, fantastic patches on the huge boulders at the foot of the cliff. Krebs did not seem like a stranger, but like one whom I had known always,—one who stood in a peculiar relationship between me and something greater I could not define. The impression was fleeting, but real.... I remember wondering how he could have known anything about Japanese prints.

"I didn't think you were still in this part of the country," I remarked awkwardly.

"I'm a reporter on a Boston newspaper, and I've been sent up here to interview old Mr. Dome, who lives in that house," and he pointed to a roof above the trees. "There is a rumour, which I hope to verify, that he has just given a hundred thousand dollars to the University."

"And—won't he see you?"

"At present he's taking a nap," said Krebs. "He comes here occasionally for a rest."

"Do you like interviewing?" I asked.

He smiled again.

"Well, I see a good many different kinds of people, and that's interesting."

"But—being a reporter?" I persisted.

This continued patronage was not a conscious expression of superiority on my part, but he did not seem to resent it. He had aroused my curiosity.

"I'm going into the law," he said.

The quiet confidence with which he spoke aroused, suddenly, a twinge of antagonism. He had every right to go into the law, of course, and yet!... my query would have made it evident to me, had I been introspective in those days, that the germ of the ideal of the profession, implanted by Mr. Watling, was expanding. Were not influential friends necessary for the proper kind of career? and where were Krebs's? In spite of the history of Daniel Webster and a long line of American tradition, I felt an incongruity in my classmate's aspiration. And as he stood there, gaunt and undoubtedly hungry, his eyes kindling, I must vaguely have classed him with the revolutionaries of all the ages; must have felt in him, instinctively, a menace to the stability of that Order with which I had thrown my fortunes. And yet there were comparatively poor men in the Law School itself who had not made me feel this way! He had impressed me against my will, taken me by surprise, commiseration had been mingled with other feelings that sprang out of the memory of the night I had called on him, when he had been sick. Now I resented something in him which Tom Peters had called "crust."

"The law!" I repeated. "Why?"

"Well," he said, "even when I was a boy, working at odd jobs, I used to think if I could ever be a lawyer I should have reached the top notch of human dignity."

Once more his smile disarmed me.

"And now" I asked curiously.

"You see, it was an ideal with me, I suppose. My father was responsible for that. He had the German temperament of '48, and when he fled to this country, he expected to find Utopia." The smile emerged again, like the sun shining through clouds, while fascination and antagonism again struggled within me. "And then came frightful troubles. For years he could get only enough work to keep him and my mother alive, but he never lost his faith in America. 'It is man,' he would say, 'man has to grow up to it—to liberty.' Without the struggle, liberty would be worth nothing. And he used to tell me that we must all do our part, we who had come here, and not expect everything to be done for us. He had made that mistake. If things were bad, why, put a shoulder to the wheel and help to make them better.

"That helped me," he continued, after a moment's pause. "For I've seen a good many things, especially since I've been working for a newspaper. I've seen, again and again, the power of the law turned against those whom it was intended to protect, I've seen lawyers who care a great deal more about winning cases than they do about justice, who prostitute their profession to profit making,—profit making for themselves and others. And they are often the respectable lawyers, too, men of high standing, whom you would not think would do such things. They are on the side of the powerful, and the best of them are all retained by rich men and corporations. And what is the result? One of the worst evils, I think, that can befall a country. The poor man goes less and less to the courts. He is getting bitter, which is bad, which is dangerous. But men won't see it."

It was on my tongue to refute this, to say that everybody had a chance. I could indeed recall many arguments that had been drilled into me; quotations, even, from court decisions. But something prevented me from doing this,—something in his manner, which was neither argumentative nor combative.

"That's why I am going into the law," he added. "And I intend to stay in it if I can keep alive. It's a great chance for me—for all of us. Aren't you at the Law School?"

I nodded. Once more, as his earnest glance fell upon me, came that suggestion of a subtle, inexplicable link between us; but before I could reply, steps were heard behind us, and an elderly servant, bareheaded, was seen coming down the path.

"Are you the reporter?" he demanded somewhat impatiently of Krebs. "If you want to see Mr. Dome, you'd better come right away. He's going out for a drive."

For a while, after he had shaken my hand and departed, I stood in the snow, looking after him....

Chapter Eight

On the Wednesday of that same week the news of my father's sudden and serious illness came to me in a telegram, and by the time I arrived at home it was too late to see him again alive. It was my first experience with death, and what perplexed me continually during the following days was an inability to feel the loss more deeply. When a child, I had been easily shaken by the spectacle of sorrow. Had I, during recent years, as a result of a discovery that emotions arising from human relationships lead to discomfort and suffering, deliberately been forming a shell, until now I was incapable of natural feelings? Of late I had seemed closer to my father, and his letters, though formal, had given evidence of his affection; in his repressed fashion he had made it clear that he looked forward to the time when I was to practise with him. Why was it then, as I gazed upon his fine features in death, that I experienced no intensity of sorrow? What was it in me that would not break down? He seemed worn and tired, yet I had never thought of him as weary, never attributed to him any yearning. And now he was released.

I wondered what had been his private thoughts about himself, his private opinions about life; and when I reflect now upon my lack of real knowledge at five and twenty, I am amazed at the futility of an expensive education which had failed to impress upon me the simple, basic fact that life was struggle; that either development or retrogression is the fate of all men, that characters are never completely made, but always in the making. I had merely a disconcerting glimpse of this truth, with no powers of formulation, as I sat beside my mother in the bedroom, where every article evoked some childhood scene. Here was the dent in the walnut foot-board of the bed made, one wintry day, by the impact of my box of blocks; the big arm-chair, covered with I know not what stiff embroidery, which had served on countless occasions as a chariot driven to victory. I even remembered how every Wednesday morning I had been banished from the room, which had been so large a part of my childhood universe, when Ella, the housemaid, had flung open all its windows and crowded its furniture into the hall.

The thought of my wanderings since then became poignant, almost terrifying. The room, with all its memories, was unchanged. How safe I had been within its walls! Why could I not have been, content with what it represented? of tradition, of custom,—of religion? And what was it within me that had lured me away from these?

I was miserable, indeed, but my misery was not of the kind I thought it ought to be. At moments, when my mother relapsed into weeping, I glanced at her almost in wonder. Such sorrow as hers was incomprehensible. Once she surprised and discomfited me by lifting her head and gazing fixedly at me through her tears.

I recall certain impressions of the funeral. There, among the pall- bearers, was my Cousin Robert Breck, tears in the furrows of his cheeks. Had he loved my father more than I? The sight of his grief moved me suddenly and strongly.... It seemed an age since I had worked in his store, and yet here he was still, coming to town every morning and returning every evening to Claremore, loving his friends, and mourning them one by one. Was this, the spectacle presented by my Cousin Robert, the reward of earthly existence? Were there no other prizes save those known as greatness of character and depth of human affections? Cousin Robert looked worn and old. The other pall-bearers, men of weight, of long standing in the community, were aged, too; Mr. Blackwood, and Mr. Jules Hollister; and out of place, somehow, in this new church building. It came to me abruptly that the old order was gone,—had slipped away during my absence. The church I had known in boyhood had been torn down to make room for a business building on Boyne Street; the edifice in which I sat was expensive, gave forth no distinctive note; seemingly transitory with its hybrid interior, its shiny oak and blue and red organ-pipes, betokening a compromised and weakened faith. Nondescript, likewise, seemed the new minister, Mr. Randlett, as he prayed unctuously in front of the flowers massed on the platform. I vaguely resented his laudatory references to my father.

The old church, with its severity, had actually stood for something. It was the Westminster Catechism in wood and stone, and Dr. Pound had been the human incarnation of that catechism, the fit representative of a wrathful God, a militant shepherd who had guarded with vigilance his respectable flock, who had protested vehemently against the sins of the world by which they were surrounded, against the "dogs, and sorcerers, and whoremongers, and murderers and idolaters, and whosoever loveth and maketh a lie." How Dr. Pound would have put the emphasis of the Everlasting into those words!

Against what was Mr. Randlett protesting?

My glance wandered to the pews which held the committees from various organizations, such as the Chamber of Commerce and the Bar Association, which had come to do honour to my father. And there, differentiated from the others, I saw the spruce, alert figure of Theodore Watling. He, too, represented a new type and a new note,—this time a forceful note, a secular note that had not belonged to the old church, and seemed likewise anomalistic in the new....

During the long, slow journey in the carriage to the cemetery my mother did not raise her veil. It was not until she reached out and seized my hand, convulsively, that I realized she was still a part of my existence.

In the days that followed I became aware that my father's death had removed a restrictive element, that I was free now to take without criticism or opposition whatever course in life I might desire. It may be that I had apprehended even then that his professional ideals would not have coincided with my own. Mingled with this sense of emancipation was a curious feeling of regret, of mourning for something I had never valued, something fixed and dependable for which he had stood, a rock and a refuge of which I had never availed myself!... When his will was opened it was found that the property had been left to my mother during her lifetime. It was larger than I had thought, four hundred thousand dollars, shrewdly invested, for the most part, in city real estate. My father had been very secretive as to money matters, and my mother had no interest in them.

Three or four days later I received in the mail a typewritten letter signed by Theodore Watling, expressing sympathy for my bereavement, and asking me to drop in on him, down town, before I should leave the city. In contrast to the somewhat dingy offices where my father had practised in the Blackwood Block, the quarters of Watling, Fowndes and Ripon on the eighth floor of the new Durrett Building were modern to a degree, finished in oak and floored with marble, with a railed-off space where young women with nimble fingers played ceaselessly on typewriters. One of them informed me that Mr. Watling was busy, but on reading my card added that she would take it in. Meanwhile, in company with two others who may have been clients, I waited. This, then, was what it meant to be a lawyer of importance, to have, like a Chesterfield, an ante-room where clients cooled their heels and awaited one's pleasure...

The young woman returned, and led me through a corridor to a door on which was painted Mr. Wailing.

I recall him tilted back in his chair in a debonnair manner beside his polished desk, the hint of a smile on his lips; and leaning close to him was a yellow, owl-like person whose eyes, as they turned to me, gave the impression of having stared for years into hard, artificial lights. Mr. Watling rose briskly.

"How are you, Hugh?" he said, the warmth of his greeting tempered by just the note of condolence suitable to my black clothes. "I'm glad you came. I wanted to see you before you went back to Cambridge. I must introduce you to Judge Bering, of our State Supreme Court. Judge, this is Mr. Paret's boy."

The judge looked me over with a certain slow impressiveness, and gave me a soft and fleshy hand.

"Glad to know you, Mr. Paret. Your father was a great loss to our bar," he declared.

I detected in his tone and manner a slight reservation that could not be called precisely judicial dignity; it was as though, in these few words, he had gone to the limit of self-commitment with a stranger—a striking contrast to the confidential attitude towards Mr. Watling in which I had surprised him.

"Judge," said Mr. Watling, sitting down again, "do you recall that time we all went up to Mr. Paret's house and tried to induce him to run for mayor? That was before you went on the lower bench."

The judge nodded gloomily, caressing his watch chain, and suddenly rose to go.

"That will be all right, then?" Mr. Watling inquired cryptically, with a smile. The other made a barely perceptible inclination of the head and departed. Mr. Watling looked at me. "He's one of the best men we have on the bench to-day," he added. There was a trace of apology in his tone.

He talked a while of my father, to whom, so he said, he had looked up ever since he had been admitted to the bar.

"It would be a pleasure to me, Hugh, as well as a matter of pride," he said cordially, but with dignity, "to have Matthew Paret's son in my office. I suppose you will be wishing to take your mother somewhere this summer, but if you care to come here in the autumn, you will be welcome. You will begin, of course, as other young men begin,—as I began.

But I am a believer in blood, and I'll be glad to have you. Mr. Fowndes and Mr. Ripon feel the same way." He escorted me to the door himself.

Everywhere I went during that brief visit home I was struck by change, by the crumbling and decay of institutions that once had held me in thrall, by the superimposition of a new order that as yet had assumed no definite character. Some of the old landmarks had disappeared; there were new and aggressive office buildings, new and aggressive residences, new and aggressive citizens who lived in them, and of whom my mother spoke with gentle deprecation. Even Claremore, that paradise of my childhood, had grown shrivelled and shabby, even tawdry, I thought, when we went out there one Sunday afternoon; all that once represented the magic word "country" had vanished. The old flat piano, made in Philadelphia ages ago, the horsehair chairs and sofa had been replaced by a nondescript furniture of the sort displayed behind plate-glass windows of the city's stores: rocking-chairs on stands, upholstered in clashing colours, their coiled springs only half hidden by tassels, and "ornamental" electric fixtures, instead of the polished coal-oil lamps. Cousin Jenny had grown white, Willie was a staid bachelor, Helen an old maid, while Mary had married a tall, anaemic young man with glasses, Walter Kinley, whom Cousin Robert had taken into the store. As I contemplated the Brecks odd questions suggested themselves: did honesty and warm-heartedness necessarily accompany a lack of artistic taste? and was virtue its own reward, after all? They drew my mother into the house, took off her wraps, set her down in the most comfortable rocker, and insisted on making her a cup of tea.

I was touched. I loved them still, and yet I was conscious of reservations concerning them. They, too, seemed a little on the defensive with me, and once in a while Mary was caustic in her remarks.

"I guess nothing but New York will be good enough for Hugh now. He'll be taking Cousin Sarah away from us."

"Not at all, my dear," said my mother, gently, "he's going into Mr. Watling's office next autumn."

"Theodore Watling?" demanded Cousin Robert, pausing in his carving.

"Yes, Robert. Mr. Watling has been good enough to say that he would like to have Hugh. Is there anything—?"

"Oh, I'm out of date, Sarah," Cousin Robert replied, vigorously severing the leg of the turkey. "These modern lawyers are too smart for me. Watling's no worse than the others, I suppose,—only he's got more ability."

"I've never heard anything against him," said my mother in a pained voice. "Only the other day McAlery Willett congratulated me that Hugh was going to be with him."

"You mustn't mind Robert, Sarah," put in Cousin Jenny,—a remark reminiscent of other days.

"Dad has a notion that his generation is the only honest one," said Helen, laughingly, as she passed a plate.

I had gained a sense of superiority, and I was quite indifferent to Cousin Robert's opinion of Mr. Watling, of modern lawyers in general. More than once a wave of self-congratulation surged through me that I had possessed the foresight and initiative to get out of the wholesale grocery business while there was yet time. I looked at Willie, still freckled, still literal, still a plodder, at Walter Kinley, and I thought of the drabness of their lives; at Cousin Robert himself as he sat smoking his cigar in the bay-window on that dark February day, and suddenly I pitied him. The suspicion struck me that he had not prospered of late, and this deepened to a conviction as he talked.

"The Republican Party is going to the dogs," he asserted.

"It used to be an honourable party, but now it is no better than the other. Politics are only conducted, now, for the purpose of making unscrupulous men rich, sir. For years I furnished this city with good groceries, if I do say it myself. I took a pride in the fact that the inmates of the hospitals, yes, and the dependent poor in the city's institutions, should have honest food. You can get anything out of the city if you are willing to pay the politicians for it. I lost my city contracts. Why? Because I refused to deal with scoundrels. Weill and Company and other unscrupulous upstarts are willing to do so, and poison the poor and the sick with adulterated groceries! The first thing I knew was that the city auditor was holding back my bills for supplies, and paying Weill's. That's what politics and business, yes, sir, and the law, have come to in these days. If a man wants to succeed, he must turn into a rascal."

I was not shocked, but I was silent, uncomfortable, wishing that it were time to take the train back to the city. Cousin Robert's face was more worn than I had thought, and I contrasted him inevitably with the forceful person who used to stand, in his worn alpaca coat, on the pavement in front of his store, greeting with clear-eyed content his fellow merchants of the city. Willie Breck, too, was silent, and Walter Kinley took off his glasses and wiped them. In the meanwhile Helen had left the group in which my mother sat, and, approaching us, laid her hands on her father's shoulders.

"Now, dad," she said, in affectionate remonstrance, "you're excited about politics again, and you know it isn't good for you. And besides, they're not worth it."

"You're right, Helen," he replied. Under the pressure of her hands he made a strong effort to control himself, and turned to address my mother across the room.

"I'm getting to be a crotchety old man," he said. "It's a good thing I have a daughter to remind me of it."

"It is a good thing, Robert," said my mother.

During the rest of our visit he seemed to have recovered something of his former spirits and poise, taking refuge in the past. They talked of their own youth, of families whose houses had been landmarks on the Second Bank.

"I'm worried about your Cousin Robert, Hugh," my mother confided to me, when we were at length seated in the train. "I've heard rumours that things are not so well at the store as they might be." We looked out at the winter landscape, so different from that one which had thrilled every fibre of my being in the days when the railroad on which we travelled had been a winding narrow gauge. The orchards—those that remained—were bare; stubble pricked the frozen ground where tassels had once waved in the hot, summer wind. We flew by row after row of ginger-bread, suburban houses built on "villa plots," and I read in large letters on a hideous sign-board, "Woodbine Park."

"Hugh, have you ever heard anything against—Mr. Watling?"

"No, mother," I said. "So far as I knew, he is very much looked up to by lawyers and business men. He is counsel, I believe, for Mr. Blackwood's street car line on Boyne Street. And I told you, I believe, that I met him once at Mr. Kyme's."

"Poor Robert!" she sighed. "I suppose business trouble does make one bitter,—I've seen it so often. But I never imagined that it would overtake Robert, and at his time of life! It is an old and respected firm, and we have always had a pride in it." ...

That night, when I was going to bed, it was evident that the subject was still in her mind. She clung to my hand a moment.

"I, too, am afraid of the new, Hugh," she said, a little tremulously. "We all grow so, as age comes on."

"But you are not old, mother," I protested.

"I have a feeling, since your father has gone, that I have lived my life, my dear, though I'd like to stay long enough to see you happily married— to have grandchildren. I was not young when you were born." And she added, after a little while, "I know nothing about business affairs, and now—now that your father is no longer here, sometimes I'm afraid—"

"Afraid of what, mother?"

She tried to smile at me through her tears. We were in the old sitting- room, surrounded by the books.

"I know it's foolish, and it isn't that I don't trust you. I know that the son of your father couldn't do anything that was not honourable. And yet I am afraid of what the world is becoming. The city is growing so fast, and so many new people are coming in. Things are not the same. Robert is right, there. And I have heard your father say the same thing. Hugh, promise me that you will try to remember always what he was, and what he would wish you to be!"

"I will, mother," I answered. "But I think you would find that Cousin Robert exaggerates a little, makes things seem worse than they really are. Customs change, you know. And politics were never well—Sunday schools." I, too, smiled a little. "Father knew that. And he would never take an active part in them."

"He was too fine!" she exclaimed.

"And now," I continued, "Cousin Robert has happened to come in contact with them through business. That is what has made the difference in him. Before, he always knew they were corrupt, but he rarely thought about them."

"Hugh," she said suddenly, after a pause, "you must remember one thing,— that you can afford to be independent. I thank God that your father has provided for that!"

I was duly admitted, the next autumn, to the bar of my own state, and was assigned to a desk in the offices of Watling, Fowndes and Ripon. Larry Weed was my immediate senior among the apprentices, and Larry was a hero- worshipper. I can see him now. He suggested a bullfrog as he sat in the little room we shared in common, his arms akimbo over a law book, his little legs doubled under him, his round, eyes fixed expectantly on the doorway. And even if I had not been aware of my good fortune in being connected with such a firm as Theodore Watling's, Larry would shortly have brought it home to me. During those weeks when I was making my first desperate attempts at briefing up the law I was sometimes interrupted by his exclamations when certain figures went by in the corridor.

"Say, Hugh, do you know who that was?"

"No."

"Miller Gorse."

"Who's he?"

"Do you mean to say you never heard of Miller Gorse?"

"I've been away a long time," I would answer apologetically. A person of some importance among my contemporaries at Harvard, I had looked forward to a residence in my native city with the complacency of one who has seen something of the world,—only to find that I was the least in the new kingdom. And it was a kingdom. Larry opened up to me something of the significance and extent of it, something of the identity of the men who controlled it.

"Miller Gorse," he said impressively, "is the counsel for the railroad."

"What railroad? You mean the—" I was adding, when he interrupted me pityingly.

"After you've been here a while you'll find out there's only one railroad in this state, so far as politics are concerned. The Ashuela and Northern, the Lake Shore and the others don't count."

I refrained from asking any more questions at that time, but afterwards I always thought of the Railroad as spelled with a capital.

"Miller Gorse isn't forty yet," Larry told me on another occasion. "That's doing pretty well for a man who comes near running this state."

For the sake of acquiring knowledge, I endured Mr. Weed's patronage. I inquired how Mr. Gorse ran the state.

"Oh, you'll find out soon enough," he assured me,

"But Mr. Barbour's president of the Railroad."

"Sure. Once in a while they take something up to him, but as a rule he leaves things to Gorse."

Whereupon I resolved to have a good look at Mr. Gorse at the first opportunity. One day Mr. Watling sent out for some papers.

"He's in there now;" said Larry. "You take 'em."

"In there" meant Mr. Watling's sanctum. And in there he was. I had only a glance at the great man, for, with a kindly but preoccupied "Thank you, Hugh," Mr. Watling took the papers and dismissed me. Heaviness, blackness and impassivity,—these were the impressions of Mr. Gorse which I carried away from that first meeting. The very solidity of his flesh seemed to suggest the solidity of his position. Such, say the psychologists, is the effect of prestige.

I remember well an old-fashioned picture puzzle in one of my boyhood books. The scene depicted was to all appearances a sylvan, peaceful one, with two happy lovers seated on a log beside a brook; but presently, as one gazed at the picture, the head of an animal stood forth among the branches, and then the body; more animals began to appear, bit by bit; a tiger, a bear, a lion, a jackal, a fox, until at last, whenever I looked at the page, I did not see the sylvan scene at all, but only the predatory beasts of the forest. So, one by one, the figures of the real rulers of the city superimposed themselves for me upon the simple and democratic design of Mayor, Council, Board of Aldermen, Police Force, etc., that filled the eye of a naive and trusting electorate which fondly imagined that it had something to say in government. Miller Gorse was one of these rulers behind the screen, and Adolf Scherer, of the Boyne Iron Works, another; there was Leonard Dickinson of the Corn National Bank; Frederick Grierson, becoming wealthy in city real estate; Judah B. Tallant, who, though outlawed socially, was deferred to as the owner of the Morning Era; and even Ralph Hambleton, rapidly superseding the elderly and conservative Mr. Lord, who had hitherto managed the great Hambleton estate. Ralph seemed to have become, in a somewhat gnostic manner, a full-fledged financier. Not having studied law, he had been home for four years when I became a legal fledgling, and during the early days of my apprenticeship I was beholden to him for many "eye openers" concerning the conduct of great affairs. I remember him sauntering into my room one morning when Larry Weed had gone out on an errand.

"Hello, Hughie," he said, with his air of having nothing to do. "Grinding it out? Where's Watling?"

"Isn't he in his office?"

"No."

"Well, what can we do for you?" I asked.

Ralph grinned.

"Perhaps I'll tell you when you're a little older. You're too young." And he sank down into Larry Weed's chair, his long legs protruding on the other side of the table. "It's a matter of taxes. Some time ago I found out that Dickinson and Tallant and others I could mention were paying a good deal less on their city property than we are. We don't propose to do it any more—that's all."

"How can Mr. Watling help you?" I inquired.

"Well, I don't mind giving you a few tips about your profession, Hughie. I'm going to get Watling to fix it up with the City Hall gang. Old Lord doesn't like it, I'll admit, and when I told him we had been contributing to the city long enough, that I proposed swinging into line with other property holders, he began to blubber about disgrace and what my grandfather would say if he were alive. Well, he isn't alive. A good deal of water has flowed under the bridges since his day. It's a mere matter of business, of getting your respectable firm to retain a City Hall attorney to fix it up with the assessor."

"How about the penitentiary?" I ventured, not too seriously.

"I shan't go to the penitentiary, neither will Watling. What I do is to pay a lawyer's fee. There isn't anything criminal in that, is there?"

For some time after Ralph had departed I sat reflecting upon this new knowledge, and there came into my mind the bitterness of Cousin Robert Breck against this City Hall gang, and his remarks about lawyers. I recalled the tone in which he had referred to Mr. Watling. But Ralph's philosophy easily triumphed. Why not be practical, and become master of a situation which one had not made, and could not alter, instead of being overwhelmed by it? Needless to say, I did not mention the conversation to Mr. Watling, nor did he dwindle in my estimation. These necessary transactions did not interfere in any way with his personal relationships, and his days were filled with kindnesses. And was not Mr. Ripon, the junior partner, one of the evangelical lights of the community, conducting advanced Bible classes every week in the Church of the Redemption?... The unfolding of mysteries kept me alert. And I understood that, if I was to succeed, certain esoteric knowledge must be acquired, as it were, unofficially. I kept my eyes and ears open, and applied myself, with all industry, to the routine tasks with which every young man in a large legal firm is familiar. I recall distinctly my pride when, the Board of Aldermen having passed an ordinance lowering the water rates, I was intrusted with the responsibility of going before the court in behalf of Mr. Ogilvy's water company, obtaining a temporary restricting order preventing the ordinance from going at once into effect. Here was an affair in point. Were it not for lawyers of the calibre of Watling, Fowndes and Ripon, hard-earned private property would soon be confiscated by the rapacious horde. Once in a while I was made aware that Mr. Watling had his eye on me.

"Well, Hugh," he would say, "how are you getting along? That's right, stick to it, and after a while we'll hand the drudgery over to somebody else."

He possessed the supreme quality of a leader of men in that he took pains to inform himself concerning the work of the least of his subordinates; and he had the gift of putting fire into a young man by a word or a touch of the hand on the shoulder. It was not difficult for me, therefore, to comprehend Larry Weed's hero-worship, the loyalty of other members of the firm or of those occupants of the office whom I have not mentioned. My first impression of him, which I had got at Jerry Kyme's, deepened as time went on, and I readily shared the belief of those around me that his legal talents easily surpassed those of any of his contemporaries. I can recall, at this time, several noted cases in the city when I sat in court listening to his arguments with thrills of pride. He made us all feel— no matter how humble may have been our contributions to the preparation— that we had a share in his triumphs. We remembered his manner with judges and juries, and strove to emulate it. He spoke as if there could be no question as to his being right as to the law and the facts, and yet, in some subtle way that bated analysis, managed not to antagonize the court. Victory was in the air in that office. I do not mean to say there were not defeats; but frequently these defeats, by resourcefulness, by a never-say-die spirit, by a consummate knowledge, not only of the law, but of other things at which I have hinted, were turned into ultimate victories. We fought cases from one court to another, until our opponents were worn out or the decision was reversed. We won, and that spirit of winning got into the blood. What was most impressed on me in those early years, I think, was the discovery that there was always a path—if one were clever enough to find it—from one terrace to the next higher. Staying power was the most prized of all the virtues. One could always, by adroitness, compel a legal opponent to fight the matter out all over again on new ground, or at least on ground partially new. If the Court of Appeals should fail one, there was the Supreme Court; there was the opportunity, also, to shift from the state to the federal courts; and likewise the much-prized device known as a change of venue, when a judge was supposed to be "prejudiced."

Chapter Nine

As my apprenticeship advanced I grew more and more to the inhabitants of our city into two kinds, the who were served, and the inefficient, who were separate efficient, neglected; but the mental process of which the classification was the result was not so deliberate as may be supposed. Sometimes, when an important client would get into trouble, the affair took me into the police court, where I saw the riff-raff of the city penned up, waiting to have justice doled out to them: weary women who had spent the night in cells, indifferent now as to the front they presented to the world, the finery rued that they had tended so carefully to catch the eyes of men on the darkened streets; brazen young girls, who blazed forth defiance to all order; derelict men, sodden and hopeless, with scrubby beards; shifty looking burglars and pickpockets. All these I beheld, at first with twinges of pity, later to mass them with the ugly and inevitable with whom society had to deal somehow. Lawyers, after all, must be practical men. I came to know the justices of these police courts, as well as other judges. And underlying my acquaintance with all of them was the knowledge—though not on the threshold of my consciousness—that they depended for their living, every man of them, those who were appointed and those who were elected, upon a political organization which derived its sustenance from the element whence came our clients. Thus by degrees the sense of belonging to a special priesthood had grown on me.

I recall an experience with that same Mr. Nathan. Weill, the wholesale grocer of whose commerce with the City Hall my Cousin Robert Breck had so bitterly complained. Late one afternoon Mr. Weill's carriage ran over a child on its way up-town through one of the poorer districts. The parents, naturally, were frantic, and the coachman was arrested. This was late in the afternoon, and I was alone in the office when the telephone rang. Hurrying to the police station, I found Mr. Weill in a state of excitement and abject fear, for an ugly crowd had gathered outside.

"Could not Mr. Watling or Mr. Fowndes come?" demanded the grocer.

With an inner contempt for the layman's state of mind on such occasions I assured him of my competency to handle the case. He was impressed, I think, by the sergeant's deference, who knew what it meant to have such an office as ours interfere with the affair. I called up the prosecuting attorney, who sent to Monahan's saloon, close by, and procured a release for the coachman on his own recognizance, one of many signed in blank and left there by the justice for privileged cases. The coachman was hustled out by a back door, and the crowd dispersed.

The next morning, while a score or more of delinquents sat in the anxious seats, Justice Garry recognized me and gave me precedence. And Mr. Weill, with a sigh of relief, paid his fine.

"Mr. Paret, is it?" he asked, as we stood together for a moment on the sidewalk outside the court. "You have managed this well. I will remember."

He was sued, of course. When he came to the office he insisted on discussing the case with Mr. Watling, who sent for me.

"That is a bright young man," Mr. Weill declared, shaking my hand. "He will get on."

"Some day," said Mr. Watling, "he may save you a lot of money, Weill."

"When my friend Mr. Watling is United States Senator,—eh?"

Mr. Watling laughed. "Before that, I hope. I advise you to compromise this suit, Weill," he added. "How would a thousand dollars strike you? I've had Paret look up the case, and he tells me the little girl has had to have an operation."

"A thousand dollars!" cried the grocer. "What right have these people to let their children play on the streets? It's an outrage."

"Where else have the children to play?" Mr. Watling touched his arm. "Weill," he said gently, "suppose it had been your little girl?" The grocer pulled out his handkerchief and mopped his bald forehead. But he rallied a little.

"You fight these damage cases for the street railroads all through the courts."

"Yes," Mr. Watling agreed, "but there a principle is involved. If the railroads once got into the way of paying damages for every careless employee, they would soon be bankrupt through blackmail. But here you have a child whose father is a poor janitor and can't afford sickness. And your coachman, I imagine, will be more particular in the future."

In the end Mr. Weill made out a cheque and departed in a good humour, convinced that he was well out of the matter. Here was one of many instances I could cite of Mr. Watling's tenderness of heart. I felt, moreover, as if he had done me a personal favour, since it was I who had recommended the compromise. For I had been to the hospital and had seen the child on the cot,—a dark little thing, lying still in her pain, with the bewildered look of a wounded animal....

Not long after this incident of Mr. Weill's damage suit I obtained a more or less definite promotion by the departure of Larry Weed. He had suddenly developed a weakness of the lungs. Mr. Watling got him a place in Denver, and paid his expenses west.

The first six or seven years I spent in the office of Wading, Fowndes and Ripon were of importance to my future career, but there is little to relate of them. I was absorbed not only in learning law, but in acquiring that esoteric knowledge at which I have hinted—not to be had from my seniors and which I was convinced was indispensable to a successful and lucrative practice. My former comparison of the organization of our city to a picture puzzle wherein the dominating figures become visible only after long study is rather inadequate. A better analogy would be the human anatomy: we lawyers, of course, were the brains; the financial and industrial interests the body, helpless without us; the City Hall politicians, the stomach that must continually be fed. All three, law, politics and business, were interdependent, united by a nervous system too complex to be developed here. In these years, though I worked hard and often late, I still found time for convivialities, for social gaieties, yet little by little without realizing the fact, I was losing zest for the companionship of my former intimates. My mind was becoming polarized by the contemplation of one object, success, and to it human ties were unconsciously being sacrificed.

Tom Peters began to feel this, even at a time when I believed myself still to be genuinely fond of him. Considering our respective temperaments in youth, it is curious that he should have been the first to fall in love and marry. One day he astonished me by announcing his engagement to Susan Blackwood.

"That ends the liquor, Hughie," he told me, beamingly. "I promised her I'd eliminate it."

He did eliminate it, save for mild relapses on festive occasions. A more seemingly incongruous marriage could scarcely be imagined, and yet it was a success from the start. From a slim, silent, self-willed girl Susan had grown up into a tall, rather rawboned and energetic young woman. She was what we called in those days "intellectual," and had gone in for kindergartens, and after her marriage she turned out to be excessively domestic; practising her theories, with entire success, upon a family that showed a tendency to increase at an alarming rate. Tom, needless to say, did not become intellectual. He settled down—prematurely, I thought—into what is known as a family man, curiously content with the income he derived from the commission business and with life in general; and he developed a somewhat critical view of the tendencies of the civilization by which he was surrounded. Susan held it also, but she said less about it. In the comfortable but unpretentious house they rented on Cedar Street we had many discussions, after the babies had been put to bed and the door of the living-room closed, in order that our voices might not reach the nursery. Perry Blackwood, now Tom's brother- in-law, was often there. He, too, had lapsed into what I thought was an odd conservatism. Old Josiah, his father, being dead, he occupied himself mainly with looking after certain family interests, among which was the Boyne Street car line. Among "business men" he was already getting the reputation of being a little difficult to deal with. I was often the subject of their banter, and presently I began to suspect that they regarded my career and beliefs with some concern. This gave me no uneasiness, though at limes I lost my temper. I realized their affection for me; but privately I regarded them as lacking in ambition, in force, in the fighting qualities necessary for achievement in this modern age. Perhaps, unconsciously, I pitied them a little.

"How is Judah B. to-day, Hughie?" Tom would inquire. "I hear you've put him up for the Boyne Club, now that Mr. Watling has got him out of that libel suit."

"Carter Ives is dead," Perry would add, sarcastically, "let bygones be bygones."

It was well known that Mr. Tallant, in the early days of his newspaper, had blackmailed Mr. Ives out of some hundred thousand dollars. And that this, more than any other act, stood in the way, with certain recalcitrant gentlemen, of his highest ambition, membership in the Boyne.

"The trouble with you fellows is that you refuse to deal with conditions as you find them," I retorted. "We didn't make them, and we can't change them. Tallant's a factor in the business life of this city, and he has to be counted with."

Tom would shake his head exasperatingly.

"Why don't you get after Ralph?" I demanded. "He doesn't antagonize Tallant, either."

"Ralph's hopeless," said Tom. "He was born a pirate, you weren't, Hughie. We think there's a chance for his salvation, don't we, Perry?"

I refused to accept the remark as flattering.

Another object of their assaults was Frederick Grierson, who by this time had emerged from obscurity as a small dealer in real estate into a manipulator of blocks and corners.

"I suppose you think it's a lawyer's business to demand an ethical bill of health of every client," I said. "I won't stand up for all of Tallant's career, of course, but Mr. Wading has a clear right to take his cases. As for Grierson, it seems to me that's a matter of giving a dog a bad name. Just because his people weren't known here, and because he has worked up from small beginnings. To get down to hard-pan, you fellows don't believe in democracy,—in giving every man a chance to show what's in him."

"Democracy is good!" exclaimed Perry. "If the kind of thing we're coming to is democracy, God save the state!"...

On the other hand I found myself drawing closer to Ralph Hambleton, sometimes present at these debates, as the only one of my boyhood friends who seemed to be able to "deal with conditions as he found them." Indeed, he gave one the impression that, if he had had the making of them, he would not have changed them.

"What the deuce do you expect?" I once heard him inquire with good- natured contempt. "Business isn't charity, it's war.

"There are certain things," maintained Perry, stoutly, "that gentlemen won't do."

"Gentlemen!" exclaimed Ralph, stretching his slim six feet two: We were sitting in the Boyne Club. "It's ungentlemanly to kill, or burn a town or sink a ship, but we keep armies and navies for the purpose. For a man with a good mind, Perry, you show a surprising inability to think things, out to a logical conclusion. What the deuce is competition, when you come down to it? Christianity? Not by a long shot! If our nations are slaughtering men and starving populations in other countries,—are carried on, in fact, for the sake of business, if our churches are filled with business men and our sky pilots pray for the government, you can't expect heathen individuals like me to do business on a Christian basis,— if there is such a thing. You can make rules for croquet, but not for a game that is based on the natural law of the survival of the fittest. The darned fools in the legislatures try it occasionally, but we all know it's a sop to the 'common people.' Ask Hughie here if there ever was a law put on the statute books that his friend Watling couldn't get 'round'? Why, you've got competition even among the churches. Yours, where I believe you teach in the Sunday school, would go bankrupt if it proclaimed real Christianity. And you'll go bankrupt if you practise it, Perry, my boy. Some early, wide-awake, competitive, red-blooded bird will relieve you of the Boyne Street car line."

It was one of this same new and "fittest" species who had already relieved poor Mr. McAlery Willett of his fortune. Mr. Willett was a trusting soul who had never known how to take care of himself or his money, people said, and now that he had lost it they blamed him. Some had been saved enough for him and Nancy to live on in the old house, with careful economy. It was Nancy who managed the economy, who accomplished remarkable things with a sum they would have deemed poverty in former days. Her mother had died while I was at Cambridge. Reverses did not subdue Mr. Willett's spirits, and the fascination modern "business" had for him seemed to grow in proportion to the misfortunes it had caused him. He moved into a tiny office in the Durrett Building, where he appeared every morning about half-past ten to occupy himself with heaven knows what short cuts to wealth, with prospectuses of companies in Mexico or Central America or some other distant place: once, I remember, it was a tea, company in which he tried to interest his friends, to raise in the South a product he maintained would surpass Orange Pekoe. In the afternoon between three and four he would turn up at the Boyne Club, as well groomed, as spruce as ever, generally with a flower in his buttonhole. He never forgot that he was a gentleman, and he had a gentleman's notions of the fitness of things, and it was against his principles to use, a gentleman's club for the furtherance of his various enterprises.

"Drop into my office some day, Dickinson," he would say. "I think I've got something there that might interest you!"

He reminded me, when I met him, that he had always predicted I would get along in life....

The portrait of Nancy at this period is not so easily drawn. The decline of the family fortunes seemed to have had as little effect upon her as upon her father, although their characters differed sharply. Something of that spontaneity, of that love of life and joy in it she had possessed in youth she must have inherited from McAlery Willett, but these qualities had disappeared in her long before the coming of financial reverses. She was nearing thirty, and in spite of her beauty and the rarer distinction that can best be described as breeding, she had never married. Men admired her, but from a distance; she kept them at arm's length, they said: strangers who visited the city invariably picked her out of an assembly and asked who she was; one man from New York who came to visit Ralph and who had been madly in love with her, she had amazed many people by refusing, spurning all he might have given her. This incident seemed a refutation of the charge that she was calculating. As might have been foretold, she had the social gift in a remarkable degree, and in spite of the limitations of her purse the knack of dressing better than other women, though at that time the organization of our social life still remained comparatively simple, the custom of luxurious and expensive entertainment not having yet set in.

The more I reflect upon those days, the more surprising does it seem that I was not in love with her. It may be that I was, unconsciously, for she troubled my thoughts occasionally, and she represented all the qualities I admired in her sex. The situation that had existed at the time of our first and only quarrel had been reversed, I was on the highroad to the worldly success I had then resolved upon, Nancy was poor, and for that reason, perhaps, prouder than ever. If she was inaccessible to others, she had the air of being peculiarly inaccessible to me—the more so because some of the superficial relics of our intimacy remained, or rather had been restored. Her very manner of camaraderie seemed paradoxically to increase the distance between us. It piqued me. Had she given me the least encouragement, I am sure I should have responded; and I remember that I used occasionally to speculate as to whether she still cared for me, and took this method of hiding her real feelings. Yet, on the whole, I felt a certain complacency about it all; I knew that suffering was disagreeable, I had learned how to avoid it, and I may have had, deep within me, a feeling that I might marry her after all. Meanwhile my life was full, and gave promise of becoming even fuller, more absorbing and exciting in the immediate future.

One of the most fascinating figures, to me, of that Order being woven, like a cloth of gold, out of our hitherto drab civilization,—an Order into which I was ready and eager to be initiated,—was that of Adolf Scherer, the giant German immigrant at the head of the Boyne Iron Works. His life would easily lend itself to riotous romance. In the old country, in a valley below the castle perched on the rack above, he had begun life by tending his father's geese. What a contrast to "Steeltown" with its smells and sickening summer heat, to the shanty where Mrs. Scherer took boarders and bent over the wash-tub! She, too, was an immigrant, but lived to hear her native Wagner from her own box at Covent Garden;

and he to explain, on the deck of an imperial yacht, to the man who might have been his sovereign certain processes in the manufacture of steel hitherto untried on that side of the Atlantic. In comparison with Adolf Scherer, citizen of a once despised democracy, the minor prince in whose dominions he had once tended geese was of small account indeed!

The Adolf Scherer of that day—though it is not so long ago as time flies —was even more solid and impressive than the man he afterwards became, when he reached the dizzier heights from which he delivered to an eager press opinions on politics and war, eugenics and woman's suffrage and other subjects that are the despair of specialists. Had he stuck to steel, he would have remained invulnerable. But even then he was beginning to abandon the field of production for that of exploitation: figuratively speaking, he had taken to soap, which with the aid of water may be blown into beautiful, iridescent bubbles to charm the eye. Much good soap, apparently, has gone that way, never to be recovered. Everybody who was anybody began to blow bubbles about that time, and the bigger the bubble the greater its attraction for investors of hard-earned savings. Outside of this love for financial iridescence, let it be called, Mr. Scherer seemed to care little then for glitter of any sort. Shortly after his elevation to the presidency of the Boyne Iron Works he had been elected a member of the Boyne Club,—an honour of which, some thought, he should have been more sensible; but generally, when in town, he preferred to lunch at a little German restaurant annexed to a saloon, where I used often to find him literally towering above the cloth,—for he was a giant with short legs,—his napkin tucked into his shirt front, engaged in lively conversation with the ministering Heinrich. The chef at the club, Mr. Scherer insisted, could produce nothing equal to Heinrich's sauer-kraut and sausage. My earliest relationship with Mr. Scherer was that of an errand boy, of bringing to him for his approval papers which might not be intrusted to a common messenger. His gruffness and brevity disturbed me more than I cared to confess. I was pretty sure that he eyed me with the disposition of the self-made to believe that college educations and good tailors were the heaviest handicaps with which a young man could be burdened: and I suspected him of an inimical attitude toward the older families of the city. Certain men possessed his confidence; and he had built, as it were, a stockade about them, sternly keeping the rest of the world outside. In Theodore Watling he had a childlike faith.

Thus I studied him, with a deliberation which it is the purpose of these chapters to confess, though he little knew that he was being made the subject of analysis. Nor did I ever venture to talk with him, but held strictly to my role of errand boy,—even after the conviction came over me that he was no longer indifferent to my presence. The day arrived, after some years, when he suddenly thrust toward me a big, hairy hand that held the document he was examining.

"Who drew this, Mr. Paret!" he demanded.

Mr. Ripon, I told him.

The Boyne Works were buying up coal-mines, and this was a contract looking to the purchase of one in Putman County, provided, after a certain period of working, the yield and quality should come up to specifications. Mr. Scherer requested me to read one of the sections, which puzzled him. And in explaining it an idea flashed over me.

"Do you mind my making a suggestion, Mr. Scherer?" I ventured.

"What is it?" he asked brusquely.

I showed him how, by the alteration of a few words, the difficulty to which he had referred could not only be eliminated, but that certain possible penalties might be evaded, while the apparent meaning of the section remained unchanged. In other words, it gave the Boyne Iron Works an advantage that was not contemplated. He seized the paper, stared at what I had written in pencil on the margin, and then stared at me. Abruptly, he began to laugh.

"Ask Mr. Wading what he thinks of it?"

"I intended to, provided it had your approval, sir," I replied.

"You have my approval, Mr. Paret," he declared, rather cryptically, and with the slight German hardening of the v's into which he relapsed at times. "Bring it to the Works this afternoon."

Mr. Wading agreed to the alteration. He looked at me amusedly.

"Yes, I think that's an improvement, Hugh," he said. I had a feeling that I had gained ground, and from this time on I thought I detected a change in his attitude toward me; there could be no doubt about the new attitude of Mr. Scherer, who would often greet me now with a smile and a joke, and sometimes went so far as to ask my opinions.... Then, about six months later, came the famous Ribblevale case that aroused the moral indignation of so many persons, among whom was Perry Blackwood.

"You know as well as I do, Hugh, how this thing is being manipulated," he declared at Tom's one Sunday evening; "there was nothing the matter with the Ribblevale Steel Company—it was as right as rain before Leonard Dickinson and Grierson and Scherer and that crowd you train with began to talk it down at the Club. Oh, they're very compassionate. I've heard 'em. Dickinson, privately, doesn't think much of Ribblevale paper, and Pugh" (the president of the Ribblevale) "seems worried and looks badly. It's all very clever, but I'd hate to tell you in plain words what I'd call it."

"Go ahead," I challenged him audaciously. "You haven't any proof that the Ribblevale wasn't in trouble."

"I heard Mr. Pugh tell my father the other day it was a d—d outrage. He couldn't catch up with these rumours, and some of his stockholders were liquidating."

"You, don't suppose Pugh would want to admit his situation, do you?" I asked.

"Pugh's a straight man," retorted Perry. "That's more than I can say for any of the other gang, saving your presence. The unpleasant truth is that Scherer and the Boyne people want the Ribblevale, and you ought to know it if you don't." He looked at me very hard through the glasses he had lately taken to wearing. Tom, who was lounging by the fire, shifted his position uneasily. I smiled, and took another cigar.

"I believe Ralph is right, Perry, when he calls you a sentimentalist. For you there's a tragedy behind every ordinary business transaction. The Ribblevale people are having a hard time to keep their heads above water, and immediately you smell conspiracy. Dickinson and Scherer have been talking it down. How about it, Tom?"

But Tom, in these debates, was inclined to be noncommittal, although it was clear they troubled him.

"Oh, don't ask me, Hughie," he said.

"I suppose I ought to cultivate the scientific point of view, and look with impartial interest at this industrial cannibalism," returned Perry, sarcastically. "Eat or be eaten that's what enlightened self-interest has come to. After all, Ralph would say, it is nature, the insect world over again, the victim duped and crippled before he is devoured, and the lawyer—how shall I put it?—facilitating the processes of swallowing and digesting...."

There was no use arguing with Perry when he was in this vein....

Since I am not writing a technical treatise, I need not go into the details of the Ribblevale suit. Since it to say that the affair, after a while, came apparently to a deadlock, owing to the impossibility of getting certain definite information from the Ribblevale books, which had been taken out of the state. The treasurer, for reasons of his own, remained out of the state also; the ordinary course of summoning him before a magistrate in another state had naturally been resorted to, but the desired evidence was not forthcoming.

"The trouble is," Mr. Wading explained to Mr. Scherer, "that there is no law in the various states with a sufficient penalty attached that will compel the witness to divulge facts he wishes to conceal."

It was the middle of a February afternoon, and they were seated in deep, leather chairs in one corner of the reading room of the Boyne Club. They had the place to themselves. Fowndes was there also, one leg twisted around the other in familiar fashion, a bored look on his long and sallow face. Mr. Wading had telephoned to the office for me to bring them some papers bearing on the case.

"Sit down, Hugh," he said kindly.

"Now we have present a genuine legal mind," said Mr. Scherer, in the playful manner he had adopted of late, while I grinned appreciatively and took a chair. Mr. Watling presently suggested kidnapping the Ribblevale treasurer until he should promise to produce the books as the only way out of what seemed an impasse. But Mr. Scherer brought down a huge fist on his knee.

"I tell you it is no joke, Watling, we've got to win that suit," he asserted.

"That's all very well," replied Mr. Watling. "But we're a respectable firm, you know. We haven't had to resort to safe-blowing, as yet."

Mr. Scherer shrugged his shoulders, as much as to say it were a matter of indifference to him what methods were resorted to. Mr. Watling's eyes met mine; his glance was amused, yet I thought I read in it a query as to the advisability, in my presence, of going too deeply into the question of ways and means. I may have been wrong. At any rate, its sudden effect was to embolden me to give voice to an idea that had begun to simmer in my mind, that excited me, and yet I had feared to utter it. This look of my chief's, and the lighter tone the conversation had taken decided me.

"Why wouldn't it be possible to draw up a bill to fit the situation?" I inquired.

Mr. Wading started.

"What do you mean?" he asked quickly.

All three looked at me. I felt the blood come into my face, but it was too late to draw back.

"Well—the legislature is in session. And since, as Mr. Watling says, there is no sufficient penalty in other states to compel the witness to produce the information desired, why not draw up a bill and—and have it passed—" I paused for breath—"imposing a sufficient penalty on home corporations in the event of such evasions. The Ribblevale Steel Company is a home corporation."

I had shot my bolt.... There followed what was for me an anxious silence, while the three of them continued to stare at me. Mr. Watling put the tips of his fingers together, and I became aware that he was not offended, that he was thinking rapidly.

"By George, why not, Fowndes?" he demanded.

"Well," said Fowndes, "there's an element of risk in such a proceeding I need not dwell upon."

"Risk!" cried the senior partner vigorously. "There's risk in everything. They'll howl, of course. But they howl anyway, and nobody ever listens to them. They'll say it's special legislation, and the Pilot will print sensational editorials for a few days. But what of it? All of that has happened before. I tell you, if we can't see those books, we'll lose the suit. That's in black and white. And, as a matter of justice, we're entitled to know what we want to know."

"There might be two opinions as to that," observed Fowndes, with his sardonic smile.

Mr. Watling paid no attention to this remark. He was already deep in thought. It was characteristic of his mind to leap forward, seize a suggestion that often appeared chimerical to a man like Fowndes and turn it into an accomplished Fact. "I believe you've hit it, Hugh," he said. "We needn't bother about the powers of the courts in other states. We'll put into this bill an appeal to our court for an order on the clerk to compel the witness to come before the court and testify, and we'll provide for a special commissioner to take depositions in the state where the witness is. If the officers of a home corporation who are outside of the state refuse to testify, the penalty will be that the ration goes into the hands of a receiver."

Fowndes whistled.

"That's going some!" he said.

"Well, we've got to go some. How about it, Scherer?"

Even Mr. Scherer's brown eyes were snapping.

"We have got to win that suit, Watling."

We were all excited, even Fowndes, I think, though he remained expressionless. Ours was the tense excitement of primitive man in chase: the quarry which had threatened to elude us was again in view, and not unlikely to fall into our hands. Add to this feeling, on my part, the thrill that it was I who had put them on the scent. I had all the sensations of an aspiring young brave who for the first time is admitted to the councils of the tribe!

"It ought to be a popular bill, too," Mr. Schemer was saying, with a smile of ironic appreciation at the thought of demagogues advocating it. "We should have one of Lawler's friends introduce it."

"Oh, we shall have it properly introduced," replied Mr. Wading.

"It may come back at us," suggested Fowndes pessimistically. "The Boyne Iron Works is a home corporation too, if I am not mistaken."

"The Boyne Iron Works has the firm of Wading, Fowndes and Ripon behind it," asserted Mr. Scherer, with what struck me as a magnificent faith.

"You mustn't forget Paret," Mr. Watling reminded him, with a wink at me.

We had risen. Mr. Scherer laid a hand on my arm.

"No, no, I do not forget him. He will not permit me to forget him."

A remark, I thought, that betrayed some insight into my character... Mr. Watling called for pen and paper and made then and there a draft of the proposed bill, for no time was to be lost. It was dark when we left the Club, and I recall the elation I felt and strove to conceal as I accompanied my chief back to the office. The stenographers and clerks were gone; alone in the library we got down the statutes and set to work. to perfect the bill from the rough draft, on which Mr. Fowndes had written his suggestions. I felt that a complete yet subtle change had come over my relationship with Mr. Watling.

In the midst of our labours he asked me to call up the attorney for the Railroad. Mr. Gorse was still at his office.

"Hello! Is that you, Miller?" Mr. Watling said. "This is Wading. When can I see you for a few minutes this evening? Yes, I am leaving for Washington at nine thirty. Eight o'clock. All right, I'll be there."

It was almost eight before he got the draft finished to his satisfaction, and I had picked it out on the typewriter. As I handed it to him, my chief held it a moment, gazing at me with an odd smile.

"You seem to have acquired a good deal of useful knowledge, here and there, Hugh," he observed.

"I've tried to keep my eyes open, Mr. Watling," I said.

"Well," he said, "there are a great many things a young man practising law in these days has to learn for himself. And if I hadn't given you credit for some cleverness, I shouldn't have wanted you here. There's only one way to look at—at these matters we have been discussing, my boy, that's the common-sense way, and if a man doesn't get that point of view by himself, nobody can teach it to him. I needn't enlarge upon it"

"No, sir," I said.

He smiled again, but immediately became serious.

"If Mr. Gorse should approve of this bill, I'm going to send you down to the capital—to-night. Can you go?"

I nodded.

"I want you to look out for the bill in the legislature. Of course there won't be much to do, except to stand by, but you will get a better idea of what goes on down there."

I thanked him, and told him I would do my best.

"I'm sure of that," he replied. "Now it's time to go to see Gorse."

The legal department of the Railroad occupied an entire floor of the Corn Bank building. I had often been there on various errands, having on occasions delivered sealed envelopes to Mr. Gorse himself, approaching him in the ordinary way through a series of offices. But now, following Mr. Watling through the dimly lighted corridor, we came to a door on which no name was painted, and which was presently opened by a stenographer. There was in the proceeding a touch of mystery that revived keenly my boyish love for romance; brought back the days when I had been, in turn, Captain Kidd and Ali Baba.

I have never realized more strongly than in that moment the psychological force of prestige. Little by little, for five years, an estimate of the extent of Miller Gorse's power had been coming home to me, and his features stood in my mind for his particular kind of power. He was a tremendous worker, and often remained in his office until ten and eleven at night. He dismissed the stenographer by the wave of a hand which seemed to thrust her bodily out of the room.

"Hello, Miller," said Mr. Watling.

"Hello, Theodore," replied Mr. Gorse.

"This is Paret, of my office."

"I know," said Mr. Gorse, and nodded toward me. I was impressed by the felicity with which a cartoonist of the Pilot had once caricatured him by the use of curved lines. The circle of the heavy eyebrows ended at the wide nostrils; the mouth was a crescent, but bowed downwards; the heavy shoulders were rounded. Indeed, the only straight line to be discerned about him was that of his hair, black as bitumen, banged across his forehead; even his polished porphyry eyes were constructed on some curvilinear principle, and never seemed to focus. It might be said of Mr. Gorse that he had an overwhelming impersonality. One could never be quite sure that one's words reached the mark.

In spite of the intimacy which I knew existed between them, in my presence at least Mr. Gorse's manner was little different with Mr. Watling than it was with other men. Mr. Wading did not seem to mind. He pulled up a chair close to the desk and began, without any preliminaries, to explain his errand.

"It's about the Ribblevale affair," he said. "You know we have a suit."

Gorse nodded.

"We've got to get at the books, Miller,—that's all there is to it. I told you so the other day. Well, we've found out a way, I think."

He thrust his hand in his pocket, while the railroad attorney remained impassive, and drew out the draft of the bill. Mr. Gorse read it, then read it over again, and laid it down in front of him.

"Well," he said.

"I want to put that through both houses and have the governor's signature to it by the end of the week."

"It seems a little raw, at first sight, Theodore," said Mr. Gorse, with the suspicion of a smile.

My chief laughed a little.

"It's not half so raw as some things I might mention, that went through like greased lightning," he replied. "What can they do? I believe it will hold water. Tallant's, and most of the other newspapers in the state, won't print a line about it, and only Socialists and Populists read the Pilot. They're disgruntled anyway. The point is, there's no other way out for us. Just think a moment, bearing in mind what I've told you about the case, and you'll see it."

Mr. Gorse took up the paper again, and read the draft over.

"You know as well as I do, Miller, how dangerous it is to leave this Ribblevale business at loose ends. The Carlisle steel people and the Lake Shore road are after the Ribblevale Company, and we can't afford to run any risk of their getting it. It's logically a part of the Boyne interests, as Scherer says, and Dickinson is ready with the money for the reorganization. If the Carlisle people and the Lake Shore get it, the product will be shipped out by the L and G, and the Railroad will lose. What would Barbour say?"

Mr. Barbour, as I have perhaps mentioned, was the president of the Railroad, and had his residence in the other great city of the state. He was then, I knew, in the West.

"We've got to act now," insisted Mr. Watling. "That's open and shut. If you have any other plan, I wish you'd trot it out. If not, I want a letter to Paul Varney and the governor. I'm going to send Paret down with them on the night train."

It was clear to me then, in the discussion following, that Mr. Watling's gift of persuasion, though great, was not the determining factor in Mr. Gorse's decision. He, too, possessed boldness, though he preferred caution. Nor did the friendship between the two enter into the transaction. I was impressed more strongly than ever with the fact that a lawsuit was seldom a mere private affair between two persons or corporations, but involved a chain of relationships and nine times out of ten that chain led up to the Railroad, which nearly always was vitally interested in these legal contests. Half an hour of masterly presentation of the situation was necessary before Mr. Gorse became convinced that the introduction of the bill was the only way out for all concerned.

"Well, I guess you're right, Theodore," he said at length. Whereupon he seized his pen and wrote off two notes with great rapidity. These he showed to Mr. Watling, who nodded and returned them. They were folded and sealed, and handed to me. One was addressed to Colonel Paul Varney, and the other to the Hon. W. W. Trulease, governor of the state.

"You can trust this young man?" demanded Mr. Gorse.

"I think so," replied Mr. Watling, smiling at me. "The bill was his own idea."

The railroad attorney wheeled about in his chair and looked at me; looked around me, would better express it, with his indefinite, encompassing yet inclusive glance. I had riveted his attention. And from henceforth, I knew, I should enter into his calculations. He had made for me a compartment in his mind.

"His own idea!" he repeated.

"I merely suggested it," I was putting in, when he cut me short.

"Aren't you the son of Matthew Paret?"

"Yes," I said.

He gave me a queer glance, the significance of which I left untranslated. My excitement was too great to analyze what he meant by this mention of my father....

When we reached the sidewalk my chief gave me a few parting instructions.

"I need scarcely say, Hugh," he added, "that your presence in the capital should not be advertised as connected with this—legislation. They will probably attribute it to us in the end, but if you're reasonably careful, they'll never be able to prove it. And there's no use in putting our cards on the table at the beginning."

"No indeed, sir!" I agreed.

He took my hand and pressed it.

"Good luck," he said. "I know you'll get along all right."

Part Two

Chapter Ten

This was not my first visit to the state capital. Indeed, some of that recondite knowledge, in which I took a pride, had been gained on the occasions of my previous visits. Rising and dressing early, I beheld out of the car window the broad, shallow river glinting in the morning sunlight, the dome of the state house against the blue of the sky. Even at that early hour groups of the gentlemen who made our laws were scattered about the lobby of the Potts House, standing or seated within easy reach of the gaily coloured cuspidors that protected the marble floor: heavy-jawed workers from the cities mingled with moon-faced but astute countrymen who manipulated votes amongst farms and villages; fat or cadaverous, Irish, German or American, all bore in common a certain indefinable stamp. Having eaten my breakfast in a large dining-room that resounded with the clatter of dishes, I directed my steps to the apartment occupied from year to year by Colonel Paul Barney, generalissimo of the Railroad on the legislative battlefield,—a position that demanded a certain uniqueness of genius.

"How do you do, sir," he said, in a guarded but courteous tone as he opened the door. I entered to confront a group of three or four figures, silent and rather hostile, seated in a haze of tobacco smoke around a marble-topped table. On it reposed a Bible, attached to a chain.

"You probably don't remember me, Colonel," I said. "My name is Pared, and I'm associated with the firm of Watling, Fowndes, and Ripon."

His air of marginality,—heightened by a grey moustache and goatee a la Napoleon Third,—vanished instantly; he became hospitable, ingratiating.

"Why—why certainly, you were down heah with Mr. Fowndes two years ago." The Colonel spoke with a slight Southern accent. "To be sure, sir. I've had the honour of meeting your father. Mr. Norris, of North Haven, meet Mr. Paret—one of our rising lawyers..." I shook hands with them all and sat down. Opening his long coat, Colonel Varney revealed two rows of cigars, suggesting cartridges in a belt. These he proceeded to hand out as he talked. "I'm glad to see you here, Mr. Paret. You must stay awhile, and become acquainted with the men who—ahem—are shaping the destinies of a great state. It would give me pleasure to escort you about."

I thanked him. I had learned enough to realize how important are the amenities in politics and business. The Colonel did most of the conversing; he could not have filled with efficiency and ease the important post that was his had it not been for the endless fund of humorous anecdotes at his disposal. One by one the visitors left, each assuring me of his personal regard: the Colonel closed the door, softly, turning the key in the lock; there was a sly look in his black eyes as he took a chair in proximity to mine.

"Well, Mr. Paret," he asked softly, "what's up?"

Without further ado I handed him Mr. Gorse's letter, and another Mr. Watling had given me for him, which contained a copy of the bill. He read these, laid them on the table, glancing at me again, stroking his goatee the while. He chuckled.

"By gum!" he exclaimed. "I take off my hat to Theodore Watling, always did." He became contemplative. "It can be done, Mr. Paret, but it's going to take some careful driving, sir, some reaching out and flicking 'em when they r'ar and buck. Paul Varney's never been stumped yet. Just as soon as this is introduced we'll have Gates and Armstrong down here— they're the Ribblevale attorneys, aren't they? I thought so,—and the best legal talent they can hire. And they'll round up all the disgruntled fellows, you know,—that ain't friendly to the Railroad. We've got to do it quick, Mr. Paret. Gorse gave you a letter to the Governor, didn't he?"

"Yes," I said.

"Well, come along. I'll pass the word around among the boys, just to let 'em know what to expect." His eyes glittered again. "I've been following this Ribblevale business," he added, "and I understand Leonard Dickinson's all ready to reorganize that company, when the time comes. He ought to let me in for a little, on the ground floor."

I did not venture to make any promises for Mr. Dickinson.

"I reckon it's just as well if you were to meet me at the Governor's office," the Colonel added reflectively, and the hint was not lost on me. "It's better not to let 'em find out any sooner than they have to where this thing comes from,—you understand." He looked at his watch. "How would nine o'clock do? I'll be there, with Trulease, when you come,—by accident, you understand. Of course he'll be reasonable, but when they get to be governors they have little notions, you know, and you've got to indulge 'em, flatter 'em a little. It doesn't hurt, for when they get their backs up it only makes more trouble."

He put on a soft, black felt hat, and departed noiselessly...

At nine o'clock I arrived at the State House and was ushered into a great square room overlooking the park. The Governor was seated at a desk under an elaborate chandelier, and sure enough, Colonel Varney was there beside him; making barely perceptible signals.

"It is a pleasure to make your acquaintance, Mr. Paret," said Mr. Trulease. "Your name is a familiar one in your city, sir. And I gather from your card that you are associated with my good friend, Theodore Watling."

I acknowledged it. I was not a little impressed by the perfect blend of cordiality, democratic simplicity and impressiveness Mr. Trulease had achieved. For he had managed, in the course of a long political career, to combine in exact proportions these elements which, in the public mind, should up the personality of a chief executive. Momentarily he overcame the feeling of superiority with which I had entered his presence; neutralized the sense I had of being associated now with the higher powers which had put him where he was. For I knew all about his "record."

"You're acquainted with Colonel Varney?" he inquired.

"Yes, Governor, I've met the Colonel," I said.

"Well, I suppose your firm is getting its share of business these days," Mr. Trulease observed. I acknowledged it was, and after discussing for a few moments the remarkable growth of my native city the Governor tapped on his desk and inquired what he could do for me. I produced the letter from the attorney for the Railroad. The Governor read it gravely.

"Ah," he said, "from Mr. Gorse." A copy of the proposed bill was enclosed, and the Governor read that also, hemmed and hawed a little, turned and handed it to Colonel Varney, who was sitting with a detached air, smoking contemplatively, a vacant expression on his face. "What do you think of this, Colonel?"

Whereupon the Colonel tore himself away from his reflections.

"What's that, Governor?"

"Mr. Gorse has called my attention to what seems to him a flaw in our statutes, an inability to obtain testimony from corporations whose books are elsewhere, and who may thus evade, he says, to a certain extent, the sovereign will of our state."

The Colonel took the paper with an admirable air of surprise, adjusted his glasses, and became absorbed in reading, clearing his throat once or twice and emitting an exclamation.

"Well, if you ask me, Governor," he said, at length, "all I can say is that I am astonished somebody didn't think of this simple remedy before now. Many times, sir, have I seen justice defeated because we had no such legislation as this."

He handed it back. The Governor studied it once more, and coughed.

"Does the penalty," he inquired, "seem to you a little severe?"

"No, sir," replied the Colonel, emphatically. "Perhaps it is because I am anxious, as a citizen, to see an evil abated. I have had an intimate knowledge of legislation, sir, for more than twenty years in this state, and in all that time I do not remember to have seen a bill more concisely drawn, or better calculated to accomplish the ends of justice. Indeed, I often wondered why this very penalty was not imposed. Foreign magistrates are notoriously indifferent as to affairs in another state than their own. Rather than go into the hands of a receiver I venture to say that hereafter, if this bill is made a law, the necessary testimony will be forthcoming."

The Governor read the bill through again.

"If it is introduced, Colonel," he said, "the legislature and the people of the state ought to have it made clear to them that its aim is to remedy an injustice. A misunderstanding on this point would be unfortunate."

"Most unfortunate, Governor."

"And of course," added the Governor, now addressing me, "it would be improper for me to indicate what course I shall pursue in regard to it if it should come to me for my signature. Yet I may go so far as to say that the defect it seeks to remedy seems to me a real one. Come in and see me, Mr. Paret, when you are in town, and give my cordial regards to Mr. Watling."

So gravely had the farce been carried on that I almost laughed, despite the fact that the matter in question was a serious one for me. The Governor held out his hand, and I accepted my dismissal.

I had not gone fifty steps in the corridor before I heard the Colonel's voice in my ear.

"We had to give him a little rope to go through with his act," he whispered confidentially. "But he'll sign it all right. And now, if you'll excuse me, Mr. Paret, I'll lay a few mines. See you at the hotel, sir."

Thus he indicated, delicately, that it would be better for me to keep out of sight. On my way to the Potts House the bizarre elements in the situation struck me again with considerable force. It seemed so ridiculous, so puerile to have to go through with this political farce in order that a natural economic evolution might be achieved. Without doubt the development of certain industries had reached a stage where the units in competition had become too small, when a greater concentration of capital was necessary. Curiously enough, in this mental argument of justification, I left out all consideration of the size of the probable profits to Mr. Scherer and his friends. Profits and brains went together. And, since the Almighty did not limit the latter, why should man attempt to limit the former? We were playing for high but justifiable stakes; and I resented the comedy which an hypocritical insistence on the forms of democracy compelled us to go through. It seemed unworthy of men who controlled the destinies of state and nation. The point of view, however, was consoling. As the day wore on I sat in the Colonel's room, admiring the skill with which he conducted the campaign: a green country lawyer had been got to introduce the bill, it had been expedited to the Committee on the Judiciary, which would have an executive session immediately after dinner. I had ventured to inquire about the hearings.

"There won't be any hearings, sir," the Colonel assured me. "We own that committee from top to bottom."

Indeed, by four o'clock in the afternoon the message came that the committee had agreed to recommend the bill.

Shortly after that the first flurry occurred. There came a knock at the door, followed by the entrance of a stocky Irish American of about forty years of age, whose black hair was plastered over his forehead. His sea- blue eyes had a stormy look.

"Hello, Jim," said the Colonel. "I was just wondering where you were."

"Sure, you must have been!" replied the gentleman sarcastically.

But the Colonel's geniality was unruffled.

"Mr. Maker," he said, "you ought to know Mr. Paret. Mr. Maker is the representative from Ward Five of your city, and we can always count on him to do the right thing, even if he is a Democrat. How about it, Jim?"

Mr. Maker relighted the stump of his cigar.

"Take a fresh one, Jim," said the Colonel, opening a bureau drawer.

Mr. Maker took two.

"Say, Colonel," he demanded, "what's this bill that went into the judiciary this morning?"

"What bill?" asked the Colonel, blandly.

"So you think I ain't on?" Mr. Maker inquired.

The Colonel laughed.

"Where have you been, Jim?"

"I've been up to the city, seem' my wife—that's where I've been."

The Colonel smiled, as at a harmless fiction.

"Well, if you weren't here, I don't see what right you've got to complain. I never leave my good Democratic friends on the outside, do I?"

"That's all right," replied Mr. Maker, doggedly, "I'm on, I'm here now, and that bill in the Judiciary doesn't pass without me. I guess I can stop it, too. How about a thousand apiece for five of us boys?"

"You're pretty good at a joke, Jim," remarked the Colonel, stroking his goatee.

"Maybe you're looking for a little publicity in this here game," retorted Mr. Maker, darkly. "Say, Colonel, ain't we always treated the Railroad on the level?"

"Jim," asked the Colonel, gently, "didn't I always take care of you?"

He had laid his hand on the shoulder of Mr. Maker, who appeared slightly mollified, and glanced at a massive silver watch.

"Well, I'll be dropping in about eight o'clock," was his significant reply, as he took his leave.

"I guess we'll have to grease the wheels a little," the Colonel remarked to me, and gazed at the ceiling....

The telegram apropos of the Ward Five leader was by no means the only cipher message I sent back during my stay. I had not needed to be told that the matter in hand would cost money, but Mr. Watling's parting instruction to me had been to take the Colonel's advice as to specific sums, and obtain confirmation from Fowndes. Nor was it any surprise to me to find Democrats on intimate terms with such a stout Republican as the Colonel. Some statesman is said to have declared that he knew neither Easterners nor Westerners, Northerners nor Southerners, but only Americans; so Colonel Varney recognized neither Democrats nor Republicans; in our legislature party divisions were sunk in a greater loyalty to the Railroad.

At the Colonel's suggestion I had laid in a liberal supply of cigars and whiskey. The scene in his room that evening suggested a session of a sublimated grand lodge of some secret order, such were the mysterious comings and goings, knocks and suspenses. One after another the "important" men duly appeared and were introduced, the Colonel supplying the light touch.

"Why, cuss me if it isn't Billy! Mr. Paret, I want you to shake hands with Mr. Donovan, the floor leader of the 'opposition,' sir. Mr. Donovan has had the habit of coming up here for a friendly chat ever since he first came down to the legislature. How long is it, Billy?"

"I guess it's nigh on to fifteen years, Colonel."

"Fifteen years!" echoed the Colonel, "and he's so good a Democrat it hasn't changed his politics a particle."

Mr. Donovan grinned in appreciation of this thrust, helped himself liberally from the bottle on the mantel, and took a seat on the bed. We had a "friendly chat."

Thus I made the acquaintance also of the Hon. Joseph Mecklin, Speaker of the House, who unbent in the most flattering way on learning my identity.

"Mr. Paret's here on that little matter, representing Watling, Fowndes and Ripon," the Colonel explained. And it appeared that Mr. Mecklin knew all about the "little matter," and that the mention of the firm of Watling, Fowndes and Ripon had a magical effect in these parts. The President of the Senate, the Hon. Lafe Giddings, went so far as to say that he hoped before long to see Mr. Watling in Washington. By no means the least among our callers was the Hon. Fitch Truesdale, editor of the St. Helen's Messenger, whose editorials were of the trite effectiveness that is taken widely for wisdom, and were assiduously copied every week by other state papers and labeled "Mr. Truesdale's Common Sense." At countless firesides in our state he was known as the spokesman of the plain man, who was blissfully ignorant of the fact that Mr. Truesdale was owned body and carcass by Mr. Cyrus Ridden, the principal manufacturer of St. Helen's and a director in several subsidiary lines of the Railroad. In the legislature, the Hon. Fitch's function was that of the moderate counsellor and bellwether for new members, hence nothing could have been more fitting than the choice of that gentleman for the honour of moving, on the morrow, that Bill No. 709 ought to pass.

Mr. Truesdale reluctantly consented to accept a small "loan" that would help to pay the mortgage on his new press....

When the last of the gathering had departed, about one o'clock in the morning, I had added considerably to my experience, gained a pretty accurate idea of who was who in the legislature and politics of the state, and established relationships—as the Colonel reminded me—likely to prove valuable in the future. It seemed only gracious to congratulate him on his management of the affair,—so far. He appeared pleased, and squeezed my hand.

"Well, sir, it did require a little delicacy of touch. And if I do say it myself, it hasn't been botched," he admitted. "There ain't an outsider, as far as I can learn, who has caught on to the nigger in the wood-pile. That's the great thing, to keep 'em ignorant as long as possible. You understand. They yell bloody murder when they do find out, but generally it's too late, if a bill's been handled right."

I found myself speculating as to who the "outsiders" might be. No Ribblevale attorneys were on the spot as yet,—of that I was satisfied. In the absence of these, who were the opposition? It seemed to me as though I had interviewed that day every man in the legislature.

I was very tired. But when I got into bed, it was impossible to sleep. My eyes smarted from the tobacco smoke; and the events of the day, in disorderly manner, kept running through my head. The tide of my exhilaration had ebbed, and I found myself struggling against a revulsion caused, apparently, by the contemplation of Colonel Varney and his associates; the instruments, in brief, by which our triumph over our opponents was to be effected. And that same idea which, when launched amidst the surroundings of the Boyne Club, had seemed so brilliant, now took on an aspect of tawdriness. Another thought intruded itself,—that of Mr. Pugh, the president of the Ribblevale Company. My father had known him, and some years before I had traveled halfway across the state in his company; his kindliness had impressed me. He had spent a large part of his business life, I knew, in building up the Ribblevale, and now it was to be wrested from him; he was to be set aside, perhaps forced to start all over again when old age was coming on! In vain I accused myself of sentimentality, and summoned all my arguments to prove that in commerce efficiency must be the only test. The image of Mr. Pugh would not down.

I got up and turned on the light, and took refuge in a novel I had in my bag. Presently I grew calmer. I had chosen. I had succeeded. And now that I had my finger at last on the nerve of power, it was no time to weaken.

It was half-past six when I awoke and went to the window, relieved to find that the sun had scattered my morbid fancies with the darkness; and I speculated, as I dressed, whether the thing called conscience were not, after all, a matter of nerves. I went downstairs through the tobacco-stale atmosphere of the lobby into the fresh air and sparkly sunlight of the mild February morning, and leaving the business district I reached the residence portion of the little town. The front steps of some of the comfortable houses were being swept by industrious servant girls, and out of the chimneys twisted, fantastically, rich blue smoke; the bare branches of the trees were silver-grey against the sky; gaining at last an old-fashioned, wooden bridge, I stood for awhile gazing at the river, over the shallows of which the spendthrift hand of nature had flung a shower of diamonds. And I reflected that the world was for the strong, for him who dared reach out his hand and take what it offered. It was not money we coveted, we Americans, but power, the self-expression conferred by power. A single experience such as I had had the night before would since to convince any sane man that democracy was a failure, that the world-old principle of aristocracy would assert itself, that the attempt of our ancestors to curtail political power had merely resulted in the growth of another and greater economic power that bade fair to be limitless. As I walked slowly back into town I felt a reluctance to return to the noisy hotel, and finding myself in front of a little restaurant on a side street, I entered it. There was but one other customer in the place, and he was seated on the far side of the counter, with a newspaper in front of him; and while I was ordering my breakfast I was vaguely aware that the newspaper had dropped, and that he was looking at me. In the slight interval that elapsed before my brain could register his identity I experienced a distinct shock of resentment; a sense of the reintrusion of an antagonistic valuc at a moment when it was most unwelcome....

The man had risen and was coming around the counter. He was Hermann Krebs.

"Paret!" I heard him say.

"You here?" I exclaimed.

He did not seem to notice the lack of cordiality in my tone. He appeared so genuinely glad to see me again that I instantly became rather ashamed of my ill nature.

"Yes, I'm here—in the legislature," he informed me.

"A Solon!"

"Exactly." He smiled. "And you?" he inquired.

"Oh, I'm only a spectator. Down here for a day or two."

He was still lanky, his clothes gave no evidence of an increased prosperity, but his complexion was good, his skin had cleared. I was more than ever baked by a resolute good humour, a simplicity that was not innocence, a whimsical touch seemingly indicative of a state of mind that refused to take too seriously certain things on which I set store. What right had he to be contented with life?

"Well, I too am only a spectator here," he laughed. "I'm neither fish, flesh nor fowl, nor good red herring."

"You were going into the law, weren't you?" I asked. "I remember you said something about it that day we met at Beverly Farms."

"Yes, I managed it, after all. Then I went back home to Elkington to try to make a living."

"But somehow I have never thought of you as being likely to develop political aspirations, Krebs," I said.

"I should say not! he exclaimed.

"Yet here you are, launched upon a political career! How did it happen?"

"Oh, I'm not worrying about the career," he assured me. "I got here by accident, and I'm afraid it won't happen again in a hurry. You see, the hands in those big mills we have in Elkington sprang a surprise on the machine, and the first thing I knew I was nominated for the legislature. A committee came to my boarding-house and told me, and there was the deuce to pay, right off. The Railroad politicians turned in and worked for the Democratic candidate, of course, and the Hutchinses, who own the mills, tried through emissaries to intimidate their operatives."

"And then?" I asked.

"Well,—I'm here," he said.

"Wouldn't you be accomplishing more," I inquired, "if you hadn't antagonized the Hutchinses?"

"It depends upon what you mean by accomplishment," he answered, so mildly that I felt more rued than ever.

"Well, from what you say, I suppose you're going in for reform, that these workmen up at Elkington are not satisfied with their conditions and imagine you can help to better them. Now, provided the conditions are not as good as they might be, how are you going to improve them if you find yourself isolated here, as you say?"

"In other words, I should cooperate with Colonel Varney and other disinterested philanthropists," he supplied, and I realized that I was losing my temper.

"Well, what can you do?" I inquired defiantly.

"I can find out what's going on," he said. "I have already learned something, by the way."

"And then?" I asked, wondering whether the implication were personal.

"Then I can help—disseminate the knowledge. I may be wrong, but I have an idea that when the people of this country learn how their legislatures are conducted they will want to change things."

"That's right!" echoed the waiter, who had come up with my griddle-cakes. "And you're the man to tell 'em, Mr. Krebs."

"It will need several thousand of us to do that, I'm afraid," said Krebs, returning his smile.

My distaste for the situation became more acute, but I felt that I was thrown on the defensive. I could not retreat, now.

"I think you are wrong," I declared, when the waiter had departed to attend to another customer. "The people the great majority of them, at least are indifferent, they don't want to be bothered with politics. There will always be labour agitation, of course,—the more wages those fellows get, the more they want. We pay the highest wages in the world to-day, and the standard of living is higher in this country than anywhere else. They'd ruin our prosperity, if we'd let 'em."

"How about the thousands of families who don't earn enough to live decently even in times of prosperity?" inquired Krebs.

"It's hard, I'll admit, but the inefficient and the shiftless are bound to suffer, no matter what form of government you adopt."

"You talk about standards of living,—I could show you some examples of standards to make your heart sick," he said. "What you don't realize, perhaps, is that low standards help to increase the inefficient of whom you complain."

He smiled rather sadly. "The prosperity you are advocating," he added, after a moment, "is a mere fiction, it is gorging the few at the expense of the many. And what is being done in this country is to store up an explosive gas that some day will blow your superstructure to atoms if you don't wake up in time."

"Isn't that a rather one-sided view, too?" I suggested.

"I've no doubt it may appear so, but take the proceedings in this legislature. I've no doubt you know something about them, and that you would maintain they are justified on account of the indifference of the public, and of other reasons, but I can cite an instance that is simply legalized thieving." For the first time a note of indignation crept into Krebs's voice. "Last night I discovered by a mere accident, in talking to a man who came in on a late train, that a bill introduced yesterday, which is being rushed through the Judiciary Committee of the House—an apparently innocent little bill—will enable, if it becomes a law, the Boyne Iron Works, of your city, to take possession of the Ribblevale Steel Company, lock, stock, and barrel. And I am told it was conceived by a lawyer who claims to be a respectable member of his profession, and who has extraordinary ability, Theodore Watling."

Krebs put his hand in his pocket and drew out a paper. "Here's a copy of it,—House Bill 709." His expression suddenly changed. "Perhaps Mr. Watling is a friend of yours."

"I'm with his firm," I replied....

Krebs's fingers closed over the paper, crumpling it.

"Oh, then, you know about this," he said. He was putting the paper back into his pocket when I took it from him. But my adroitness, so carefully schooled, seemed momentarily to have deserted me. What should I say? It was necessary to decide quickly.

"Don't you take rather a—prejudiced view of this, Krebs?" I said. "Upon my word, I can't see why you should accept a rumour running around the lobbies that Mr. Watling drafted this bill for a particular purpose."

He was silent. But his eyes did not leave my face.

"Why should any sensible man, a member of the legislature, take stock in that kind of gossip?" I insisted. "Why not judge this bill by its face, without heeding a cock and bull story as to how it may have originated? It is a good bill, or a bad bill? Let's see what it says."

I read it.

"So far as I can see, it is legislation which we ought to have had long ago, and tends to compel a publicity in corporation affairs that is much needed, to put a stop to practices which every decent citizen deplores."

He drew the paper out of my hand.

"You needn't go on, Paret," he told me. "It's no use."

"Well, I'm sorry we don't agree," I said, and got up. I left him twisting the paper in his fingers.

Beside the clerk's desk in the Potts House, relating one of his anecdotes, I spied Colonel Varney, and managed presently to draw him upstairs to his room. "What's the matter?" he asked.

"Do you know a man named Krebs in the House?" I said.

"From Elkington? Why, that's the man the Hutchinses let slip through,— the Hutchinses, who own the mills over there. The agitators put up a job on them." The Colonel was no longer the genial and social purveyor of anecdotes. He had become tense, alert, suspicious. "What's he up to?"

"He's found out about this bill," I replied.

"How?"

"I don't know. But someone told him that it originated in our office, and that we were going to use it in our suit against the Ribblevale."

I related the circumstances of my running across Krebs, speaking of having known him at Harvard. Colonel Varney uttered an oath, and strode across to the window, where he stood looking down into the street from between the lace curtains.

"We'll have to attend to him, right off," he said.

I was surprised to find myself resenting the imputation, and deeply. "I'm afraid he's one of those who can't be 'attended to,'" I answered.

"You mean that he's in the employ of the Ribblevale people?" the Colonel inquired.

"I don't mean anything of the kind," I retorted, with more heat, perhaps, than I realized. The Colonel looked at me queerly.

"That's all right, Mr. Paret. Of course I don't want to question your judgment, sir. And you say he's a friend of yours."

"I said I knew him at college."

"But you will pardon me," the Colonel went on, "when I tell you that I've had some experience with that breed, and I have yet to see one of 'em you couldn't come to terms with in some way—in some way," he added, significantly. I did not pause to reflect that the Colonel's attitude, from his point of view (yes, and from mine,—had I not adopted it?) was the logical one. In that philosophy every man had his price, or his weakness. Yet, such is the inconsistency of human nature, I was now unable to contemplate this attitude with calmness.

"Mr. Krebs is a lawyer. Has he accepted a pass from the Railroad?" I demanded, knowing the custom of that corporation of conferring this delicate favour on the promising young talent in my profession.

"I reckon he's never had the chance," said Mr. Varney.

"Well, has he taken a pass as a member of the legislature?"

"No,—I remember looking that up when he first came down. Sent that back, if I recall the matter correctly." Colonel Varney went to a desk in the corner of the room, unlocked it, drew forth a black book, and running his fingers through the pages stopped at the letter K. "Yes, sent back his legislative pass, but I've known 'em to do that when they were holding out for something more. There must be somebody who can get close to him."

The Colonel ruminated awhile. Then he strode to the door and called out to the group of men who were always lounging in the hall.

"Tell Alf Young I want to see him, Fred."

I waited, by no means free from uneasiness and anxiety, from a certain lack of self-respect that was unfamiliar. Mr. Young, the Colonel explained, was a legal light in Galesburg, near Elkington,—the Railroad lawyer there. And when at last Mr. Young appeared he proved to be an oily gentleman of about forty, inclining to stoutness, with one of those "blue," shaven faces.

"Want me, Colonel?" he inquired blithely, when the door had closed behind him; and added obsequiously, when introduced to me, "Glad to meet you, Mr. Paret. My regards to Mr. Watling, when you go back.

"Alf," demanded the Colonel, "what do you know of this fellow Krebs?"

Mr. Young laughed. Krebs was "nutty," he declared—that was all there was to it.

"Won't he—listen to reason?"

"It's been tried, Colonel. Say, he wouldn't know a hundred-dollar bill if you showed him one."

"What does he want?"

"Oh, something,—that's sure, they all want something." Mr. Young shrugged his shoulder expressively, and by a skillful manipulation of his lips shifted his cigar from one side of his mouth to the other without raising his hands. "But it ain't money. I guess he's got a notion that later on the labour unions'll send him to the United States Senate some day. He's no slouch, either, when it comes to law. I can tell you that."

"No—no flaw in his—record?" Colonel Varney's agate eyes sought those of Mr. Young, meaningly.

"That's been tried, too," declared the Galesburg attorney. "Say, you can believe it or not, but we've never dug anything up so far. He's been too slick for us, I guess."

"Well," exclaimed the Colonel, at length, "let him squeal and be d—d! He can't do any more than make a noise. Only I hoped we'd be able to grease this thing along and slide it through the Senate this afternoon, before they got wind of it."

"He'll squeal, all right, until you smother him," Mr. Young observed.

"We'll smother him some day!" replied the Colonel, savagely.

Mr. Young laughed.

But as I made my way toward the State House I was conscious of a feeling of relief. I had no sooner gained a front seat in the gallery of the House of Representatives when the members rose, the Senate marched gravely in, the Speaker stopped jesting with the Chaplain, and over the Chaplain's face came suddenly an agonized expression. Folding his hands across his stomach he began to call on God with terrific fervour, in an intense and resounding voice. I was struck suddenly by the irony of it all. Why have a legislature when Colonel Paul Varney was so efficient! The legislature was a mere sop to democratic prejudice, to pray over it heightened the travesty. Suppose there were a God after all? not necessarily the magnified monarch to whom these pseudo-democrats prayed, but an Intelligent Force that makes for righteousness. How did He, or It, like to be trifled with in this way? And, if He existed, would not His disgust be immeasurable as He contemplated that unctuous figure in the "Prince Albert" coat, who pretended to represent Him?

As the routine business began I searched for Krebs, to find him presently at a desk beside a window in the rear of the hall making notes on a paper; there was, confessedly, little satisfaction in the thought that the man whose gaunt features I contemplated was merely one of those impractical idealists who beat themselves to pieces against the forces that sway the world and must forever sway it. I should be compelled to admit that he represented something unique in that assembly if he had the courage to get up and oppose House Bill 709. I watched him narrowly; the suggestion intruded itself—perhaps he had been "seen," as the Colonel expressed it. I repudiated it. I grew impatient, feverish; the monotonous reading of the clerk was interrupted now and then by the sharp tones of the Speaker assigning his various measures to this or that committee, "unless objection is offered," while the members moved about and murmured among themselves; Krebs had stopped making notes; he was looking out of the window. At last, without any change of emphasis in his droning voice, the clerk announced the recommendation of the Committee on Judiciary that House Bill 709 ought to pass.

Down in front a man had risen from his seat—the felicitous Mr. Truesdale. Glancing around at his fellow-members he then began to explain in the impressive but conversational tone of one whose counsels are in the habit of being listened to, that this was merely a little measure to remedy a flaw in the statutes. Mr. Truesdale believed in corporations when corporations were good, and this bill was calculated to make them good, to put an end to jugglery and concealment. Our great state, he said, should be in the forefront of such wise legislation, which made for justice and a proper publicity; but the bill in question was of greater interest to lawyers than to laymen, a committee composed largely of lawyers had recommended it unanimously, and he was sure that no opposition would develop in the House. In order not to take up their time he asked: therefore, that it be immediately put on its second and third reading and allowed to pass.

He sat down, and I looked at Krebs. Could he, could any man, any lawyer, have the presumption to question such an obviously desirable measure, to arraign the united judgment of the committee's legal talent? Such was the note Mr. Truesdale so admirably struck. As though fascinated, I continued to gaze at Krebs. I hated him, I desired to see him humiliated, and yet amazingly I found myself wishing with almost equal vehemence that he would be true to himself. He was rising,—slowly, timidly, I thought, his hand clutching his desk lid, his voice sounding wholly inadequate as he addressed the Speaker. The Speaker hesitated, his tone palpably supercilious.

"The gentleman from—from Elkington, Mr. Krebs."

There was a craning of necks, a staring, a tittering. I burned with vicarious shame as Krebs stood there awkwardly, his hand still holding the desk. There were cries of "louder" when he began; some picked up their newspapers, while others started conversations. The Speaker rapped with his gavel, and I failed to hear the opening words. Krebs paused, and began again. His speech did not, at first, flow easily.

"Mr. Speaker, I rise to protest against this bill, which in my opinion is not so innocent as the gentleman from St. Helen's would have the House believe. It is on a par, indeed, with other legislation that in past years has been engineered through this legislature under the guise of beneficent law. No, not on a par. It is the most arrogant, the most monstrous example of special legislation of them all. And while I do not expect to be able to delay its passage much longer than the time I shall be on my feet—"

"Then why not sit down?" came a voice, just audible.

As he turned swiftly toward the offender his profile had an eagle-like effect that startled me, seemingly realizing a new quality in the man. It was as though he had needed just the stimulus of that interruption to electrify and transform him. His awkwardness disappeared; and if he was a little bombastic, a little "young," he spoke with the fire of conviction.

"Because," he cried, "because I should lose my self-respect for life if I sat here and permitted the political organization of a railroad, the members of which are here under the guise of servants of the people, to cow me into silence. And if it be treason to mention the name of that Railroad in connection with its political tyranny, then make the most of it." He let go of the desk, and tapped the copy of the bill. "What are the facts? The Boyne Iron Works, under the presidency of Adolf Scherer, has been engaged in litigation with the Ribblevale Steel Company for some years: and this bill is intended to put into the hands of the attorneys for Mr. Scherer certain information that will enable him to get possession of the property. Gentlemen, that is what 'legal practice' has descended to in the hands of respectable lawyers. This device originated with the resourceful Mr. Theodore Watling, and if it had not had the approval of Mr. Miller Gorse, it would never have got any farther than the judiciary committee. It was confided to the skillful care of Colonel Paul Varney to be steered through this legislature, as hundreds of other measures have been steered through,—without unnecessary noise. It may be asked why the Railroad should bother itself by lending its political organization to private corporations? I will tell you. Because corporations like the Boyne corporation are a part of a network of interests, these corporations aid the Railroad to maintain its monopoly, and in return receive rebates."

Krebs had raised his voice as the murmurs became louder. At this point a sharp-faced lawyer from Belfast got to his feet and objected that the gentleman from Elkington was wasting the time of the House, indulging in hearsay. His remarks were not germane, etc. The Speaker rapped again, with a fine show of impartiality, and cautioned the member from Elkington.

"Very well," replied Krebs. "I have said what I wanted to say on that score, and I know it to be the truth. And if this House does not find it germane, the day is coming when its constituents will."

Whereupon he entered into a discussion of the bill, dissecting it with more calmness, with an ability that must have commanded, even from some hostile minds, an unwilling respect. The penalty, he said, was outrageous, hitherto unheard of in law,—putting a corporation in the hands of a receiver, at the mercy of those who coveted it, because one of its officers refused, or was unable, to testify. He might be in China, in Timbuctoo when the summons was delivered at his last or usual place of abode. Here was an enormity, an exercise of tyrannical power exceeding all bounds, a travesty on popular government.... He ended by pointing out the significance of the fact that the committee had given no hearings; by declaring that if the bill became a law, it would inevitably react upon the heads of those who were responsible for it.

He sat down, and there was a flutter of applause from the scattered audience in the gallery.

"By God, that's the only man in the whole place!"

I was aware, for the first time, of a neighbour at my side,—a solid, red-faced man, evidently a farmer. His trousers were tucked into his boots, and his gnarled and powerful hands, ingrained with dirt, clutched the arms of the seat as he leaned forward.

"Didn't he just naturally lambaste 'em?" he cried excitedly. "They'll down him, I guess,—but say, he's right. A man would lose his self- respect if he didn't let out his mind at them hoss thieves, wouldn't he? What's that fellow's name?"

I told him.

"Krebs," he repeated. "I want to remember that. Durned if I don't shake hands with him."

His excitement astonished me. Would the public feel like that, if they only knew?... The Speaker's gavel had come down like a pistol shot.

One "war-hoss"—as my neighbour called them—after another proceeded to crush the member from Elkington. It was, indeed, very skillfully done, and yet it was a process from which I did not derive, somehow, much pleasure. Colonel Varney's army had been magnificently trained to meet just this kind of situation: some employed ridicule, others declared, in impassioned tones, that the good name of their state had been wantonly assailed, and pointed fervently to portraits on the walls of patriots of the past,—sentiments that drew applause from the fickle gallery. One gentleman observed that the obsession of a "railroad machine" was a sure symptom of a certain kind of insanity, of which the first speaker had given many other evidences. The farmer at my side remained staunch.

"They can't fool me," he said angrily, "I know 'em. Do you see that fellow gettin' up to talk now? Well, I could tell you a few things about him, all right. He comes from Glasgow, and his name's Letchworth. He's done more harm in his life than all the criminals he's kept out of prison,—belongs to one of the old families down there, too."

I had, indeed, remarked Letchworth's face, which seemed to me peculiarly evil, its lividity enhanced by a shock of grey hair. His method was withering sarcasm, and he was clearly unable to control his animus....

No champion appeared to support Krebs, who sat pale and tense while this denunciation of him was going on. Finally he got the floor. His voice trembled a little, whether with passion, excitement, or nervousness it was impossible to say. But he contented himself with a brief defiance. If the bill passed, he declared, the men who voted for it, the men who were behind it, would ultimately be driven from political life by an indignant public. He had a higher opinion of the voters of the state than those who accused him of slandering it, than those who sat silent and had not lifted their voices against this crime.

When the bill was put to a vote he demanded a roll call. Ten members besides himself were recorded against House Bill No. 709!

In spite of this overwhelming triumph my feelings were not wholly those of satisfaction when I returned to the hotel and listened to the exultations and denunciations of such politicians as Letchworth, Young, and Colonel Varney. Perhaps an image suggesting Hermann Krebs as some splendid animal at bay, dragged down by the hounds, is too strong: he had been ingloriously crushed, and defeat, even for the sake of conviction, was not an inspiring spectacle.... As the chase swept on over his prostrate figure I rapidly regained poise and a sense of proportion; a "master of life" could not permit himself to be tossed about by sentimentality; and gradually I grew ashamed of my bad quarter of an hour in the gallery of the House, and of the effect of it—which lingered awhile—as of a weakness suddenly revealed, which must at all costs be overcome. I began to see something dramatic and sensational in Krebs's performance....

The Ribblevale Steel Company was the real quarry, after all. And such had been the expedition, the skill and secrecy, with which our affair was conducted, that before the Ribblevale lawyers could arrive, alarmed and breathless, the bill had passed the House, and their only real chance of halting it had been lost. For the Railroad controlled the House, not by owning the individuals composing it, but through the leaders who dominated it,—men like Letchworth and Truesdale. These, and Colonel Varney, had seen to it that men who had any parliamentary ability had been attended to; all save Krebs, who had proved a surprise. There were indeed certain members who, although they had railroad passes in their pockets (which were regarded as just perquisites,—the Railroad being so rich!), would have opposed the bill if they had felt sufficiently sure of themselves to cope with such veterans as Letchworth. Many of these had allowed themselves to be won over or cowed by the oratory which had crushed Krebs.

Nor did the Ribblevale people—be it recorded—scruple to fight fire with fire. Their existence, of course, was at stake, and there was no public to appeal to. A part of the legal army that rushed to the aid of our adversaries spent the afternoon and most of the night organizing all those who could be induced by one means or another to reverse their sentiments, and in searching for the few who had grievances against the existing power. The following morning a motion was introduced to reconsider; and in the debate that followed, Krebs, still defiant, took an active part. But the resolution required a two-thirds vote, and was lost.

When the battle was shifted to the Senate it was as good as lost. The Judiciary Committee of the august body did indeed condescend to give hearings, at which the Ribblevale lawyers exhausted their energy and ingenuity without result with only two dissenting votes the bill was calmly passed. In vain was the Governor besieged, entreated, threatened,—it was said; Mr. Trulease had informed protesters—so Colonel Varney gleefully reported—that he had "become fully convinced of the inherent justice of the measure." On Saturday morning he signed it, and it became a law....

Colonel Varney, as he accompanied me to the train, did not conceal his jubilation.

"Perhaps I ought not to say it, Mr. Paret, but it couldn't have been done neater. That's the art in these little affairs, to get 'em runnin' fast, to get momentum on 'em before the other party wakes up, and then he can't stop 'em." As he shook hands in farewell he added, with more gravity: "We'll see each other often, sir, I guess. My very best regards to Mr. Watling."

Needless to say, I had not confided to him the part I had played in originating House Bill No. 709, now a law of the state. But as the train rolled on through the sunny winter landscape a sense of well-being, of importance and power began to steal through me. I was victoriously bearing home my first scalp,—one which was by no means to be despised.... It was not until we reached Rossiter, about five o'clock, that I was able to get the evening newspapers. Such was the perfection of the organization of which I might now call myself an integral part that the "best" publications contained only the barest mention,—and that in the legislative news,—of the signing of the bill. I read with complacency and even with amusement the flaring headlines I had anticipated in Mr. Lawler's 'Pilot.'

"The Governor Signs It!"

"Special legislation, forced through by the Railroad Lobby, which will drive honest corporations from this state."

"Ribblevale Steel Company the Victim."

It was common talk in the capital, the article went on to say, that Theodore Watling himself had drawn up the measure.... Perusing the editorial page my eye fell on the name, Krebs. One member of the legislature above all deserved the gratitude of the people of the state,- -the member from Elkington. "An unknown man, elected in spite of the opposition of the machine, he had dared to raise his voice against this iniquity," etc., etc.

We had won. That was the essential thing. And my legal experience had taught me that victory counts; defeat is soon forgotten. Even the discontented, half-baked and heterogeneous element from which the Pilot got its circulation had short memories.

Chapter Eleven

The next morning, which was Sunday, I went to Mr. Watling's house in, Fillmore Street—a new residence at that time, being admired as the dernier cri in architecture. It had a mediaeval look, queer dormers in a steep roof of red tiles, leaded windows buried deep in walls of rough stone. Emerging from the recessed vestibule on a level with the street were the Watling twins, aglow with health, dressed in identical costumes of blue. They had made their bow to society that winter.

"Why, here's Hugh!" said Frances. "Doesn't he look pleased with himself?"

"He's come to take us to church," said Janet.

"Oh, he's much too important," said Frances. "He's made a killing of some sort,—haven't you, Hugh?“...

I rang the bell and stood watching them as they departed, reflecting that I was thirty-two years of age and unmarried. Mr. Watling, surrounded with newspapers and seated before his library fire, glanced up at me with a welcoming smile: how had I borne the legislative baptism of fire? Such, I knew, was its implication.

"Everything went through according to schedule, eh? Well, I congratulate you, Hugh," he said.

"Oh, I didn't have much to do with it," I answered, smiling back at him. "I kept out of sight."

"That's an art in itself."

"I had an opportunity, at close range, to study the methods of our lawmakers."

"They're not particularly edifying," Mr. Watling replied. "But they seem, unfortunately, to be necessary."

Such had been my own thought.

"Who is this man Krebs?" he inquired suddenly. "And why didn't Varney get hold of him and make him listen to reason?"

"I'm afraid it wouldn't have been any use," I replied. "He was in my class at Harvard. I knew him—slightly. He worked his way through, and had a pretty hard time of it. I imagine it affected his ideas."

"What is he, a Socialist?"

"Something of the sort." In Theodore Watling's vigorous, sanity-exhaling presence Krebs's act appeared fantastic, ridiculous. "He has queer notions about a new kind of democracy which he says is coming. I think he is the kind of man who would be willing to die for it."

"What, in these days!" Mr. Watling looked at me incredulously. "If that's so, we must keep an eye on him, a sincere fanatic is a good deal more dangerous than a reformer who wants something. There are such men," he added, "but they are rare. How was the Governor, Trulease?" he asked suddenly. "Tractable?"

"Behaved like a lamb, although he insisted upon going through with his little humbug," I said.

Mr. Watling laughed. "They always do," he observed, "and waste a lot of valuable time. You'll find some light cigars in the corner, Hugh."

I sat down beside him and we spent the morning going over the details of the Ribblevale suit, Mr. Watling delegating to me certain matters connected with it of a kind with which I had not hitherto been entrusted; and he spoke again, before I left, of his intention of taking me into the firm as soon as the affair could be arranged. Walking homeward, with my mind intent upon things to come, I met my mother at the corner of Lyme Street coming from church. Her face lighted up at sight of me.

"Have you been working to-day, Hugh?" she asked.

I explained that I had spent the morning with Mr. Watling.

"I'll tell you a secret, mother. I'm going to be taken into the firm."

"Oh, my dear, I'm so glad!" she exclaimed. "I often think, if only your father were alive, how happy he would be, and how proud of you. I wish he could know. Perhaps he does know."

Theodore Watling had once said to me that the man who can best keep his own counsel is the best counsel for other men to keep. I did not go about boasting of the part I had played in originating the now famous Bill No. 709, the passage of which had brought about the capitulation of the Ribblevale Steel Company to our clients. But Ralph Hambleton knew of it, of course.

"That was a pretty good thing you pulled off, Hughie," he said. "I didn't think you had it in you."

It was rank patronage, of course, yet I was secretly pleased. As the years went on I was thrown more and more with him, though in boyhood there had been between us no bond of sympathy. About this time he was beginning to increase very considerably the Hambleton fortune, and a little later I became counsel for the Crescent Gas and Electric Company, in which he had shrewdly gained a controlling interest. Even toward the colossal game of modern finance his attitude was characteristically that of the dilettante, of the amateur; he played it, as it were, contemptuously, even as he had played poker at Harvard, with a cynical audacity that had a peculiarly disturbing effect upon his companions. He bluffed, he raised the limit in spite of protests, and when he lost one always had the feeling that he would ultimately get his money back twice over. At the conferences in the Boyne Club, which he often attended, his manner toward Mr. Dickinson and Mr. Scherer and even toward Miller Gorse was frequently one of thinly veiled amusement at their seriousness. I often wondered that they did not resent it. But he was a privileged person.

His cousin, Ham Durrett, whose inheritance was even greater than Ralph's had been, had also become a privileged person whose comings and goings and more reputable doings were often recorded in the newspapers. Ham had attained to what Gene Hollister aptly but inadvertently called "notoriety": as Ralph wittily remarked, Ham gave to polo and women that which might have gone into high finance. He spent much of his time in the East; his conduct there and at home would once have created a black scandal in our community, but we were gradually leaving our Calvinism behind us and growing more tolerant: we were ready to Forgive much to wealth especially if it was inherited. Hostesses lamented the fact that Ham was "wild," but they asked him to dinners and dances to meet their daughters.

If some moralist better educated and more far-seeing than Perry Blackwood (for Perry had become a moralist) had told these hostesses that Hambleton Durrett was a victim of our new civilization, they would have raised their eyebrows. They deplored while they coveted. If Ham had been told he was a victim of any sort, he would have laughed.

He enjoyed life; he was genial and jovial, both lavish and parsimonious,- -this latter characteristic being the curious survival of the trait of the ancestors to which he owed his millions. He was growing even heavier, and decidedly red in the face.

Perry used to take Ralph to task for not saving Ham from his iniquities, and Ralph would reply that Ham was going to the devil anyway, and not even the devil himself could stop him.

"You can stop him, and you know it," Perry retorted indignantly.

"What do you want me to do with him?" asked Ralph. "Convert him to the saintly life I lead?"

This was a poser.

"That's a fact," sand Perry, "you're no better than he is."

"I don't know what you mean by 'better,'" retorted Ralph, grinning. "I'm wiser, that's all." (We had been talking about the ethics of business when Perry had switched off to Ham.) "I believe, at least, in restraint of trade. Ham doesn't believe in restraint of any kind."

When, therefore, the news suddenly began to be circulated in the Boyne Club that Ham was showing a tendency to straighten up, surprise and incredulity were genuine. He was drinking less,—much less; and it was said that he had severed certain ties that need not again be definitely mentioned. The theory of religious regeneration not being tenable, it was naturally supposed that he had fallen in love; the identity of the unknown lady becoming a fruitful subject of speculation among the feminine portion of society. The announcement of the marriage of Hambleton Durrett would be news of the first magnitude, to be absorbed eagerly by the many who had not the honour of his acquaintance,— comparable only to that of a devastating flood or a murder mystery or a change in the tariff.

Being absorbed in affairs that seemed more important, the subject did not interest me greatly. But one cold Sunday afternoon, as I made my way, in answer to her invitation, to see Nancy Willett, I found myself wondering idly whether she might not be by way of making a shrewd guess as to the object of Hambleton's affections. It was well known that he had entertained a hopeless infatuation for her; and some were inclined to attribute his later lapses to her lack of response. He still called on her, and her lectures, which she delivered like a great aunt with a recondite knowledge of the world, he took meekly. But even she had seemed powerless to alter his habits....

Powell Street, that happy hunting-ground of my youth, had changed its character, become contracted and unfamiliar, sooty. The McAlerys and other older families who had not decayed with the neighbourhood were rapidly deserting it, moving out to the new residence district known as "the Heights." I came to the Willett House. That, too, had an air of shabbiness,—of well-tended shabbiness, to be sure; the stone steps had been scrupulously scrubbed, but one of them was cracked clear across, and the silver on the polished name-plate was wearing off; even the act of pulling the knob of a door-bell was becoming obsolete, so used had we grown to pushing porcelain buttons in bright, new vestibules. As I waited for my summons to be answered it struck me as remarkable that neither Nancy nor her father had been contaminated by the shabbiness that surrounded them.

She had managed rather marvellously to redeem one room from the old- fashioned severity of the rest of the house, the library behind the big "parlour." It was Nancy's room, eloquent of her daintiness and taste, of her essential modernity and luxuriousness; and that evening, as I was ushered into it, this quality of luxuriousness, of being able to shut out the disagreeable aspects of life that surrounded and threatened her, particularly impressed me. She had not lacked opportunities to escape. I wondered uneasily as I waited why she had not embraced them. I strayed about the room. A coal fire burned in the grate, the red-shaded lamps gave a subdued but cheerful light; some impulse led me to cross over to the windows and draw aside the heavy hangings. Dusk was gathering over that garden, bleak and frozen now, where we had romped together as children. How queer the place seemed! How shrivelled! Once it had had the wide range of a park. There, still weathering the elements, was the old-fashioned latticed summer-house, but the fruit-trees that I recalled as clouds of pink and white were gone.... A touch of poignancy was in these memories. I dropped the curtain, and turned to confront Nancy, who had entered noiselessly.

"Well, Hugh, were you dreaming?" she said.

"Not exactly," I replied, embarrassed. "I was looking at the garden."

"The soot has ruined it. My life seems to be one continual struggle against the soot,—the blacks, as the English call them. It's a more expressive term. They are like an army, you know, overwhelming in their relentless invasion. Well, do sit down. It is nice of you to come. You'll have some tea, won't you?"

The maid had brought in the tray. Afternoon tea was still rather a new custom with us, more of a ceremony than a meal; and as Nancy handed me my cup and the thinnest of slices of bread and butter I found the intimacy of the situation a little disquieting. Her manner was indeed intimate, and yet it had the odd and disturbing effect of making her seem more remote. As she chatted I answered her perfunctorily, while all the time I was asking myself why I had ceased to desire her, whether the old longing for her might not return—was not even now returning? I might indeed go far afield to find a wife so suited to me as Nancy. She had beauty, distinction, and position. She was a woman of whom any man might be proud....

"I haven't congratulated you yet, Hugh," she said suddenly, "now that you are a partner of Mr. Watling's. I hear on all sides that you are on the high road to a great success."

"Of course I'm glad to be in the firm," I admitted.

It was a new tack for Nancy, rather a disquieting one, this discussion of my affairs, which she had so long avoided or ignored. "You are getting what you have always wanted, aren't you?"

I wondered in some trepidation whether by that word "always" she was making a deliberate reference to the past.

"Always?" I repeated, rather fatuously.

"Nearly always, ever since you have been a man."

I was incapable of taking advantage of the opening, if it were one. She was baffling.

"A man likes to succeed in his profession, of course," I said.

"And you made up your mind to succeed more deliberately than most men. I needn't ask you if you are satisfied, Hugh. Success seems to agree with you,—although I imagine you will never be satisfied."

"Why do you say that?" I demanded.

"I haven't known you all your life for nothing. I think I know you much better than you know yourself."

"You haven't acted as if you did," I exclaimed.

She smiled.

"Have you been interested in what I thought about you?" she asked.

"That isn't quite fair, Nancy," I protested. "You haven't given me much evidence that you did think about me."

"Have I received much encouragement to do so?" she inquired.

"But you haven't seemed to invite—you've kept me at arm's length."

"Oh, don't fence!" she cried, rather sharply.

I had become agitated, but her next words gave me a shock that was momentarily paralyzing.

"I asked you to come here to-day, Hugh, because I wished you to know that I have made up my mind to marry Hambleton Durrett."

"Hambleton Durrett!" I echoed stupidly. "Hambleton Durrett!"

"Why not?"

"Have you—have you accepted him?"

"No. But I mean to do so."

"You—you love him?"

"I don't see what right you have to ask."

"But you just said that you invited me here to talk frankly."

"No, I don't love him."

"Then why, in heaven's name, are you going to marry him?"

She lay back in her chair, regarding me, her lips slightly parted. All at once the full flavour of her, the superfine quality was revealed after years of blindness.—Nor can I describe the sudden rebellion, the revulsion that I experienced. Hambleton Durrett! It was an outrage, a sacrilege! I got up, and put my hand on the mantel. Nancy remained motionless, inert, her head lying back against the chair. Could it be that she were enjoying my discomfiture? There is no need to confess that I knew next to nothing of women; had I been less excited, I might have made the discovery that I still regarded them sentimentally. Certain romantic axioms concerning them, garnered from Victorian literature, passed current in my mind for wisdom; and one of these declared that they were prone to remain true to an early love. Did Nancy still care for me? The query, coming as it did on top of my emotion, brought with it a strange and overwhelming perplexity. Did I really care for her? The many years during which I had practised the habit of caution began to exert an inhibiting pressure. Here was a situation, an opportunity suddenly thrust upon me which might never return, and which I was utterly unprepared to meet. Would I be happy with Nancy, after all? Her expression was still enigmatic.

"Why shouldn't I marry him?" she demanded.

"Because he's not good enough for you."

"Good!" she exclaimed, and laughed. "He loves me. He wants me without reservation or calculation." There was a sting in this. "And is he any worse," she asked slowly, "than many others who might be mentioned?"

"No," I agreed. I did not intend to be led into the thankless and disagreeable position of condemning Hambleton Durrett. "But why have you waited all these years if you did not mean to marry a man of ability, a man who has made something of himself?"

"A man like you, Hugh?" she said gently.

I flushed.

"That isn't quite fair, Nancy."

"What are you working for?" she suddenly inquired, straightening up.

"What any man works for, I suppose."

"Ah, there you have hit it,—what any man works for in our world. Power,—personal power. You want to be somebody,—isn't that it? Not the noblest ambition, you'll have to admit,—not the kind of thing we used to dream about, when we did dream. Well, when we find we can't realize our dreams, we take the next best thing. And I fail to see why you should blame me for taking it when you yourself have taken it. Hambleton Durrett can give it to me. He'll accept me on my own terms, he won't interfere with me, I shan't be disillusionized,—and I shall have a position which I could not hope to have if I remained unmarried, a very marked position as Hambleton Durrett's wife. I am thirty, you know."

Her frankness appalled me.

"The trouble with you, Hugh, is that you still deceive yourself. You throw a glamour over things. You want to keep your cake and eat it too.

"I don't see why you say that. And marriage especially—"

She took me up.

"Marriage! What other career is open to a woman? Unless she is married, and married well, according to the money standard you men have set up, she is nobody. We can't all be Florence Nightingales, and I am unable to imagine myself a Julia Ward Howe or a Harriet Beecher Stowe. What is left? Nothing but marriage. I'm hard and cynical, you will say, but I have thought, and I'm not afraid, as I have told you, to look things in the face. There are very few women, I think, who would not take the real thing if they had the chance before it were too late, who wouldn't be willing to do their own cooking in order to get it."

She fell silent suddenly. I began to pace the room.

"For God's sake, don't do this, Nancy!" I begged.

But she continued to stare into the fire, as though she had not heard me.

"If you had made up your mind to do it, why did you tell me?" I asked.

"Sentiment, I suppose. I am paying a tribute to what I once was, to what you once were," she said. A—a sort of good-bye to sentiment."

"Nancy!" I said hoarsely.

She shook her head.

"No, Hugh. Surely you can't misjudge me so!" she answered reproachfully. "Do you think I should have sent for you if I had meant—that!"

"No, no, I didn't think so. But why not? You—you cared once, and you tell me plainly you don't love him. It was all a terrible mistake. We were meant for each other."

"I did love you then," she said. "You never knew how much. And there is nothing I wouldn't give to bring it all back again. But I can't. It's gone. You're gone, and I'm gone. I mean what we were. Oh, why did you change?"

"It was you who changed," I declared, bewildered.

"Couldn't you see—can't you see now what you did? But perhaps you couldn't help it. Perhaps it was just you, after all."

"What I did?"

"Why couldn't you have held fast to your faith? If you had, you would have known what it was I adored in you. Oh, I don't mind telling you now, it was just that faith, Hugh, that faith you had in life, that faith you had in me. You weren't cynical and calculating, like Ralph Hambleton, you had imagination. I—I dreamed, too. And do you remember the time when you made the boat, and we went to Logan's Pond, and you sank in her?"

"And you stayed," I went on, "when all the others ran away? You ran down the hill like a whirlwind."

She laughed.

"And then you came here one day, to a party, and said you were going to Harvard, and quarrelled with me."

"Why did you doubt met" I asked agitatedly. "Why didn't you let me see that you still cared?"

"Because that wasn't you, Hugh, that wasn't your real self. Do you suppose it mattered to me whether you went to Harvard with the others? Oh, I was foolish too, I know. I shouldn't have said what I did. But what is the use of regrets?" she exclaimed. "We've both run after the practical gods, and the others have hidden their faces from us. It may be that we are not to blame, either of us, that the practical gods are too strong. We've learned to love and worship them, and now we can't do without them."

"We can try, Nancy," I pleaded.

"No," she answered in a low voice, "that's the difference between you and me. I know myself better than you know yourself, and I know you better." She smiled again. "Unless we could have it all back again, I shouldn't want any of it. You do not love me—"

I started once more to protest.

"No, no, don't say it!" she cried.

"You may think you do, just this moment, but it's only because—you've been moved. And what you believe you want isn't me, it's what I was. But I'm not that any more,—I'm simply recalling that, don't you see? And even then you wouldn't wish me, now, as I was. That sounds involved, but you must understand. You want a woman who will be wrapped up in your career, Hugh, and yet who will not share it,—who will devote herself body and soul to what you have become. A woman whom you can shape. And you won't really love her, but only just so much of her as may become the incarnation of you. Well, I'm not that kind of woman. I might have been, had you been different. I'm not at all sure. Certainly I'm not that kind now, even though I know in my heart that the sort of career you have made for yourself, and that I intend to make for myself is all dross. But now I can't do without it."

"And yet you are going to marry Hambleton Durrett!" I said.

She understood me, although I regretted my words at once.

"Yes, I am going to marry him." There was a shade of bitterness, of defiance in her voice. "Surely you are not offering me the—the other thing, now. Oh, Hugh!"

"I am willing to abandon it all, Nancy."

"No," she said, "you're not, and I'm not. What you can't see and won't see is that it has become part of you. Oh, you are successful, you will be more and more successful. And you think I should be somebody, as your wife, Hugh, more perhaps, eventually, than I shall be as Hambleton's. But I should be nobody, too. I couldn't stand it now, my dear. You must realize that as soon as you have time to think it over. We shall be friends."

The sudden gentleness in her voice pierced me through and through. She held out her hand. Something in her grasp spoke of a resolution which could not be shaken.

"And besides," she added sadly, "I don't love you any more, Hugh. I'm mourning for something that's gone. I wanted to have just this one talk with you. But we shan't mention it again,—we'll close the book."...

At that I fled out of the house, and at first the thought of her as another man's wife, as Hambleton Durrett's wife, was seemingly not to be borne. It was incredible! "We'll close the book." I found myself repeating the phrase; and it seemed then as though something within me I had believed dead—something that formerly had been all of me—had revived again to throb with pain.

It is not surprising that the acuteness of my suffering was of short duration, though I remember certain sharp twinges when the announcement of the engagement burst on the city. There was much controversy over the question as to whether or not Ham Durrett's reform would be permanent; but most people were willing to give him the benefit of the doubt; it was time he settled down and took the position in the community that was to be expected of one of his name; and as for Nancy, it was generally agreed that she had done well for herself. She was not made for poverty—and who so well as she was fitted for the social leadership of our community?

They were married in Trinity Church in the month of May, and I was one of Ham's attendants. Ralph was "best man." For the last time the old Willett mansion in Powell Street wore the gala air of former days; carpets were spread over the sidewalk, and red and white awnings; rooms were filled with flowers and flung open to hundreds of guests. I found the wedding something of an ordeal. I do not like to dwell upon it— especially upon that moment when I came to congratulate Nancy as she stood beside Ham at the end of the long parlour. She seemed to have no regrets. I don't know what I expected of her—certainly not tears and tragedy. She seemed taller than ever, and very beautiful in her veil and white satin gown and the diamonds Ham had given her; very much mistress of herself, quite a contrast to Ham, who made no secret of his elation. She smiled when I wished her happiness.

"We'll be home in the autumn, Hugh, and expect to see a great deal of you," she said.

As I paused in a corner of the room my eye fell upon Nancy's father. McAlery Willett's elation seemed even greater than Ham's. With a gardenia in his frock-coat and a glass of champagne in his hand he went from group to group; and his familiar laughter, which once had seemed so full of merriment and fun, gave me to-day a somewhat scandalized feeling. I heard Ralph's voice, and turned to discover him standing beside me, his long legs thrust slightly apart, his hands in his pockets, overlooking the scene with typical, semi-contemptuous amusement.

"This lets old McAlery out, anyway," he said.

"What do you mean?" I demanded.

"One or two little notes of his will be cancelled, sooner or later— that's all."

For a moment I was unable to speak.

"And do you think that she—that Nancy found out—?" I stammered.

"Well, I'd be willing to take that end of the bet," he replied. "Why the deuce should she marry Ham? You ought to know her well enough to understand how she'd feel if she discovered some of McAlery's financial coups? Of course it's not a thing I talk about, you understand. Are you going to the Club?"

"No, I'm going home," I said. I was aware of his somewhat compassionate smile as I left him....

Chapter Twelve

One November day nearly two years after my admission as junior member of the firm of Watling, Fowndes and Ripon seven gentlemen met at luncheon in the Boyne Club; Mr. Barbour, President of the Railroad, Mr. Scherer, of the Boyne Iron Works and other corporations, Mr. Leonard Dickinson, of the Corn National Bank, Mr. Halsey, a prominent banker from the other great city of the state, Mr. Grunewald, Chairman of the Republican State Committee, and Mr. Frederick Grierson, who had become a very important man in our community. At four o'clock they emerged from the club: citizens in Boyne Street who saw them chatting amicably on the steps little suspected that in the last three hours these gentlemen had chosen and practically elected the man who was to succeed Mr. Wade as United States Senator in Washington. Those were the days in which great affairs were simply and efficiently handled. No democratic nonsense about leaving the choice to an electorate that did not know what it wanted.

The man chosen to fill this high position was Theodore Watling. He said he would think about the matter.

In the nation at large, through the defection of certain Northern states neither so conservative nor fortunate as ours, the Democratic party was in power, which naturally implies financial depression. There was no question about our ability to send a Republican Senator; the choice in the Boyne Club was final; but before the legislature should ratify it, a year or so hence, it were just as well that the people of the state should be convinced that they desired Mr. Watling more than any other man; and surely enough, in a little while such a conviction sprang up spontaneously. In offices and restaurants and hotels, men began to suggest to each other what a fine thing it would be if Theodore Watling might be persuaded to accept the toga; at the banks, when customers called to renew their notes and tight money was discussed and Democrats excoriated, it was generally agreed that the obvious thing to do was to get a safe man in the Senate. From the very first, Watling sentiment stirred like spring sap after a hard winter.

The country newspapers, watered by providential rains, began to put forth tender little editorial shoots, which Mr. Judah B. Tallant presently collected and presented in a charming bouquet in the Morning Era. "The Voice of the State Press;" thus was the column headed; and the remarks of the Hon. Fitch Truesdale, of the St. Helen's Messenger, were given a special prominence. Mr. Truesdale was the first, in his section, to be inspired by the happy thought that the one man preeminently fitted to represent the state in the present crisis, when her great industries had been crippled by Democratic folly, was Mr. Theodore Watling. The Rossiter Banner, the Elkington Star, the Belfast Recorder, and I know not how many others simultaneously began to sing Mr. Watling's praises.

"Not since the troublous times of the Civil War," declared the Morning Era, "had the demand for any man been so unanimous." As a proof of it, there were the country newspapers, "which reflected the sober opinion of the firesides of the common people."

There are certain industrious gentlemen to whom little credit is given, and who, unlike the average citizen who reserves his enthusiasm for election time, are patriotic enough to labour for their country's good all the year round. When in town, it was their habit to pay a friendly call on the Counsel for the Railroad, Mr. Miller Gorse, in the Corn Bank Building. He was never too busy to converse with them; or, it might better be said, to listen to them converse. Let some legally and politically ambitious young man observe Mr. Gorse's method. Did he inquire what the party worker thought of Mr. Watling for the Senate? Not at all! But before the party worker left he was telling Mr. Gorse that public sentiment demanded Mr. Watling. After leaving Mr. Gorse they wended their way to the Durrett Building and handed their cards over the rail of the offices of Watling, Fowndes and Ripon. Mr. Watling shook hands with scores of them, and they departed, well satisfied with the flavour of his cigars and intoxicated by his personality. He had a marvellous way of cutting short an interview without giving offence. Some of them he turned over to Mr. Paret, whom he particularly desired they should know. Thus Mr. Paret acquired many valuable additions to his acquaintance, cultivated a memory for names and faces that was to stand him in good stead; and kept, besides, an indexed note-book into which he put various bits of interesting information concerning each. Though not immediately lucrative, it was all, no doubt, part of a lawyer's education.

During the summer and the following winter Colonel Paul Varney came often to town and spent much of his time in Mr. Paret's office smoking Mr. Watling's cigars and discussing the coming campaign, in which he took a whole-souled interest.

"Say, Hugh, this is goin' slick!" he would exclaim, his eyes glittering like round buttons of jet. "I never saw a campaign where they fell in the way they're doing now. If it was anybody else but Theodore Watling, it would scare me. You ought to have been in Jim Broadhurst's campaign," he added, referring to the junior senator, "they wouldn't wood up at all, they was just listless. But Gorse and Barbour and the rest wanted him, and we had to put him over. I reckon he is useful down there in Washington, but say, do you know what he always reminded me of? One of those mud-turtles I used to play with as a boy up in Columbia County,— shuts up tight soon as he sees you coming. Now Theodore Watling ain't like that, any way of speaking. We can get up some enthusiasm for a man of his sort. He's liberal and big. He's made his pile, and he don't begrudge some of it to the fellows who do the work. Mark my words, when you see a man who wants a big office cheap, look out for him."

This, and much more wisdom I imbibed while assenting to my chief's greatness. For Mr. Varney was right,—one could feel enthusiasm for Theodore Watling; and my growing intimacy with him, the sense that I was having a part in his career, a share in his success, became for the moment the passion of my life. As the campaign progressed I gave more and more time to it, and made frequent trips of a confidential nature to the different counties of the state. The whole of my being was energized. The national fever had thoroughly pervaded my blood—the national fever to win. Prosperity—writ large—demanded it, and Theodore Watling personified, incarnated the cause. I had neither the time nor the desire to philosophize on this national fever, which animated all my associates: animated, I might say, the nation, which was beginning to get into a fever about games. If I remember rightly, it was about this time that golf was introduced, tennis had become a commonplace, professional baseball was in full swing; Ham Durrett had even organized a local polo team.... The man who failed to win something tangible in sport or law or business or politics was counted out. Such was the spirit of America, in the closing years of the nineteenth century.

And yet, when one has said this, one has failed to express the national Geist in all its subtlety. In brief, the great American sport was not so much to win the game as to beat it; the evasion of rules challenged our ingenuity; and having won, we set about devising methods whereby it would be less and less possible for us winners to lose in the future. No better illustration of this tendency could be given than the development which had recently taken place in the field of our city politics, hitherto the battle-ground of Irish politicians who had fought one another for supremacy. Individualism had been rampant, competition the custom; you bought an alderman, or a boss who owned four or five aldermen, and then you never could be sure you were to get what you wanted, or that the aldermen and the bosses would "stay bought." But now a genius had appeared, an American genius who had arisen swiftly and almost silently, who appealed to the imagination, and whose name was often mentioned in a whisper,—the Hon. Judd Jason, sometimes known as the Spider, who organized the City Hall and capitalized it; an ultimate and logical effect—if one had considered it—of the Manchester school of economics. Enlightened self-interest, stripped of sentiment, ends on Judd Jasons. He ran the city even as Mr. Sherrill ran his department store; you paid your price. It was very convenient. Being a genius, Mr. Jason did not wholly break with tradition, but retained those elements of the old muddled system that had their value, chartering steamboats for outings on the river, giving colossal picnics in Lowry Park. The poor and the wanderer and the criminal (of the male sex at least) were cared for. But he was not loved, as the rough-and-tumble Irishmen had been loved; he did not make himself common; he was surrounded by an aura of mystery which I confess had not failed of effect on me. Once, and only once during my legal apprenticeship, he had been pointed out to me on the street, where he rarely ventured. His appearance was not impressive....

Mr. Jason could not, of course, prevent Mr. Watling's election, even did he so desire, but he did command the allegiance of several city candidates—both democratic and republican—for the state legislature, who had as yet failed to announce their preferences for United States Senator. It was important that Mr. Watling's vote should be large, as indicative of a public reaction and repudiation of Democratic national folly. This matter among others was the subject of discussion one July morning when the Republican State Chairman was in the city; Mr. Grunewald expressed anxiety over Mr. Jason's continued silence. It was expedient that somebody should "see" the boss.

"Why not Paret?" suggested Leonard Dickinson. Mr. Watling was not present at this conference. "Paret seems to be running Watling's campaign, anyway."

It was settled that I should be the emissary. With lively sensations of curiosity and excitement, tempered by a certain anxiety as to my ability to match wits with the Spider, I made my way to his "lair" over Monahan's saloon, situated in a district that was anything but respectable. The saloon, on the ground floor, had two apartments; the bar-room proper where Mike Monahan, chamberlain of the establishment, was wont to stand, red faced and smiling, to greet the courtiers, big and little, the party workers, the district leaders, the hangers-on ready to be hired, the city officials, the police judges,—yes, and the dignified members of state courts whose elections depended on Mr. Jason's favour: even Judge Bering, whose acquaintance I had made the day I had come, as a law student, to Mr. Watling's office, unbent from time to time sufficiently to call there for a small glass of rye and water, and to relate, with his owl-like gravity, an anecdote to the "boys." The saloon represented Democracy, so dear to the American public. Here all were welcome, even the light- fingered gentlemen who enjoyed the privilege of police protection; and who sometimes, through fortuitous circumstances, were hauled before the very magistrates with whom they had rubbed elbows on the polished rail. Behind the bar-room, and separated from it by swinging doors only the elite ventured to thrust apart, was an audience chamber whither Mr. Jason occasionally descended. Anecdote and political reminiscence gave place here to matters of high policy.

I had several times come to the saloon in the days of my apprenticeship in search of some judge or official, and once I had run down here the city auditor himself. Mike Monahan, whose affair it was to know everyone, recognized me. It was part of his business, also, to understand that I was now a member of the firm of Watling, Fowndes and Ripon.

"Good morning to you, Mr. Paret," he said suavely. We held a colloquy in undertones over the bar, eyed by the two or three customers who were present. Mr. Monahan disappeared, but presently returned to whisper: "Sure, he'll see you," to lead the way through the swinging doors and up a dark stairway. I came suddenly on a room in the greatest disorder, its tables and chairs piled high with newspapers and letters, its windows streaked with soot. From an open door on its farther side issued a voice.

"Is that you, Mr. Paret? Come in here."

It was little less than a command.

"Heard of you, Mr. Paret. Glad to know you. Sit down, won't you?"

The inner room was almost dark. I made out a bed in the corner, and propped up in the bed a man; but for the moment I was most aware of a pair of eyes that flared up when the man spoke, and died down again when he became silent. They reminded me of those insects which in my childhood days we called "lightning bugs." Mr. Jason gave me a hand like a woman's. I expressed my pleasure at meeting him, and took a chair beside the bed.

"I believe you're a partner of Theodore Watling's now aren't you? Smart man, Watling."

"He'll make a good senator," I replied, accepting the opening.

"You think he'll get elected—do you?" Mr. Jason inquired.

I laughed.

"Well, there isn't much doubt about that, I imagine."

"Don't know—don't know. Seen some dead-sure things go wrong in my time."

"What's going to defeat him?" I asked pleasantly.

"I don't say anything," Mr. Jason replied. "But I've known funny things to happen—never does to be dead sure."

"Oh, well, we're as sure as it's humanly possible to be," I declared. The eyes continued to fascinate me, they had a peculiar, disquieting effect. Now they died down, and it was as if the man's very presence had gone out, as though I had been left alone; and I found it exceedingly difficult, under the circumstances, to continue to address him. Suddenly he flared up again.

"Watling send you over here?" he demanded.

"No. As a matter of fact, he's out of town. Some of Mr. Watling's friends, Mr. Grunewald and Mr. Dickinson, Mr. Gorse and others, suggested that I see you, Mr. Jason."

There came a grunt from the bed.

"Mr. Watling has always valued your friendship and support," I said.

"What makes him think he ain't going to get it?"

"He hasn't a doubt of it," I went on diplomatically. "But we felt—and I felt personally, that we ought to be in touch with you, to work along with you, to keep informed how things are going in the city."

"What things?"

"Well—there are one or two representatives, friends of yours, who haven't come out for Mr. Watling. We aren't worrying, we know you'll do the right thing, but we feel that it would have a good deal of influence in some other parts of the state if they declared themselves. And then you know as well as I do that this isn't a year when any of us can afford to recognize too closely party lines; the Democratic administration has brought on a panic, the business men in that party are down on it, and it ought to be rebuked. And we feel, too, that some of the city's Democrats ought to be loyal to Mr. Watling,—not that we expect them to vote for him in caucus, but when it comes to the joint ballot—"

"Who?" demanded Mr. Jason.

"Senator Dowse and Jim Maher, for instance," I suggested.

"Jim voted for Bill 709 all right—didn't he?" said Mr. Jason abruptly.

"That's just it," I put in boldly. "We'd like to induce him to come in with us this time. But we feel that—the inducement would better come through you."

I thought Mr. Jason smiled. By this time I had grown accustomed to the darkness, the face and figure of the man in the bed had become discernible. Power, I remember thinking, chooses odd houses for itself. Here was no overbearing, full-blooded ward ruffian brimming with vitality, but a thin, sallow little man in a cotton night-shirt, with iron-grey hair and a wiry moustache; he might have been an overworked clerk behind a dry-goods counter; and yet somehow, now that I had talked to him, I realized that he never could have been. Those extraordinary eyes of his, when they were functioning, marked his individuality as unique. It were almost too dramatic to say that he required darkness to make his effect, but so it seemed. I should never forget him. He had in truth been well named the Spider.

"Of course we haven't tried to get in touch with them. We are leaving them to you," I added.

"Paret," he said suddenly, "I don't care a damn about Grunewald—never did. I'd turn him down for ten cents. But you can tell Theodore Watling for me, and Dickinson, that I guess the 'inducement' can be fixed."

I felt a certain relief that the interview had come to an end, that the moment had arrived for amenities. To my surprise, Mr. Jason anticipated me.

"I've been interested in you, Mr. Paret," he observed. "Know who you are, of course, knew you were in Watling's office. Then some of the boys spoke about you when you were down at the legislature on that Ribblevale matter. Guess you had more to do with that bill than came out in the newspapers—eh?"

I was taken off my guard.

"Oh, that's talk," I said.

"All right, it's talk, then? But I guess you and I will have some more talk after a while,—after Theodore Watling gets to be United States Senator. Give him my regards, and—and come in when I can do anything for you, Mr. Paret."

Thanking him, I groped my way downstairs and let myself out by a side door Monahan had shown me into an alleyway, thus avoiding the saloon. As I walked slowly back to the office, seeking the shade of the awnings, the figure in the darkened room took on a sinister aspect that troubled me....

The autumn arrived, the campaign was on with a whoop, and I had my first taste of "stump" politics. The acrid smell of red fire brings it back to me. It was a medley of railroad travel, of committees provided with badges—and cigars, of open carriages slowly drawn between lines of bewildered citizens, of Lincoln clubs and other clubs marching in serried ranks, uniformed and helmeted, stalwarts carrying torches and banners. And then there were the draughty opera-houses with the sylvan scenery pushed back and plush chairs and sofas pushed forward; with an ominous table, a pitcher of water on it and a glass, near the footlights. The houses were packed with more bewildered citizens. What a wonderful study of mob-psychology it would have offered! Men who had not thought of the grand old Republican party for two years, and who had not cared much about it when they had entered the dooms, after an hour or so went mad with fervour. The Hon. Joseph Mecklin, ex-Speaker of the House, with whom I traveled on occasions, had a speech referring to the martyred President, ending with an appeal to the revolutionary fathers who followed Washington with bleeding feet. The Hon. Joseph possessed that most valuable of political gifts, presence; and when with quivering voice he finished his peroration, citizens wept with him. What it all had to do with the tariff was not quite clear. Yet nobody seemed to miss the connection.

We were all of us most concerned, of course, about the working-man and his dinner pail,—whom the Democrats had wantonly thrown out of employment for the sake of a doctrinaire theory. They had put him in competition with the serf of Europe. Such was the subject-matter of my own modest addresses in this, my maiden campaign. I had the sense to see myself in perspective; to recognize that not for me, a dignified and substantial lawyer of affairs, were the rhetorical flights of the Hon. Joseph Mecklin. I spoke with a certain restraint. Not too dryly, I hope. But I sought to curb my sentiments, my indignation, at the manner in which the working-man had been treated; to appeal to the common sense rather than to the passions of my audiences. Here were the statistics! (drawn, by the way, from the Republican Campaign book). Unscrupulous demagogues—Democratic, of course—had sought to twist and evade them. Let this terrible record of lack of employment and misery be compared with the prosperity under Republican rule.

"One of the most effective speakers in this campaign for the restoration of Prosperity," said the Rossiter Banner, "is Mr. Hugh Paret, of the firm of Watling, Fowndes and Ripon. Mr. Paret's speech at the Opera-House last evening made a most favourable impression. Mr. Paret deals with facts. And his thoughtful analysis of the situation into which the Democratic party has brought this country should convince any sane-minded voter that the time has come for a change."

I began to keep a scrap-book, though I locked it up in the drawer of my desk. In it are to be found many clippings of a similarly gratifying tenor....

Mecklin and I were well contrasted. In this way, incidentally, I made many valuable acquaintances among the "solid" men of the state, the local capitalists and manufacturers, with whom my manner of dealing with public questions was in particular favour. These were practical men; they rather patronized the Hon. Joseph, thus estimating, to a nicety, a mans value; or solidity, or specific gravity, it might better be said, since our universe was one of checks and balances. The Hon. Joseph and his like, skyrocketing through the air, were somehow necessary in the scheme of things, but not to be taken too seriously. Me they did take seriously, these provincial lords, inviting me to their houses and opening their hearts. Thus, when we came to Elkington, Mr. Mecklin reposed in the Commercial House, on the noisy main street. Fortunately for him, the clanging of trolley cars never interfered with his slumbers. I slept in a wide chamber in the mansion of Mr. Ezra Hutchins. There were many Hutchinses in Elkington,—brothers and cousins and uncles and great-uncles,—and all were connected with the woollen mills. But there is always one supreme Hutchins, and Ezra was he: tall, self-contained, elderly, but well preserved through frugal living, essentially American and typical of his class, when he entered the lobby of the Commercial House that afternoon the babel of political discussion was suddenly hushed; politicians, traveling salesmen and the members of the local committee made a lane for him; to him, the Hon. Joseph and I were introduced. Mr. Hutchins knew what he wanted. He was cordial to Mr. Mecklin, but he took me. We entered a most respectable surrey with tassels, driven by a raw-boned coachman in a black overcoat, drawn by two sleek horses.

"How is this thing going, Paret?" he asked.

I gave him Mr. Grunewald's estimated majority.

"What do you think?" he demanded, a shrewd, humorous look in his blue eyes.

"Well, I think we'll carry the state. I haven't had Grunewald's experience in estimating."

Ezra Hutchins smiled appreciatively.

"What does Watling think?"

"He doesn't seem to be worrying much."

"Ever been in Elkington before?"

I said I hadn't.

"Well, a drive will do you good."

It was about four o'clock on a mild October afternoon. The little town, of fifteen thousand inhabitants or so, had a wonderful setting in the widening valley of the Scopanong, whose swiftly running waters furnished the power for the mills. We drove to these through a gateway over which the words "No Admittance" were conspicuously painted, past long brick buildings that bordered the canals; and in the windows I caught sight of drab figures of men and women bending over the machines. Half of the buildings, as Mr. Hutchins pointed out, were closed,—mute witnesses of tariff-tinkering madness. Even more eloquent of democratic folly was that part of the town through which we presently passed, streets lined with rows of dreary houses where the workers lived. Children were playing on the sidewalks, but theirs seemed a listless play; listless, too, were the men and women who sat on the steps,—listless, and somewhat sullen, as they watched us passing. Ezra Hutchins seemed to read my thought.

"Since the unions got in here I've had nothing but trouble," he said. "I've tried to do my duty by my people, God knows. But they won't see which side their bread's buttered on. They oppose me at every step, they vote against their own interests. Some years ago they put up a job on us, and sent a scatter-brained radical to the legislature."

"Krebs."

"Do you know him?"

"Slightly. He was in my class at Harvard.... Is he still here?" I asked, after a pause.

"Oh, yes. But he hasn't gone to the legislature this time, we've seen to that. His father was a respectable old German who had a little shop and made eye-glasses. The son is an example of too much education. He's a notoriety seeker. Oh, he's clever, in a way. He's given us a good deal of trouble, too, in the courts with damage cases."...

We came to a brighter, more spacious, well-to-do portion of the town, where the residences faced the river. In a little while the waters widened into a lake, which was surrounded by a park, a gift to the city of the Hutchins family. Facing it, on one side, was the Hutchins Library; on the other, across a wide street, where the maples were turning, were the Hutchinses' residences of various dates of construction, from that of the younger George, who had lately married a wife, and built in bright yellow brick, to the old-fashioned mansion of Ezra himself. This, he told me, had been good enough for his father, and was good enough for him. The picture of it comes back to me, now, with singular attractiveness. It was of brick, and I suppose a modification of the Georgian; the kind of house one still sees in out-of-the way corners of London, with a sort of Dickensy flavour; high and square and uncompromising, with small-paned windows, with a flat roof surrounded by a low balustrade, and many substantial chimneys. The third storey was lower than the others, separated from them by a distinct line. On one side was a wide porch. Yellow and red leaves, the day's fall, scattered the well-kept lawn. Standing in the doorway of the house was a girl in white, and as we descended from the surrey she came down the walk to meet us. She was young, about twenty. Her hair was the colour of the russet maple leaves.

"This is Mr. Paret, Maude." Mr. Hutchins looked at his watch as does a man accustomed to live by it. "If you'll excuse me, Mr. Paret, I have something important to attend to. Perhaps Mr. Paret would like to look about the grounds?" He addressed his daughter.

I said I should be delighted, though I had no idea what grounds were meant. As I followed Maude around the house she explained that all the Hutchins connection had a common back yard, as she expressed it. In reality, there were about two blocks of the property, extending behind all the houses. There were great trees with swings, groves, orchards where the late apples glistened between the leaves, an old-fashioned flower garden loath to relinquish its blooming. In the distance the shadowed western ridge hung like a curtain of deep blue velvet against the sunset.

"What a wonderful spot!" I exclaimed.

"Yes, it is nice," she agreed, "we were all brought up here—I mean my cousins and myself. There are dozens of us. And dozens left," she added, as the shouts and laughter of children broke the stillness.

A boy came running around the corner of the path. He struck out at Maude. With a remarkably swift movement she retaliated.

"Ouch!" he exclaimed.

"You got him that time," I laughed, and, being detected, she suddenly blushed. It was this act that drew my attention to her, that defined her as an individual. Before that I had regarded her merely as a shy and provincial girl. Now she was brimming with an unsuspected vitality. A certain interest was aroused, although her shyness towards me was not altered. I found it rather a flattering shyness.

"It's Hugh," she explained, "he's always trying to be funny. Speak to Mr. Paret, Hugh."

"Why, that's my name, too," I said.

"Is it?"

"She knocked my hat off a little while ago," said Hugh. "I was only getting square."

"Well, you didn't get square, did you?" I asked.

"Are you going to speak in the tows hall to-night?" the boy demanded. I admitted it. He went off, pausing once to stare back at me.... Maude and I walked on.

"It must be exciting to speak before a large audience," she said. "If I were a man, I think I should like to be in politics."

"I cannot imagine you in politics," I answered.

She laughed.

"I said, if I were a man."

"Are you going to the meeting?"

"Oh, yes. Father promised to take me. He has a box."

I thought it would be pleasant to have her there.

"I'm afraid you'll find what I have to say rather dry," I said.

"A woman can't expect to understand everything," she answered quickly.

This remark struck me favourably. I glanced at her sideways. She was not a beauty, but she was distinctly well-formed and strong. Her face was oval, her features not quite regular,—giving them a certain charm; her colour was fresh, her eyes blue, the lighter blue one sees on Chinese ware: not a poetic comparison, but so I thought of them. She was apparently not sophisticated, as were most of the young women at home whom I knew intimately (as were the Watling twins, for example, with one of whom, Frances, I had had, by the way, rather a lively flirtation the spring before); she seemed refreshingly original, impressionable and plastic....

We walked slowly back to the house, and in the hallway I met Mrs. Hutchins, a bustling, housewifely lady, inclined to stoutness, whose creased and kindly face bore witness to long acquiescence in the discipline of matrimony, to the contentment that results from an essentially circumscribed and comfortable life. She was, I learned later, the second Mrs. Hutchins, and Maude their only child. The children of the first marriage, all girls, had married and scattered.

Supper was a decorous but heterogeneous meal of the old-fashioned sort that gives one the choice between tea and cocoa. It was something of an occasion, I suspected. The minister was there, the Reverend Mr. Doddridge, who would have made, in appearance at least, a perfect Puritan divine in a steeple hat and a tippet. Only—he was no longer the leader of the community; and even in his grace he had the air of deferring to the man who provided the bounties of which we were about to partake rather than to the Almighty. Young George was there, Mr. Hutchins's nephew, who was daily becoming more and more of a factor in the management of the mills, and had built the house of yellow brick that stood out so incongruously among the older Hutchinses' mansions, and marked a transition. I thought him rather a yellow-brick gentleman himself for his assumption of cosmopolitan manners. His wife was a pretty, discontented little woman who plainly deplored her environment, longed for larger fields of conquest: George, she said, must remain where he was, for the present at least,—Uncle Ezra depended on him; but Elkington was a prosy place, and Mrs. George gave the impression that she did not belong here. They went to the city on occasions; both cities. And when she told me we had a common acquaintance in Mrs. Hambleton Durrett—whom she thought so lovely!—I knew that she had taken Nancy as an ideal: Nancy, the social leader of what was to Mrs. George a metropolis.

Presently the talk became general among the men, the subject being the campaign, and I the authority, bombarded with questions I strove to answer judicially. What was the situation in this county and in that? the national situation? George indulged in rather a vigorous arraignment of the demagogues, national and state, who were hurting business in order to obtain political power. The Reverend Mr. Doddridge assented, deploring the poverty that the local people had brought on themselves by heeding the advice of agitators; and Mrs. Hutchins, who spent much of her time in charity work, agreed with the minister when he declared that the trouble was largely due to a decline in Christian belief. Ezra Hutchins, too, nodded at this.

"Take that man Krebs, for example," the minister went on, stimulated by this encouragement, "he's an atheist, pure and simple." A sympathetic shudder went around the table at the word. George alone smiled. "Old Krebs was a free-thinker; I used to get my glasses of him. He was at least a conscientious man, a good workman, which is more than can be said for the son. Young Krebs has talent, and if only he had devoted himself to the honest practice of law, instead of stirring up dissatisfaction among these people, he would be a successful man to-day."

Mr. Hutchins explained that I was at college with Krebs.

"These people must like him," I said, "or they wouldn't have sent him to the legislature."

"Well, a good many of them do like him," the minister admitted. "You see, he actually lives among them. They believe his socialistic doctrines because he's a friend of theirs."

"He won't represent this town again, that's sure," exclaimed George. "You didn't see in the papers that he was nominated,—did you, Paret?"

"But if the mill people wanted him, George, how could it be prevented?" his wife demanded.

George winked at me.

"There are more ways of skinning a cat than one," he said cryptically.

"Well, it's time to go to the meeting, I guess," remarked Ezra, rising. Once more he looked at his watch.

We were packed into several family carriages and started off. In front of the hall the inevitable red fire was burning, its quivering light reflected on the faces of the crowd that blocked the street. They stood silent, strangely apathetic as we pushed through them to the curb, and the red fire went out suddenly as we descended. My temporary sense of depression, however, deserted me as we entered the hall, which was well lighted and filled with people, who clapped when the Hon. Joseph and I, accompanied by Mr. Doddridge and the Hon. Henry Clay Mellish from Pottstown, with the local chairman, walked out on the stage. A glance over the audience sufficed to ascertain that that portion of the population whose dinner pails we longed to fill was evidently not present in large numbers. But the farmers had driven in from the hills, while the merchants and storekeepers of Elkington had turned out loyally.

The chairman, in introducing me, proclaimed me as a coming man, and declared that I had already achieved, in the campaign, considerable notoriety. As I spoke, I was pleasantly aware of Maude Hutchins leaning forward a little across the rail of the right-hand stage box—for the town hall was half opera-house; her attitude was one of semi-absorbed admiration; and the thought that I had made an impression on her stimulated me. I spoke with more aplomb. Somewhat to my surprise, I found myself making occasional, unexpected witticisms that drew laughter and applause. Suddenly, from the back of the hall, a voice called out:—

"How about House Bill 709?"

There was a silence, then a stirring and craning of necks. It was my first experience of heckling, and for the moment I was taken aback. I thought of Krebs. He had, indeed, been in my mind since I had risen to my feet, and I had scanned the faces before me in search of his. But it was not his voice.

"Well, what about Bill 709?" I demanded.

"You ought to know something about it, I guess," the voice responded.

"Put him out!" came from various portions of the hall.

Inwardly, I was shaken. Not—in orthodox language from any "conviction of sin." Yet it was my first intimation that my part in the legislation referred to was known to any save a select few. I blamed Krebs, and a hot anger arose within me against him. After all, what could they prove?

"No, don't put him out," I said. "Let him come up here to the platform. I'll yield to him. And I'm entirely willing to discuss with him and defend any measures passed in the legislature of this state by a Republican majority. Perhaps," I added, "the gentleman has a copy of the law in his pocket, that I may know what he is talking about, and answer him intelligently."

At this there was wild applause. I had the audience with me. The offender remained silent and presently I finished my speech. After that Mr. Mecklin made them cheer and weep, and Mr. Mellish made them laugh. The meeting had been highly successful.

"You polished him off, all right," said George Hutchins, as he took my hand.

"Who was he?"

"Oh, one of the local sore-heads. Krebs put him up to it, of course."

"Was Krebs here?" I asked.

"Sitting in the corner of the balcony. That meeting must have made him feel sick." George bent forward and whispered in my ear: "I thought Bill 709 was Watling's idea."

"Oh, I happened to be in the Potts House about that time," I explained.

George, of whom it may be gathered that he was not wholly unsophisticated, grinned at me appreciatively.

"Say, Paret," he replied, putting his hand through my arm, "there's a little legal business in prospect down here that will require some handling, and I wish you'd come down after the campaign and talk it over, with us. I've just about made up my mind that you're he man to tackle it."

"All right, I'll come," I said.

"And stay with me," said George....

We went to his yellow-brick house for refreshments, salad and ice-cream and (in the face of the Hutchins traditions) champagne. Others had been invited in, some twenty persons.... Once in a while, when I looked up, I met Maude's eyes across the room. I walked home with her, slowly, the length of the Hutchinses' block. Floating over the lake was a waning October moon that cast through the thinning maples a lace-work of shadows at our feet; I had the feeling of well-being that comes to heroes, and the presence of Maude Hutchins was an incense, a vestal incense far from unpleasing. Yet she had reservations which appealed to me. Hers was not a gushing provincialism, like that of Mrs. George.

"I liked your speech so much, Mr. Paret," she told me. "It seemed so sensible and—controlled, compared to the others. I have never thought a great deal about these things, of course, and I never understood before why taking away the tariff caused so much misery. You made that quite plain.

"If so, I'm glad," I said.

She was silent a moment.

"The working people here have had a hard time during the last year," she went on. "Some of the mills had to be shut down, you know. It has troubled me. Indeed, it has troubled all of us. And what has made it more difficult, more painful is that many of them seem actually to dislike us. They think it's father's fault, and that he could run all the mills if he wanted to. I've been around a little with mother and sometimes the women wouldn't accept any help from us; they said they'd rather starve than take charity, that they had the right to work. But father couldn't run the mills at a loss—could he?"

"Certainly not," I replied.

"And then there's Mr. Krebs, of whom we were speaking at supper, and who puts all kinds of queer notions into their heads. Father says he's an anarchist. I heard father say at supper that he was at Harvard with you. Did you like him?"

"Well," I answered hesitatingly, "I didn't know him very well."

"Of course not," she put in. "I suppose you couldn't have."

"He's got these notions," I explained, "that are mischievous and crazy— but I don't dislike him."

"I'm glad to hear you say that!" she answered quietly. "I like him, too- -he seems so kind, so understanding."

"Do you know him?"

"Well,—"she hesitated—"I feel as though I do. I've only met him once, and that was by accident. It was the day the big strike began, last spring, and I had been shopping, and started for the mills to get father to walk home with me, as I used to do. I saw the crowds blocking the streets around the canal. At first I paid no attention to them, but after a while I began to be a little uneasy, there were places where I had to squeeze through, and I couldn't help seeing that something was wrong, and that the people were angry. Men and women were talking in loud voices. One woman stared at me, and called my name, and said something that frightened me terribly. I went into a doorway—and then I saw Mr. Krebs. I didn't know who he was. He just said, 'You'd better come with me, Miss Hutchins,' and I went with him. I thought afterwards that it was a very courageous thing for him to do, because he was so popular with the mill people, and they had such a feeling against us. Yet they didn't seem to resent it, and made way for us, and Mr. Krebs spoke to many of them as we passed. After we got to State Street, I asked him his name, and when he told me I was speechless. He took off his hat and went away. He had such a nice face—not at all ugly when you look at it twice—and kind eyes, that I just couldn't believe him to be as bad as father and George think he is. Of course he is mistaken," she added hastily, "but I am sure he is sincere, and honestly thinks he can help those people by telling them what he does."

The question shot at me during the meeting rankled still; I wanted to believe that Krebs had inspired it, and her championship of him gave me a twinge of jealousy,—the slightest twinge, to be sure, yet a perceptible one. At the same time, the unaccountable liking I had for the man stirred to life. The act she described had been so characteristic.

"He's one of the born rebels against society," I said glibly. "Yet I do think he's sincere."

Maude was grave. "I should be sorry to think he wasn't," she replied. After I had bidden her good night at the foot of the stairs, and gone to my room, I reflected how absurd it was to be jealous of Krebs. What was Maude Hutchins to me? And even if she had been something to me, she never could be anything to Krebs. All the forces of our civilization stood between the two; nor was she of a nature to take plunges of that sort. The next day, as I lay back in my seat in the parlour-car and gazed at the autumn landscape, I indulged in a luxurious contemplation of the picture she had made as she stood on the lawn under the trees in the early morning light, when my carriage had driven away; and I had turned, to perceive that her eyes had followed me. I was not in love with her, of course. I did not wish to return at once to Elkington, but I dwelt with a pleasant anticipation upon my visit, when the campaign should be over, with George.

Chapter Thirteen

The good old days of the Watling campaign," as Colonel Paul Varney is wont to call them, are gone forever. And the Colonel himself, who stuck to his gods, has been through the burning, fiery furnace of Investigation, and has come out unscathed and unrepentant. The flames of investigation, as a matter of fact, passed over his head in their vain attempt to reach the "man higher up," whose feet they licked; but him they did not devour, either. A veteran in retirement, the Colonel is living under his vine and fig tree on the lake at Rossiter; the vine bears Catawba grapes, of which he is passionately fond; the fig tree, the Bartlett pears he gives to his friends. He has saved something from the spoils of war, but other veterans I could mention are not so fortunate. The old warriors have retired, and many are dead; the good old methods are becoming obsolete. We never bothered about those mischievous things called primaries. Our county committees, our state committees chose the candidates for the conventions, which turned around and chose the committees. Both the committees and the conventions—under advice—chose the candidates. Why, pray, should the people complain, when they had everything done for them? The benevolent parties, both Democratic and Republican, even undertook the expense of printing the ballots! And generous ballots they were (twenty inches long and five wide!), distributed before election, in order that the voters might have the opportunity of studying and preparing them: in order that Democrats of delicate feelings might take the pains to scratch out all the Democratic candidates, and write in the names of the Republican candidates. Patriotism could go no farther than this....

I spent the week before election in the city, where I had the opportunity of observing what may be called the charitable side of politics. For a whole month, or more, the burden of existence had been lifted from the shoulders of the homeless. No church or organization, looked out for these frowsy, blear-eyed and ragged wanderers who had failed to find a place in the scale of efficiency. For a whole month, I say, Mr. Judd Jason and his lieutenants made them their especial care; supported them in lodging-houses, induced the night clerks to give them attention; took the greatest pains to ensure them the birth-right which, as American citizens, was theirs,—that of voting. They were not only given homes for a period, but they were registered; and in the abundance of good feeling that reigned during this time of cheer, even the foreigners were registered! On election day they were driven, like visiting notables, in carryalls and carriages to the polls! Some of them, as though in compensation for ills endured between elections, voted not once, but many times; exercising judicial functions for which they should be given credit. For instance, they were convinced that the Hon. W. W. Trulease had made a good governor; and they were Watling enthusiasts,—intent on sending men to the legislature who would vote for him for senator; yet there were cases in which, for the minor offices, the democrat was the better man!

It was a memorable day. In spite of Mr. Lawler's Pilot, which was as a voice crying in the wilderness, citizens who had wives and homes and responsibilities, business men and clerks went to the voting booths and recorded their choice for Trulease, Watling and Prosperity: and working- men followed suit. Victory was in the air. Even the policemen wore happy smiles, and in some instances the election officers themselves in absent-minded exuberance thrust bunches of ballots into the boxes!

In response to an insistent demand from his fellow-citizens Mr. Watling, the Saturday evening before, had made a speech in the Auditorium, decked with bunting and filled with people. For once the Morning Era did not exaggerate when it declared that the ovation had lasted fully ten minutes. "A remarkable proof" it went on to say, "of the esteem and confidence in which our fellow-citizen is held by those who know him best, his neighbours in the city where he has given so many instances of his public spirit, where he has achieved such distinction in the practice of the law. He holds the sound American conviction that the office should seek the man. His address is printed in another column, and we believe it will appeal to the intelligence and sober judgment of the state. It is replete with modesty and wisdom."

Mr. Watling was introduced by Mr. Bering of the State Supreme Court (a candidate for re-election), who spoke with deliberation, with owl-like impressiveness. He didn't believe in judges meddling in politics, but this was an unusual occasion. (Loud applause.) Most unusual. He had come here as a man, as an American, to pay his tribute to another man, a long-time friend, whom he thought to stand somewhat aside and above mere party strife, to represent values not merely political.... So accommodating and flexible is the human mind, so "practical" may it become through dealing with men and affairs, that in listening to Judge Bering I was able to ignore the little anomalies such a situation might have suggested to the theorist, to the mere student of the institutions of democracy. The friendly glasses of rye and water Mr. Bering had taken in Monahan's saloon, the cases he had "arranged" for the firm of Watling, Fowndes and Ripon were forgotten. Forgotten, too, when Theodore Watling stood up and men began, to throw their hats in the air,—were the cavilling charges of Mr. Lawler's Pilot that, far from the office seeking the man, our candidate had spent over a hundred thousand dollars of his own money, to say nothing of the contributions of Mr. Scherer, Mr. Dickinson and the Railroad! If I had been troubled with any weak, ethical doubts, Mr. Watling would have dispelled them; he had red blood in his veins, a creed in which he believed, a rare power of expressing himself in plain, everyday language that was often colloquial, but never —as the saying goes—"cheap." The dinner-pail predicament was real to him. He would present a policy of our opponents charmingly, even persuasively, and then add, after a moment's pause: "There is only one objection to this, my friends—that it doesn't work." It was all in the way he said it, of course. The audience would go wild with approval, and shouts of "that's right" could be heard here and there. Then he proceeded to show why it didn't work. He had the faculty of bringing his lessons home, the imagination to put himself into the daily life of those who listened to him,—the life of the storekeeper, the clerk, of the labourer and of the house-wife. The effect of this can scarcely be overestimated. For the American hugs the delusion that there are no class distinctions, even though his whole existence may be an effort to rise out of once class into another. "Your wife," he told them once, "needs a dress. Let us admit that the material for the dress is a little cheaper than it was four years ago, but when she comes to look into the family stocking—" (Laughter.) "I needn't go on. If we could have things cheaper, and more money to buy them with, we should all be happy, and the Republican party could retire from business."

He did not once refer to the United States Senatorship.

It was appropriate, perhaps, that many of us dined on the evening of election day at the Boyne Club. There was early evidence of a Republican land-slide. And when, at ten o'clock, it was announced that Mr. Trulease was re-elected by a majority which exceeded Mr. Grunewald's most hopeful estimate, that the legislature was "safe," that Theodore Watling would be the next United States Senator, a scene of jubilation ensued within those hallowed walls which was unprecedented. Chairs were pushed back, rugs taken up, Gene Hollister played the piano and a Virginia reel started; in a burst of enthusiasm Leonard Dickinson ordered champagne for every member present. The country was returning to its senses. Theodore Watling had preferred, on this eventful night, to remain quietly at home. But presently carriages were ordered, and a "delegation" of enthusiastic friends departed to congratulate him; Dickinson, of course, Grierson, Fowndes, Ogilvy, and Grunewald. We found Judah B. Tallant there,—in spite of the fact that it was a busy night for the Era; and Adolf Scherer himself, in expansive mood, was filling the largest of the library chairs. Mr. Watling was the least excited of them all; remarkably calm, I thought, for a man on the verge of realizing his life's high ambition. He had some old brandy, and a box of cigars he had been saving for an occasion. He managed to convey to everyone his appreciation of the value of their cooperation....

It was midnight before Mr. Scherer arose to take his departure. He seized Mr. Watling's hand, warmly, in both of his own.

"I have never," he said, with a relapse into the German f's, "I have never had a happier moment in my life, my friend, than when I congratulate you on your success." His voice shook with emotion. "Alas, we shall not see so much of you now."

"He'll be on guard, Scherer," said Leonard Dickinson, putting his arm around my chief.

"Good night, Senator," said Tallant, and all echoed the word, which struck me as peculiarly appropriate. Much as I had admired Mr. Watling before, it seemed indeed as if he had undergone some subtle change in the last few hours, gained in dignity and greatness by the action of the people that day. When it came my turn to bid him good night, he retained my hand in his.

"Don't go yet, Hugh," he said.

"But you must be tired," I objected.

"This sort of thing doesn't make a man tired," he laughed, leading me back to the library, where he began to poke the fire into a blaze. "Sit down awhile. You must be tired,

I think,—you've worked hard in this campaign, a good deal harder than I have. I haven't said much about it, but I appreciate it, my boy." Mr. Watling had the gift of expressing his feelings naturally, without sentimentality. I would have given much for that gift.

"Oh, I liked it," I replied awkwardly.

I read a gentle amusement in his eyes, and also the expression of something else, difficult to define. He had seated himself, and was absently thrusting at the logs with the poker.

"You've never regretted going into law?" he asked suddenly, to my surprise.

"Why, no, sir," I said.

"I'm glad to hear that. I feel, to a considerable extent, responsible for your choice of a profession."

"My father intended me to be a lawyer," I told him. "But it's true that you gave me my—my first enthusiasm."

He looked up at me at the word.

"I admired your father. He seemed to me to be everything that a lawyer should be. And years ago, when I came to this city a raw country boy from upstate, he represented and embodied for me all the fine traditions of the profession. But the practice of law isn't what it was in his day, Hugh."

"No," I agreed, "that could scarcely be expected."

"Yes, I believe you realize that," he said. "I've watched you, I've taken a personal pride in you, and I have an idea that eventually you will succeed me here—neither Fowndes nor Ripon have the peculiar ability you have shown. You and I are alike in a great many respects, and I am inclined to think we are rather rare, as men go. We are able to keep one object vividly in view, so vividly as to be able to work for it day and night. I could mention dozens who had and have more natural talent for the law than I, more talent for politics than I. The same thing may be said about you. I don't regard either of us as natural lawyers, such as your father was. He couldn't help being a lawyer."

Here was new evidence of his perspicacity.

"But surely," I ventured, "you don't feel any regrets concerning your career, Mr. Watling?"

"No," he said, "that's just the point. But no two of us are made wholly alike. I hadn't practised law very long before I began to realize that conditions were changing, that the new forces at work in our industrial life made the older legal ideals impracticable. It was a case of choosing between efficiency and inefficiency, and I chose efficiency. Well, that was my own affair, but when it comes to influencing others—" He paused. "I want you to see this as I do, not for the sake of justifying myself, but because I honestly believe there is more to it than expediency,—a good deal more. There's a weak way of looking at it, and a strong way. And if I feel sure you understand it, I shall be satisfied.

"Because things are going to change in this country, Hugh. They are changing, but they are going to change more. A man has got to make up his mind what he believes in, and be ready to fight for it. We'll have to fight for it, sooner perhaps than we realize. We are a nation divided against ourselves; democracy—Jacksonian democracy, at all events, is a flat failure, and we may as well acknowledge it. We have a political system we have outgrown, and which, therefore, we have had to nullify. There are certain needs, certain tendencies of development in nations as well as in individuals,—needs stronger than the state, stronger than the law or constitution. In order to make our resources effective, combinations of capital are more and more necessary, and no more to be denied than a chemical process, given the proper ingredients, can be thwarted. The men who control capital must have a free hand, or the structure will be destroyed. This compels us to do many things which we would rather not do, which we might accomplish openly and unopposed if conditions were frankly recognized, and met by wise statesmanship which sought to bring about harmony by the reshaping of laws and policies. Do you follow me?"

"Yes," I answered. "But I have never heard the situation stated so clearly. Do you think the day will come when statesmanship will recognize this need?"

"Ah," he said, "I'm afraid not—in my time, at least. But we shall have to develop that kind of statesmen or go on the rocks. Public opinion in the old democratic sense is a myth; it must be made by strong individuals who recognize and represent evolutionary needs, otherwise it's at the mercy of demagogues who play fast and loose with the prejudice and ignorance of the mob. The people don't value the vote, they know nothing about the real problems. So far as I can see, they are as easily swayed to-day as the crowd that listened to Mark Antony's oration about Caesar. You've seen how we have to handle them, in this election and—in other matters. It isn't a pleasant practice, something we'd indulge in out of choice, but the alternative is unthinkable. We'd have chaos in no time. We've just got to keep hold, you understand—we can't leave it to the irresponsible."

"Yes," I said. In this mood he was more impressive than I had ever known him, and his confidence flattered and thrilled me.

"In the meantime, we're criminals," he continued. "From now on we'll have to stand more and more denunciation from the visionaries, the dissatisfied, the trouble makers. We may as well make up our minds to it. But we've got something on our side worth fighting for, and the man who is able to make that clear will be great."

"But you—you are going to the Senate," I reminded him.

He shook his head.

"The time has not yet come," he said. "Confusion and misunderstanding must increase before they can diminish. But I have hopes of you, Hugh, or I shouldn't have spoken. I shan't be here now—of course I'll keep in touch with you. I wanted to be sure that you had the right view of this thing."

"I see it now," I said. "I had thought of it, but never—never as a whole—not in the large sense in which you have expressed it." To attempt to acknowledge or deprecate the compliment he had paid me was impossible; I felt that he must have read my gratitude and appreciation in my manner.

"I mustn't keep you up until morning." He glanced at the clock, and went with me through the hall into the open air. A meteor darted through the November night. "We're like that," he observed, staring after it, a "flash across the darkness, and we're gone."

"Only—there are many who haven't the satisfaction of a flash," I was moved to reply.

He laughed and put his hand on my shoulder as he bade me good night.

"Hugh, you ought to get married. I'll have to find a nice girl for you," he said. With an elation not unmingled with awe I made my way homeward.

Theodore Watling had given me a creed.

A week or so after the election I received a letter from George Hutchins asking me to come to Elkington. I shall not enter into the details of the legal matter involved. Many times that winter I was a guest at the yellow-brick house, and I have to confess, as spring came on, that I made several trips to Elkington which business necessity did not absolutely demand.

I considered Maude Hutchins, and found the consideration rather a delightful process. As became an eligible and successful young man, I was careful not to betray too much interest; and I occupied myself at first with a review of what I deemed her shortcomings. Not that I was thinking of marriage—but I had imagined the future Mrs. Paret as tall; Maude was up to my chin: again, the hair of the fortunate lady was to be dark, and Maude's was golden red: my ideal had esprit, lightness of touch, the faculty of seizing just the aspect of a subject that delighted me, and a knowledge of the world; Maude was simple, direct, and in a word provincial. Her provinciality, however, was negative rather than positive, she had no disagreeable mannerisms, her voice was not nasal; her plasticity appealed to me. I suppose I was lost without knowing it when I began to think of moulding her.

All of this went on at frequent intervals during the winter, and while I was organizing the Elkington Power and Traction Company for George I found time to dine and sup at Maude's house, and to take walks with her. I thought I detected an incense deliciously sweet; by no means overpowering, like the lily's, but more like the shy fragrance of the wood flower. I recall her kind welcomes, the faint deepening of colour in her cheeks when she greeted me, and while I suspected that she looked up to me she had a surprising and tantalizing self-command.

There came moments when I grew slightly alarmed, as, for instance, one Sunday in the early spring when I was dining at the Ezra Hutchins's house and surprised Mrs. Hutchins's glance on me, suspecting her of seeking to divine what manner of man I was. I became self-conscious; I dared not look at Maude, who sat across the table; thereafter I began to feel that the Hutchins connection regarded me as a suitor. I had grown intimate with George and his wife, who did not refrain from sly allusions; and George himself once remarked, with characteristic tact, that I was most conscientious in my attention to the traction affair; I have reason to believe they were even less delicate with Maude. This was the logical time to withdraw—but I dallied. The experience was becoming more engrossing,—if I may so describe it,—and spring was approaching. The stars in their courses were conspiring. I was by no means as yet a self- acknowledged wooer, and we discussed love in its lighter phases through the medium of literature. Heaven forgive me for calling it so! About that period, it will be remembered, a mushroom growth of volumes of a certain kind sprang into existence; little books with "artistic" bindings and wide margins, sweetened essays, some of them written in beautiful English by dilettante authors for drawing-room consumption; and collections of short stories, no doubt chiefly bought by philanderers like myself, who were thus enabled to skate on thin ice over deep water. It was a most delightful relationship that these helped to support, and I fondly believed I could reach shore again whenever I chose.

There came a Sunday in early May, one of those days when the feminine assumes a large importance. I had been to the Hutchinses' church; and Maude, as she sat and prayed decorously in the pew beside me, suddenly increased in attractiveness and desirability. Her voice was very sweet, and I felt a delicious and languorous thrill which I identified not only with love, but also with a reviving spirituality. How often the two seem to go hand in hand!

She wore a dress of a filmy material, mauve, with a design in gold thread running through it. Of late, it seemed, she had had more new dresses: and their modes seemed more cosmopolitan; at least to the masculine eye. How delicately her hair grew, in little, shining wisps, around her white neck! I could have reached out my hand and touched her. And it was this desire,—although by no means overwhelming,—that startled me. Did I really want her? The consideration of this vital question occupied the whole time of the sermon; made me distrait at dinner,—a large family gathering. Later I found myself alone with heron a bench in the Hutchinses' garden where we had walked the day of my arrival, during the campaign.

The gardens were very different, now. The trees had burst forth again into leaf, the spiraea bushes seemed weighted down with snow, and with a note like that of the quivering bass string of a 'cello the bees hummed among the fruit blossoms. And there beside me in her filmy dress was Maude, a part of it all—the meaning of all that set my being clamouring. She was like some ripened, delicious flower ready to be picked.... One of those pernicious, make-believe volumes had fallen on the bench between us, for I could not read any more; I could not think; I touched her hand, and when she drew it gently away I glanced at her. Reason made a valiant but hopeless effort to assert itself. Was I sure that I wanted her—for life? No use! I wanted her now, no matter what price that future might demand. An awkward silence fell between us—awkward to me, at least—and I, her guide and mentor, became banal, apologetic, confused. I made some idiotic remark about being together in the Garden of Eden.

"I remember Mr. Doddridge saying in Bible class that it was supposed to be on the Euphrates," she replied. "But it's been destroyed by the flood."

"Let's make another—one of our own," I suggested.

"Why, how silly you are this afternoon."

"What's to prevent us—Maude?" I demanded, with a dry throat.

"Nonsense!" she laughed. In proportion as I lost poise she seemed to gain it.

"It's not nonsense," I faltered. "If we were married."

At last the fateful words were pronounced—irrevocably. And, instead of qualms, I felt nothing but relief, joy that I had been swept along by the flood of feeling. She did not look at me, but gazed straight ahead of her.

"If I love you, Maude?" I stammered, after a moment.

"But I don't love you," she replied, steadily.

Never in my life had I been so utterly taken aback.

"Do you mean," I managed to say, "that after all these months you don't like me a little?"

"'Liking' isn't loving." She looked me full in the face. "I like you very much."

"But—" there I stopped, paralyzed by what appeared to me the quintessence of feminine inconsistency and caprice. Yet, as I stared at her, she certainly did not appear capricious. It is not too much to say that I was fairly astounded at this evidence of self-command and decision, of the strength of mind to refuse me. Was it possible that she had felt nothing and I all? I got to my feet.

"I hate to hurt your feelings," I heard her say. "I'm very sorry."... She looked up at me. Afterwards, when reflecting on the scene, I seemed to remember that there were tears in her eyes. I was not in a condition to appreciate her splendid sincerity. I was overwhelmed and inarticulate. I left her there, on the bench, and went back to George's, announcing my intention of taking the five o'clock train....

Maude Hutchins had become, at a stroke, the most desirable of women. I have often wondered how I should have felt on that five-hour journey back to the city if she had fallen into my arms! I should have persuaded myself, no doubt, that I had not done a foolish thing in yielding to an impulse and proposing to an inexperienced and provincial young woman, yet there would have been regrets in the background. Too deeply chagrined to see any humour in the situation, I settled down in a Pullman seat and went over and over again the event of that afternoon until the train reached the city.

As the days wore on, and I attended to my cases, I thought of Maude a great deal, and in those moments when the pressure of business was relaxed, she obsessed me. She must love me,—only she did not realize it. That was the secret! Her value had risen amazingly, become supreme; the very act of refusing me had emphasized her qualifications as a wife, and I now desired her with all the intensity of a nature which had been permitted always to achieve its objects. The inevitable process of idealization began. In dusty offices I recalled her freshness as she had sat beside me in the garden,—the freshness of a flower; with

Berkeleyan subjectivism I clothed the flower with colour, bestowed it with fragrance. I conferred on Maude all the gifts and graces that woman had possessed since the creation. And I recalled, with mingled bitterness and tenderness, the turn of her head, the down on her neck, the half- revealed curve of her arm.... In spite of the growing sordidness of Lyme Street, my mother and I still lived in the old house, for which she very naturally had a sentiment. In vain I had urged her from time to time to move out into a brighter and fresher neighbourhood. It would be time enough, she said, when I was married.

"If you wait for that, mother," I answered, "we shall spend the rest of our lives here."

"I shall spend the rest of my life here," she would declare. "But you— you have your life before you, my dear. You would be so much more contented if—if you could find some nice girl. I think you live—too feverishly."

I do not know whether or not she suspected me of being in love, nor indeed how much she read of me in other ways. I did not confide in her, nor did it strike me that she might have yearned for confidences; though sometimes, when I dined at home, I surprised her gentle face—framed now with white hair—lifted wistfully toward me across the table. Our relationship, indeed, was a pathetic projection of that which had existed in my childhood; we had never been confidants then. The world in which I lived and fought, of great transactions and merciless consequences frightened her; her own world was more limited than ever. She heard disquieting things, I am sure, from Cousin Robert Breck, who had become more and more querulous since the time-honoured firm of Breck and Company had been forced to close its doors and the home at Claremore had been sold. My mother often spent the day in the scrolled suburban cottage with the coloured glass front door where he lived with the Kinleys and Helen....

If my mother suspected that I was anticipating marriage, and said nothing, Nancy Durrett suspected and spoke out.

Life is such a curious succession of contradictions and surprises that I record here without comment the fact that I was seeing much more of Nancy since her marriage than I had in the years preceding it. A comradeship existed between us. I often dined at her house and had fallen into the habit of stopping there frequently on my way home in the evening. Ham did not seem to mind. What was clear, at any rate, was that Nancy, before marriage, had exacted some sort of an understanding by which her "freedom" was not to be interfered with. She was the first among us of the "modern wives."

Ham, whose heartstrings and purse-strings were oddly intertwined, had stipulated that they were to occupy the old Durrett mansion; but when Nancy had made it "livable," as she expressed it, he is said to have remarked that he might as well have built a new house and been done with it. Not even old Nathaniel himself would have recognized his home when Nancy finished what she termed furnishing: out went the horsehair, the hideous chandeliers, the stuffy books, the Recamier statuary, and an army of upholsterers, wood-workers, etc., from Boston and New York invaded the place. The old mahogany doors were spared, but matched now by Chippendale and Sheraton; the new, polished floors were covered with Oriental rugs, the dreary Durrett pictures replaced by good canvases and tapestries. Nancy had what amounted to a genius for interior effects, and she was the first to introduce among us the luxury that was to grow more and more prevalent as our wealth increased by leaps and bounds. Only Nancy's luxury, though lavish, was never vulgar, and her house when completed had rather marvellously the fine distinction of some old London mansion filled with the best that generations could contribute. It left Mrs. Frederick Grierson—whose residence on the Heights had hitherto been our "grandest"—breathless with despair.

With characteristic audacity Nancy had chosen old Nathaniel's sanctum for her particular salon, into which Ham himself did not dare to venture without invitation. It was hung in Pompeiian red and had a little wrought-iron balcony projecting over the yard, now transformed by an expert into a garden. When I had first entered this room after the metamorphosis had taken place I inquired after the tombstone mantel.

"Oh, I've pulled it up by the roots," she said.

"Aren't you afraid of ghosts?" I inquired.

"Do I look it?" she asked. And I confessed that she didn't. Indeed, all ghosts were laid, nor was there about her the slightest evidence of mourning or regret. One was forced to acknowledge her perfection in the part she had chosen as the arbitress of social honours. The candidates were rapidly increasing; almost every month, it seemed, someone turned up with a fortune and the aspirations that go with it, and it was Mrs. Durrett who decided the delicate question of fitness. With these, and with the world at large, her manner might best be described as difficult; and I was often amused at the way in which she contrived to keep them at arm's length and make them uncomfortable. With her intimates—of whom there were few—she was frank.

"I suppose you enjoy it," I said to her once.

"Of course I enjoy it, or I shouldn't do it," she retorted. "It isn't the real thing, as I told you once. But none of us gets the real thing. It's power.... Just as you enjoy what you're doing—sorting out the unfit. It's a game, it keeps us from brooding over things we can't help. And after all, when we have good appetites and are fairly happy, why should we complain?"

"I'm not complaining," I said, taking up a cigarette, "since I still enjoy your favour."

She regarded me curiously.

"And when you get married, Hugh?"

"Sufficient unto the day," I replied.

"How shall I get along, I wonder, with that simple and unsophisticated lady when she appears?"

"Well," I said, "you wouldn't marry me."

She shook her head at me, and smiled....

"No," she corrected me, "you like me better as Hams' wife than you would have as your own."

I merely laughed at this remark.... It would indeed have been difficult to analyze the new relationship that had sprung up between us, to say what elements composed it. The roots of it went back to the beginning of our lives; and there was much of sentiment in it, no doubt. She understood me as no one else in the world understood me, and she was fond of me in spite of it.

Hence, when I became infatuated with Maude Hutchins, after that Sunday when she so unexpectedly had refused me, I might have known that Nancy's suspicions would be aroused. She startled me by accusing me, out of a clear sky, of being in love. I denied it a little too emphatically.

"Why shouldn't you tell me, Hugh, if it's so?" she asked. "I didn't hesitate to tell you."

It was just before her departure for the East to spend the summer. We were on the balcony, shaded by the big maple that grew at the end of the garden.

"But there's nothing to tell," I insisted.

She lay back in her chair, regarding me.

"Did you think that I'd be jealous?"

"There's nothing to be jealous about."

"I've always expected you to get married, Hugh. I've even predicted the type."

She had, in truth, with an accuracy almost uncanny.

"The only thing I'm afraid of is that she won't like me. She lives in that place you've been going to so much, lately,—doesn't she?"

Of course she had put two and two together, my visits to Elkington and my manner, which I had flattered myself had not been distrait. On the chance that she knew more, from some source, I changed my tactics.

"I suppose you mean Maude Hutchins," I said.

Nancy laughed.

"So that's her name!"

"It's the name of a girl in Elkington. I've been doing legal work for the Hutchinses, and I imagine some idiot has been gossiping. She's just a young girl—much too young for me."

"Men are queer creatures," she declared. "Did you think I should be jealous?"

It was exactly what I had thought, but I denied it.

"Why should you be—even if there were anything to be jealous about? You didn't consult me when you got married. You merely announced an irrevocable decision."

Nancy leaned forward and laid her hand on my arm.

"My dear," she said, "strange as it may seem, I want you to be happy. I don't want you to make a mistake, Hugh, too great a mistake."

I was surprised and moved. Once more I had a momentary glimpse of the real Nancy....

Our conversation was interrupted by the arrival of Ralph Hambleton....

Chapter Fourteen

However, thoughts of Maude continued to possess me. She still appeared the most desirable of beings, and a fortnight after my repulse, without any excuse at all, I telegraphed the George Hutchinses that I was coming to pay them a visit. Mrs. George, wearing a knowing smile, met me at the station in a light buck-board.

"I've asked Maude to dinner," she said....

Thus with masculine directness I returned to the charge, and Maude's continued resistance but increased my ardour; could not see why she continued to resist me.

"Because I don't love you," she said.

This was incredible. I suggested that she didn't know what love was, and she admitted it was possible: she liked me very, very much. I told her, sagely, that this was the best foundation for matrimony. That might be, but she had had other ideas. For one thing, she felt that she did not know me.... In short, she was charming and maddening in her defensive ruses, in her advances and retreats, for I pressed her hard during the four weeks which followed, and in them made four visits. Flinging caution to the winds, I did not even pretend to George that I was coming to see him on business. I had the Hutchins family on my side, for they had the sense to see that the match would be an advantageous one; I even summoned up enough courage to talk to Ezra Hutchins on the subject.

"I'll not attempt to influence Maude, Mr. Paret—I've always said I wouldn't interfere with her choice. But as you are a young man of sound habits, sir, successful in your profession, I should raise no objection. I suppose we can't keep her always."

To conceal his emotion, he pulled out the watch he lived by. "Why, it's church time!" he said.... I attended church regularly at Elkington....

On a Sunday night in June, following a day during which victory seemed more distant than ever, with startling unexpectedness Maude capitulated. She sat beside me on the bench, obscured, yet the warm night quivered with her presence. I felt her tremble.... I remember the first exquisite touch of her soft cheek. How strange it was that in conquest the tumult of my being should be stilled, that my passion should be transmuted into awe that thrilled yet disquieted! What had I done? It was as though I had suddenly entered an unimagined sanctuary filled with holy flame....

Presently, when we began to talk, I found myself seeking more familiar levels. I asked her why she had so long resisted me, accusing her of having loved me all the time.

"Yes, I think I did, Hugh. Only—I didn't know it."

"You must have felt something, that afternoon when I first proposed to you!"

"You didn't really want me, Hugh. Not then."

Surprised, and a little uncomfortable at this evidence of intuition, I started to protest. It seemed to me then as though I had always wanted her.

"No, no," she exclaimed, "you didn't. You were carried away by your feelings—you hadn't made up your mind. Indeed, I can't see why you want me now."

"You believe I do," I said, and drew her toward me.

"Yes, I—I believe it, now. But I can't see why. There must be so many attractive girls in the city, who know so much more than I do."

I sought fervidly to reassure her on this point.... At length when we went into the house she drew away from me at arm's length and gave me one long searching look, as though seeking to read my soul.

"Hugh, you will always love me—to the very end, won't you?"

"Yes," I whispered, "always."

In the library, one on each side of the table, under the lamp, Ezra Hutchins and his wife sat reading. Mrs. Hutchins looked up, and I saw that she had divined.

"Mother, I am engaged to Hugh," Maude said, and bent over and kissed her. Ezra and I stood gazing at them. Then he turned to me and pressed my hand.

"Well, I never saw the man who was good enough for her, Hugh. But God bless you, my son. I hope you will prize her as we prize her."

Mrs. Hutchins embraced me. And through her tears she, too, looked long into my face. When she had released me Ezra had his watch in his hand.

"If you're going on the ten o'clock train, Hugh—"

"Father!" Maude protested, laughing, "I must say I don't call that very polite."...

In the train I slept but fitfully, awakening again and again to recall the extraordinary fact that I was now engaged to be married, to go over the incidents of the evening. Indifferent to the backings and the bumpings of the car, the voices in the stations, the clanging of locomotive bells and all the incomprehensible startings and stoppings, exalted yet troubled I beheld Maude luminous with the love I had amazingly awakened, a love somewhere beyond my comprehension. For her indeed marriage was made in heaven. But for me? Could I rise now to the ideal that had once been mine, thrust henceforth evil out of my life? Love forever, live always in this sanctuary she had made for me? Would the time come when I should feel a sense of bondage?...

The wedding was set for the end of September. I continued to go every week to Elkington, and in August, Maude and I spent a fortnight at the sea. There could be no doubt as to my mother's happiness, as to her approval of Maude; they loved each other from the beginning. I can picture them now, sitting together with their sewing on the porch of the cottage at Mattapoisett. Out on the bay little white-caps danced in the sunlight, sail-boats tacked hither and thither, the strong cape breeze, laden with invigorating salt, stirred Maude's hair, and occasionally played havoc with my papers.

"She is just the wife for you, Hugh," my mother confided to me. "If I had chosen her myself I could not have done better," she added, with a smile.

I was inclined to believe it, but Maude would have none of this illusion.

"He just stumbled across me," she insisted....

We went on long sails together, towards Wood's Hole and the open sea, the sprays washing over us. Her cheeks grew tanned.... Sometimes, when I praised her and spoke confidently of our future, she wore a troubled expression.

"What are you thinking about?" I asked her once.

"You mustn't put me on a pedestal," she said gently. "I want you to see me as I am—I don't want you to wake up some day and be disappointed. I'll have to learn a lot of things, and you'll have to teach me. I can't get used to the fact that you, who are so practical and successful in business, should be such a dreamer where I am concerned."

I laughed, and told her, comfortably, that she was talking nonsense.

"What did you think of me, when you first knew me?" I inquired.

"Well," she answered, with the courage that characterized her, "I thought you were rather calculating, that you put too high a price on success. Of course you attracted me. I own it."

"You hid your opinions rather well," I retorted, somewhat discomfited.

She flushed.

"Have you changed them?" I demanded.

"I think you have that side, and I think it a weak side, Hugh. It's hard to tell you this, but it's better to say so now, since you ask me. I do think you set too high a value on success.'

"Well, now that I know what success really is, perhaps I shall reform," I told her.

"I don't like to think that you fool yourself," she replied, with a perspicacity I should have found extraordinary.

Throughout my life there have been days and incidents, some trivial, some important, that linger in my memory because they are saturated with "atmosphere." I recall, for instance, a gala occasion in youth when my mother gave one of her luncheon parties; on my return from school, the house and its surroundings wore a mysterious, exciting and unfamiliar look, somehow changed by the simple fact that guests sat decorously chatting in a dining-room shining with my mother's best linen and treasured family silver and china. The atmosphere of my wedding-day is no less vivid. The house of Ezra Hutchins was scarcely recognizable: its doors and windows were opened wide, and all the morning people were being escorted upstairs to an all-significant room that contained a collection like a jeweller's exhibit,—a bewildering display. There was a massive punch-bowl from which dangled the card of Mr. and Mrs. Adolf Scherer, a really wonderful tea set of old English silver given by Senator and Mrs. Watling, and Nancy Willett, with her certainty of good taste, had sent an old English tankard of the time of the second Charles. The secret was in that room. And it magically transformed for me (as I stood, momentarily alone, in the doorway where I had first beheld Maude) the accustomed scene, and charged with undivined significance the blue shadows under the heavy foliage of the maples. The September sunlight was heavy, tinged with gold....

So fragmentary and confused are the events of that day that a cubist literature were necessary to convey the impressions left upon me. I had something of the feeling of a recruit who for the first time is taking part in a brilliant and complicated manoeuvre.

Tom and Susan Peters flit across the view, and Gene Hollister and Perry Blackwood and the Ewanses,- -all of whom had come up in a special car; Ralph Hambleton was "best man," looking preternaturally tall in his frock-coat: and his manner, throughout the whole proceeding, was one of good-natured tolerance toward a folly none but he might escape.

"If you must do it, Hughie, I suppose you must," he had said to me. "I'll see you through, of course. But don't blame me afterwards."

Maude was a little afraid of him....

I dressed at George's; then, like one of those bewildering shifts of a cinematograph, comes the scene in church, the glimpse of my mother's wistful face in the front pew; and I found myself in front of the austere Mr. Doddridge standing beside Maude—or rather beside a woman I tried hard to believe was Maude—so veiled and generally encased was she. I was thinking of this all the time I was mechanically answering Mr. Doddridge, and even when the wedding march burst forth and I led her out of the church. It was as though they had done their best to disguise her, to put our union on the other-worldly plane that was deemed to be its only justification, to neutralize her sex at the very moment it should have been most enhanced. Well, they succeeded. If I had not been as conventional as the rest, I should have preferred to have run away with her in the lavender dress she wore when I first proposed to her. It was only when we had got into the carriage and started for the house and she turned to me her face from which the veil had been thrown back that I realized what a sublime meaning it all had for her. Her eyes were wet. Once more I was acutely conscious of my inability to feel deeply at supreme moments. For months I had looked forward with anticipation and impatience to my wedding-day.

I kissed her gently. But I felt as though she had gone to heaven, and that the face I beheld enshrouded were merely her effigy. Commonplace words were inappropriate, yet it was to these I resorted.

"Well—it wasn't so bad after all! Was it?"

She smiled at me.

"You don't want to take it back?"

She shook her head.

"I think it was a beautiful wedding, Hugh. I'm so glad we had a good day."...

She seemed shy, at once very near and very remote. I held her hand awkwardly until the carriage stopped.

A little later we were standing in a corner of the parlour, the atmosphere of which was heavy with the scent of flowers, submitting to the onslaught of relatives. Then came the wedding breakfast: croquettes, champagne, chicken salad, ice-cream, the wedding-cake, speeches and more kisses.... I remember Tom Peters holding on to both my hands.

"Good-bye, and God bless you, old boy," he was saying. Susan, in view of the occasion, had allowed him a little more champagne than usual—enough to betray his feelings, and I knew that these had not changed since our college days. I resolved to see more of him. I had neglected him and undervalued his loyalty.... He had followed me to my room in George's house where I was dressing for the journey, and he gave it as his deliberate judgment that in Maude I had "struck gold."

"She's just the girl for you, Hughie," he declared. "Susan thinks so, too."

Later in the afternoon, as we sat in the state-room of the car that was bearing us eastward, Maude began to cry. I sat looking at her helplessly, unable to enter into her emotion, resenting it a little. Yet I tried awkwardly to comfort her.

"I can't bear to leave them," she said.

"But you will see them often, when we come back," I reassured her. It was scarcely the moment for reminding her of what she was getting in return. This peculiar family affection she evinced was beyond me; I had never experienced it in any poignant degree since I had gone as a freshman to Harvard, and yet I was struck by the fact that her emotions were so rightly placed. It was natural to love one's family. I began to feel, vaguely, as I watched her, that the new relationship into which I had entered was to be much more complicated than I had imagined. Twilight was coming on, the train was winding through the mountain passes, crossing and re-crossing a swift little stream whose banks were massed with alder; here and there, on the steep hillsides, blazed the goldenrod.... Presently I turned, to surprise in her eyes a wide, questioning look,—the look of a child. Even in this irrevocable hour she sought to grasp what manner of being was this to whom she had confided her life, and with whom she was faring forth into the unknown. The experience was utterly unlike my anticipation. Yet I responded. The kiss I gave her had no passion in it.

"I'll take good care of you, Maude," I said.

Suddenly, in the fading light, she flung her arms around me, pressing me tightly, desperately.

"Oh, I know you will, Hugh, dear. And you'll forgive me, won't you, for being so horrid to-day, of all days? I do love you!"

Neither of us had ever been abroad. And although it was before the days of swimming-pools and gymnasiums and a la carte cafes on ocean liners, the Atlantic was imposing enough. Maude had a more lasting capacity for pleasure than I, a keener enjoyment of new experiences, and as she lay beside me in the steamer-chair where I had carefully tucked her she would exclaim:

"I simply can't believe it, Hugh! It seems so unreal. I'm sure I shall wake up and find myself back in Elkington."

"Don't speak so loud, my dear," I cautioned her. There were some very formal-looking New Yorkers next us.

"No, I won't," she whispered. "But I'm so happy I feel as though I should like to tell everyone."

"There's no need," I answered smiling.

"Oh, Hugh, I don't want to disgrace you!" she exclaimed, in real alarm. "Otherwise, so far as I am concerned, I shouldn't care who knew."

People smiled at her. Women came up and took her hands. And on the fourth day the formidable New Yorkers unexpectedly thawed.

I had once thought of Maude as plastic. Then I had discovered she had a mind and will of her own. Once more she seemed plastic; her love had made her so. Was it not what I had desired? I had only to express a wish, and it became her law. Nay, she appealed to me many times a day to know whether she had made any mistakes, and I began to drill her in my silly traditions,—gently, very gently.

"Well, I shouldn't be quite so familiar with people, quite so ready to make acquaintances, Maude. You have no idea who they may be. Some of them, of course, like the Sardells, I know by reputation."

The Sardells were the New Yorkers who sat next us.

"I'll try, Hugh, to be more reserved, more like the wife of an important man." She smiled.

"It isn't that you're not reserved," I replied, ignoring the latter half of her remark. "Nor that I want you to change," I said. "I only want to teach you what little of the world I know myself."

"And I want to learn, Hugh. You don't know how I want to learn!"

The sight of mist-ridden Liverpool is not a cheering one for the American who first puts foot on the mother country's soil, a Liverpool of yellow- browns and dingy blacks, of tilted funnels pouring out smoke into an atmosphere already charged with it. The long wharves and shed roofs glistened with moisture.

"Just think, Hugh, it's actually England!" she cried, as we stood on the wet deck. But I felt as though I'd been there before.

"No wonder they're addicted to cold baths," I replied. "They must feel perfectly at home in them, especially if they put a little lampblack in the water."

Maude laughed.

"You grumpy old thing!" she exclaimed.

Nothing could dampen her ardour, not the sight of the rain-soaked stone houses when we got ashore, nor even the frigid luncheon we ate in the lugubrious hotel. For her it was all quaint and new. Finally we found ourselves established in a compartment upholstered in light grey, with tassels and arm-supporters, on the window of which was pasted a poster with the word reserved in large, red letters. The guard inquired respectfully, as the porter put our new luggage in the racks, whether we had everything we wanted. The toy locomotive blew its toy whistle, and we were off for the north; past dingy, yellow tenements of the smoking factory towns, and stretches of orderly, hedge-spaced rain-swept country. The quaint cottages we glimpsed, the sight of distant, stately mansions on green slopes caused Maude to cry out with rapture:—

"Oh, Hugh, there's a manor-house!"

More vivid than were the experiences themselves of that journey are the memories of them. We went to windswept, Sabbath-keeping Edinburgh, to high Stirling and dark Holyrood, and to Abbotsford. It was through Sir Walter's eyes we beheld Melrose bathed in autumn light, by his aid repeopled it with forgotten monks eating their fast-day kale.

And as we sat reading and dreaming in the still, sunny corners I forgot, that struggle for power in which I had been so furiously engaged since leaving Cambridge. Legislatures, politicians and capitalists receded into a dim background; and the gift I had possessed, in youth, of living in a realm of fancy showed astonishing signs of revival.

"Why, Hugh," Maude exclaimed, "you ought to have been a writer!"

"You've only just begun to fathom my talents," I replied laughingly. "Did you think you'd married just a dry old lawyer?"

"I believe you capable of anything," she said....

I grew more and more to depend on her for little things.

She was a born housewife. It was pleasant to have her do all the packing, while I read or sauntered in the queer streets about the inns. And she took complete charge of my wardrobe.

She had a talent for drawing, and as we went southward through England she made sketches of the various houses that took our fancy—suggestions for future home-building; we spent hours in the evenings in the inn sitting-rooms incorporating new features into our residence, continually modifying our plans. Now it was a Tudor house that carried us away, now a Jacobean, and again an early Georgian with enfolding wings and a wrought-iron grill. A stage of bewilderment succeeded.

Maude, I knew, loved the cottages best. She said they were more "homelike." But she yielded to my liking for grandeur.

"My, I should feel lost in a palace like that!" she cried, as we gazed at the Marquis of So-and-So's country-seat.

"Well, of course we should have to modify it," I admitted. "Perhaps— perhaps our family will be larger."

She put her hand on my lips, and blushed a fiery red....

We examined, with other tourists, at a shilling apiece historic mansions with endless drawing-rooms, halls, libraries, galleries filled with family portraits; elaborate, formal bedrooms where famous sovereigns had slept, all roped off and carpeted with canvas strips to protect the floors. Through mullioned windows we caught glimpses of gardens and geometrical parterres, lakes, fountains, statuary, fantastic topiary and distant stretches of park. Maude sighed with admiration, but did not covet. She had me. But I was often uncomfortable, resenting the vulgar, gaping tourists with whom we were herded and the easy familiarity of the guides. These did not trouble Maude, who often annoyed me by asking naive questions herself. I would nudge her.

One afternoon when, with other compatriots, we were being hurried through a famous castle, the guide unwittingly ushered us into a drawing-room where the owner and several guests were seated about a tea-table. I shall never forget the stares they gave us before we had time precipitately to retreat, nor the feeling of disgust and rebellion that came over me. This was heightened by the remark of a heavy, six-foot Ohioan with an infantile face and a genial manner.

"I notice that they didn't invite us to sit down and have a bite," he said. "I call that kind of inhospitable."

"It was 'is lordship himself!" exclaimed the guide, scandalized.

"You don't say!" drawled our fellow-countryman. "I guess I owe you another shilling, my friend."

The guide, utterly bewildered, accepted it. The transatlantic point of view towards the nobility was beyond him.

"His lordship could make a nice little income if he set up as a side show," added the Ohioan.

Maude giggled, but I was furious. And no sooner were we outside the gates than I declared I should never again enter a private residence by the back door.

"Why, Hugh, how queer you are sometimes," she said.

"I maybe queer, but I have a sense of fitness," I retorted.

She asserted herself.

"I can't see what difference it makes. They didn't know us. And if they admit people for money—"

"I can't help it. And as for the man from Ohio—"

"But he was so funny!" she interrupted. "And he was really very nice."

I was silent. Her point of view, eminently sensible as it was, exasperated me. We were leaning over the parapet of a little-stone bridge. Her face was turned away from me, but presently I realized that she was crying. Men and women, villagers, passing across the bridge, looked at us curiously. I was miserable, and somewhat appalled; resentful, yet striving to be gentle and conciliatory. I assured her that she was talking nonsense, that I loved her. But I did not really love her at that moment; nor did she relent as easily as usual. It was not until we were together in our sitting-room, a few hours later, that she gave in. I felt a tremendous sense of relief.

"Hugh, I'll try to be what you want. You know I am trying. But don't kill what is natural in me."

I was touched by the appeal, and repentant...

It is impossible to say when the little worries, annoyances and disagreements began, when I first felt a restlessness creeping over me. I tried to hide these moods from her, but always she divined them. And yet I was sure that I loved Maude; in a surprisingly short period I had become accustomed to her, dependent on her ministrations and the normal, cosy intimacy of our companionship. I did not like to think that the keen edge of the enjoyment of possession was wearing a little, while at the same time I philosophized that the divine fire, when legalized, settles down to a comfortable glow. The desire to go home that grew upon me I attributed to the irritation aroused by the spectacle of a fixed social order commanding such unquestioned deference from the many who were content to remain resignedly outside of it. Before the setting in of the Liberal movement and the "American invasion" England was a country in which (from my point of view) one must be "somebody" in order to be happy. I was "somebody" at home; or at least rapidly becoming so....

London was shrouded, parliament had risen, and the great houses were closed. Day after day we issued forth from a musty and highly respectable hotel near Piccadilly to a gloomy Tower, a soggy Hampton Court or a mournful British Museum. Our native longing for luxury—or rather my native longing—impelled me to abandon Smith's Hotel for a huge hostelry where our suite overlooked the Thames, where we ran across a man I had known slightly at Harvard, and other Americans with whom we made excursions and dined and went to the theatre. Maude liked these persons; I did not find them especially congenial. My life-long habit of unwillingness to accept what life sent in its ordinary course was asserting itself; but Maude took her friends as she found them, and I was secretly annoyed by her lack of discrimination. In addition to this, the sense of having been pulled up by the roots grew upon me.

"Suppose," Maude surprised me by suggesting one morning as we sat at breakfast watching the river craft flit like phantoms through the yellow- green fog—" suppose we don't go to France, after all, Hugh?"

"Not go to France!" I exclaimed. "Are you tired of the trip?"

"Oh, Hugh!" Her voice caught. "I could go on, always, if you were content."

"And—what makes you think that I'm not content?"

Her smile had in it just a touch of wistfulness.

"I understand you, Hugh, better than you think. You want to get back to your work, and—and I should be happier. I'm not so silly and so ignorant as to think that I can satisfy you always. And I'd like to get settled at home,—I really should."

There surged up within me a feeling of relief. I seized her hand as it lay on the table.

"We'll come abroad another time, and go to France," I said. "Maude, you're splendid!"

She shook her head.

"Oh, no, I'm not."

"You do satisfy me," I insisted. "It isn't that at all. But I think, perhaps, it would be wiser to go back. It's rather a crucial time with me, now that Mr. Watling's in Washington. I've just arrived at a position where I shall be able to make a good deal of money, and later on—"

"It isn't the money, Hugh," she cried, with a vehemence which struck me as a little odd. "I sometimes think we'd be a great deal happier without—without all you are going to make."

I laughed.

"Well, I haven't made it yet."

She possessed the frugality of the Hutchinses. And some times my lavishness had frightened her, as when we had taken the suite of rooms we now occupied.

"Are you sure you can afford them, Hugh?" she had asked when we first surveyed them.

I began married life, and carried it on without giving her any conception of the state of my finances. She had an allowance from the first.

As the steamer slipped westward my spirits rose, to reach a climax of exhilaration when I saw the towers of New York rise gleaming like huge stalagmites in the early winter sun. Maude likened them more happily—to gigantic ivory chessmen. Well, New York was America's chessboard, and the Great Players had already begun to make moves that astonished the world. As we sat at breakfast in a Fifth Avenue hotel I ran my eye eagerly over the stock-market reports and the financial news, and rallied Maude for a lack of spirits.

"Aren't you glad to be home?" I asked her, as we sat in a hansom.

"Of course I am, Hugh!" she protested. "But—I can't look upon New York as home, somehow. It frightens me."

I laughed indulgently.

"You'll get used to it," I said. "We'll be coming here a great deal, off and on."

She was silent. But later, when we took a hansom and entered the streams of traffic, she responded to the stimulus of the place: the movement, the colour, the sight of the well-appointed carriages, of the well-fed, well- groomed people who sat in them, the enticement of the shops in which we made our purchases had their effect, and she became cheerful again....

In the evening we took the "Limited" for home.

We lived for a month with my mother, and then moved into our own house. It was one which I had rented from Howard Ogilvy, and it stood on the corner of Baker and Clinton streets, near that fashionable neighbourhood called "the Heights." Ogilvy, who was some ten years older than I, and who belonged to one of our old families, had embarked on a career then becoming common, but which at first was regarded as somewhat meteoric: gradually abandoning the practice of law, and perceiving the possibilities of the city of his birth, he had "gambled" in real estate and other enterprises, such as our local water company, until he had quadrupled his inheritance. He had built a mansion on Grant Avenue, the wide thoroughfare bisecting the Heights. The house he had vacated was not large, but essentially distinctive; with the oddity characteristic of the revolt against the banal architecture of the 80's. The curves of the tiled roof enfolded the upper windows; the walls were thick, the note one of mystery. I remember Maude's naive delight when we inspected it.

"You'd never guess what the inside was like, would you, Hugh?" she cried.

From the panelled box of an entrance hall one went up a few steps to a drawing-room which had a bowed recess like an oriel, and window-seats. The dining-room was an odd shape, and was wainscoted in oak; it had a tiled fireplace and (according to Maude) the "sweetest" china closet built into the wall. There was a "den" for me, and an octagonal reception-room on the corner. Upstairs, the bedrooms were quite as unusual, the plumbing of the new pattern, heavy and imposing. Maude expressed the air of seclusion when she exclaimed that she could almost imagine herself in one of the mediaeval towns we had seen abroad.

"It's a dream, Hugh," she sighed. "But—do you think we can afford it?"...

"This house," I announced, smiling, "is only a stepping-stone to the palace I intend to build you some day."

"I don't want a palace!" she cried. "I'd rather live here, like this, always."

A certain vehemence in her manner troubled me. I was charmed by this disposition for domesticity, and yet I shrank from the contemplation of its permanency. I felt vaguely, at the time, the possibility of a future conflict of temperaments. Maude was docile, now. But would she remain docile? and was it in her nature to take ultimately the position that was desirable for my wife? Well, she must be moulded, before it were too late. Her ultra-domestic tendencies must be halted. As yet blissfully unaware of the inability of the masculine mind to fathom the subtleties of feminine relationships, I was particularly desirous that Maude and Nancy Durrett should be intimates. The very day after our arrival, and while we were still at my mother's, Nancy called on Maude, and took her out for a drive. Maude told me of it when I came home from the office.

"Dear old Nancy!" I said. "I know you liked her."

"Of course, Hugh. I should like her for your sake, anyway. She's—she's one of your oldest and best friends."

"But I want you to like her for her own sake."

"I think I shall," said Maude. She was so scrupulously truthful! "I was a little afraid of her, at first."

"Afraid of Nancy!" I exclaimed.

"Well, you know, she's much older than I. I think she is sweet. But she knows so much about the world—so much that she doesn't say. I can't describe it."

I smiled.

"It's only her manner. You'll get used to that, when you know what she really is."

"Oh, I hope so," answered Maude. "I'm very anxious to like her—I do like her. But it takes me such a lot of time to get to know people."

Nancy asked us to dinner.

"I want to help Maude all I can,—if she'll let me," Nancy said.

"Why shouldn't she let you?" I asked.

"She may not like me," Nancy replied.

"Nonsense!" I exclaimed.

Nancy smiled.

"It won't be my fault, at any rate, if she doesn't," she said. "I wanted her to meet at first just the right people your old friends and a few others. It is hard for a woman—especially a young woman—coming among strangers." She glanced down the table to where Maude sat talking to Ham. "She has an air about her,—a great deal of self-possession."

I, too, had noticed this, with pride and relief. For I knew Maude had been nervous.

"You are luckier than you deserve to be," Nancy reminded me. "But I hope you realize that she has a mind of her own, that she will form her own opinions of people, independently of you."

I must have betrayed the fact that I was a little startled, for the remark came as a confirmation of what I had dimly felt.

"Of course she has," I agreed, somewhat lamely. "Every woman has, who is worth her salt."

Nancy's smile bespoke a knowledge that seemed to transcend my own.

"You do like her?" I demanded.

"I like her very much indeed," said Nancy, a little gravely. "She's simple, she's real, she has that which so few of us possess nowadays— character. But—I've got to be prepared for the possibility that she may not get along with me."

"Why not?" I demanded.

"There you are again, with your old unwillingness to analyze a situation and face it. For heaven's sake, now that you have married her, study her. Don't take her for granted. Can't you see that she doesn't care for the things that amuse me, that make my life?"

"Of course, if you insist on making yourself out a hardened, sophisticated woman—" I protested. But she shook her head.

"Her roots are deeper,—she is in touch, though she may not realize it, with the fundamentals. She is one of those women who are race-makers."

Though somewhat perturbed, I was struck by the phrase. And I lost sight of Nancy's generosity. She looked me full in the face.

"I wonder whether you can rise to her," she said. "If I were you, I should try. You will be happier—far happier than if you attempt to use her for your own ends, as a contributor to your comfort and an auxiliary to your career. I was afraid—I confess it—that you had married an aspiring, simpering and empty-headed provincial like that Mrs. George Hutchins' whom I met once, and who would sell her soul to be at my table. Well, you escaped that, and you may thank God for it. You've got a chance, think it over.

"A chance!" I repeated, though I gathered something of her meaning.

"Think it over, said Nancy again. And she smiled.

"But—do you want me to bury myself in domesticity?" I demanded, without grasping the significance of my words.

"You'll find her reasonable, I think. You've got a chance now, Hugh. Don't spoil it."

She turned to Leonard Dickinson, who sat on her other side....

When we got home I tried to conceal my anxiety as to Maude's impressions of the evening. I lit a cigarette, and remarked that the dinner had been a success.

"Do you know what I've been wondering all evening?" Maude asked. "Why you didn't marry Nancy instead of me."

"Well," I replied, "it just didn't come off. And Nancy was telling me at dinner how fortunate I was to have married you."

Maude passed this.

"I can't see why she accepted Hambleton Durrett. It seems horrible that such a woman as she is could have married—just for money.

"Nancy has an odd streak in her," I said. "But then we all have odd streaks. She's the best friend in the world, when she is your friend."

"I'm sure of it," Maude agreed, with a little note of penitence.

"You enjoyed it," I ventured cautiously.

"Oh, yes," she agreed. "And everyone was so nice to me—for your sake of course."

"Don't be ridiculous!" I said. "I shan't tell you what Nancy and the others said about you."

Maude had the gift of silence.

"What a beautiful house!" she sighed presently. "I know you'll think me silly, but so much luxury as that frightens me a little. In England, in those places we saw, it seemed natural enough, but in America—! And they all your friends—seem to take it as a matter of course."

"There's no reason why we shouldn't have beautiful things and well served dinners, too, if we have the money to pay for them."

"I suppose not," she agreed, absently.

Chapter Fifteen

That winter many other entertainments were given in our honour. But the conviction grew upon me that Maude had no real liking for the social side of life, that she acquiesced in it only on my account. Thus, at the very outset of our married career, an irritant developed: signs of it, indeed, were apparent from the first, when we were preparing the house we had rented for occupancy. Hurrying away from my office at odd times to furniture and department stores to help decide such momentous questions as curtains, carpets, chairs and tables I would often spy the tall, uncompromising figure of Susan Peters standing beside Maude's, while an obliging clerk spread out, anxiously, rugs or wall-papers for their inspection.

"Why don't you get Nancy to help you, too!" I ventured to ask her once.

"Ours is such a little house—compared to Nancy's, Hugh."

My attitude towards Susan had hitherto remained undefined. She was Tom's wife and Tom's affair. In spite of her marked disapproval of the modern trend in business and social life,—a prejudice she had communicated to Tom, as a bachelor I had not disliked her; and it was certain that these views had not mitigated Tom's loyalty and affection for me. Susan had been my friend, as had her brother Perry, and Lucia, Perry's wife: they made no secret of the fact that they deplored in me what they were pleased to call plutocratic obsessions, nor had their disapproval always been confined to badinage. Nancy, too, they looked upon as a renegade. I was able to bear their reproaches with the superior good nature that springs from success, to point out why the American tradition to which they so fatuously clung was a things of the past. The habit of taking dinner with them at least once a week had continued, and their arguments rather amused me. If they chose to dwell in a backwater out of touch with the current of great affairs, this was a matter to be deplored, but I did not feel strongly enough to resent it. So long as I remained a bachelor the relationship had not troubled me, but now that I was married I began to consider with some alarm its power to affect my welfare.

It had remained for Nancy to inform me that I had married a woman with a mind of her own. I had flattered myself that I should be able to control Maude, to govern her predilections, and now at the very beginning of our married life she was showing a disquieting tendency to choose for herself. To be sure, she had found my intimacy with the Peterses and Blackwoods already formed; but it was an intimacy from which I was growing away. I should not have quarrelled with her if she had not discriminated: Nancy made overtures, and Maude drew back; Susan presented herself, and with annoying perversity and in an extraordinarily brief time Maude had become her intimate. It seemed to me that she was always at Susan's, lunching or playing with the children, who grew devoted to her; or with Susan, choosing carpets and clothes; while more and more frequently we dined with the Peterses and the Blackwoods, or they with us. With Perry's wife Maude was scarcely less intimate than with Susan. This was the more surprising to me since Lucia Blackwood was a dyed-in- the-wool "intellectual," a graduate of Radcliffe, the daughter of a Harvard professor. Perry had fallen in love with her during her visit to Susan. Lucia was, perhaps, the most influential of the group; she scorned the world, she held strong views on the higher education of women; she had long discarded orthodoxy for what may be called a Cambridge stoicism of simple living and high thinking; while Maude was a strict Presbyterian, and not in the least given to theories. When, some months after our homecoming, I ventured to warn her gently of the dangers of confining one's self to a coterie—especially one of such narrow views—her answer was rather bewildering.

"But isn't Tom your best friend?" she asked.

I admitted that he was.

"And you always went there such a lot before we were married."

This, too, was undeniable. "At the same time," I replied, "I have other friends. I'm fond of the Blackwoods and the Peterses, I'm not advocating seeing less of them, but their point of view, if taken without any antidote, is rather narrowing. We ought to see all kinds," I suggested, with a fine restraint.

"You mean—more worldly people," she said with her disconcerting directness.

"Not necessarily worldly," I struggled on. "People who know more of the world—yes, who understand it better."

Maude sighed.

"I do try, Hugh,—I return their calls,—I do try to be nice to them. But somehow I don't seem to get along with them easily—I'm not myself, they make me shy. It's because I'm provincial."

"Nonsense!" I protested, "you're not a bit provincial." And it was true; her dignity and self-possession redeemed her.

Nancy was not once mentioned. But I think she was in both our minds....

Since my marriage, too, I had begun to resent a little the attitude of Tom and Susan and the Blackwoods of humorous yet affectionate tolerance toward my professional activities and financial creed, though Maude showed no disposition to take this seriously. I did suspect, however, that they were more and more determined to rescue Maude from what they would have termed a frivolous career; and on one of these occasions—so exasperating in married life when a slight cause for pique tempts husband or wife to try to ask myself whether this affair were only a squall, something to be looked for once in a while on the seas of matrimony, and weathered: or whether Maude had not, after all, been right when she declared that I had made a mistake, and that we were not fitted for one another? In this gloomy view endless years of incompatibility stretched ahead; and for the first time I began to rehearse with a certain cold detachment the chain of apparently accidental events which had led up to my marriage: to consider the gradual blindness that had come over my faculties; and finally to wonder whether judgment ever entered into sexual selection. Would Maude have relapsed into this senseless fit if she had realized how fortunate she was? For I was prepared to give her what thousands of women longed for, position and influence. My resentment rose again against Perry and Tom, and I began to attribute their lack of appreciation of my achievements to jealousy. They had not my ability; this was the long and short of it.... I pondered also, regretfully, on my bachelor days. And for the first time, I, who had worked so hard to achieve freedom, felt the pressure of the yoke I had fitted over my own shoulders. I had voluntarily, though unwittingly, returned to slavery. This was what had happened. And what was to be done about it? I would not consider divorce.

Well, I should have to make the best of it. Whether this conclusion brought on a mood of reaction, I am unable to say. I was still annoyed by what seemed to the masculine mind a senseless and dramatic performance on Maude's part, an incomprehensible case of "nerves." Nevertheless, there stole into my mind many recollections of Maude's affection, many passages between us; and my eye chanced to fall on the ink-well she had bought me out of the allowance I gave her. An unanticipated pity welled up within me for her loneliness, her despair in that room upstairs. I got up—and hesitated. A counteracting, inhibiting wave passed through me. I hardened. I began to walk up and down, a prey to conflicting impulses. Something whispered, "go to her"; another voice added, "for your own peace of mind, at any rate." I rejected the intrusion of this motive as unworthy, turned out the light and groped my way upstairs. The big clock in the hall struck twelve.

I listened outside the door of the bedroom, but all was silent within. I knocked.

"Maude!" I said, in a low voice.

There was no response.

"Maude—let me in! I didn't mean to be unkind—I'm sorry."

After an interval I heard her say: "I'd rather stay here,—to-night."

But at length, after more entreaty and self-abasement on my part, she opened the door. The room was dark. We sat down together on the window- seat, and all at once she relaxed and her head fell on my shoulder, and she began weeping again. I held her, the alternating moods still running through me.

"Hugh," she said at length, "how could you be so cruel? when you know I love you and would do anything for you."

"I didn't mean to be cruel, Maude," I answered.

"I know you didn't. But at times you seem so—indifferent, and you can't understand how it hurts. I haven't anybody but you, now, and it's in your power to make me happy or—or miserable."

Later on I tried to explain my point of view, to justify myself.

"All I mean," I concluded at length, "is that my position is a little different from Perry's and Tom's. They can afford to isolate themselves, but I'm thrown professionally with the men who are building up this city. Some of them, like Ralph Hambleton and Mr. Ogilvy, I've known all my life. Life isn't so simple for us, Maude—we can't ignore the social side."

"I understand," she said contentedly. "You are more of a man of affairs —much more than Tom or Perry, and you have greater responsibilities and wider interests. I'm really very proud of you. Only—don't you think you are a little too sensitive about yourself, when you are teased?"

I let this pass....

I give a paragraph from a possible biography of Hugh Paret which, as then seemed not improbable, might in the future have been written by some aspiring young worshipper of success.

"On his return from a brief but delightful honeymoon in England Mr. Paret took up again, with characteristic vigour, the practice of the law. He was entering upon the prime years of manhood; golden opportunities confronted him as, indeed, they confronted other men—but Paret had the foresight to take advantage of them. And his training under Theodore Watling was now to produce results.... The reputations had already been made of some of that remarkable group of financial geniuses who were chiefly instrumental in bringing about the industrial evolution begun after the Civil War: at the same time, as is well known, a political leadership developed that gave proof of a deplorable blindness to the logical necessity of combinations in business. The lawyer with initiative and brains became an indispensable factor," etc., etc.

The biography might have gone on to relate my association with and important services to Adolf Scherer in connection with his constructive dream. Shortly after my return from abroad, in answer to his summons, I found him at Heinrich's, his napkin tucked into his shirt front, and a dish of his favourite sausages before him.

"So, the honeymoon is over!" he said, and pressed my hand. "You are right to come back to business, and after awhile you can have another honeymoon, eh? I have had many since I married. And how long do you think was my first? A day! I was a foreman then, and the wedding was at six o'clock in the morning. We went into the country, the wife and I."

He laid down his knife and fork, possessed by the memory. "I have grown rich since, and we've been to Europe and back to Germany, and travelled on the best ships and stayed at the best hotels, but I never enjoyed a holiday more than that day. It wasn't long afterwards I went to Mr. Durrett and told him how he could save much money. He was always ready to listen, Mr. Durrett, when an employee had anything to say. He was a big man,—an iron-master. Ah, he would be astonished if only he could wake up now!"

"He would not only have to be an iron-master," I agreed, "but a financier and a railroad man to boot."

"A jack of all trades," laughed Mr. Scherer. "That's what we are—men in my position. Well, it was comparatively simple then, when we had no Sherman law and crazy statutes, such as some of the states are passing, to bother us. What has got into the politicians, that they are indulging in such foolishness?" he exclaimed, more warmly. "We try to build up a trade for this country, and they're doing their best to tie our hands and tear it down. When I was in Washington the other day I was talking with one of those Western senators whose state has passed those laws. He said to me, 'Mr. Scherer, I've been making a study of the Boyne Iron Works. You are clever men, but you are building up monopolies which we propose to stop.' 'By what means?'" I asked. "'Rebates, for one,' said he, 'you get preferential rates from your railroad which give you advantages over your competitors.' Foolishness!" Mr. Scherer exclaimed. "I tell him the railroad is a private concern, built up by private enterprise, and it has a right to make special rates for large shippers. No,—railroads are public carriers with no right to make special rates. I ask him what else he objects to, and he says patented processes. As if we don't have a right to our own patents! We buy them. I buy them, when other steel companies won't touch 'em. What is that but enterprise, and business foresight, and taking risks? And then he begins to talk about the tariff taking money out of the pockets of American consumers and making men like me rich. I have come to Washington to get the tariff raised on steel rails; and Watling and other senators we send down there are raising it for us. We are building up monopolies! Well, suppose we are. We can't help it, even if we want to. Has he ever made a study of the other side of the question—the competition side? Of course he hasn't."

He brought down his beer mug heavily on the table. In times of excitement his speech suggested the German idiom. Abruptly his air grew mysterious; he glanced around the room, now becoming empty, and lowered his voice.

"I have been thinking a long time, I have a little scheme," he said, "and I have been to Washington to see Watling, to talk over it. Well, he thinks much of you. Fowndes and Ripon are good lawyers, but they are not smart like you. See Paret, he says, and he can come down and talk to me. So I ask you to come here. That is why I say you are wise to get home. Honeymoons can wait—eh?"

I smiled appreciatively.

"They talk about monopoly, those Populist senators, but I ask you what is a man in my place to do? If you don't eat, somebody eats you—is it not so? Like the boa-constrictors—that is modern business. Look at the Keystone Plate people, over there at Morris. For years we sold them steel billets from which to make their plates, and three months ago they serve notice on us that they are getting ready to make their own billets, they buy mines north of the lakes and are building their plant. Here is a big customer gone. Next year, maybe, the Empire Tube Company goes into the business of making crude steel, and many more thousands of tons go from us. What is left for us, Paret?"

"Obviously you've got to go into the tube and plate business yourselves," I said.

"So!" cried Mr. Scherer, triumphantly, "or it is close up. We are not fools, no, we will not lie down and be eaten like lambs for any law. Dickinson can put his hand on the capital, and I—I have already bought a tract on the lakes, at Bolivar, I have already got a plant designed with the latest modern machinery. I can put the ore right there, I can send the coke back from here in cars which would otherwise be empty, and manufacture tubes at eight dollars a ton less than they are selling. If we can make tubes we can make plates, and if we can make plates we can make boilers, and beams and girders and bridges.... It is not like it was but where is it all leading, my friend? The time will come—is right on us now, in respect to many products—when the market will be flooded with tubes and plates and girders, and then we'll have to find a way to limit production. And the inefficient mills will all be forced to shut down."

The logic seemed unanswerable, even had I cared to answer it.... He unfolded his campaign. The Boyne Iron Works was to become the Boyne Iron Works, Ltd., owner of various subsidiary companies, some of which were as yet blissfully ignorant of their fate. All had been thought out as calmly as the partition of Poland—only, lawyers were required; and ultimately, after the process of acquisition should have been completed, a delicate document was to be drawn up which would pass through the meshes of that annoying statutory net, the Sherman Anti-trust Law. New mines were to be purchased, extending over a certain large area; wide coal deposits; little strips of railroad to tap them. The competition of the Keystone Plate people was to be met by acquiring and bringing up to date the plate mills of King and Son, over the borders of a sister state; the Somersworth Bridge and Construction Company and the Gring Steel and Wire Company were to be absorbed. When all of this should have been accomplished, there would be scarcely a process in the steel industry, from the smelting of the ore to the completion of a bridge, which the Boyne Iron Works could not undertake. Such was the beginning of the "lateral extension" period.

"Two can play at that game," Mr. Scherer said. "And if those fellows could only be content to let well enough alone, to continue buying their crude steel from us, there wouldn't be any trouble."...

It was evident, however, that he really welcomed the "trouble," that he was going into battle with enthusiasm. He had already picked out his points of attack and was marching on them. Life, for him, would have been a poor thing without new conflicts to absorb his energy; and he had already made of the Boyne Iron Works, with its open-hearth furnaces, a marvel of modern efficiency that had opened the eyes of the Steel world, and had drawn the attention of a Personality in New York,—a Personality who was one of the new and dominant type that had developed with such amazing rapidity, the banker-dinosaur; preying upon and superseding the industrial-dinosaur, conquering type of the preceding age, builder of the railroads, mills and manufactories. The banker-dinosaurs, the gigantic ones, were in Wall Street, and strove among themselves for the industrial spoils accumulated by their predecessors. It was characteristic of these monsters that they never fought in the open unless they were forced to. Then the earth rocked, huge economic structures tottered and fell, and much dust arose to obscure the vision of smaller creatures, who were bewildered and terrified. Such disturbances were called "panics," and were blamed by the newspapers on the Democratic party, or on the reformers who had wantonly assailed established institutions. These dominant bankers had contrived to gain control of the savings of thousands and thousands of fellow-citizens who had deposited them in banks or paid them into insurance companies, and with the power thus accumulated had sallied forth to capture railroads and industries. The railroads were the strategic links. With these in hand, certain favoured industrial concerns could be fed, and others starved into submission.

Adolf Scherer might be said to represent a transitional type. For he was not only an iron-master who knew every detail of his business, who kept it ahead of the times; he was also a strategist, wise in his generation, making friends with the Railroad while there had yet been time, at length securing rebates and favours. And when that Railroad (which had been constructed through the enterprise and courage of such men as Nathaniel Durrett) had passed under the control of the banker-personality to whom I have referred, and had become part of a system, Adolf Scherer remained in alliance, and continued to receive favours.... I can well remember the time when the ultimate authority of our Railroad was transferred, quietly, to Wall Street. Alexander Barbour, its president, had been a great man, but after that he bowed, in certain matters, to a greater one.

I have digressed.... Mr. Scherer unfolded his scheme, talking about "units" as calmly as though they were checkers on a board instead of huge, fiery, reverberating mills where thousands and thousands of human beings toiled day and night—beings with families, and hopes and fears, whose destinies were to be dominated by the will of the man who sat opposite me. But—did not he in his own person represent the triumph of that American creed of opportunity? He, too, had been through the fire, had sweated beside the blasts, had handled the ingots of steel. He was one of the "fittest" who had survived, and looked it. Had he no memories of the terrors of that struggle?... Adolf Scherer had grown to be a giant. And yet without me, without my profession he was a helpless giant, at the mercy of those alert and vindictive lawmakers who sought to restrain and hamper him, to check his growth with their webs. How stimulating the idea of his dependence! How exhilarating too, the thought that that vision which had first possessed me as an undergraduate—on my visit to Jerry Kyme—was at last to be realized! I had now become the indispensable associate of the few who divided the spoils, I was to have a share in these myself.

"You're young, Paret," Mr. Scherer concluded. "But Watling has confidence in you, and you will consult him frequently. I believe in the young men, and I have alreadyseen something of you—so?"...

When I returned to the office I wrote Theodore Watling a letter expressing my gratitude for the position he had, so to speak, willed me, of confidential legal adviser to Adolf Scherer. Though the opportunity had thrust itself upon me suddenly, and sooner than I expected it, I was determined to prove myself worthy of it. I worked as I had never worked before, making trips to New York to consult leading members of this new branch of my profession there, trips to Washington to see my former chief. There were, too, numerous conferences with local personages, with Mr. Dickinson and Mr. Grierson, and Judah B. Tallant,—whose newspaper was most useful; there were consultations and negotiations of a delicate nature with the owners and lawyers of other companies to be "taken in." Nor was it all legal work, in the older and narrower sense. Men who are playing for principalities are making war. Some of our operations had all the excitement of war. There was information to be got, and it was got—somehow. Modern war involves a spy system, and a friendly telephone company is not to be despised. And all of this work from first to last had to be done with extreme caution. Moribund distinctions of right and wrong did not trouble me, for the modern man labours religiously when he knows that Evolution is on his side.

For all of these operations a corps of counsel had been employed, including the firm of Harrington and Bowes next to Theodore Watling, Joel Harrington was deemed the ablest lawyer in the city. We organized in due time the corporation known as the Boyne Iron Works, Limited; a trust agreement was drawn up that was a masterpiece of its kind, one that caused, first and last, meddling officials in the Department of Justice at Washington no little trouble and perplexity. I was proud of the fact that I had taken no small part in its composition.... In short, in addition to certain emoluments and opportunities for investment, I emerged from the affair firmly established in the good graces of Adolf Scherer, and with a reputation practically made.

A year or so after the Boyne Company, Ltd., came into existence I chanced one morning to go down to the new Ashuela Hotel to meet a New Yorker of some prominence, and was awaiting him in the lobby, when I overheard a conversation between two commercial travellers who were sitting with their backs to me.

"Did you notice that fellow who went up to the desk a moment ago?" asked one.

"The young fellow in the grey suit? Sure. Who is he? He looks as if he was pretty well fixed."

"I guess he is," replied the first. "That's Paret. He's Scherer's confidential counsel. He used to be Senator Watling's partner, but they say he's even got something on the old man."

In spite of the feverish life I led, I was still undoubtedly young- looking, and in this I was true to the incoming type of successful man. Our fathers appeared staid at six and thirty. Clothes, of course, made some difference, and my class and generation did not wear the sombre and cumbersome kind, with skirts and tails; I patronized a tailor in New York. My chestnut hair, a little darker than my father's had been, showed no signs of turning grey, although it was thinning a little at the crown of the forehead, and I wore a small moustache, clipped in a straight line above the mouth. This made me look less like a college youth. Thanks to a strong pigment in my skin, derived probably from Scotch-Irish ancestors, my colour was fresh. I have spoken of my life as feverish, and yet I am not so sure that this word completely describes it. It was full to overflowing—one side of it; and I did not miss (save vaguely, in rare moments of weariness) any other side that might have been developed. I was busy all day long, engaged in affairs I deemed to be alone of vital importance in the universe. I was convinced that the welfare of the city demanded that supreme financial power should remain in the hands of the group of men with whom I was associated, and whose battles I fought in the courts, in the legislature, in the city council, and sometimes in Washington,—although they were well cared for there. By every means ingenuity could devise, their enemies were to be driven from the field, and they were to be protected from blackmail.

A sense of importance sustained me; and I remember in that first flush of a success for which I had not waited too long—what a secret satisfaction it was to pick up the Era and see my name embedded in certain dignified notices of board meetings, transactions of weight, or cases known to the initiated as significant. "Mr. Scherer's interests were taken care of by Mr. Hugh Paret." The fact that my triumphs were modestly set forth gave me more pleasure than if they had been trumpeted in headlines. Although I might have started out in practice for myself, my affection and regard for Mr. Watling kept me in the firm, which became Watling, Fowndes and Paret, and a new, arrangement was entered into: Mr. Ripon retired on account of ill health.

There were instances, however, when a certain amount of annoying publicity was inevitable. Such was the famous Galligan case, which occurred some three or four years after my marriage. Aloysius Galligan was a brakeman, and his legs had become paralyzed as the result of an accident that was the result of defective sills on a freight car. He had sued, and been awarded damages of $15,000. To the amazement and indignation of Miller Gorse, the Supreme Court, to which the Railroad had appealed, affirmed the decision. It wasn't the single payment of $15,000 that the Railroad cared about, of course; a precedent might be established for compensating maimed employees which would be expensive in the long run. Carelessness could not be proved in this instance. Gorse sent for me. I had been away with Maude at the sea for two months, and had not followed the case.

"You've got to take charge, Paret, and get a rehearing. See Bering, and find out who in the deuce is to blame for this. Chesley's one, of course. We ought never to have permitted his nomination for the Supreme Bench. It was against my judgment, but Varney and Gill assured me that he was all right."

I saw Judge Bering that evening. We sat on a plush sofa in the parlour of his house in Baker Street.

"I had a notion Gorse'd be mad," he said, "but it looked to me as if they had it on us, Paret. I didn't see how we could do anything else but affirm without being too rank. Of course, if he feels that way, and you want to make a motion for a rehearing, I'll see what can be done."

"Something's got to be done," I replied. "Can't you see what such a decision lets them in for?"

"All right," said the judge, who knew an order when he heard one, "I guess we can find an error." He was not a little frightened by the report of Mr. Gorse's wrath, for election-day was approaching. "Say, you wouldn't take me for a sentimental man, now, would you?"

I smiled at the notion of it.

"Well, I'll own up to you this kind of got under my skin. That Galligan is a fine-looking fellow, if there ever was one, and he'll never be of a bit of use any more. Of course the case was plain sailing, and they ought to have had the verdict, but that lawyer of his handled it to the queen's taste, if I do say so. He made me feel real bad, by God,—as if it was my own son Ed who'd been battered up. Lord, I can't forget the look in that man Galligan's eyes. I hate to go through it again, and reverse it, but I guess I'll have to, now."

The Judge sat gazing at the flames playing over his gas log.

"Who was the lawyer?" I asked.

"A man by the name of Krebs," he replied. "Never heard of him before. He's just moved to the city."

"This city?" I ejaculated.

The Judge glanced at me interestedly.

"This city, of course. What do you know about him?"

"Well," I answered, when I had recovered a little from the shock—for it was a distinct shock—"he lived in Elkington. He was the man who stirred up the trouble in the legislature about Bill 709."

The Judge slapped his knee.

"That fellow!" he exclaimed, and ruminated. "Why didn't somebody tell me?" he added, complainingly. "Why didn't Miller Gorse let me know about it, instead of licking up a fuss after it's all over?"...

Of all men of my acquaintance I had thought the Judge the last to grow maudlin over the misfortunes of those who were weak or unfortunate enough to be defeated and crushed in the struggle for existence, and it was not without food for reflection that I departed from his presence. To make Mr. Bering "feel bad" was no small achievement, and Krebs had been responsible for it, of course,—not Galligan. Krebs had turned up once more! It seemed as though he were destined to haunt me. Well, I made up my mind that he should not disturb me again, at any rate: I, at least, had learned to eliminate sentimentality from business, and it was not without deprecation I remembered my experience with him at the Capital, when he had made me temporarily ashamed of my connection with Bill 709. I had got over that. And when I entered the court room (the tribunal having graciously granted a rehearing on the ground that it had committed an error in the law!) my feelings were of lively curiosity and zest. I had no disposition to underrate his abilities, but I was fortified by the consciousness of a series of triumphs behind me, by a sense of association with prevailing forces against which he was helpless. I could afford to take a superior attitude in regard to one who was destined always to be dramatic.

As the case proceeded I was rather disappointed on the whole that he was not dramatic—not even as dramatic as he had been when he defied the powers in the Legislature. He had changed but little, he still wore ill- fitting clothes, but I was forced to acknowledge that he seemed to have gained in self-control, in presence. He had nodded at me before the case was called, as he sat beside his maimed client; and I had been on the alert for a hint of reproach in his glance: there was none. I smiled back at him....

He did not rant. He seemed to have rather a remarkable knowledge of the law. In a conversational tone he described the sufferings of the man in the flannel shirt beside him, but there could be no question of the fact that he did produce an effect. The spectators were plainly moved, and it was undeniable that some of the judges wore rather a sheepish look as they toyed with their watch chains or moved the stationery in front of them. They had seen maimed men before, they had heard impassioned, sentimental lawyers talk about wives and families and God and justice. Krebs did none of this. Just how he managed to bring the thing home to those judges, to make them ashamed of their role, just how he managed—in spite of my fortified attitude to revive something of that sense of discomfort I had experienced at the State House is difficult to say. It was because, I think, he contrived through the intensity of his own sympathy to enter into the body of the man whose cause he pleaded, to feel the despair in Galligan's soul—an impression that was curiously conveyed despite the dignified limits to which he confined his speech. It was strange that I began to be rather sorry for him, that I felt a certain reluctant regret that he should thus squander his powers against overwhelming odds. What was the use of it all!

At the end his voice became more vibrant—though he did not raise it—as he condemned the Railroad for its indifference to human life, for its contention that men were cheaper than rolling-stock.

I encountered him afterward in the corridor. I had made a point of seeking him out, perhaps from some vague determination to prove that our last meeting in the little restaurant at the Capital had left no traces of embarrassment in me: I was, in fact, rather aggressively anxious to reveal myself to him as one who has thriven on the views he condemned, as one in whose unity of mind there is no rift. He was alone, apparently waiting for someone, leaning against a steam radiator in one of his awkward, angular poses, looking out of the court-house window.

"How are you?" I said blithely. "So you've left Elkington for a wider field." I wondered whether my alert cousin-in-law, George Hutchins, had made it too hot for him.

He turned to me unexpectedly a face of profound melancholy; his expression had in it, oddly, a trace of sternness; and I was somewhat taken aback by this evidence that he was still bearing vicariously the troubles of his client. So deep had been the thought I had apparently interrupted that he did not realize my presence at first.

"Oh, it's you, Paret. Yes, I've left Elkington," he said.

"Something of a surprise to run up against you suddenly, like this."

"I expected to see you," he answered gravely, and the slight emphasis he gave the pronoun implied not only a complete knowledge of the situation and of the part I had taken in it, but also a greater rebuke than if his accusation had been direct. But I clung to my affability.

"If I can do anything for you, let me know," I told him. He said nothing, he did not even smile. At this moment he was opportunely joined by a man who had the appearance of a labour leader, and I walked away. I was resentful; my mood, in brief, was that of a man who has done something foolish and is inclined to talk to himself aloud: but the mood was complicated, made the more irritating by the paradoxical fact that that last look he had given me seemed to have borne the traces of affection....

It is perhaps needless to add that the court reversed its former decision.

Chapter Sixteen

The Pilot published a series of sensational articles and editorials about the Galligan matter, a picture of Galligan, an account of the destitute state of his wife and family. The time had not yet arrived when such newspapers dared to attack the probity of our courts, but a system of law that permitted such palpable injustice because of technicalities was bitterly denounced. What chance had a poor man against such a moloch as the railroad, even with a lawyer of such ability as had been exhibited by Hermann Krebs? Krebs was praised, and the attention of Mr. Lawler's readers was called to the fact that Krebs was the man who, some years before, had opposed single-handed in the legislature the notorious Bill No. 709. It was well known in certain circles—the editorial went on to say—that this legislation had been drawn by Theodore Watling in the interests of the Boyne Iron Works, etc., etc. Hugh Paret had learned at the feet of an able master. This first sight of my name thus opprobriously flung to the multitude gave me an unpleasant shock. I had seen Mr. Scherer attacked, Mr. Gorse attacked, and Mr. Watling: I had all along realized, vaguely, that my turn would come, and I thought myself to have acquired a compensating philosophy. I threw the sheet into the waste basket, presently picked it out again and reread the sentence containing my name. Well, there were certain penalties that every career must pay. I had become, at last, a marked man, and I recognized the fact that this assault would be the forerunner of many.

I tried to derive some comfort and amusement from the thought of certain operations of mine that Mr. Lawler had not discovered, that would have been matters of peculiar interest to his innocent public: certain extra- legal operations at the time when the Bovine corporation was being formed, for instance. And how they would have licked their chops had they learned of that manoeuvre by which I had managed to have one of Mr. Scherer's subsidiary companies in another state, with property and assets amounting to more than twenty millions, reorganized under the laws of New Jersey, and the pending case thus transferred to the Federal court, where we won hands down! This Galligan affair was nothing to that. Nevertheless, it was annoying. As I sat in the street car on my way homeward, a man beside me was reading the Pilot. I had a queer sensation as he turned the page, and scanned the editorial; and I could not help wondering what he and the thousands like him thought of me; what he would say if I introduced myself and asked his opinion. Perhaps he did not think at all: undoubtedly he, and the public at large, were used to Mr. Lawler's daily display of "injustices." Nevertheless, like slow acid, they must be eating into the public consciousness. It was an outrage— this freedom of the press.

With renewed exasperation I thought of Krebs, of his disturbing and almost uncanny faculty of following me up. Why couldn't he have remained in Elkington? Why did he have to follow me here, to make capital out of a case that might never have been heard of except for him?... I was still in this disagreeable frame of mind when I turned the corner by my house and caught sight of Maude, in the front yard, bending bareheaded over a bed of late flowers which the frost had spared. The evening was sharp, the dusk already gathering.

"You'll catch cold," I called to her.

She looked up at the sound of my voice.

"They'll soon be gone," she sighed, referring to the flowers. "I hate winter."

She put her hand through my arm, and we went into the house. The curtains were drawn, a fire was crackling on the hearth, the lamps were lighted, and as I dropped into a chair this living-room of ours seemed to take on the air of a refuge from the vague, threatening sinister things of the world without. I felt I had never valued it before. Maude took up her sewing and sat down beside the table.

"Hugh," she said suddenly, "I read something in the newspaper—"

My exasperation flared up again.

"Where did you get that disreputable sheet?" I demanded.

"At the dressmaker's!" she answered. "I—I just happened to see the name, Paret."

"It's just politics," I declared, "stirring up discontent by misrepresentation. Jealousy."

She leaned forward in her chair, gazing into the flames.

"Then it isn't true that this poor man, Galligan—isn't that his name?— was cheated out of the damages he ought to have to keep himself and his family alive?"

"You must have been talking to Perry or Susan," I said. "They seem to be convinced that I am an oppressor of the poor.

"Hugh!" The tone in which she spoke my name smote me. "How can you say that? How can you doubt their loyalty, and mine? Do you think they would undermine you, and to me, behind your back?"

"I didn't mean that, of course, Maude. I was annoyed about something else. And Tom and Perry have an air of deprecating most of the enterprises in which I am professionally engaged. It's very well for them to talk. All Perry has to do is to sit back and take in receipts from the Boyne Street car line, and Tom is content if he gets a few commissions every week. They're like militiamen criticizing soldiers under fire. I know they're good friends of mine, but sometimes I lose patience with them."

I got up and walked to the window, and came back again and stood before her.

"I'm sorry for this man, Galligan," I went on, "I can't tell you how sorry. But few people who are not on the inside, so to speak, grasp the fact that big corporations, like the Railroad, are looked upon as fair game for every kind of parasite. Not a day passes in which attempts are not made to bleed them. Some of these cases are pathetic. It had cost the Railroad many times fifteen thousand dollars to fight Galligan's case. But if they had paid it, they would have laid themselves open to thousands of similar demands. Dividends would dwindle. The stockholders have a right to a fair return on their money. Galligan claims that there was a defective sill on the car which is said to have caused the wreck. If damages are paid on that basis, it means the daily inspection of every car which passes over their lines. And more than that: there are certain defects, as in the present case, which an inspection would not reveal. When a man accepts employment on a railroad he assumes a certain amount of personal risk,—it's not precisely a chambermaid's job. And the lawyer who defends such cases, whatever his personal feelings may be, cannot afford to be swayed by them. He must take the larger view."

"Why didn't you tell me about it before?" she asked.

"Well, I didn't think it of enough importance—these things are all in the day's work."

"But Mr. Krebs? How strange that he should be here, connected with the case!"

I made an effort to control myself.

"Your old friend," I said. "I believe you have a sentiment about him."

She looked up at me.

"Scarcely that," she replied gravely, with the literalness that often characterized her, "but he isn't a person easily forgotten. He may be queer, one may not agree with his views, but after the experience I had with him I've never been able to look at him in the way George does, for instance, or even as father does."

"Or even as I do," I supplied.

"Well, perhaps not even as you do," she answered calmly. "I believe you once told me, however, that you thought him a fanatic, but sincere."

"He's certainly a fanatic!" I exclaimed.

"But sincere, Hugh-you still think him sincere."

"You seem a good deal concerned about a man you've laid eyes on but once."

She considered this.

"Yes, it is surprising," she admitted, "but it's true. I was sorry for him, but I admired him. I was not only impressed by his courage in taking charge of me, but also by the trust and affection the work-people showed. He must be a good man, however mistaken he may be in the methods he employs. And life is cruel to those people."

"Life is-life," I observed. "Neither you nor I nor Krebs is able to change it."

"Has he comc here to practice?" she asked, after a moment.

"Yes. Do you want me to invite him to dinner?" and seeing that she did not reply I continued: "In spite of my explanation I suppose you think, because Krebs defended the man Galligan, that a monstrous injustice has been done."

"That is unworthy of you," she said, bending over her stitch.

I began to pace the room again, as was my habit when overwrought.

"Well, I was going to tell you about this affair if you had not forestalled me by mentioning it yourself. It isn't pleasant to be vilified by rascals who make capital out of vilification, and a man has a right to expect some sympathy from his wife."

"Did I ever deny you that, Hugh?" she asked. "Only you don't ever seem to need it, to want it."

"And there are things," I pursued, "things in a man's province that a woman ought to accept from her husband, things which in the very nature of the case she can know nothing about."

"But a woman must think for herself," she declared. "She shouldn't become a mere automaton,—and these questions involve so much! People are discussing them, the magazines and periodicals are beginning to take them up."

I stared at her, somewhat appalled by this point of view. There had, indeed, been signs of its development before now, but I had not heeded them. And for the first time I beheld Maude in a new light.

"Oh, it's not that I don't trust you," she continued, "I'm open to conviction, but I must be convinced. Your explanation of this Galligan case seems a sensible one, although it's depressing. But life is hard and depressing sometimes I've come to realize that. I want to think over what you've said, I want to talk over it some more. Why won't you tell me more of what you are doing? If you only would confide in me—as you have now! I can't help seeing that we are growing farther and farther apart, that business, your career, is taking all of you and leaving me nothing." She faltered, and went on again. "It's difficult to tell you this—you never give me the chance. And it's not for my sake alone, but for yours, too. You are growing more and more self-centred, surrounding yourself with a hard shell. You don't realize it, but Tom notices it, Perry notices it, it hurts them, it's that they complain of. Hugh!" she cried appealingly, sensing my resentment, forestalling the words of defence ready on my lips. "I know that you are busy, that many men depend on you, it isn't that I'm not proud of you and your success, but you don't understand what a woman craves,—she doesn't want only to be a good housekeeper, a good mother, but she wants to share a little, at any rate, in the life of her husband, in his troubles as well as in his successes. She wants to be of some little use, of some little help to him."

My feelings were reduced to a medley.

"But you are a help to me—a great help," I protested.

She shook her head. "I wish I were," she said.

It suddenly occurred to me that she might be. I was softened, and alarmed by the spectacle she had revealed of the widening breach between us. I laid my hand on her shoulder.

"Well, I'll try to do better, Maude."

She looked up at me, questioningly yet gratefully, through a mist of tears. But her reply—whatever it might have been—was forestalled by the sound of shouts and laughter in the hallway. She sprang up and ran to the door.

"It's the children," she exclaimed, "they've come home from Susan's party!"

It begins indeed to look as if I were writing this narrative upside down, for I have said nothing about children. Perhaps one reason for this omission is that I did not really appreciate them, that I found it impossible to take the same minute interest in them as Tom, for instance, who was, apparently, not content alone with the six which he possessed, but had adopted mine. One of them, little Sarah, said "Uncle Tom" before "Father." I do not mean to say that I had not occasional moments of tenderness toward them, but they were out of my thoughts much of the time. I have often wondered, since, how they regarded me; how, in their little minds, they defined the relationship. Generally, when I arrived home in the evening I liked to sit down before my study fire and read the afternoon newspapers or a magazine; but occasionally I went at once to the nursery for a few moments, to survey with complacency the medley of toys on the floor, and to kiss all three. They received my caresses with a certain shyness—the two younger ones, at least, as though they were at a loss to place me as a factor in the establishment. They tumbled over each other to greet Maude, and even Tom. If I were an enigma to them, what must they have thought of him? Sometimes I would discover him on the nursery floor, with one or two of his own children, building towers and castles and railroad stations, or forts to be attacked and demolished by regiments of lead soldiers. He was growing comfortable-looking, if not exactly stout; prematurely paternal, oddly willing to renounce the fiercer joys of life, the joys of acquisition, of conquest, of youth.

"You'd better come home with me, Chickabiddy," he would say, "that father of yours doesn't appreciate you. He's too busy getting rich."

"Chickabiddy," was his name for little Sarah. Half of the name stuck to her, and when she was older we called her Biddy.

She would gaze at him questioningly, her eyes like blue flower cups, a strange little mixture of solemnity and bubbling mirth, of shyness and impulsiveness. She had fat legs that creased above the tops of the absurd little boots that looked to be too tight; sometimes she rolled and tumbled in an ecstasy of abandon, and again she would sit motionless, as though absorbed in dreams. Her hair was like corn silk in the sun, twisting up into soft curls after her bath, when she sat rosily presiding over her supper table.

As I look back over her early infancy, I realize that I loved her, although it is impossible for me to say how much of this love is retrospective. Why I was not mad about her every hour of the day is a puzzle to me now. Why, indeed, was I not mad about all three of them? There were moments when I held and kissed them, when something within me melted:

moments when I was away from them, and thought of them. But these moments did not last. The something within me hardened again, I became indifferent, my family was wiped out of my consciousness as though it had never existed.

There was Matthew, for instance, the oldest. When he arrived, he was to Maude a never-ending miracle, she would have his crib brought into her room, and I would find her leaning over the bedside, gazing at him with a rapt expression beyond my comprehension. To me he was just a brick-red morsel of humanity, all folds and wrinkles, and not at all remarkable in any way. Maude used to annoy me by getting out of bed in the middle of the night when he cried, and at such times I was apt to wonder at the odd trick the life-force had played me, and ask myself why I got married at all. It was a queer method of carrying on the race. Later on, I began to take a cursory interest in him, to watch for signs in him of certain characteristics of my own youth which, in the philosophy of my manhood, I had come to regard as defects. And it disturbed me somewhat to see these signs appear. I wished him to be what I had become by force of will—a fighter. But he was a sensitive child, anxious for approval; not robust, though spiritual rather than delicate; even in comparative infancy he cared more for books than toys, and his greatest joy was in being read to. In spite of these traits—perhaps because of them—there was a sympathy between us. From the time that he could talk the child seemed to understand me. Occasionally I surprised him gazing at me with a certain wistful look that comes back to me as I write.

Moreton, Tom used to call Alexander the Great because he was a fighter from the cradle, beating his elder brother, too considerate to strike back, and likewise—when opportunity offered—his sister; and appropriating their toys. A self-sufficient, doughty young man, with the round head that withstands many blows, taking by nature to competition and buccaneering in general. I did not love him half so much as I did Matthew—if such intermittent emotions as mine may be called love. It was a standing joke of mine—which Maude strongly resented—that Moreton resembled Cousin George of Elkington.

Imbued with the highest ambition of my time, I had set my barque on a great circle, and almost before I realized it the barque was burdened with a wife and family and the steering had insensibly become more difficult; for Maude cared nothing about the destination, and when I took any hand off the wheel our ship showed a tendency to make for a quiet harbour. Thus the social initiative, which I believed should have been the woman's, was thrust back on me. It was almost incredible, yet indisputable, in a day when most American women were credited with a craving for social ambition that I, of all men, should have married a wife in whom the craving was wholly absent! She might have had what other women would have given their souls for. There were many reasons why I wished her to take what I deemed her proper place in the community as my wife—not that I cared for what is called society in the narrow sense; with me, it was a logical part of a broader scheme of life; an auxiliary rather than an essential, but a needful auxiliary; a means of dignifying and adorning the position I was taking. Not only that, but I felt the need of intercourse—of intercourse of a lighter and more convivial nature with men and women who saw life as I saw it. In the evenings when we did not go out into that world our city afforded ennui took possession of me: I had never learned to care for books, I had no resources outside of my profession, and when I was not working on some legal problem I dawdled over the newspapers and went to bed. I don't mean to imply that our existence, outside of our continued intimacy with the Peterses and the Blackwoods, was socially isolated. We gave little dinners that Maude carried out with skill and taste; but it was I who suggested them; we went out to other dinners, sometimes to Nancy's— though we saw less and less of her—sometimes to other houses. But Maude had given evidence of domestic tastes and a disinclination for gaiety that those who entertained more were not slow to sense. I should have liked to take a larger house, but I felt the futility of suggesting it; the children were still small, and she was occupied with them. Meanwhile I beheld, and at times with considerable irritation, the social world changing, growing larger and more significant, a more important function of that higher phase of American existence the new century seemed definitely to have initiated. A segregative process was away to which Maude was wholly indifferent. Our city was throwing off its social conservatism; wealth (which implied ability and superiority) was playing a greater part, entertainments were more luxurious, lines more strictly drawn. We had an elaborate country club for those who could afford expensive amusements. Much of this transformation had been due to the initiative and leadership of Nancy Durrett....

Great and sudden wealth, however, if combined with obscure antecedents and questionable qualifications, was still looked upon askance. In spite of the fact that Adolf Scherer had "put us on the map," the family of the great iron-master still remained outside of the social pale. He himself might have entered had it not been for his wife, who was supposed to be "queer," who remained at home in her house opposite Gallatin Park and made little German cakes,—a huge house which an unknown architect had taken unusual pains to make pretentious and hideous, for it was Rhenish, Moorish and Victorian by turns. Its geometric grounds matched those of the park, itself a monument to bad taste in landscape. The neighbourhood was highly respectable, and inhabited by families of German extraction. There were two flaxen-haired daughters who had just graduated from an expensive boarding-school in New York, where they had received the polish needful for future careers. But the careers were not forthcoming.

I was thrown constantly with Adolf Scherer; I had earned his gratitude, I had become necessary to him. But after the great coup whereby he had fulfilled Mr. Watling's prophecy and become the chief factor in our business world he began to show signs of discontent, of an irritability that seemed foreign to his character, and that puzzled me. One day, however, I stumbled upon the cause of this fermentation, to wonder that I had not discovered it before. In many ways Adolf Scherer was a child. We were sitting in the Boyne Club.

"Money—yes!" he exclaimed, apropos of some demand made upon him by a charitable society. "They come to me for my money—there is always Scherer, they say. He will make up the deficit in the hospitals. But what is it they do for me? Nothing. Do they invite me to their houses, to their parties?"

This was what he wanted, then,—social recognition. I said nothing, but I saw my opportunity: I had the clew, now, to a certain attitude he had adopted of late toward me, an attitude of reproach; as though, in return for his many favours to me, there were something I had left undone. And when I went home I asked Maude to call on Mrs. Scherer.

"On Mrs. Scherer!" she repeated.

"Yes, I want you to invite them to dinner." The proposal seemed to take away her breath. "I owe her husband a great deal, and I think he feels hurt that the wives of the men he knows down town haven't taken up his family." I felt that it would not be wise, with Maude, to announce my rather amazing discovery of the iron-master's social ambitions.

"But, Hugh, they must be very happy, they have their friends. And after all this time wouldn't it seem like an intrusion?"

"I don't think so," I said, "I'm sure it would please him, and them. You know how kind he's been to us, how he sent us East in his private car last year."

"Of course I'll go if you wish it, if you're sure they feel that way." She did make the call, that very week, and somewhat to my surprise reported that she liked Mrs. Scherer and the daughters: Maude's likes and dislikes, needless to say, were not governed by matters of policy.

" You were right, Hugh," she informed me, almost with enthusiasm, "they did seem lonely. And they were so glad to see me, it was rather pathetic. Mr. Scherer, it seems, had talked to them a great deal about you. They wanted to know why I hadn't come before. That was rather embarrassing. Fortunately they didn't give me time to talk, I never heard people talk as they do. They all kissed me when I went away, and came down the steps with me. And Mrs. Scherer went into the conservatory and picked a huge bouquet. There it is," she said, laughingly, pointing to several vases. "I separated the colours as well as I could when I got home. We had coffee, and the most delicious German cakes in the Turkish room, or the Moorish room, whichever it is. I'm sure I shan't be able to eat anything more for days. When do you wish to have them for dinner?"

"Well," I said, "we ought to have time to get the right people to meet them. We'll ask Nancy and Ham."

Maude opened her eyes.

"Nancy! Do you think Nancy would like them?"

"I'm going to give her a chance, anyway," I replied....

It was, in some ways, a memorable dinner. I don't know what I expected in Mrs. Scherer—from Maude's description a benevolent and somewhat stupid, blue-eyed German woman, of peasant extraction. There could be no doubt about the peasant extraction, but when she hobbled into our little parlour with the aid of a stout, gold-headed cane she dominated it. Her very lameness added to a distinction that evinced itself in a dozen ways. Her nose was hooked, her colour high,—despite the years in Steelville,— her peculiar costume heightened the effect of her personality; her fire- lit black eyes bespoke a spirit accustomed to rule, and instead of being an aspirant for social honours, she seemed to confer them. Conversation ceased at her entrance.

"I'm sorry we are late, my dear," she said, as she greeted Maude affectionately, "but we have far to come. And this is your husband!" she exclaimed, as I was introduced. She scrutinized me. "I have heard something of you, Mr. Paret. You are smart. Shall I tell you the smartest thing you ever did?" She patted Maude's shoulder. "When you married your wife—that was it. I have fallen in love with her. If you do not know it, I tell you."

Next, Nancy was introduced.

"So you are Mrs. Hambleton Durrett?"

Nancy acknowledged her identity with a smile, but the next remark was a bombshell.

"The leader of society."

"Alas!" exclaimed Nancy, "I have been accused of many terrible things."

Their glances met. Nancy's was amused, baffling, like a spark in amber. Each, in its way, was redoubtable. A greater contrast between two women could scarcely have been imagined. It was well said (and not snobbishly) that generations had been required to make Nancy's figure: she wore a dress of blue sheen, the light playing on its ripples; and as she stood, apparently wholly at ease, looking down at the wife of Adolf Scherer, she reminded me of an expert swordsman who, with remarkable skill, was keeping a too pressing and determined aspirant at arm's length. I was keenly aware that Maude did not possess this gift, and I realized for the first time something of the similarity between Nancy's career and my own. She, too, in her feminine sphere, exercised, and subtly, a power in which human passions were deeply involved.

If Nancy Durrett symbolized aristocracy, established order and prestige, what did Mrs. Scherer represent? Not democracy, mob rule—certainly. The stocky German peasant woman with her tightly drawn hair and heavy jewels seemed grotesquely to embody something that ultimately would have its way, a lusty and terrible force in the interests of which my own services were enlisted; to which the old American element in business and industry, the male counterpart of Nancy Willett, had already succumbed. And now it was about to storm the feminine fastnesses! I beheld a woman who had come to this country with a shawl aver her head transformed into a new species of duchess, sure of herself, scorning the delicate euphemisms in which Fancy's kind were wont to refer to asocial realm, that was no less real because its boundaries had not definitely been defined. She held her stick firmly, and gave Nancy an indomitable look.

"I want you to meet my daughters. Gretchen, Anna, come here and be introduced to Mrs. Durrett."

It was not without curiosity I watched these of the second generation as they made their bows, noted the differentiation in the type for which an American environment and a "finishing school" had been responsible. Gretchen and Anna had learned—in crises, such as the present—to restrain the superabundant vitality they had inherited. If their cheekbones were a little too high, their Delft blue eyes a little too small, their colour was of the proverbial rose-leaves and cream. Gene Hollister's difficulty was to know which to marry. They were nice girls,—of that there could be no doubt; there was no false modesty in their attitude toward "society"; nor did they pretend—as so many silly people did, that they were not attempting to get anywhere in particular, that it was less desirable to be in the centre than on the dubious outer walks. They, too, were so glad to meet Mrs. Durrett.

Nancy's eyes twinkled as they passed on.

"You see what I have let you in for?" I said.

"My dear Hugh," she replied, "sooner or later we should have had to face them anyhow. I have recognized that for some time. With their money, and Mr. Scherer's prestige, and the will of that lady with the stick, in a few years we should have had nothing to say. Why, she's a female Napoleon. Hilda's the man of the family."

After that, Nancy invariably referred to Mrs. Scherer as Hilda.

If Mrs. Scherer was a surprise to us, her husband was a still greater one; and I had difficulty in recognizing the Adolf Scherer who came to our dinner party as the personage of the business world before whom lesser men were wont to cringe. He seemed rather mysteriously to have shed that personality; become an awkward, ingratiating, rather too exuberant, ordinary man with a marked German accent. From time to time I found myself speculating uneasily on this phenomenon as I glanced down the table at his great torso, white waist-coated for the occasion. He was plainly "making up" to Nancy, and to Mrs. Ogilvy, who sat opposite him. On the whole, the atmosphere of our entertainment was rather electric. "Hilda" was chiefly responsible for this; her frankness was of the breath-taking kind. Far from attempting to hide or ignore the struggle by which she and her husband had attained their present position, she referred with the utmost naivete to incidents in her career, while the whole table paused to listen.

"Before we had a carriage, yes, it was hard for me to get about. I had to be helped by the conductors into the streetcars. I broke my hip when we lived in Steelville, and the doctor was a numbskull. He should be put in prison, is what I tell Adolf. I was standing on a clothes-horse, when it fell. I had much washing to do in those days."

"And—can nothing be done, Mrs. Scherer?" asked Leonard Dickinson, sympathetically.

"For an old woman? I am fifty-five. I have had many doctors. I would put them all in prison. How much was it you paid Dr. Stickney, in New York, Adolf? Five thousand dollars? And he did nothing—nothing. I'd rather be poor again, and work. But it is well to make the best of it."...

"Your grandfather was a fine man, Mr. Durrett," she informed Hambleton. "It is a pity for you, I think, that you do not have to work."

Ham, who sat on her other side, was amused.

"My grandfather did enough work for both of us," he said.

"If I had been your grandfather, I would have started you in puddling," she observed, as she eyed with disapproval the filling of his third glass of champagne. "I think there is too much gay life, too much games for rich young men nowadays. You will forgive me for saying what I think to young men?"

"I'll forgive you for not being my grandfather, at any rate," replied Ham, with unaccustomed wit.

She gazed at him with grim humour.

"It is bad for you I am not," she declared.

There was no gainsaying her. What can be done with a lady who will not recognize that morality is not discussed, and that personalities are tabooed save between intimates. Hilda was a personage as well as a Tartar. Laws, conventions, usages—to all these she would conform when it pleased her. She would have made an admirable inquisitorial judge, and quite as admirable a sick nurse. A rare criminal lawyer, likewise, was wasted in her. She was one of those individuals, I perceived, whose loyalties dominate them; and who, in behalf of those loyalties, carry chips on their shoulders.

"It is a long time that I have been wanting to meet you," she informed me. "You are smart."

I smiled, yet I was inclined to resent her use of the word, though I was by no means sure of the shade of meaning she meant to put into it. I had, indeed, an uneasy sense of the scantiness of my fund of humour to meet and turn such a situation; for I was experiencing, now, with her, the same queer feeling I had known in my youth in the presence of Cousin Robert Breck—the suspicion that this extraordinary person saw through me. It was as though she held up a mirror and compelled me to look at my soul features. I tried to assure myself that the mirror was distorted. I lost, nevertheless, the sureness of touch that comes from the conviction of being all of a piece. She contrived to resolve me again into conflicting elements. I was, for the moment, no longer the self- confident and triumphant young attorney accustomed to carry all before him, to command respect and admiration, but a complicated being whose unity had suddenly been split. I glanced around the table at Ogilvy, at Dickinson, at Ralph Hambleton. These men were functioning truly. But was I? If I were not, might not this be the reason for the lack of synthesis—of which I was abruptly though vaguely aware between my professional life, my domestic relationships, and my relationships with friends. The loyalty of the woman beside me struck me forcibly as a supreme trait. Where she had given, she did not withdraw. She had conferred it instantly on Maude. Did I feel that loyalty towards a single human being? towards Maude herself—my wife? or even towards Nancy? I pulled myself together, and resolved to give her credit for using the word "smart" in its unobjectionable sense. After all; Dickens had so used it.

"A lawyer must needs know something of what he is about, Mrs. Scherer, if he is to be employed by such a man as your husband," I replied.

Her black eyes snapped with pleasure.

"Ah, I suppose that is so," she agreed. "I knew he was a great man when I married him, and that was before Mr. Nathaniel Durrett found it out."

"But surely you did not think, in those days, that he would be as big as he has become? That he would not only be president of the Boyne Iron Works, but of a Boyne Iron Works that has exceeded Mr. Durrett's wildest dreams."

She shook her head complacently.

"Do you know what I told him when he married me? I said, 'Adolf, it is a pity you are born in Germany.' And when he asked me why, I told him that some day he might have been President of the United States."

"Well, that won't be a great deprivation to him," I remarked. "Mr. Scherer can do what he wants, and the President cannot."

"Adolf always does as he wants," she declared, gazing at him as he sat beside the brilliant wife of the grandson of the man whose red-shirted foreman he had been. "He does what he wants, and gets what he wants. He is getting what he wants now," she added, with such obvious meaning that I found no words to reply. "She is pretty, that Mrs. Durrett, and clever,—is it not so?"

I agreed. A new and indescribable note had come into Mrs. Scherer's voice, and I realized that she, too, was aware of that flaw in the redoubtable Mr. Scherer which none of his associates had guessed. It would have been strange if she had not discovered it. "She is beautiful, yes," the lady continued critically, "but she is not to compare with your wife. She has not the heart,—it is so with all your people of society. For them it is not what you are, but what you have done, and what you have."

The banality of this observation was mitigated by the feeling she threw into it.

"I think you misjudge Mrs. Durrett," I said, incautiously. "She has never before had the opportunity of meeting Mr. Scherer of appreciating him."

"Mrs. Durrett is an old friend of yours?" she asked.

"I was brought up with her."

"Ah!" she exclaimed, and turned her penetrating glance upon me. I was startled. Could it be that she had discerned and interpreted those renascent feelings even then stirring within me, and of which I myself was as yet scarcely conscious? At this moment, fortunately for me, the women rose; the men remained to smoke; and Scherer, as they discussed matters of finance, became himself again. I joined in the conversation, but I was thinking of those instants when in flashes of understanding my eyes had met Nancy's; instants in which I was lifted out of my humdrum, deadly serious self and was able to look down objectively upon the life I led, the life we all led—and Nancy herself; to see with her the comic irony of it all. Nancy had the power to give me this exquisite sense of detachment that must sustain her. And was it not just this sustenance she could give that I needed? For want of it I was hardening, crystallizing, growing blind to the joy and variety of existence. Nancy could have saved me; she brought it home to me that I needed salvation.... I was struck by another thought; in spite of our separation, in spite of her marriage and mine, she was still nearer to me—far nearer—than any other being.

Later, I sought her out. She looked up at me amusedly from the window- seat in our living-room, where she had been talking to the Scherer girls.

"Well, how did you get along with Hilda?" she asked. "I thought I saw you struggling."

"She's somewhat disconcerting," I said. "I felt as if she were turning me inside out."

Nancy laughed.

"Hilda's a discovery—a genius. I'm going to have them to dinner myself."

"And Adolf?" I inquired. "I believe she thought you were preparing to run away with him. You seemed to have him hypnotized."

"I'm afraid your great man won't be able to stand—elevation," she declared. "He'll have vertigo. He's even got it now, at this little height, and when he builds his palace on Grant Avenue, and later moves to New York, I'm afraid he'll wobble even more."

"Is he thinking of doing all that?" I asked.

"I merely predict New York—it's inevitable," she replied. "Grant Avenue, yes; he wants me to help him choose a lot. He gave me ten thousand dollars for our Orphans' Home, but on the whole I think I prefer Hilda even if she doesn't approve of me."

Nancy rose. The Scherers were going. While Mr. Scherer pressed my hand in a manner that convinced me of his gratitude, Hilda was bidding an affectionate good night to Maude. A few moments later she bore her husband and daughters away, and we heard the tap-tap of her cane on the walk outside....

Chapter Seventeen

The remembrance of that dinner when with my connivance the Scherers made their social debut is associated in my mind with the coming of the fulness of that era, mad and brief, when gold rained down like manna from our sooty skies. Even the church was prosperous; the Rev. Carey Heddon, our new minister, was well abreast of the times, typical of the new and efficient Christianity that has finally buried the hatchet with enlightened self-interest. He looked like a young and prosperous man of business, and indeed he was one.

The fame of our city spread even across the Atlantic, reaching obscure hamlets in Europe, where villagers gathered up their lares and penates, mortgaged their homes, and bought steamship tickets from philanthropists,—philanthropists in diamonds. Our Huns began to arrive, their Attilas unrecognized among them: to drive our honest Americans and Irish and Germans out of the mills by "lowering the standard of living." Still—according to the learned economists in our universities, enlightened self-interest triumphed. Had not the honest Americans and Germans become foremen and even presidents of corporations? What greater vindication for their philosophy could be desired?

The very aspect of the city changed like magic. New buildings sprang high in the air; the Reliance Trust (Mr. Grierson's), the Scherer Building, the Hambleton Building; a stew hotel, the Ashuela, took proper care of our visitors from the East,—a massive, grey stone, thousand- awninged affair on Boyne Street, with a grill where it became the fashion to go for supper after the play, and a head waiter who knew in a few weeks everyone worth knowing.

To return for a moment to the Huns. Maude had expressed a desire to see a mill, and we went, one afternoon, in Mr. Scherer's carriage to Steelville, with Mr. Scherer himself,—a bewildering, educative, almost terrifying experience amidst fumes and flames, gigantic forces and titanic weights. It seemed a marvel that we escaped being crushed or burned alive in those huge steel buildings reverberating with sound. They appeared a very bedlam of chaos, instead of the triumph of order, organization and human skill. Mr. Scherer was very proud of it all, and ours was a sort of triumphal procession, accompanied by superintendents, managers and other factotums. I thought of my childhood image of Shadrach, Meshach and Abednego, and our progress through the flames seemed no less remarkable and miraculous.

Maude, with alarm in her eyes, kept very close to me, as I supplemented the explanations they gave her. I had been there many times before.

"Why, Hugh," she exclaimed, "you seem to know a lot about it!"

Mr. Scherer laughed.

"He's had to talk about it once or twice in court—eh, Hugh? You didn't realize how clever your husband was did you, Mrs. Paret?"

"But this is so—complicated," she replied. "It is overwhelming."

"When I found out how much trouble he had taken to learn about my business," added Mr. Scherer, "there was only one thing to do. Make him my lawyer. Hugh, you have the floor, and explain the open-hearth process."

I had almost forgotten the Huns. I saw Maude gazing at them with a new kind of terror. And when we sat at home that evening they still haunted her.

"Somehow, I can't bear to think about them," she said. "I'm sure we'll have to pay for it, some day."

"Pay for what?" I asked.

"For making them work that way. And twelve hours! It can't be right, while we have so much, and are so comfortable."

"Don't be foolish," I exclaimed. "They're used to it. They think themselves lucky to get the work—and they are. Besides, you give them credit for a sensitiveness that they don't possess. They wouldn't know what to do with such a house as this if they had it."

"I never realized before that our happiness and comfort were built on such foundations;" she said, ignoring my remark.

"You must have seen your father's operatives, in Elkington, many times a week."

"I suppose I was too young to think about such things," she reflected. "Besides, I used to be sorry for them, sometimes. But these men at the steel mills—I can't tell you what I feel about them. The sight of their great bodies and their red, sullen faces brought home to me the cruelty of life. Did you notice how some of them stared at us, as though they were but half awake in the heat, with that glow on their faces? It made me afraid—afraid that they'll wake up some day, and then they will be terrible. I thought of the children. It seems not only wicked, but mad to bring ignorant foreigners over here and make them slaves like that, and so many of them are hurt and maimed. I can't forget them."

"You're talking Socialism," I said crossly, wondering whether Lucia had taken it up as her latest fad.

"Oh, no, I'm not," said Maude, "I don't know what Socialism is. I'm talking about something that anyone who is not dazzled by all this luxury we are living in might be able to see, about something which, when it comes, we shan't be able to help."

I ridiculed this. The prophecy itself did not disturb me half as much as the fact that she had made it, as this new evidence that she was beginning to think for herself, and along lines so different from my own development.

While it lasted, before novelists, playwrights, professors and ministers of the Gospel abandoned their proper sphere to destroy it, that Golden Age was heaven; the New Jerusalem—in which we had ceased to believe— would have been in the nature of an anticlimax to any of our archangels of finance who might have attained it. The streets of our own city turned out to be gold; gold likewise the acres of unused, scrubby land on our outskirts, as the incident of the Riverside Franchise—which I am about to relate—amply proved.

That scheme originated in the alert mind of Mr. Frederick Grierson, and in spite of the fact that it has since become notorious in the eyes of a virtue-stricken public, it was entered into with all innocence at the time: most of the men who were present at the "magnate's" table at the Boyne Club the day Mr. Grierson broached it will vouch for this. He casually asked Mr. Dickinson if he had ever noticed a tract lying on the river about two miles beyond the Heights, opposite what used to be in the old days a road house.

"This city is growing so fast, Leonard," said Grierson, lighting a special cigar the Club kept for him, "that it might pay a few of us to get together and buy that tract, have the city put in streets and sewers and sell it in building lots. I think I can get most of it at less than three hundred dollars an acre."

Mr. Dickinson was interested. So were Mr. Ogilvy and Ralph Hambleton, and Mr. Scherer, who chanced to be there. Anything Fred Grierson had to say on the question of real estate was always interesting. He went on to describe the tract, its size and location.

"That's all very well, Fred," Dickinson objected presently, "but how are your prospective householders going to get out there?"

"Just what I was coming to," cried Grierson, triumphantly, "we'll get a franchise, and build a street-railroad out Maplewood Avenue, an extension of the Park Street line. We can get the franchise for next to nothing, if we work it right." (Mr. Grierson's eye fell on me), "and sell it out to the public, if you underwrite it, for two million or so."

"Well, you've got your nerve with you, Fred, as usual," said Dickinson. But he rolled his cigar in his mouth, an indication, to those who knew him well, that he was considering the matter. When Leonard Dickinson didn't say "no" at once, there was hope. "What do you think the property holders on Maplewood Avenue would say? Wasn't it understood, when that avenue was laid out, that it was to form part of the system of boulevards?"

"What difference does it make what they say?" Ralph interposed.

Dickinson smiled. He, too, had an exaggerated respect for Ralph. We all thought the proposal daring, but in no way amazing; the public existed to be sold things to, and what did it matter if the Maplewood residents, as Ralph said; and the City Improvement League protested?

Perry Blackwood was the Secretary of the City Improvement League, the object of which was to beautify the city by laying out a system of parkways.

The next day some of us gathered in Dickinson's office and decided that Grierson should go ahead and get the options. This was done; not, of course, in Grierson's name. The next move, before the formation of the Riverside Company, was to "see" Mr. Judd Jason. The success or failure of the enterprise was in his hands. Mahomet must go to the mountain, and I went to Monahan's saloon, first having made an appointment. It was not the first time I had been there since I had made that first memorable visit, but I never quite got over the feeling of a neophyte before Buddha, though I did not go so far as to analyze the reason,—that in Mr. Jason I was brought face to face with the concrete embodiment of the philosophy I had adopted, the logical consequence of enlightened self- interest. If he had ever heard of it, he would have made no pretence of being anything else. Greatness, declares some modern philosopher, has no connection with virtue; it is the continued, strong and logical expression of some instinct; in Mr. Jason's case, the predatory instinct.

And like a true artist, he loved his career for itself—not for what its fruits could buy. He might have built a palace on the Heights with the tolls he took from the disreputable houses of the city; he was contented with Monahan's saloon: nor did he seek to propitiate a possible God by endowing churches and hospitals with a portion of his income. Try though I might, I never could achieve the perfection of this man's contempt for all other philosophies. The very fact of my going there in secret to that dark place of his from out of the bright, respectable region in which I lived was in itself an acknowledgment of this. I thought him a thief—a necessary thief—and he knew it: he was indifferent to it; and it amused him, I think, to see clinging to me, when I entered his presence, shreds of that morality which those of my world who dealt with him thought so needful for the sake of decency.

He was in bed, reading newspapers, as usual. An empty coffee-cup and a plate were on the littered table.

"Sit down, sit down, Paret," he said. "What do you hear from the Senator?"

I sat down, and gave him the news of Mr. Watling. He seemed, as usual, distrait, betraying no curiosity as to the object of my call, his lean, brown fingers playing with the newspapers on his lap. Suddenly, he flashed out at me one of those remarks which produced the uncanny conviction that, so far as affairs in the city were concerned, he was omniscient.

"I hear somebody has been getting options on that tract of land beyond the Heights, on the river."

He had "focussed."

"How did you hear that?" I asked.

He smiled.

"It's Grierson, ain't it?"

"Yes, it's Grierson," I said.

"How are you going to get your folks out there?" he demanded.

"That's what I've come to see you about. We want a franchise for Maplewood Avenue."

"Maplewood Avenue!" He lay back with his eyes closed, as though trying to visualize such a colossal proposal....

When I left him, two hours later, the details were all arranged, down to Mr. Jason's consideration from Riverside Company and the "fee" which his lawyer, Mr. Bitter, was to have for "presenting the case" before the Board of Aldermen. I went back to lunch at the Boyne Club, and to receive the congratulations of my friends. The next week the Riverside Company was formed, and I made out a petition to the Board of Aldermen for a franchise; Mr. Bitter appeared and argued: in short, the procedure so familiar to modern students of political affairs was gone through. The Maplewood Avenue residents rose en masse, supported by the City Improvement League. Perry Blackwood, as soon as he heard of the petition, turned up at my office. By this time I was occupying Mr. Watling's room.

"Look here," he began, as soon as the office-boy had closed the door behind him, "this is going it a little too strong."

"What is?" I asked, leaning back in my chair and surveying him.

"This proposed Maplewood Avenue Franchise. Hugh," he said, "you and I have been friends a good many years, Lucia and I are devoted to Maude."

I did not reply.

"I've seen all along that we've been growing apart," he added sadly. "You've got certain ideas about things which I can't share. I suppose I'm old fashioned. I can't trust myself to tell you what I think—what Tom and I think about this deal."

"Go ahead, Perry," I said.

He got up, plainly agitated, and walked to the window. Then he turned to me appealingly.

"Get out of it, for God's sake get out of it, before it's too late. For your own sake, for Maude's, for the children's. You don't realize what you are doing. You may not believe me, but the time will come when these fellows you are in with will be repudiated by the community,—their money won't help them. Tom and I are the best friends you have," he added, a little irrelevantly.

"And you think I'm going to the dogs."

"Now don't take it the wrong way," he urged.

"What is it you object to about the Maplewood franchise?" I asked. "If you'll look at a map of the city, you'll see that development is bound to come on that side. Maplewood Avenue is the natural artery, somebody will build a line out there, and if you'd rather have eastern capitalists—"

"Why are you going to get this franchise?" he demanded. "Because we haven't a decent city charter, and a healthy public spirit, you fellows are buying it from a corrupt city boss, and bribing a corrupt board of aldermen. That's the plain language of it. And it's only fair to warn you that I'm going to say so, openly."

"Be sensible," I answered. "We've got to have street railroads,—your family has one. We know what the aldermen are, what political conditions are. If you feel this way about it, the thing to do is to try to change them. But why blame me for getting a franchise for a company in the only manner in which, under present conditions, a franchise can be got? Do you want the city to stand still? If not, we have to provide for the new population."

"Every time you bribe these rascals for a franchise you entrench them," he cried. "You make it more difficult to oust them. But you mark my words, we shall get rid of them some day, and when that fight comes, I want to be in it."

He had grown very much excited; and it was as though this excitement suddenly revealed to me the full extent of the change that had taken place in him since he had left college. As he stood facing me, almost glaring at me through his eye-glasses, I beheld a slim, nervous, fault- finding doctrinaire, incapable of understanding the world as it was, lacking the force of his pioneer forefathers. I rather pitied him.

"I'm sorry we can't look at this thing alike, Perry," I told him. "You've said solve pretty hard things, but I realize that you hold your point of view in good faith, and that you have come to me as an old friend. I hope it won't make any difference in our personal relations."

"I don't see how it can help making a difference," he answered slowly. His excitement had cooled abruptly: he seemed dazed. At this moment my private stenographer entered to inform me that I was being called up on the telephone from New York. "Well, you have more important affairs to attend to, I won't bother you any more," he added.

"Hold on," I exclaimed, "this call can wait. I'd like to talk it over with you."

"I'm afraid it wouldn't be any use, Hugh," he said, and went out.

After talking with the New York client whose local interests I represented I sat thinking over the conversation with Perry. Considering Maude's intimacy with and affection for the Blackwoods, the affair was awkward, opening up many uncomfortable possibilities; and it was the prospect of discomfort that bothered me rather than regret for the probable loss of Perry's friendship. I still believed myself to have an affection for him: undoubtedly this was a sentimental remnant....

That evening after dinner Tom came in alone, and I suspected that Perry had sent him. He was fidgety, ill at ease, and presently asked if I could see him a moment in my study. Maude's glance followed us.

"Say, Hugh, this is pretty stiff," he blurted out characteristically, when the door was closed.

"I suppose you mean the Riverside Franchise," I said. He looked up at me, miserably, from the chair into which he had sunk, his hands in his pockets.

"You'll forgive me for talking about it, won't you? You used to lecture me once in a while at Cambridge, you know."

"That's all right—go ahead," I replied, trying to speak amiably.

"You know I've always admired you, Hugh,—I never had your ability," he began painfully, "you've gone ahead pretty fast,—the truth is that Perry and I have been worried about you for some time. We've tried not to be too serious in showing it, but we've felt that these modern business methods were getting into your system without your realizing it. There are some things a man's friends can tell him, and it's their duty to tell him. Good God, haven't you got enough, Hugh,—enough success and enough money, without going into a thing like this Riverside scheme?"

I was intensely annoyed, if not angry; and I hesitated a moment to calm myself.

"Tom, you don't understand my position," I said. "I'm willing to discuss it with you, now that you've opened up the subject. Perry's been talking to you, I can see that. I think Perry's got queer ideas,—to be plain with you, and they're getting queerer."

He sat down again while, with what I deemed a rather exemplary patience, I went over the arguments in favour of my position; and as I talked, it clarified in my own mind. It was impossible to apply to business an individual code of ethics,—even to Perry's business, to Tom's business: the two were incompatible, and the sooner one recognized that the better: the whole structure of business was built up on natural, as opposed to ethical law. We had arrived at an era of frankness—that was the truth— and the sooner we faced this truth the better for our peace of mind. Much as we might deplore the political system that had grown up, we had to acknowledge, if we were consistent, that it was the base on which our prosperity was built. I was rather proud of having evolved this argument; it fortified my own peace of mind, which had been disturbed by Tom's attitude. I began to pity him. He had not been very successful in life, and with the little he earned, added to Susan's income, I knew that a certain ingenuity was required to make both ends meet. He sat listening with a troubled look. A passing phase of feeling clouded for a brief moment my confidence when there arose in my mind an unbidden memory of my youth, of my father. He, too, had mistrusted my ingenuity. I recalled how I had out-manoeuvred him and gone to college; I remembered the March day so long ago, when Tom and I had stood on the corner debating how to deceive him, and it was I who had suggested the nice distinction between a boat and a raft. Well, my father's illogical attitude towards boyhood nature, towards human nature, had forced me into that lie, just as the senseless attitude of the public to-day forced business into a position of hypocrisy.

"Well, that's clever," he said, slowly and perplexedly, when I had finished. "It's damned clever, but somehow it looks to me all wrong. I can't pick it to pieces." He got up rather heavily. "I—I guess I ought to be going. Susan doesn't know where I am."

I was exasperated. It was clear, though he did not say so, that he thought me dishonest. The pain in his eyes had deepened.

"If you feel that way—" I said.

"Oh, God, I don't know how I feel!" he cried. "You're the oldest friend I have, Hugh,—I can't forget that. We'll say nothing more about it." He picked up his hat and a moment later I heard the front door close behind him. I stood for a while stock-still, and then went into the livingroom, where Maude was sewing.

"Why, where's Tom?" she inquired, looking up.

"Oh, he went home. He said Susan didn't know where he was."

"How queer! Hugh, was there anything the matter? Is he in trouble?" she asked anxiously.

I stood toying with a book-mark, reflecting. She must inevitably come to suspect that something had happened, and it would be as well to fortify her.

"The trouble is," I said after a moment, "that Perry and Tom would like to run modern business on the principle of a charitable institution. Unfortunately, it is not practical. They're upset because I have been retained by a syndicate whose object is to develop some land out beyond Maplewood Avenue. They've bought the land, and we are asking the city to give us a right to build a line out Maplewood Avenue, which is the obvious way to go. Perry says it will spoil the avenue. That's nonsense, in the first place. The avenue is wide, and the tracks will be in a grass plot in the centre. For the sake of keeping tracks off that avenue he would deprive people of attractive homes at a small cost, of the good air they can get beyond the heights; he would stunt the city's development."

"That does seem a little unreasonable," Maude admitted. "Is that all he objects to?"

"No, he thinks it an outrage because, in order to get the franchise, we have to deal with the city politicians. Well, it so happens, and always has happened, that politics have been controlled by leaders, whom Perry calls 'bosses,' and they are not particularly attractive men. You wouldn't care to associate with them. My father once refused to be mayor of the city for this reason. But they are necessities. If the people didn't want them, they'd take enough interest in elections to throw them out. But since the people do want them, and they are there, every time a new street-car line or something of that sort needs to be built they have to be consulted, because, without their influence nothing could be done. On the other hand, these politicians cannot afford to ignore men of local importance like Leonard Dickinson and Adolf Scherer and Miller Gorse who represent financial substance and' responsibility. If a new street- railroad is to be built, these are the logical ones to build it. You have just the same situation in Elkington, on a smaller scale.

"Your family, the Hutchinses, own the mills and the street-railroads, and any new enterprise that presents itself is done with their money, because they are reliable and sound."

"It isn't pleasant to think that there are such people as the politicians, is it?" said Maude, slowly.

"Unquestionably not," I agreed. "It isn't pleasant to think of some other crude forces in the world. But they exist, and they have to be dealt with. Suppose the United States should refuse to trade with Russia because, from our republican point of view, we regarded her government as tyrannical and oppressive? or to cooperate with England in some undertaking for the world's benefit because we contended that she ruled India with an iron hand? In such a case, our President and Senate would be scoundrels for making and ratifying a treaty. Yet here are Perry and Tom, and no doubt Susan and Lucia, accusing me, a lifetime friend, of dishonesty because I happen to be counsel for a syndicate that wishes to build a street-railroad for the convenience of the people of the city."

"Oh, no, not of dishonesty!" she exclaimed. "I can't—I won't believe they would do that."

"Pretty near it," I said. "If I listened to them, I should have to give up the law altogether."

"Sometimes," she answered in a low voice, "sometimes I wish you would."

"I might have expected that you would take their point of view."

As I was turning away she got up quickly and put her hand on my shoulder.

"Hugh, please don't say such things—you've no right to say them."

"And you?" I asked.

"Don't you see," she continued pleadingly, "don't you see that we are growing apart? That's the only reason I said what I did. It isn't that I don't trust you, that I don't want you to have your work, that I demand all of you. I know a woman can't ask that,—can't have it. But if you would only give me—give the children just a little, if I could feel that we meant something to you and that this other wasn't gradually becoming everything, wasn't absorbing you more and more, killing the best part of you. It's poisoning our marriage, it's poisoning all your relationships."

In that appeal the real Maude, the Maude of the early days of our marriage flashed forth again so vividly that I was taken aback. I understood that she had had herself under control, had worn a mask—a mask I had forced on her; and the revelation of the continued existence of that other Maude was profoundly disturbing. Was it true, as she said, that my absorption in the great game of modern business, in the modern American philosophy it implied was poisoning my marriage? or was it that my marriage had failed to satisfy and absorb me? I was touched—but sentimentally touched: I felt that this was a situation that ought to touch me; I didn't wish to face it, as usual: I couldn't acknowledge to myself that anything was really wrong... I patted her on the shoulder, I bent over and kissed her.

"A man in my position can't altogether choose just how busy he will be," I said smiling. "Matters are thrust upon me which I have to accept, and I can't help thinking about some of them when I come home. But we'll go off for a real vacation soon, Maude, to Europe—and take the children."

"Oh, I hope so," she said.

From this time on, as may be supposed, our intercourse with both the Blackwoods began to grow less frequent, although Maude continued to see a great deal of Lucia; and when we did dine in their company, or they with us, it was quite noticeable that their former raillery was suppressed. Even Tom had ceased to refer to me as the young Napoleon of the Law: he clung to me, but he too kept silent on the subject of business. Maude of course must have noticed this, must have sensed the change of atmosphere, have known that the Blackwoods, at least, were maintaining appearances for her sake. She did not speak to me of the change, nor I to her; but when I thought of her silence, it was to suspect that she was weighing the question which had led up to the difference between Perry and me, and I had a suspicion that the fact that I was her husband would not affect her ultimate decision. This faculty of hers of thinking things out instead of accepting my views and decisions was, as the saying goes, getting a little "on my nerves": that she of all women should have developed it was a recurring and unpleasant surprise. I began at times to pity myself a little, to feel the need of sympathetic companionship— feminine companionship....

I shall not go into the details of the procurement of what became known as the Riverside Franchise. In spite of the Maplewood residents, of the City Improvement League and individual protests, we obtained it with absurd ease. Indeed Perry Blackwood himself appeared before the Public Utilities Committee of the Board. of Aldermen, anal vas listened to with deference and gravity while he discoursed on the defacement of a beautiful boulevard to satisfy the greed of certain private individuals. Mr. Otto Bitter and myself, who appeared for the petitioners, had a similar reception. That struggle was a tempest in a tea-pot. The reformer raged, but he was feeble in those days, and the great public believed what it read in the respectable newspapers. In Mr. Judah B. Tallant's newspaper, for instance, the Morning Era, there were semi- playful editorials about "obstructionists." Mr. Perry Blackwood was a well-meaning, able gentleman of an old family, etc., but with a sentiment for horse-cars. The Era published also the resolutions which (with interesting spontaneity!) had been passed by our Board of Trade and Chamber of Commerce and other influential bodies in favour of the franchise; the idea—unknown to the public—of Mr. Hugh Paret, who wrote drafts of the resolutions and suggested privately to Mr. Leonard Dickinson that a little enthusiasm from these organizations might be helpful. Mr. Dickinson accepted the suggestion eagerly, wondering why he hadn't thought of it himself. The resolutions carried some weight with a public that did not know its right hand from its left.

After fitting deliberation, one evening in February the Board of Aldermen met and granted the franchise. Not unanimously, oh, no! Mr. Jason was not so simple as that! No further visits to Monahan's saloon on my part, in this connection were necessary; but Mr. Otto Bitter met me one day in the hotel with a significant message from the boss.

"It's all fixed," he informed me. "Murphy and Scott and Ottheimer and Grady and Loth are the decoys. You understand?"

"I think I gather your meaning," I said.

Mr. Bitter smiled by pulling down one corner of a crooked mouth.

"They'll vote against it on principle, you know," he added. "We get a little something from the Maple Avenue residents."

I've forgotten what the Riverside Franchise cost. The sum was paid in a lump sum to Mr. Bitter as his "fee,"—so, to their chagrin, a grand jury discovered in later years, when they were barking around Mr. Jason's hole with an eager district attorney snapping his whip over them. I remember the cartoon. The municipal geese were gone, but it was impossible to prove that this particular fox had used his enlightened reason in their procurement. Mr. Bitter was a legally authorized fox, and could take fees. How Mr. Jason was to be rewarded by the land company's left-hand, unknown, to the land company's right hand, became a problem worthy of a genius. The genius was found, but modesty forbids me to mention his name, and the problem was solved, to wit: the land company bought a piece of downtown property from—Mr. Ryerson, who was Mr. Grierson's real estate man and the agent for the land company, for a consideration of thirty thousand dollars. An unconfirmed rumour had it that Mr. Ryerson turned over the thirty thousand to Mr. Jason. Then the Riverside Company issued a secret deed of the same property back to Mr. Ryerson, and this deed was not recorded until some years later.

Such are the elaborate transactions progress and prosperity demand. Nature is the great teacher, and we know that her ways are at times complicated and clumsy. Likewise, under the "natural" laws of economics, new enterprises are not born without travail, without the aid of legal physicians well versed in financial obstetrics. One hundred and fifty to two hundred thousand, let us say, for the right to build tracks on Maplewood Avenue, and we sold nearly two million dollars worth of the securities back to the public whose aldermen had sold us the franchise. Is there a man so dead as not to feel a thrill at this achievement? And let no one who declares that literary talent and imagination are nonexistent in America pronounce final judgment until he reads that prospectus, in which was combined the best of realism and symbolism, for the labours of Alonzo Cheyne were not to be wasted, after all. Mr. Dickinson, who was a director in the Maplewood line, got a handsome underwriting percentage, and Mr. Berringer, also a director, on the bonds and preferred stock he sold. Mr. Paret, who entered both companies on the ground floor, likewise got fees. Everybody was satisfied except the trouble makers, who were ignored. In short, the episode of the Riverside Franchise is a triumphant proof of the contention that business men are the best fitted to conduct the politics of their country.

We had learned to pursue our happiness in packs, we knew that the Happy Hunting-Grounds are here and now, while the Reverend Carey Heddon continued to assure the maimed, the halt and the blind that their kingdom was not of this world, that their time was coming later. Could there have been a more idyl arrangement! Everybody should have been satisfied, but everybody was not. Otherwise these pages would never have been written.

Part Three

Chapter Eighteen

As the name of our city grew to be more and more a byword for sudden and fabulous wealth, not only were the Huns and the Slavs, the Czechs and the Greeks drawn to us, but it became the fashion for distinguished Englishmen and Frenchmen and sometimes Germans and Italians to pay us a visit when they made the grand tour of America. They had been told that they must not miss us; scarcely a week went by in our community—so it was said—in which a full-fledged millionaire was not turned out. Our visitors did not always remain a week,—since their rapid journeyings from the Atlantic to the Pacific, from Canada to the Gulf rarely occupied more than four,—but in the books embodying their mature comments on the manners, customs and crudities of American civilization no less than a chapter was usually devoted to us; and most of the adjectives in their various languages were exhausted in the attempt to prove how symptomatic we were of the ambitions and ideals of the Republic. The fact that many of these gentlemen—literary and otherwise—returned to their own shores better fed and with larger balances in the banks than when they departed is neither here nor there. Egyptians are proverbially created to be spoiled.

The wiser and more fortunate of these travellers and students of life brought letters to Mr. and Mrs. Hambleton Durrett. That household was symptomatic—if they liked—of the new order of things; and it was rare indeed when both members of it were at home to entertain them. If Mr. Durrett were in the city, and they did not happen to be Britons with sporting proclivities, they simply were not entertained: when Mrs. Durrett received them dinners were given in their honour on the Durrett gold plate, and they spent cosey and delightful hours conversing with her in the little salon overlooking the garden, to return to their hotels and jot down paragraphs on the superiority of the American women over the men. These particular foreigners did not lay eyes on Mr. Durrett, who was in Florida or in the East playing polo or engaged in some other pursuit. One result of the lavishness and luxury that amazed them they wrote—had been to raise the standard of culture of the women, who were our leisure class. But the travellers did not remain long enough to arrive at any conclusions of value on the effect of luxury and lavishness on the sacred institution of marriage.

If Mr. Nathaniel Durrett could have returned to his native city after fifteen years or so in the grave, not the least of the phenomena to startle him would have been that which was taking place in his own house. For he would have beheld serenely established in that former abode of Calvinism one of the most reprehensible of exotic abominations, a 'mariage de convenance;' nor could he have failed to observe, moreover, the complacency with which the descendants of his friends, the pew holders in Dr. Pound's church, regarded the matter: and not only these, but the city at large. The stronghold of Scotch Presbyterianism had become a London or a Paris, a Gomorrah!

Mrs. Hambleton Durrett went her way, and Mr. Durrett his. The less said about Mr. Durrett's way—even in this suddenly advanced age—the better. As for Nancy, she seemed to the distant eye to be walking through life in a stately and triumphant manner. I read in the newspapers of her doings, her comings and goings; sometimes she was away for months together, often abroad; and when she was at home I saw her, but infrequently, under conditions more or less formal. Not that she was formal,—or I: our intercourse seemed eloquent of an intimacy in a tantalizing state of suspense. Would that intimacy ever be renewed? This was a question on which I sometimes speculated. The situation that had suspended or put an end to it, as the case might be, was never referred to by either of us.

One afternoon in the late winter of the year following that in which we had given a dinner to the Scherers (where the Durretts had rather marvellously appeared together) I left my office about three o'clock—a most unusual occurrence. I was restless, unable to fix my mind on my work, filled with unsatisfied yearnings the object of which I sought to keep vague, and yet I directed my steps westward along Boyne Street until I came to the Art Museum, where a loan exhibition was being held. I entered, bought a catalogue, and presently found myself standing before number 103, designated as a portrait of Mrs.

Hambleton Durrett,—painted in Paris the autumn before by a Polish artist then much in vogue, Stanislaus Czesky. Nancy—was it Nancy?—was standing facing me, tall, superb in the maturity of her beauty, with one hand resting on an antique table, a smile upon her lips, a gentle mockery in her eyes as though laughing at the world she adorned. With the smile and the mockery— somehow significant, too, of an achieved inaccessibility—went the sheen of her clinging gown and the glint of the heavy pearls drooping from her high throat to her waist. These caught the eye, but failed at length to hold it, for even as I looked the smile faded, the mockery turned to wistfulness. So I thought, and looked again—to see the wistfulness: the smile had gone, the pearls seemed heavier. Was it a trick of the artist? had he seen what I saw, or thought I saw? or was it that imagination which by now I might have learned to suspect and distrust. Wild longings took possession of me, for the portrait had seemed to emphasize at once how distant now she was from me, and yet how near! I wanted to put that nearness to the test. Had she really changed? did anyone really change? and had I not been a fool to accept the presentment she had given me? I remembered those moments when our glances had met as across barriers in flashes of understanding. After all, the barriers were mere relics of the superstition of the past. What if I went to her now? I felt that I needed her as I never had needed anyone in all my life.... I was aroused by the sound of lowered voices beside me.

"That's Mrs. Hambleton Durrett," I heard a woman say. "Isn't she beautiful?"

The note of envy struck me sharply—horribly. Without waiting to listen to the comment of her companion I hurried out of the building into the cold, white sunlight that threw into bold relief the mediocre houses of the street. Here was everyday life, but the portrait had suggested that which might have been—might be yet. What did I mean by this? I didn't know, I didn't care to define it,—a renewal of her friendship, of our intimacy. My being cried out for it, and in the world in which I lived we took what we wanted—why not this? And yet for an instant I stood on the sidewalk to discover that in new situations I was still subject to unaccountable qualms of that thing I had been taught to call "conscience"; whether it were conscience or not must be left to the psychologists. I was married—terrible word! the shadow of that Institution fell athwart me as the sun went under a cloud; but the sun came out again as I found myself walking toward the Durrett house reflecting that numbers of married men called on Nancy, and that what I had in mind in regard to her was nothing that the court would have pronounced an infringement upon the Institution.... I reached her steps, the long steps still guarded by the curved wrought-iron railings reminiscent of Nathaniel's day, though the "portals" were gone, a modern vestibule having replaced them; I rang the bell; the butler, flung open the doors. He, at any rate, did not seem surprised to see me here, he greeted me with respectful cordiality and led me, as a favoured guest, through the big drawing-room into the salon.

"Mr. Paret, Madam!"

Nancy, rose quickly from the low chair where she sat cutting the pages of a French novel.

"Hugh!" she exclaimed. "I'm out if anyone calls. Bring tea," she added to the man, who retired. For a moment we stood gazing at each other, questioningly. "Well, won't you sit down and stay awhile?" she asked.

I took a chair on the opposite side of the fire.

"I just thought I'd drop in," I said.

"I am flattered," said Nancy, "that a person so affaire should find time to call on an old friend. Why, I thought you never left your office until seven o'clock."

"I don't, as a rule, but to-day I wasn't particularly busy, and I thought I'd go round to the Art Museum and look at your portrait."

"More flattery! Hugh, you're getting quite human. What do you think of it?"

"I like it. I think it quite remarkable."

"Have a cigarette!"

I took one.

"So you really like it," she said.

"Don't you?"

"Oh, I think it's a trifle—romantic," she replied "But that's Czesky. He made me quite cross,—the feminine presentation of America, the spoiled woman who has shed responsibilities and is beginning to have a glimpse—just a little one—of the emptiness of it all."

I was stirred.

"Then why do you accept it, if it isn't you?" I demanded. "One doesn't refuse Czesky's canvases," she replied. "And what difference does it make? It amused him, and he was fairly subtle about it. Only those who are looking for romance, like you, are able to guess what he meant, and they would think they saw it anyway, even if he had painted me—extinct."

"Extinct!" I repeated.

She laughed.

"Hugh, you're a silly old goose!"

"That's why I came here, I think, to be told so," I said.

Tea was brought in. A sense of at-homeness stole over me,—I was more at home here in this room with Nancy, than in any other place in the world; here, where everything was at once soothing yet stimulating, expressive of her, even the smaller objects that caught my eye,—the crystal inkstand tipped with gold, the racks for the table books, her paper-cutter. Nancy's was a discriminating luxury. And her talk! The lightness with which she touched life, the unexplored depths of her, guessed at but never fathomed! Did she feel a little the need of me as I felt the need of her?

"Why, I believe you're incurably romantic, Hugh," she said laughingly, when the men had left the room. "Here you are, what they call a paragon of success, a future senator, Ambassador to England. I hear of those remarkable things you have done—even in New York the other day a man was asking me if I knew Mr. Paret, and spoke of you as one of the coming men. I suppose you will be moving there, soon. A practical success! It always surprises me when I think of it, I find it difficult to remember what a dreamer you were and here you turn out to be still a dreamer! Have you discovered, too, the emptiness of it all?" she inquired provokingly. "I must say you don't look it"—she gave me a critical, quizzical glance—"you look quite prosperous and contented, as though you enjoyed your power."

I laughed uneasily.

"And then," she continued, "and then one day when your luncheon has disagreed with you—you walk into a gallery and see a portrait of—of an old friend for whom in youth, when you were a dreamer, you professed a sentimental attachment, and you exclaim that the artist is a discerning man who has discovered the secret that she has guarded so closely. She's sorry that she ever tried to console herself with baubles it's what you've suspected all along. But you'll just run around to see for yourself—to be sure of it." And she handed me my tea. "Come now, confess. Where are your wits—I hear you don't lack them in court."

"Well," I said, "if that amuses you—"

"It does amuse me," said Nancy, twining her fingers across her knee and regarding me smilingly, with parted lips, "it amuses me a lot—it's so characteristic."

"But it's not true, it's unjust," I protested vigorously, smiling, too, because the attack was so characteristic of her.

"What then?" she demanded.

"Well, in the first place, my luncheon didn't disagree with me. It never does."

She laughed. "But the sentiment—come now—the sentiment? Do you perceive any hint of emptiness—despair?"

Our chairs were very close, and she leaned forward a little.

"Emptiness or no emptiness," I said a little tremulously, "I know that I haven't been so contented, so happy for a long time."

She sat very still, but turned her gaze on the fire.

"You really wouldn't want to find that, Hugh," she said in another voice, at which I exclaimed. "No, I'm not being sentimental. But, to be serious, I really shouldn't care to think that of you. I'd like to think of you as a friend—a good friend—although we don't see very much of one another."

"But that's why I came, Nancy," I explained. "It wasn't just an impulse- -that is, I've been thinking of you a great deal, all along. I miss you, I miss the way you look at things—your point of view. I can't see any reason why we shouldn't see something of each other—now—"

She continued to stare into the fire.

"No," she said at length, "I suppose there isn't any reason." Her mood seemed suddenly to change as she bent over and extinguished the flame under the kettle. "After all," she added gaily, "we live in a tolerant age, we've reached the years of discretion, and we're both too conventional to do anything silly—even if we wanted to—which we don't. We're neither of us likely to quarrel with the world as it is, I think, and we might as well make fun of it together. We'll begin with our friends. What do you think of Mr. Scherer's palace?"

"I hear you're building it for him."

"I told him to get Eyre," said Nancy, laughingly, "I was afraid he'd repeat the Gallatin Park monstrosity on a larger scale, and Eyre's the only man in this country who understands the French. It's been rather amusing," she went on, "I've had to fight Hilda, and she's no mean antagonist. How she hates me! She wanted a monstrosity, of course, a modernized German rock-grotto sort of an affair, I can imagine. She's been so funny when I've met her at dinner. 'I understand you take a great interest in the house, Mrs. Durrett.' Can't you hear her?"

"Well, you did get ahead of her," I said.

"I had to. I couldn't let our first citizen build a modern Rhine castle, could I? I have some public spirit left. And besides, I expect to build on Grant Avenue myself."

"And leave here?"

"Oh, it's too grubby, it's in the slums," said Nancy. "But I really owe you a debt of gratitude, Hugh, for the Scherers."

"I'm told Adolf's lost his head over you."

"It's not only over me, but over everything. He's so ridiculously proud of being on the board of the Children's Hospital.... You ought to hear him talking to old Mrs. Ogilvy, who of course can't get used to him at all,—she always has the air of inquiring what he's doing in that galley. She still thinks of him as Mr. Durrett's foreman."

The time flew. Her presence was like a bracing, tingling atmosphere in which I felt revived and exhilarated, self-restored. For Nancy did not question—she took me as I was. We looked out on the world, as it were, from the same window, and I could not help thinking that ours, after all, was a large view. The topics didn't matter—our conversation was fragrant with intimacy; and we were so close to each other it seemed incredible that we ever should be parted again. At last the little clock on the mantel chimed an hour, she started and looked up.

"Why, it's seven, Hugh!" she exclaimed, rising. "I'd no idea it was so late, and I'm dining with the Dickinsons. I've only just time to dress."

"It's been like a reunion, hasn't it?—a reunion after many years," I said. I held her hand unconsciously—she seemed to be drawing me to her, I thought she swayed, and a sudden dizziness seized me. Then she drew away abruptly, with a little cry. I couldn't be sure about the cry, whether I heard it or not, a note was struck in the very depths of me.

"Come in again," she said, "whenever you're not too busy." And a minute later I found myself on the street.

This was the beginning of a new intimacy with Nancy, resembling the old intimacy yet differing from it. The emotional note of our parting on the occasion I have just related was not again struck, and when I went eagerly to see her again a few days later I was conscious of limitations,—not too conscious: the freedom she offered and which I gladly accepted was a large freedom, nor am I quite sure that even I would have wished it larger, though there were naturally moments when I thought so: when I asked myself what I did wish, I found no answer. Though I sometimes chafed, it would have been absurd of me to object to a certain timidity or caution I began to perceive in her that had been absent in the old Nancy; but the old Nancy had ceased to exist, and here instead was a highly developed, highly specialized creature in whom I delighted; and after taking thought I would not have robbed her of fine acquired attribute. As she had truly observed, we were both conventional; conventionality was part of the price we had willingly paid for membership in that rarer world we had both achieved. It was a world, to be sure, in which we were rapidly learning to take the law into our own hands without seeming to defy it, in order that the fear of it might remain in those less fortunately placed and endowed: we had begun with the appropriation of the material property of our fellow-citizens, which we took legally; from this point it was, of course, merely a logical step to take—legally, too other gentlemen's human property—their wives, in short: the more progressive East had set us our example, but as yet we had been chary to follow it.

About this time rebellious voices were beginning to make themselves heard in the literary wilderness proclaiming liberty—liberty of the sexes. There were Russian novels and French novels, and pioneer English novels preaching liberty with Nietzschean stridency, or taking it for granted. I picked these up on Nancy's table.

"Reading them?" she said, in answer to my query. "Of course I'm reading them. I want to know what these clever people are thinking, even if I don't always agree with them, and you ought to read them too. It's quite true what foreigners say about our men,—that they live in a groove, that they haven't any range of conversation."

"I'm quite willing to be educated," I replied. "I haven't a doubt that I need it."

She was leaning back in her chair, her hands behind her head, a posture she often assumed. She looked up at me amusedly.

"I'll acknowledge that you're more teachable than most of them," she said. "Do you know, Hugh, sometimes you puzzle me greatly. When you are here and we're talking together I can never think of you as you are out in the world, fighting for power—and getting it. I suppose it's part of your charm, that there is that side of you, but I never consciously realize it. You're what they call a dual personality."

"That's a pretty hard name!" I exclaimed.

She laughed.

"I can't help it—you are. Oh, not disagreeably so, quite normally— that's the odd thing about you. Sometimes I believe that you were made for something different, that in spite of your success you have missed your 'metier.'"

"What ought I to have been?"

"How can I tell? A Goethe, perhaps—a Goethe smothered by a twentieth- century environment. Your love of adventure isn't dead, it's been merely misdirected, real adventure, I mean, forth faring, straying into unknown paths. Perhaps you haven't yet found yourself."

"How uncanny!" I said, stirred and startled.

"You have a taste for literature, you know, though you've buried it. Give me Turgeniev. We'll begin with him...."

Her reading and the talks that followed it were exciting, amazingly stimulating.... Once Nancy gave me an amusing account of a debate which had taken place in the newly organized woman's discussion club to which she belonged over a rather daring book by an English novelist. Mrs. Dickinson had revolted.

"No, she wasn't really shocked, not in the way she thought she was," said Nancy, in answer to a query of mine.

"How was she shocked, then?"

"As you and I are shocked."

"But I'm not shocked," I protested.

"Oh, yes, you are, and so am I—not on the moral side, nor is it the moral aspect that troubles Lula Dickinson. She thinks it's the moral aspect, but it's really the revolutionary aspect, the menace to those precious institutions from which we derive our privileges and comforts."

I considered this, and laughed.

"What's the use of being a humbug about it," said Nancy.

"But you're talking like a revolutionary," I said.

"I may be talking like one, but I'm not one. I once had the makings of one—of a good one,—a 'proper' one, as the English would say." She sighed.

"You regret it?" I asked curiously.

"Of course I regret it!" she cried. "What woman worth her salt doesn't regret it, doesn't want to live, even if she has to suffer for it? And those people—the revolutionaries, I mean, the rebels—they live, they're the only ones who do live. The rest of us degenerate in a painless paralysis we think of as pleasure. Look at me! I'm incapable of committing a single original act, even though I might conceive one. Well, there was a time when I should have been equal to anything and wouldn't have cared a—a damn."

I believed her....

I fell into the habit of dropping in on Nancy at least twice a week on my way from the office, and I met her occasionally at other houses. I did not tell Maude of that first impulsive visit; but one evening a few weeks later she asked me where I had been, and when I told her she made no comment. I came presently to the conclusion that this renewed intimacy did not trouble her—which was what I wished to believe. Of course I had gone to Nancy for a stimulation I failed to get at home, and it is the more extraordinary, therefore, that I did not become more discontented and restless: I suppose this was because I had grown to regard marriage as most of the world regarded it, as something inevitable and humdrum, as a kind of habit it is useless to try to shake off. But life is so full of complexities and anomalies that I still had a real affection for Maude, and I liked her the more because she didn't expect too much of me, and because she didn't complain of my friendship with Nancy although I should vehemently have denied there was anything to complain of. I respected Maude. If she was not a squaw, she performed religiously the traditional squaw duties, and made me comfortable: and the fact that we lived separate mental existences did not trouble me because I never thought of hers—or even that she had one. She had the children, and they seemed to suffice. She never renewed her appeal for my confidence, and I forgot that she had made it.

Nevertheless I always felt a tug at my heartstrings when June came around and it was time for her and the children to go to Mattapoisett for the summer; when I accompanied them, on the evening of their departure, to the smoky, noisy station and saw deposited in the sleeping-car their luggage and shawls and bundles. They always took the evening train to Boston; it was the best. Tom and Susan were invariably there with candy and toys to see them off—if Susan and her children had not already gone —and at such moments my heart warmed to Tom. And I was astonished as I clung to Matthew and Moreton and little Biddy at the affection that welled up within me, saddened when I kissed Maude good-bye. She too was sad, and always seemed to feel compunctions for deserting me.

"I feel so selfish in leaving you all alone!" she would say. "If it weren't for the children—they need the sea air. But I know you don't miss me as I miss you. A man doesn't, I suppose.... Please don't work so hard, and promise me you'll come on and stay a long time. You can if you want to. We shan't starve." She smiled. "That nice room, which is yours, at the southeast corner, is always waiting for you. And you do like the sea, and seeing the sail-boats in the morning."

I felt an emptiness when the train pulled out. I did love my family, after all! I would go back to the deserted house, and I could not bear to look in at the nursery door, at the little beds with covers flung over them. Why couldn't I appreciate these joys when I had them?

One evening, as we went home in an open street-car together, after such a departure, Tom blurted out:—

"Hugh, I believe I care for your family as much as for my own. I often wonder if you realize how wonderful these children are! My boys are just plain ruffians—although I think they're pretty decent ruffians, but Matthew has a mind—he's thoughtful—and an imagination. He'll make a name for himself some day if he's steered properly and allowed to develop naturally. Moreton's more like my boys. And as for Chickabiddy!—" words failed him.

I put my hand on his knee. I actually loved him again as I had loved and yearned for him as a child,—he was so human, so dependable. And why couldn't this feeling last? He disapproved—foolishly, I thought—of my professional career, and this was only one of his limitations. But I knew that he was loyal. Why hadn't I been able to breathe and be reasonably happy in that atmosphere of friendship and love in which I had been placed—or rather in which I had placed myself?.... Before the summer was a day or two older I had grown accustomed to being alone, and enjoyed the liberty; and when Maude and the children returned in the autumn, similarly, it took me some days to get used to the restrictions imposed by a household. I run the risk of shocking those who read this by declaring that if my family had been taken permanently out of my life, I should not long have missed them. But on the whole, in those years my marriage relation might be called a negative one. There were moments, as I have described, when I warmed to Maude, moments when I felt something akin to a violent antagonism aroused by little mannerisms and tricks she had. The fact that we got along as well as we did was probably due to the orthodox teaching with which we had been inoculated,—to the effect that matrimony was a moral trial, a shaking-down process. But moral trials were ceasing to appeal to people, and more and more of them were refusing to be shaken down. We didn't cut the Gordian knot, but we managed to loosen it considerably.

I have spoken of a new species of titans who inhabited the giant buildings in Wall Street, New York, and fought among themselves for possession of the United States of America. It is interesting to note that in these struggles a certain chivalry was observed among the combatants, no matter how bitter the rivalry: for instance, it was deemed very bad form for one of the groups of combatants to take the public into their confidence; cities were upset and stirred to the core by these conflicts, and the citizens never knew who was doing the fighting, but imagined that some burning issue was at stake that concerned them. As a matter of fact the issue always did concern them, but not in the way they supposed.

Gradually, out of the chaotic melee in which these titans were engaged had emerged one group more powerful than the rest and more respectable, whose leader was the Personality to whom I have before referred. He and his group had managed to gain control of certain conservative fortresses in various cities such as the Corn National Bank and the Ashuela Telephone Company—to mention two of many: Adolf Scherer was his ally, and the Boyne Iron Works, Limited, was soon to be merged by him into a greater corporation still. Leonard Dickinson might be called his local governor-general. We manned the parapets and kept our ears constantly to the ground to listen for the rumble of attacks; but sometimes they burst upon us fiercely and suddenly, without warning. Such was the assault on the Ashuela, which for years had exercised an apparently secure monopoly of the city's telephone service, which had been able to ignore with complacency the shrillest protests of unreasonable subscribers. Through the Pilot it was announced to the public that certain benevolent "Eastern capitalists" were ready to rescue them from their thraldom if the city would grant them a franchise. Mr. Lawler, the disinterestedness of whose newspaper could not be doubted, fanned the flame day by day, sent his reporters about the city gathering instances of the haughty neglect of the Ashuela, proclaiming its instruments antiquated compared with those used in more progressive cities, as compared with the very latest inventions which the Automatic Company was ready to install provided they could get their franchise. And the prices! These, too, would fall— under competition. It was a clever campaign. If the city would give them a franchise, that Automatic Company—so well named! would provide automatic instruments. Each subscriber, by means of a numerical disk, could call up any other, subscriber; there would be no central operator, no listening, no tapping of wires; the number of calls would be unlimited. As a proof of the confidence of these Eastern gentlemen in our city, they were willing to spend five millions, and present more than six hundred telephones free to the city departments! What was fairer, more generous than this! There could be no doubt that popular enthusiasm was enlisted in behalf of the "Eastern Capitalists," who were made to appear in the light of Crusaders ready to rescue a groaning people from the thrall of monopoly. The excitement approached that of a presidential election, and became the dominant topic at quick-lunch counters and in street-cars. Cheap and efficient service! Down with the Bastille of monopoly!

As counsel for the Ashuela, Mr. Ogilvy sent for me, and by certain secret conduits of information at my disposal I was not long in discovering the disquieting fact that a Mr. Orthwein, who was described as a gentleman with fat fingers and a plausible manner, had been in town for a week and had been twice seen entering and emerging from Monahan's saloon. In short, Mr. Jason had already been "seen." Nevertheless I went to him myself, to find him for the first time in my experience absolutely non- committal.

"What's the Ashuela willing to do?" he demanded.

I mentioned a sum, and he shook his head. I mentioned another, and still he shook his head.

"Come 'round again," he said...

I was compelled to report this alarming situation to Ogilvy and Dickinson and a few chosen members of a panicky board of directors.

"It's that damned Grannis crowd," said Dickinson, mentioning an aggressive gentleman who had migrated from Chicago to Wall Street some five years before in a pink collar.

"But what's to be done?" demanded Ogilvy, playing nervously with a gold pencil on the polished table. He was one of those Americans who in a commercial atmosphere become prematurely white, and today his boyish, smooth-shaven face was almost as devoid of colour as his hair. Even Leonard Dickinson showed anxiety, which was unusual for him.

"You've got to fix it, Hugh," he said.

I did not see my way, but I had long ago learned to assume the unruffled air and judicial manner of speaking that inspires the layman with almost superstitious confidence in the lawyer....

"We'll find a way out," I said.

Mr. Jason, of course, held the key to the situation, and just how I was to get around him was problematical. In the meantime there was the public: to permit the other fellow to capture that was to be lacking in ordinary prudence; if its votes counted for nothing, its savings were desirable; and it was fast getting into a state of outrage against monopoly. The chivalry of finance did not permit of a revelation that Mr. Grannis and his buccaneers were behind the Automatic, but it was possible to direct and strengthen the backfire which the Era and other conservative newspapers had already begun. Mr. Tallant for delicate reasons being persona non grata at the Boyne Club, despite the fact that he had so many friends there, we met for lunch in a private room at the new hotel, and as we sipped our coffee and smoked our cigars we planned a series of editorials and articles that duly appeared. They made a strong appeal to the loyalty of our citizens to stand by the home company and home capital that had taken generous risks to give them service at a time when the future of the telephone business was by no means assured; they belittled the charges made by irresponsible and interested "parties," and finally pointed out, not without effect, that one logical consequence of having two telephone companies would be to compel subscribers in self- defence to install two telephones instead of one. And where was the saving in that?

"Say, Paret," said Judah B. when we had finished our labours; "if you ever get sick of the law, I'll give you a job on the Era's staff. This is fine, the way you put it. It'll do a lot of good, but how in hell are you going to handle Judd?...."

For three days the inspiration was withheld. And then, as I was strolling down Boyne Street after lunch gazing into the store windows it came suddenly, without warning. Like most inspirations worth anything, it was very simple. Within half an hour I had reached Monahan's saloon and found Mr. Jason out of bed, but still in his bedroom, seated meditatively at the window that looked over the alley.

"You know the crowd in New York behind this Automatic company as well as I do, Jason," I said. "Why do you want to deal with them when we've always been straight with you, when we're ready to meet them and go one better? Name your price."

"Suppose I do—what then," he replied. "This thing's gone pretty far. Under that damned new charter the franchise has got to be bid for—hasn't it? And the people want this company. There'll be a howl from one end of this town to the other if we throw 'em down."

"We'll look out for the public," I assured him, smiling.

"Well," he said, with one of his glances that were like flashes, "what you got up your sleeve?"

"Suppose another telephone company steps in, and bids a little higher for the franchise. That relieves, your aldermen of all responsibility, doesn't it?"

"Another telephone company!" he repeated.

I had already named it on my walk.

"The Interurban," I said.

"A dummy company?" said Mr. Jason.

"Lively enough to bid something over a hundred thousand to the city for its franchise," I replied.

Judd Jason, with a queer look, got up and went to a desk in a dark corner, and after rummaging for a few moments in one of the pigeon-holes, drew forth a glass cylinder, which he held out as he approached me.

"You get it, Mr. Paret," he said.

"What is it?" I asked, "a bomb!"

"That," he announced, as he twisted the tube about in his long fingers, holding it up to the light, "is the finest brand of cigars ever made in Cuba. A gentleman who had every reason to be grateful to me—I won't say who he was—gave me that once. Well, the Lord made me so's I can't appreciate any better tobacco than those five-cent 'Bobtails' Monahan's got downstairs, and I saved it. I saved it for the man who would put something over me some day, and—you get it."

"Thank you," I said, unconsciously falling in with the semi-ceremony of his manner. "I do not flatter myself that the solution I have suggested did not also occur to you."

"You'll smoke it?" he asked.

"Surely."

"Now? Here with me?"

"Certainly," I agreed, a little puzzled. As I broke the seal, pulled out the cork and unwrapped the cigar from its gold foil he took a stick and rapped loudly on the floor. After a brief interval footsteps were heard on the stairs and Mike Monahan, white aproned and scarlet faced, appeared at the door.

"Bobtails," said Mr. Jason, laconically.

"It's them I thought ye'd be wanting," said the saloon-keeper, holding out a handful. Judd Jason lighted one, and began smoking reflectively.

I gazed about the mean room, with its litter of newspapers and reports, its shabby furniture, and these seemed to have become incongruous, out of figure in the chair facing me keeping with the thoughtful figure in the chair facing me.

"You had a college education, Mr. Paret," he remarked at length.

"Yes."

"Life's a queer thing. Now if I'd had a college education, like you, and you'd been thrown on the world, like me, maybe I'd be livin' up there on Grant Avenue and you'd be down here over the saloon."

"Maybe," I said, wondering uneasily whether he meant to imply a similarity in our gifts. But his manner remained impassive, speculative.

"Ever read Carlyle's 'French Revolution'?" he asked suddenly.

"Why, yes, part of it, a good while ago."

"When you was in college?"

"Yes."

"I've got a little library here," he said, getting up and raising the shades and opening the glass doors of a bookcase which had escaped my attention. He took down a volume of Carlyle, bound in half calf.

"Wouldn't think I cared for such things, would you?" he demanded as he handed it to me.

"Well, you never can tell what a man's real tastes are until you know him," I observed, to conceal my surprise.

"That's so," he agreed. "I like books—some books. If I'd had an education, I'd have liked more of 'em, known more about 'em. Now I can read this one over and over. That feller Carlyle was a genius, he could look right into the bowels of the volcano, and he was on to how men and women feet down there, how they hate, how they square 'emselves when they get a chance."

He had managed to bring before me vividly that terrible, volcanic flow on Versailles of the Paris mob. He put back the book and resumed his seat.

"And I know how these people fed down here, below the crust," he went on, waving his cigar out of the window, as though to indicate the whole of that mean district. "They hate, and their hate is molten hell. I've been through it."

"But you've got on top," I suggested.

"Sure, I've got on top. Do you know why? it's because I hated—that's why. A man's feelings, if they're strong enough, have a lot to do with what he becomes."

"But he has to have ability, too," I objected.

"Sure, he has to have ability, but his feeling is the driving power if he feels strong enough, he can make a little ability go a long way."

I was struck by the force of this remark. I scarcely recognized Judd Jason. The man, as he revealed himself, had become at once more sinister and more fascinating.

"I can guess how some of those Jacobins felt when they had the aristocrats in the dock. They'd got on top—the Jacobins, I mean. It's human nature to want to get on top—ain't it?" He looked at me and smiled, but he did not seem to expect a reply. "Well, what you call society, rich, respectable society like you belong to would have made a bum and a criminal out of me if I hadn't been too smart for 'em, and it's a kind of satisfaction to have 'em coming down here to Monahan's for things they can't have without my leave. I've got a half Nelson on 'em. I wouldn't live up on Grant Avenue if you gave me Scherer's new house."

I was silent.

"Instead of starting my career in college, I started in jail," he went on, apparently ignoring any effect he may have produced. So subtly, so dispassionately indeed was he delivering himself of these remarks that it was impossible to tell whether he meant their application to be personal, to me, or general, to my associates. "I went to jail when I was fourteen because I wanted a knife to make kite sticks, and I stole a razor from a barber. I was bitter when they steered me into a lockup in Hickory Street. It was full of bugs and crooks, and they put me in the same cell with an old-timer named 'Red' Waters; who was one of the slickest safe- blowers around in those days. Red took a shine to me, found out I had a head piece, and said their gang could use a clever boy. If I'd go in with him, I could make all kinds of money. I guess I might have joined the gang if Red hadn't kept talking—about how the boss of his district named Gallagher would come down and get him out,—and sure enough Gallagher did come down and get him out. I thought I'd rather be Gallagher than Red—Red had to serve time once in a while. Soon as he got out I went down to Gallagher's saloon, and there was Red leaning over the bar. 'Here's a smart kid! he says, 'He and me were room-mates over in Hickory Street.' He got to gassing me, and telling me I'd better come along with him, when Gallagher came in. 'What is it ye'd like to be, my son?' says he. A politician, I told him. I was through going to jail. Gallagher had a laugh you could hear all over the place. He took me on as a kind of handy boy around the establishment, and by and by I began to run errands and find out things for him. I was boss of that ward myself when I was twenty-six.... How'd you like that cigar?"

I praised it.

"It ought to have been a good one," he declared. "Well, I don't want to keep you here all afternoon telling you my life story."

I assured him I had been deeply interested.

"Pretty slick idea of yours, that dummy company, Mr. Paret. Go ahead and organize it." He rose, which was contrary to his custom on the departure of a visitor. "Drop in again. We'll talk about the books."...

I walked slowly back reflecting on this conversation, upon the motives impelling Mr. Jason to become thus confidential; nor was it the most comforting thought in the world that the artist in me had appealed to the artist in him, that he had hailed me as a breather. But for the grace of God I might have been Mr. Jason and he Mr. Paret: undoubtedly that was what he had meant to imply... And I was forced to admit that he had succeeded—deliberately or not—in making the respectable Mr. Paret just a trifle uncomfortable.

In the marble vestibule of the Corn National Bank I ran into Tallant, holding his brown straw hat in his hand and looking a little more moth- eaten than usual.

"Hello, Paret," he said "how is that telephone business getting along?"

"Is Dickinson in?" I asked.

Tallant nodded.

We went through the cool bank, with its shining brass and red mahogany, its tiled floor, its busy tellers attending to files of clients, to the president's sanctum in the rear. Leonard Dickinson, very spruce and dignified in a black cutaway coat, was dictating rapidly to a woman, stenographer, whom he dismissed when he saw us. The door was shut.

"I was just asking Paret about the telephone affair," said Mr. Tallant.

"Well, have you found a way out?" Leonard Dickinson looked questioningly at me.

"It's all right," I answered. "I've seen Jason."

"All right!" they both ejaculated at once.

"We win," I said.

They stood gazing at me. Even Dickinson, who was rarely ruffled, seemed excited.

"Do you mean to say you've fixed it?" he demanded.

I nodded. They stared at me in amazement.

"How the deuce did you manage it?"

"We organize the Interurban Telephone Company, and bid for the franchise —that's all."

"A dummy company!" cried Tallant. "Why, it's simple as ABC!"

Dickinson smiled. He was tremendously relieved, and showed it.

"That's true about all great ideas, Tallant," he said. "They're simple, only it takes a clever man to think of them."

"And Jason agrees?" Tallant demanded.

I nodded again. "We'll have to outbid the Automatic people. I haven't seen Bitter yet about the—about the fee."

"That's all right," said Leonard Dickinson, quickly. "I take off my hat to you. You've saved us. You can ask any fee you like," he added genially. "Let's go over to—to the Ashuela and get some lunch." He had been about to say the Club, but he remembered Mr. Tallant's presence in time. "Nothing's worrying you, Hugh?" he added, as we went out, followed by the glances of his employees.

"Nothing," I said....

Chapter Nineteen

Making money in those days was so ridiculously easy! The trouble was to know how to spend it. One evening when I got home I told Maude I had a surprise for her.

"A surprise?" she asked, looking up from a little pink smock she was making for Chickabiddy.

"I've bought that lot on Grant Avenue, next to the Ogilvys'."

She dropped her sewing, and stared at me.

"Aren't you pleased?" I asked. "At last we are going to have a house of our very own. What's the matter?"

"I can't bear the thought of leaving here. I'm so used to it. I've grown to love it. It's part of me."

"But," I exclaimed, a little exasperated, "you didn't expect to live here always, did you? The house has been too small for us for years. I thought you'd be delighted." (This was not strictly true, for I had rather expected some such action on her part.) "Most women would. Of course, if it's going to make such a difference to you as that, I'll sell the lot. That won't be difficult."

I got up, and started to go into my study. She half rose, and her sewing fell to the floor.

"Oh, why are we always having misunderstandings? Do sit down a minute, Hugh. Don't think I'm not appreciative," she pleaded. "It was—such a shock."

I sat down rather reluctantly.

"I can't express what I think," she continued, rather breathlessly, "but sometimes I'm actually frightened, we're going through life so fast in these days, and it doesn't seem as if we were getting the real things out of it. I'm afraid of your success, and of all the money you're making."

I smiled.

"I'm not so rich yet, as riches go in these days, that you need be alarmed," I said.

She looked at me helplessly a moment.

"I feel that it isn't—right, somehow, that you'll pay for it, that we'll pay for it. Goodness knows, we have everything we want, and more too. This house—this house is real, and I'm afraid that won't be a home, won't be real. That we'll be overwhelmed with—with things!"...

She was interrupted by the entrance of the children. But after dinner, when she had seen them to bed, as was her custom, she came downstairs into my study and said quietly:—

"I was wrong, Hugh. If you want to build a house, if you feel that you'd be happier, I have no right to object. Of course my sentiment for this house is natural, the children were born here, but I've realized we couldn't live here always."

"I'm glad you look at it that way," I replied. "Why, we're already getting cramped, Maude, and now you're going to have a governess I don't know where you'd put her."

"Not too large, a house," she pleaded. "I know you think I'm silly, but this extravagance we see everywhere does make me uneasy. Perhaps it's because I'm provincial, and always shall be."

"Well, we must have a house large enough to be comfortable in," I said. "There's no reason why we shouldn't be comfortable." I thought it as well not to confess my ambitions, and I was greatly relieved that she did not reproach me for buying the lot without consulting her. Indeed, I was grateful for this unanticipated acquiescence, I felt nearer to her, than I had for a long time. I drew up another chair to my desk.

"Sit down and we'll make a few sketches, just for fun," I urged.

"Hugh," she said presently, as we were blacking out prospective rooms, "do you remember all those drawings and plans we made in England, on our wedding trip, and how we knew just what we wanted, and changed our minds every few days? And now we're ready to build, and haven't any ideas at all!"

"Yes," I answered—but I did not look at her.

"I have the book still—it's in the attic somewhere, packed away in a box. I suppose those plans would seem ridiculous now."

It was quite true,—now that we were ready to build the home that had been deferred so long, now that I had the money to spend without stint on its construction, the irony of life had deprived me of those strong desires and predilections I had known on my wedding trip. What a joy it would have been to build then! But now I found myself: wholly lacking in definite ideas as to style and construction. Secretly, I looked forward to certain luxuries, such as a bedroom and dressing-room and warm tiled bathroom all to myself bachelor privacies for which I had longed. Two mornings later at the breakfast table Maude asked me if I had thought of an architect.

"Why, Archie Lammerton, I suppose. Who else is there? Have you anyone else in mind?"

"N-no," said Maude. "But I heard of such a clever man in Boston, who doesn't charge Mr. Lammerton's prices; and who designs such beautiful private houses."

"But we can afford to pay Lammerton's prices," I replied, smiling. "And why shouldn't we have the best?"

"Are you sure—he is the best, Hugh?"

"Everybody has him," I said.

Maude smiled in return.

"I suppose that's a good reason," she answered.

"Of course it's a good reason," I assured her. "These people—the people we know—wouldn't have had Lammerton unless he was satisfactory. What's the matter with his houses?"

"Well," said Maude, "they're not very original. I don't say they're not good, in away, but they lack a certain imagination. It's difficult for me to express what I mean, 'machine made' isn't precisely the idea, but there should be a certain irregularity in art—shouldn't there? I saw a reproduction in one of the architectural journals of a house in Boston by a man named Frey, that seemed to me to have great charm."

Here was Lucia, unmistakably.

"That's all very well," I said impatiently, "but when one has to live in a house, one wants something more than artistic irregularity. Lammerton knows how to build for everyday existence; he's a practical man, as well as a man of taste, he may not be a Christopher Wrenn, but he understands conveniences and comforts. His chimneys don't smoke, his windows are tight, he knows what systems of heating are the best, and whom to go to: he knows what good plumbing is. I'm rather surprised you don't appreciate that, Maude, you're so particular as to what kind of rooms the children shall have, and you want a schoolroom-nursery with all the latest devices, with sun and ventilation. The Berringers wouldn't have had him, the Hollisters and Dickinsons wouldn't have had him if his work lacked taste."

"And Nancy wouldn't have had him," added Maude, and she smiled once more.

"Well, I haven't consulted Nancy, or anyone else," I replied—a little tartly, perhaps. "You don't seem to realize that some fashions may have a basis of reason. They are not all silly, as Lucia seems to think. If Lammerton builds satisfactory houses, he ought to be forgiven for being the fashion, he ought to have a chance." I got up to leave. "Let's see what kind of a plan he'll draw up, at any rate."

Her glance was almost indulgent.

"Of course, Hugh. I want you to be satisfied, to be pleased," she said.

"And you?" I questioned, "you are to live in the house more than I."

"Oh, I'm sure it will turn out all right," she replied. "Now you'd better run along, I know you're late."

"I am late," I admitted, rather lamely. "If you don't care for Lammerton's drawings, we'll get another architect."

Several years before Mr. Lammerton had arrived among us with a Beaux Arts moustache and letters of introduction to Mrs. Durrett and others. We found him the most adaptable, the most accommodating of young men, always ready to donate his talents and his services to private theatricals, tableaux, and fancy-dress balls, to take a place at a table at the last moment. One of his most appealing attributes was his "belief" in our city,—a form of patriotism that culminated, in later years, in "million population" clubs. I have often heard him declare, when the ladies had left the diningroom, that there was positively no limit to our future growth; and, incidentally, to our future wealth. Such sentiments as these could not fail to add to any man's popularity, and his success was a foregone conclusion. Almost before we knew it he was building the new Union Station of which he had foreseen the need, to take care of the millions to which our population was to be swelled; building the new Post Office that the unceasing efforts of Theodore Watling finally procured for us: building, indeed, Nancy's new house, the largest of our private mansions save Mr. Scherer's, a commission that had immediately brought about others from the Dickinsons and the Berringers.... That very day I called on him in his offices at the top of one of our new buildings, where many young draftsmen were bending over their boards. I was ushered into his private studio.

"I suppose you want something handsome, Hugh," he said, looking at me over his cigarette, "something commensurate with these fees I hear you are getting."

"Well, I want to be comfortable," I admitted.

We lunched at the Club together, where we talked over the requirements.

When he came to dinner the next week and spread out his sketch on the living-room table Maude drew in her breath.

"Why, Hugh," she exclaimed in dismay, "it's as big as—as big as the White House!"

"Not quite," I answered, laughing with Archie. "We may as well take our ease in our old age."

"Take our ease!" echoed Maude. "We'll rattle 'round in it. I'll never get used to it."

"After a month, Mrs. Paret, I'll wager you'll be wondering how you ever got along without it," said Archie.

It was not as big as the White House, yet it could not be called small. I had seen, to that. The long facade was imposing, dignified, with a touch of conventionality and solidity in keeping with my standing in the city. It was Georgian, of plum-coloured brick with marble trimmings and marble wedges over the ample windows, some years later I saw the house by Ferguson, of New York, from which Archie had cribbed it. At one end, off the dining-room, was a semicircular conservatory. There was a small portico, with marble pillars, and in the ample, swift sloping roof many dormers; servants' rooms, Archie explained. The look of anxiety on Maude's face deepened as he went over the floor plans, the reception-room; dining room to seat thirty, the servants' hall; and upstairs Maude's room, boudoir and bath and dress closet, my "apartments" adjoining on one side and the children's on the other, and the guest-rooms with baths....

Maude surrendered, as one who gives way to the inevitable. When the actual building began we both of us experienced, I think; a certain mild excitement; and walked out there, sometimes with the children, in the spring evenings, and on Sunday afternoons. "Excitement" is, perhaps, too strong a word for my feelings: there was a pleasurable anticipation on my part, a looking forward to a more decorous, a more luxurious existence; a certain impatience at the delays inevitable in building. But a new legal commercial enterprise of magnitude began to absorb me at his time, and somehow the building of this home—the first that we possessed was not the event it should have been; there were moments when I felt cheated, when I wondered what had become of that capacity for enjoyment which in my youth had been so keen. I remember indeed, one grey evening when I went there alone, after the workmen had departed, and stood in the litter of mortar and bricks and boards gazing at the completed front of the house. It was even larger than I had imagined it from the plans; in the Summer twilight there was an air about it,—if not precisely menacing, at least portentous, with its gaping windows and towering roof. I was a little tired from a hard day; I had the odd feeding of having raised up something with which—momentarily at least—I doubted my ability to cope: something huge, impersonal; something that ought to have represented a fireside, a sanctuary, and yet was the embodiment of an element quite alien to the home; a restless element with which our American atmosphere had, by invisible degrees, become charged. As I stared at it, the odd fancy seized me that the building somehow typified my own career.... I had gained something, in truth, but had I not also missed something? something a different home would have embodied?

Maude and the children had gone, to the seaside.

With a vague uneasiness I turned away from the contemplation of those walls. The companion mansions were closed, their blinds tightly drawn; the neighbourhood was as quiet as the country, save for a slight but persistent noise that impressed itself on my consciousness. I walked around the house to spy in the back yard; a young girl rather stealthily gathering laths, and fragments of joists and flooring, and loading them into a child's express-wagon. She started when she saw me. She was little, more than a child, and the loose calico dress she wore seemed to emphasize her thinness. She stood stock-still, staring at me with frightened yet defiant eyes. I, too, felt a strange timidity in her presence.

"Why do you stop?" I asked at length.

"Say, is this your heap?" she demanded.

I acknowledged it. A hint of awe widened her eyes. Then site glanced at the half-filled wagon.

"This stuff ain't no use to you, is it?"

"No, I'm glad to have you take it."

She shifted to the other foot, but did not continue her gathering. An impulse seized me, I put down my walkingstick and began picking up pieces of wood, flinging them into the wagon. I looked at her again, rather furtively; she had not moved. Her attitude puzzled me, for it was one neither of surprise nor of protest. The spectacle of the "millionaire" owner of the house engaged in this menial occupation gave her no thrills. I finished the loading.

"There!" I said, and drew a dollar bill out of my pocket and gave it to her. Even then she did not thank me, but took up the wagon tongue and went off, leaving on me a disheartening impression of numbness, of life crushed out. I glanced up once more at the mansion I had built for myself looming in the dusk, and walked hurriedly away....

One afternoon some three weeks after we had moved into the new house, I came out of the Club, where I had been lunching in conference with Scherer and two capitalists from New York. It was after four o'clock, the day was fading, the street lamps were beginning to cast sickly streaks of jade-coloured light across the slush of the pavements. It was the sight of this slush (which for a brief half hour that morning had been pure snow, and had sent Matthew and Moreton and Biddy into ecstasies at the notion of a "real Christmas"), that brought to my mind the immanence of the festival, and the fact that I had as yet bought no presents. Such was the predicament in which I usually found myself on Christmas eve; and it was not without a certain sense of annoyance at the task thus abruptly confronting me that I got into my automobile and directed the chauffeur to the shopping district. The crowds surged along the wet sidewalks and overflowed into the street, and over the heads of the people I stared at the blazing shop-windows decked out in Christmas greens. My chauffeur, a bristly-haired Parisian, blew his horn insolently, men and women jostled each other to get out of the way, their holiday mood giving place to resentment as they stared into the windows of the limousine. With the American inability to sit still I shifted from one corner of the seat to another, impatient at the slow progress of the machine: and I felt a certain contempt for human beings, that they should make all this fuss, burden themselves with all these senseless purchases, for a tradition. The automobile stopped, and I fought my way across the sidewalk into the store of that time-honoured firm, Elgin, Yates and Garner, pausing uncertainly before the very counter where, some ten years before, I had bought an engagement ring. Young Mr. Garner himself spied me, and handing over a customer to a tired clerk, hurried forward to greet me, his manner implying that my entrance was in some sort an event. I had become used to this aroma of deference.

"What can I show you, Mr. Paret?" he asked.

"I don't know—I'm looking around," I said, vaguely, bewildered by the glittering baubles by which I was confronted. What did Maude want? While I was gazing into the case, Mr. Garner opened a safe behind him, laying before me a large sapphire set with diamonds in a platinum brooch; a beautiful stone, in the depths of it gleaming a fire like a star in an arctic sky. I had not given Maude anything of value of late. Decidedly, this was of value; Mr. Garner named the price glibly; if Mrs. Paret didn't care for it, it might be brought back or exchanged. I took it, with a sigh of relief. Leaving the store, I paused on the edge of the rushing stream of humanity, with the problem of the children's gifts still to be solved. I thought of my own childhood, when at Christmastide I had walked with my mother up and down this very street, so changed and modernized now; recalling that I had had definite desires, desperate ones; but my imagination failed me when I tried to summon up the emotions connected with them. I had no desires now: I could buy anything in reason in the whole street. What did Matthew and Moreton want? and little Biddy? Maude had not "spoiled" them; but they didn't seem to have any definite wants. The children made me think, with a sudden softening, of Tom Peters, and I went into a tobacconist's and bought him a box of expensive cigars. Then I told the chauffeur to take me to a toy-shop, where I stood staring through a plate-glass window at the elaborate playthings devised for the modern children of luxury. In the centre was a toy man-of-war, three feet in length, with turrets and guns, and propellers and a real steam-engine. As a boy I should have dreamed about it, schemed for it, bartered my immortal soul for it. But—if I gave it to Matthew, what was there for Moreton? A steam locomotive caught my eye, almost as elaborate. Forcing my way through the doors, I captured a salesman, and from a state bordering on nervous collapse he became galvanized into an intense alertness and respect when he understood my desires. He didn't know the price of the objects in question. He brought the proprietor, an obsequious little German who, on learning my name, repeated it in every sentence. For Biddy I chose a doll that was all but human; when held by a young woman for my inspection, it elicited murmurs of admiration from the women shoppers by whom we were surrounded. The proprietor promised to make a special delivery of the three articles before seven o'clock....

Presently the automobile, after speeding up the asphalt of Grant Avenue, stopped before the new house. In spite of the change that house had made in my life, in three weeks I had become amazingly used to it; yet I had an odd feeling that Christmas eve as I stood under the portico with my key in the door, the same feeling of the impersonality of the place which I had experienced before. Not that for one moment I would have exchanged it for the smaller house we had left. I opened the door. How often, in that other house, I had come in the evening seeking quiet, my brain occupied with a problem, only to be annoyed by the romping of the children on the landing above. A noise in one end of it echoed to the other. But here, as I entered the hall, all was quiet: a dignified, deep-carpeted stairway swept upward before me, and on either side were wide, empty rooms; and in the subdued light of one of them I saw a dark figure moving silently about—the butler. He came forward to relieve me, deftly, of my hat and overcoat. Well, I had it at last, this establishment to which I had for so long looked forward. And yet that evening, as I hesitated in the hall, I somehow was unable to grasp that it was real and permanent, the very solidity of the walls and doors paradoxically suggested transientness, the butler a flitting ghost. How still the place was! Almost oppressively still. I recalled oddly a story of a peasant who, yearning for the great life, had stumbled upon an empty palace, its tables set with food in golden dishes. Before two days had passed he had fled from it in horror back to his crowded cottage and his drudgery in the fields. Never once had the sense of possession of the palace been realized. Nor did I feel that I possessed this house, though I had the deeds of it in my safe and the receipted bills in my files. It eluded me; seemed, in my, bizarre mood of that evening, almost to mock me. "You have built me," it seemed to say, "but I am stronger than you, because you have not earned me." Ridiculous, when the years of my labour and the size of my bank account were considered! Such, however, is the verbal expression of my feeling. Was the house empty, after all? Had something happened? With a slight panicky sensation I climbed the stairs, with their endless shallow treads, to hurry through the silent hallway to the schoolroom. Reassuring noises came faintly through the heavy door. I opened it. Little Biddy was careening round and round, crying out:—

"To-morrow's Chris'mas! Santa Claus is coming tonight."

Matthew was regarding her indulgently, sympathetically, Moreton rather scornfully. The myth had been exploded for both, but Matthew still hugged it. That was the difference between them. Maude, seated on the floor, perceived me first, and glanced up at me with a smile.

"It's father!" she said.

Biddy stopped in the midst of a pirouette. At the age of seven she was still shy with me, and retreated towards Maude.

"Aren't we going to have a tree, father?" demanded Moreton, aggressively. "Mother won't tell us—neither will Miss Allsop."

Miss Allsop was their governess.

"Why do you want a tree?" I asked.

"Oh, for Biddy," he said.

"It wouldn't be Christmas without a tree," Matthew declared, "—and Santa Claus," he added, for his sister's benefit.

"Perhaps Santa Claus, when he sees we've got this big house, will think we don't need anything, and go on to some poorer children," said Maude. "You wouldn't blame him if he did that,—would you?"

The response to this appeal cannot be said to have been enthusiastic....

After dinner, when at last all of them were in bed, we dressed the tree; it might better be said that Maude and Miss Allsop dressed it, while I gave a perfunctory aid. Both the women took such a joy in the process, vying with each other in getting effects, and as I watched them eagerly draping the tinsel and pinning on the glittering ornaments I wondered why it was that I was unable to find the same joy as they. Thus it had been every Christmas eve. I was always tired when I got home, and after dinner relaxation set in.

An electrician had come while we were at the table, and had fastened on the little electric bulbs which did duty as candles.

"Oh," said Maude, as she stood off to survey the effect, "isn't it beautiful! Come, Miss Allsop, let's get the presents."

They flew out of the room, and presently hurried back with their arms full of the usual parcels: parcels from Maude's family in Elkington, from my own relatives, from the Blackwoods and the Peterses, from Nancy. In the meantime I had had my own contributions brought up, the man of war, the locomotive, the big doll. Maude stood staring.

"Hugh, they'll be utterly ruined!" she exclaimed.

"The boys might as well have something instructive," I replied, "and as for Biddy—nothing's too good for her."

"I might have known you wouldn't forget them, although you are so busy."....

We filled the three stockings hung by the great fireplace. Then, with a last lingering look at the brightness of the tree, she stood in the doorway and turned the electric switch.

"Not before seven to-morrow morning, Miss Allsop," she said. "Hugh, you will get up, won't you? You mustn't miss seeing them. You can go back to bed again."

I promised.

Evidently, this was Reality to Maude. And had it not been one of my dreams of marriage, this preparing for the children's Christmas, remembering the fierce desires of my own childhood? It struck me, after I had kissed her good night and retired to my dressing-room, that fierce desires burned within me still, but the objects towards which their flames leaped out differed. That was all. Had I remained a child, since my idea of pleasure was still that of youth? The craving far excitement, adventure, was still unslaked; the craving far freedom as keen as ever. During the whole of my married life, I had been conscious of an inner protest against "settling down," as Tom Peters had settled down. The smaller house from which we had moved, with its enforced propinquity, hard emphasized the bondage of marriage. Now I had two rooms to myself, in the undisputed possession of which I had taken a puerile delight. On one side of my dressing-room Archie Lammerton had provided a huge closet containing the latest devices for the keeping of a multitudinous wardrobe; there was a reading-lamp, and the easiest of easy-chairs, imported from England, while between the windows were shelves of Italian walnut which I had filled with the books I had bought while at Cambridge, and had never since opened. As I sank down in my chair that odd feeling of uneasiness, of transience and unreality, of unsatisfaction I had had ever since we had moved suddenly became intensified, and at the very moment when I had gained everything I had once believed a man could desire! I was successful, I was rich, my health had not failed, I had a wife who catered to my wishes, lovable children who gave no trouble and yet—there was still the void to be filled, the old void I had felt as a boy, the longing for something beyond me, I knew not what; there was the strange inability to taste any of these things, the need at every turn for excitement, for a stimulus. My marriage had been a disappointment, though I strove to conceal this from myself; a disappointment because it had not filled the requirements of my category—excitement and mystery: I had provided the setting and lacked the happiness. Another woman Nancy— might have given me the needed stimulation; and yet my thoughts did not dwell on Nancy that night, my longings were not directed towards her, but towards the vision of a calm, contented married happiness I had looked forward to in youth,—a vision suddenly presented once more by the sight of Maude's simple pleasure in dressing the Christmas tree. What restless, fiendish element in me prevented my enjoying that? I had something of the fearful feeling of a ghost in my own house and among my own family, of a spirit doomed to wander, unable to share in what should have been my own, in what would have saved me were I able to partake of it. Was it too late to make that effort?.... Presently the strains of music pervaded my consciousness, the chimes of Trinity ringing out in the damp night the Christmas hymn, Adeste Fideles. It was midnight it was Christmas. How clear the notes rang through the wet air that came in at my window! Back into the dim centuries that music led me, into candle- lit Gothic chapels of monasteries on wind-swept heights above the firs, and cathedrals in mediaeval cities. Twilight ages of war and scourge and stress and storm—and faith. "Oh, come, all ye Faithful!" What a strange thing, that faith whose flame so marvellously persisted, piercing the gloom; the Christmas myth, as I had heard someone once call it. Did it possess the power to save me? Save me from what? Ah, in this hour I knew. In the darkness the Danger loomed up before me, vague yet terrible, and I trembled. Why was not this Thing ever present, to chasten and sober me? The Thing was myself.

Into my remembrance, by what suggestion I know not, came that March evening when I had gone to Holder Chapel at Harvard to listen to a preacher, a personality whose fame and influence had since spread throughout the land. Some dim fear had possessed me then. I recalled vividly the man, and the face of Hermann Krebs as I drew back from the doorway....

When I awoke my disquieting, retrospective mood had disappeared, and yet there clung to me, minus the sanction of fear or reward or revealed truth, a certain determination to behave, on this day at least, more like a father and a husband: to make an effort to enter into the spirit of the festival, and see what happened. I dressed in cheerful haste, took the sapphire pendant from its velvet box, tiptoed into the still silent schoolroom and hung it on the tree, flooding on the electric light that set the tinsel and globes ablaze. No sooner had I done this than I heard the patter of feet in the hallway, and a high-pitched voice—Biddy's— crying out:—

"It's Santa Claus!"

Three small, flannel-wrappered figures stood in the doorway.

"Why, it's father!" exclaimed Moreton.

"And he's all dressed!" said Matthew.

"Oh-h-h!" cried Biddy, staring at the blazing tree, "isn't it beautiful!"

Maude was close behind them. She gave an exclamation of delighted surprise when she saw me, and then stood gazing with shining eyes at the children, especially at Biddy, who stood dazzled by the glory of the constellation confronting her.... Matthew, too, wished to prolong the moment of mystery. It was the practical Moreton who cried:—

"Let's see what we've got!"

The assault and the sacking began. I couldn't help thinking as I watched them of my own wildly riotous, Christmas-morning sensations, when all the gifts had worn the aura of the supernatural; but the arrival of these toys was looked upon by my children as a part of the natural order of the universe. At Maude's suggestion the night before we had placed my presents, pieces de resistance, at a distance from the tree, in the hope that they would not be spied at once, that they would be in some sort a climax. It was Matthew who first perceived the ship, and identified it, by the card, as his property. To him it was clearly wonderful, but no miracle. He did not cry out, or call the attention of the others to it, but stood with his feet apart, examining it, his first remark being a query as to why it didn't fly the American flag. It's ensign was British. Then Moreton saw the locomotive, was told that it was his, and took possession of it violently. Why wasn't there more track? Wouldn't I get more track? I explained that it would go by steam, and he began unscrewing the cap on the little boiler until he was distracted by the man-of-war, and with natural acquisitiveness started to take possession of that. Biddy was bewildered by the doll, which Maude had taken up and was holding in her lap. She had had talking dolls before, and dolls that closed their eyes; she recognized this one, indeed, as a sort of super- doll, but her little mind was modern, too, and set no limits on what might be accomplished. She patted it, but was more impressed by the raptures of Miss Allsop, who had come in and was admiring it with some extravagance. Suddenly the child caught sight of her stocking, until now forgotten, and darted for the fireplace.

I turned to Maude, who stood beside me, watching them.

"But you haven't looked on the tree yourself," I reminded her.

She gave me an odd, questioning glance, and got up and set down the doll. As she stood for a moment gazing at the lights, she seemed very girlish in her dressing-gown, with her hair in two long plaits down her back.

"Oh, Hugh!" She lifted the pendant from the branch and held it up. Her gratitude, her joy at receiving a present was deeper than the children's!

"You chose it for me?"

I felt something like a pang when I thought how little trouble it had been.

"If you don't like it," I said, "or wish to have it changed—"

"Changed!" she exclaimed reproachfully. "Do you think I'd change it? Only—it's much too valuable—"

I smiled.... Miss Allsop deftly undid the clasp and hung it around Maude's neck.

"How it suits you, Mrs. Paret!" she cried....

This pendant was by no means the only present I had given Maude in recent years, and though she cared as little for jewels as for dress she seemed to attach to it a peculiar value and significance that disturbed and smote me, for the incident had revealed a love unchanged and unchangeable. Had she taken my gift as a sign that my indifference was melting?

As I went downstairs and into the library to read the financial page of the morning newspaper I asked myself, with a certain disquiet, whether, in the formal, complicated, and luxurious conditions in which we now lived it might be possible to build up new ties and common interests. I reflected that this would involve confessions and confidences on my part, since there was a whole side of my life of which Maude knew nothing. I had convinced myself long ago that a man's business career was no affair of his wife's: I had justified that career to myself: yet I had always had a vague feeling that Maude, had she known the details, would not have approved of it. Impossible, indeed, for a woman to grasp these problems. They were outside of her experience.

Nevertheless, something might be done to improve our relationship, something which would relieve me of that uneasy lack of unity I felt when at home, of the lassitude and ennui I was wont to feel creeping over me on Sundays and holidays....

Chapter Twenty

I find in relating those parts of my experience that seem to be of most significance I have neglected to tell of my mother's death, which occurred the year before we moved to Grant Avenue. She had clung the rest of her days to the house in which I had been born. Of late years she had lived in my children, and Maude's devotion to her had been unflagging. Truth compels me to say that she had long ceased to be a factor in my life. I have thought of her in later years.

Coincident with the unexpected feeling of fruitlessness that came to me with the Grant Avenue house, of things achieved but not realized or appreciated, was the appearance of a cloud on the business horizon; or rather on the political horizon, since it is hard to separate the two realms. There were signs, for those who could read, of a rising popular storm. During the earliest years of the new century the political atmosphere had changed, the public had shown a tendency to grow restless; and everybody knows how important it is for financial operations, for prosperity, that the people should mind their own business. In short, our commercial-romantic pilgrimage began to meet with unexpected resistance. It was as though the nation were entering into a senseless conspiracy to kill prosperity.

In the first place, in regard to the Presidency of the United States, a cog had unwittingly been slipped. It had always been recognized—as I have said—by responsible financial personages that the impulses of the majority of Americans could not be trusted, that these—who had inherited illusions of freedom—must be governed firmly yet with delicacy; unknown to them, their Presidents must be chosen for them, precisely as Mr. Watling had been chosen for the people of our state, and the popular enthusiasm manufactured later. There were informal meetings in New York, in Washington, where candidates were discussed; not that such and such a man was settled upon,—it was a process of elimination. Usually the affair had gone smoothly. For instance, a while before, a benevolent capitalist of the middle west, an intimate of Adolf Scherer, had become obsessed with the idea that a friend of his was the safest and sanest man for the head of the nation, had convinced his fellow-capitalists of this, whereupon he had gone ahead to spend his energy and his money freely to secure the nomination and election of this gentleman.

The Republican National Committee, the Republican National Convention were allowed to squabble to their hearts' content as to whether Smith, Jones or Brown should be nominated, but it was clearly understood that if Robinson or White were chosen there would be no corporation campaign funds. This applied also to the Democratic party, on the rare occasions when it seemed to have an opportunity of winning. Now, however, through an unpardonable blunder, there had got into the White House a President who was inclined to ignore advice, who appealed over the heads of the "advisers" to the populace; who went about tilting at the industrial structures we had so painfully wrought, and in frequent blasts of presidential messages enunciated new and heretical doctrines; who attacked the railroads, encouraged the brazen treason of labour unions, inspired an army of "muck-rakers" to fill the magazines with the wildest and most violent of language. State legislatures were emboldened to pass mischievous and restrictive laws, and much of my time began to be occupied in inducing, by various means, our courts to declare these unconstitutional. How we sighed for a business man or a lawyer in the White House! The country had gone mad, the stock-market trembled, the cry of "corporation control" resounded everywhere, and everywhere demagogues arose to inaugurate "reform campaigns," in an abortive attempt to "clean up politics." Down with the bosses, who were the tools of the corporations!

In our own city, which we fondly believed to be proof against the prevailing madness, a slight epidemic occurred; slight, yet momentarily alarming. Accidents will happen, even in the best regulated political organizations,—and accidents in these days appeared to be the rule. A certain Mr. Edgar Greenhalge, a middle-aged, mild-mannered and inoffensive man who had made a moderate fortune in wholesale drugs, was elected to the School Board. Later on some of us had reason to suspect that Perry Blackwood—with more astuteness than he had been given credit for—was responsible for Mr. Greenhalge's candidacy. At any rate, he was not a man to oppose, and in his previous life had given no hint that he might become a trouble maker. Nothing happened for several months. But one day on which I had occasion to interview Mr. Jason on a little matter of handing over to the Railroad a piece of land belonging to the city, which was known as Billings' Bowl, he inferred that Mr. Greenhaige might prove a disturber of that profound peace with which the city administration had for many years been blessed.

"Who the hell is he?" was Mr. Jason's question.

It appeared that Mr. G.'s private life had been investigated, with disappointingly barren results; he was, seemingly, an anomalistic being in our Nietzschean age, an unaggressive man; he had never sold any drugs to the city; he was not a church member; nor could it be learned that he had ever wandered into those byways of the town where Mr. Jason might easily have got trace of him: if he had any vices, he kept them locked up in a safe-deposit box that could not be "located." He was very genial, and had a way of conveying disturbing facts—when he wished to convey them—under cover of the most amusing stories. Mr. Jason was not a man to get panicky. Greenhalge could be handled all right, only—what was there in it for Greenhalge?—a nut difficult for Mr. Jason to crack. The two other members of the School Board were solid. Here again the wisest of men was proved to err, for Mr. Greenhalge turned out to have powers of persuasion; he made what in religious terms would have been called a conversion in the case of another member of the board, an hitherto staunch old reprobate by the name of Muller, an ex-saloon-keeper in comfortable circumstances to whom the idea of public office had appealed.

Mr. Greenhalge, having got wind of certain transactions that interested him extremely, brought them in his good-natured way to the knowledge of Mr. Gregory, the district attorney, suggesting that he investigate. Mr. Gregory smiled; undertook, as delicately as possible, to convey to Mr. Greenhalge the ways of the world, and of the political world in particular, wherein, it seemed, everyone was a good fellow. Mr. Greenhalge was evidently a good fellow, and didn't want to make trouble over little things. No, Mr. Greenhalge didn't want to make trouble; he appreciated a comfortable life as much as Mr. Gregory; he told the district attorney a funny story which might or might not have had an application to the affair, and took his leave with the remark that he had been happy to make Mr. Gregory's acquaintance. On his departure the district attorney's countenance changed. He severely rebuked a subordinate for some trivial mistake, and walked as rapidly as he could carry his considerable weight to Monahan's saloon.... One of the things Mr. Gregory had pointed out incidentally was that Mr. Greenhalge's evidence was vague, and that a grand jury wanted facts, which might be difficult to obtain. Mr. Greenhalge, thinking over the suggestion, sent for Krebs. In the course of a month or two the investigation was accomplished, Greenhalge went back to Gregory; who repeated his homilies, whereupon he was handed a hundred or so typewritten pages of evidence.

It was a dramatic moment.

Mr. Gregory resorted to pleading. He was sure that Mr. Greenhalge didn't want to be disagreeable, it was true and unfortunate that such things were so, but they would be amended: he promised all his influence to amend them. The public conscience, said Mr. Gregory, was being aroused. Now how much better for the party, for the reputation, the fair name of the city if these things could be corrected quietly, and nobody indicted or tried! Between sensible and humane men, wasn't that the obvious way? After the election, suit could be brought to recover the money. But Mr. Greenhalge appeared to be one of those hopeless individuals without a spark of party loyalty; he merely continued to smile, and to suggest that the district attorney prosecute. Mr. Gregory temporized, and presently left the city on a vacation. A day or two after his second visit to the district attorney's office Mr. Greenhalge had a call from the city auditor and the purchasing agent, who talked about their families,—which was very painful. It was also intimated to Mr. Greenhalge by others who accosted him that he was just the man for mayor. He smiled, and modestly belittled his qualifications....

Suddenly, one fine morning, a part of the evidence Krebs had gathered appeared in the columns of the Mail and State, a new and enterprising newspaper for which the growth and prosperity of our city were responsible; the sort of "revelations" that stirred to amazement and wrath innocent citizens of nearly every city in our country: politics and "graft" infesting our entire educational system, teachers and janitors levied upon, prices that took the breath away paid to favoured firms for supplies, specifications so worded that reasonable bids were barred. The respectable firm of Ellery and Knowles was involved. In spite of our horror, we were Americans and saw the humour of the situation, and laughed at the caricature in the Mail and State representing a scholar holding up a pencil and a legend under it, "No, it's not gold, but it ought to be."

Here I must enter into a little secret history. Any affair that threatened the integrity of Mr. Jason's organization was of serious moment to the gentlemen of the financial world who found that organization invaluable and who were also concerned about the fair name of their community; a conference in the Boyne Club decided that the city officials were being persecuted, and entitled therefore to "the very best of counsel,"—in this instance, Mr. Hugh Paret. It was also thought wise by Mr. Dickinson, Mr. Gorse, and Mr. Grierson, and by Mr. Paret himself that he should not appear in the matter; an aspiring young attorney, Mr. Arbuthnot, was retained to conduct the case in public. Thus capital came to the assistance of Mr. Jason, a fund was raised, and I was given carte blanche to defend the miserable city auditor and purchasing agent, both of whom elicited my sympathy; for they were stout men, and rapidly losing weight. Our first care was to create a delay in the trial of the case in order to give the public excitement a chance to die down. For the public is proverbially unable to fix its attention for long on one object, continually demanding the distraction that our newspapers make it their business to supply. Fortunately, a murder was committed in one of our suburbs, creating a mystery that filled the "extras" for some weeks, and this was opportunely followed by the embezzlement of a considerable sum by the cashier of one of our state banks. Public interest was divided between baseball and the tracking of this criminal to New Zealand.

Our resentment was directed, not so much against Commissioner Greenhalge as against Krebs. It is curious how keen is the instinct of men like Grierson, Dickinson, Tallant and Scherer for the really dangerous opponent. Who the deuce was this man Krebs? Well, I could supply them with some information: they doubtless recalled the Galligan, case; and Miller Gorse, who forgot nothing, also remembered his opposition in the legislature to House Bill 709. He had continued to be the obscure legal champion of "oppressed" labour, but how he had managed to keep body and soul together I knew not. I had encountered him occasionally in court corridors or on the street; he did not seem to change much; nor did he appear in our brief and perfunctory conversations to bear any resentment against me for the part I had taken in the Galligan affair. I avoided him when it was possible.... I had to admit that he had done a remarkably good piece of work in collecting Greenhalge's evidence, and how the, erring city officials were to be rescued became a matter of serious concern. Gregory, the district attorney, was in an abject funk; in any case a mediocre lawyer, after the indictment he was no help at all. I had to do all the work, and after we had selected the particular "Railroad" judge before whom the case was to be tried, I talked it over with him. His name was Notting, he understood perfectly what was required of him, and that he was for the moment the chief bulwark on which depended the logical interests of capital and sane government for their defence; also, his re-election was at stake. It was indicated to newspapers (such as the Mail and State) showing a desire to keep up public interest in the affair that their advertising matter might decrease; Mr. Sherrill's great department store, for instance, did not approve of this sort of agitation. Certain stationers, booksellers and other business men had got "cold feet," as Mr. Jason put it, the prospect of bankruptcy suddenly looming ahead of them,—since the Corn National Bank held certain paper....

In short, when the case did come to trial, it "blew up," as one of our ward leaders dynamically expressed it. Several important witnesses were mysteriously lacking, and two or three school-teachers had suddenly decided—to take a trip to Europe. The district attorney was ill, and assigned the prosecution to a mild assistant; while a sceptical jury—composed largely of gentlemen who had the business interests of the community, and of themselves, at heart returned a verdict of "not guilty." This was the signal for severely dignified editorials in Mr. Tallant's and other conservative newspapers, hinting that it might be well in the future for all well-meaning but misguided reformers to think twice before subjecting the city to the cost of such trials, and uselessly attempting to inflame public opinion and upset legitimate business. The Era expressed the opinion that no city in the United States was "more efficiently and economically governed than our own." "Irregularities" might well occur in every large organization; and it would better have become Mr. Greenhalge if, instead of hiring an unknown lawyer thirsting for notoriety to cook up charges, he had called the attention of the proper officials to the matter, etc., etc. The Pilot alone, which relied on sensation for its circulation, kept hammering away for a time with veiled accusations. But our citizens had become weary....

As a topic, however, this effective suppression of reform was referred to with some delicacy by my friends and myself. Our interference had been necessary and therefore justified, but we were not particularly proud of it, and our triumph had a temporarily sobering effect. It was about this time, if I remember correctly, that Mr. Dickinson gave the beautiful stained-glass window to the church....

Months passed. One day, having occasion to go over to the Boyne Iron Works to get information at first hand from certain officials, and having finished my business, I boarded a South Side electric car standing at the terminal. Just before it started Krebs came down the aisle of the car and took the seat in front of me.

"Well," I said, "how are you?" He turned in surprise, and thrust his big, bony hand across the back of the seat. "Come and sit here." He came. "Do you ever get back to Cambridge in these days?" I asked cordially.

"Not since I graduated from newspaper work in Boston. That's a good many years ago. By the way, our old landlady died this year."

"Do you mean—?" "Granite Face," I was about to say. I had forgotten her name, but that homesick scene when Tom and I stood before our open trunks, when Krebs had paid us a visit, came back to me. "You've kept in touch with her?" I asked, in surprise.

"Well," said Krebs, "she was one of the few friends I had at Cambridge. I had a letter from the daughter last week. She's done very well, and is an instructor in biology in one of the western universities."

I was silent a moment.

"And you,—you never married, did you?" I inquired, somewhat irrelevantly.

His semi-humorous gesture seemed to deny that such a luxury was for him. The conversation dragged a little; I began to feel the curiosity he invariably inspired. What was his life? What were his beliefs? And I was possessed by a certain militancy, a desire to "smoke him out." I did not stop to reflect that mine was in reality a defensive rather than an aggressive attitude.

"Do you live down here, in this part of the city?" I asked.

No, he boarded in Fowler Street. I knew it as in a district given over to the small houses of working-men.

"I suppose you are still a socialist."

"I suppose I am," he admitted, and added, "at any rate, that is as near as you can get to it."

"Isn't it fairly definite?"

"Fairly, if my notions are taken in general as the antithesis of what you fellows believe."

"The abolition of property, for instance."

"The abolition of too much property."

"What do you mean by 'too much'?"

"When it ceases to be real to a man, when it represents more than his need, when it drives him and he becomes a slave to it."

Involuntarily I thought of my new house,—not a soothing reflection.

"But who is going to decree how much property, a man should have?"

"Nobody—everybody. That will gradually tend to work itself out as we become more sensible and better educated, and understand more clearly what is good for us."

I retorted with the stock, common-sense phrase.

"If we had a division to-morrow, within a few years or so the most efficient would contrive to get the bulk of it back in their hands."

"That's so," he admitted. "But we're not going to have a division to- morrow."

"Thank God!" I exclaimed.

He regarded me.

"The 'efficient' will have to die or be educated first. That will take time."

"Educated!"

"Paret, have you ever read any serious books on what you call socialism?" he asked.

I threw out an impatient negative. I was going on to protest that I was not ignorant of the doctrine.

"Oh, what you call socialism is merely what you believe to be the more or less crude and utopian propaganda of an obscure political party. That isn't socialism. Nor is the anomalistic attempt that the Christian Socialists make to unite modern socialistic philosophy with Christian orthodoxy, socialism."

"What is socialism, then?" I demanded, somewhat defiantly.

"Let's call it education, science," he said smilingly, "economics and government based on human needs and a rational view of religion. It has been taught in German universities, and it will be taught in ours whenever we shall succeed in inducing your friends, by one means or another, not to continue endowing them. Socialism, in the proper sense, is merely the application of modern science to government."

I was puzzled and angry. What he said made sense somehow, but it sounded to me like so much gibberish.

"But Germany is a monarchy," I objected.

"It is a modern, scientific system with monarchy as its superstructure. It is anomalous, but frank. The monarchy is there for all men to see, and some day it will be done away with. We are supposedly a democracy, and our superstructure is plutocratic. Our people feel the burden, but they have not yet discovered what the burden is."

"And when they do?" I asked, a little defiantly.

"When they do," replied Krebs, "they will set about making the plutocrats happy. Now plutocrats are discontented, and never satisfied; the more they get, the more they want, the more they are troubled by what other people have."

I smiled in spite of myself.

"Your interest in—in plutocrats is charitable, then?"

"Why, yes," he said, "my interest in all kinds of people is charitable. However improbable it may seem, I have no reason to dislike or envy people who have more than they know what to do with." And the worst of it was he looked it. He managed somehow simply by sitting there with his strange eyes fixed upon me—in spite of his ridiculous philosophy—to belittle my ambitions, to make of small worth my achievements, to bring home to me the fact that in spite of these I was neither contented nor happy though he kept his humour and his poise, he implied an experience that was far deeper, more tragic and more significant than mine. I was goaded into making an injudicious remark.

"Well, your campaign against Ennerly and Jackson fell through, didn't it?" Ennerly and Jackson were the city officials who had been tried.

"It wasn't a campaign against them," he answered. "And considering the subordinate part I took in it, it could scarcely be called mine."

"Greenhalge turned to you to get the evidence."

"Well, I got it," he said.

"What became of it?"

"You ought to know."

"What do you mean?"

"Just what I say, Paret," he answered slowly. "You ought to know, if anyone knows."

I considered this a moment, more soberly. I thought I might have counted on my fingers the number of men cognizant of my connection with the case. I decided that he was guessing.

"I think you should explain that," I told him.

"The time may come, when you'll have to explain it."

"Is that a threat?" I demanded.

"A threat?" he repeated. "Not at all."

"But you are accusing me—"

"Of what?" he interrupted suddenly.

He had made it necessary for me to define the nature of his charges.

"Of having had some connection with the affair in question."

"Whatever else I may be, I'm not a fool," he said quietly. "Neither the district attorney's office, nor young Arbuthnot had brains enough to get them out of that scrape. Jason didn't have influence enough with the judiciary, and, as I happen to know, there was a good deal of money spent."

"You may be called upon to prove it," I retorted, rather hotly.

"So I may."

His tone, far from being defiant, had in it a note of sadness. I looked at him. What were his potentialities? Was it not just possible that I should have to revise my idea of him, acknowledge that he might become more formidable than I had thought?

There was an awkward silence.

"You mustn't imagine, Paret, that I have any personal animus against you, or against any of the men with whom you're associated," he went on, after a moment. "I'm sorry you're on that side, that's all,—I told you so once before. I'm not calling you names, I'm not talking about morality and immorality. Immorality, when you come down to it, is often just the opposition to progress that comes from blindness. I don't make the mistake of blaming a few individuals for the evils of modern industrial society, and on the other hand you mustn't blame individuals for the discomforts of what you call the reform movement, for that movement is merely a symptom—a symptom of a disease due to a change in the structure of society. We'll never have any happiness or real prosperity until we cure that disease. I was inclined to blame you once, at the capital that time, because it seemed to me that a man with all the advantages you have had and a mind like yours didn't have much excuse. But I've thought about it since; I realize now that I've had a good many more 'advantages' than you, and to tell you the truth, I don't see how you could have come out anywhere else than where you are,—all your surroundings and training were against it. That doesn't mean that you won't grasp the situation some day—I have an idea you will. It's just an idea. The man who ought to be condemned isn't the man that doesn't understand what's going on, but the man who comes to understand and persists in opposing it." He rose and looked down at me with the queer, disturbing smile I remembered. "I get off at this corner," he added, rather diffidently. "I hope you'll forgive me for being personal. I didn't mean to be, but you rather forced it on me."

"Oh, that's all right," I replied. The car stopped, and he hurried off. I watched his tall figure as it disappeared among the crowd on the sidewalk....

I returned to my office in one of those moods that are the more disagreeable because conflicting. To-day in particular I had been aroused by what Tom used to call Krebs's "crust," and as I sat at my desk warm waves of resentment went through me at the very notion of his telling me that my view was limited and that therefore my professional conduct was to be forgiven! It was he, the fanatic, who saw things in the larger scale! an assumption the more exasperating because at the moment he made it he almost convinced me that he did, and I was unable to achieve for him the measure of contempt I desired, for the incident, the measure of ridicule it deserved. My real animus was due to the fact that he had managed to shake my self-confidence, to take the flavour out of my achievements,—a flavour that was in the course of an hour to be completely restored by one of those interesting coincidences occasionally occurring in life. A young member of my staff entered with a telegram; I tore it open, and sat staring at it a moment before I realized that it brought to me the greatest honour of my career.

The Banker-Personality in New York had summoned me for consultation. To be recognized by him conferred indeed an ennoblement, the Star and Garter, so to speak, of the only great realm in America, that of high finance; and the yellow piece of paper I held in my hand instantly re- magnetized me, renewed my energy, and I hurried home to pack my bag in order to catch the seven o'clock train. I announced the news to Maude.

"I imagine it's because he knows I have made something of a study of the coal roads situation," I added.

"I'm glad, Hugh," she said. "I suppose it's a great compliment."

Never had her inadequacy to appreciate my career been more apparent! I looked at her curiously, to realize once more with peculiar sharpness how far we were apart; but now the resolutions I had made—and never carried out—on that first Christmas in the new home were lacking. Indeed, it was the futility of such resolutions that struck me at this moment. If her manner had been merely one of indifference, it would in a way have been easier to bear; she was simply incapable of grasping the significance of the event, the meaning to me of the years of unceasing, ambitious effort it crowned.

"Yes, it is something of a recognition," I replied. "Is there anything I can get for you in New York? I don't know how long I shall have to stay- -I'll telegraph you when I'm getting back." I kissed her and hurried out to the automobile. As I drove off I saw her still standing in the doorway looking after me.... In the station I had a few minutes to telephone Nancy.

"If you don't see me for a few days it's because I've gone to New York," I informed her.

"Something important, I'm sure."

"How did you guess?" I demanded, and heard her laugh.

"Come back soon and tell me about it," she said, and I walked, exhilarated, to the train.... As I sped through the night, staring out of the window into the darkness, I reflected on the man I was going to see. But at that time, although he represented to me the quintessence of achievement and power, I did not by any means grasp the many sided significance of the phenomenon he presented, though I was keenly aware of his influence, and that men spoke of him with bated breath. Presidents came and went, kings and emperors had responsibilities and were subject daily to annoyances, but this man was a law unto himself. He did exactly what he chose, and compelled other men to do it. Wherever commerce reigned,—and where did it not?—he was king and head of its Holy Empire, Pope and Emperor at once. For he had his code of ethics, his religion, and those who rebelled, who failed to conform, he excommunicated; a code something like the map of Europe,—apparently inconsistent in places. What I did not then comprehend was that he was the American Principle personified, the supreme individual assertion of the conviction that government should remain modestly in the background while the efficient acquired the supremacy that was theirs by natural right; nor had I grasped at that time the crowning achievement of a unity that fused Christianity with those acquisitive dispositions said to be inherent in humanity. In him the Lion and the Lamb, the Eagle and the Dove dwelt together in amity and power.

New York, always a congenial place to gentlemen of vitality and means and influential connections, had never appeared to me more sparkling, more inspiring. Winter had relented, spring had not as yet begun. And as I sat in a corner of the dining-room of my hotel looking out on the sunlit avenue I was conscious of partaking of the vigour and confidence of the well-dressed, clear-eyed people who walked or drove past my window with the air of a conquering race. What else was there in the world more worth having than this conquering sense? Religion might offer charms to the weak. Yet here religion itself became sensible, and wore the garb of prosperity. The stonework of the tall church on the corner was all lace; and the very saints in their niches, who had known martyrdom and poverty, seemed to have renounced these as foolish, and to look down complacently on the procession of wealth and power.. Across the street, behind a sheet of glass, was a carrosserie where were displayed the shining yellow and black panels of a closed automobile, the cost of which would have built a farm-house and stocked a barn.

At eleven o'clock, the appointed hour, I was in Wall Street. Sending in my name, I was speedily ushered into a room containing a table, around which were several men; but my eyes were drawn at once to the figure of the great banker who sat, massive and preponderant, at one end, smoking a cigar, and listening in silence to the conversation I had interrupted. He rose courteously and gave me his hand, and a glance that is unforgettable.

"It is good of you to come, Mr. Paret," he said simply, as though his summons had not been a command. "Perhaps you know some of these gentlemen."

One of them was our United States Senator, Theodore Watling. He, as it turned out, had been summoned from Washington. Of course I saw him frequently, having from time to time to go to Washington on various errands connected with legislation. Though spruce and debonnair as ever, in the black morning coat he invariably wore, he appeared older than he had on the day when I had entered his office. He greeted me warmly, as always.

"Hugh, I'm glad to see you here," he said, with a slight emphasis on the last word. My legal career was reaching its logical climax, the climax he had foreseen. And he added, to the banker, that he had brought me up.

"Then he was trained in a good school," remarked that personage, affably.

Mr. Barbour, the president of our Railroad, was present, and nodded to me kindly; also a president of a smaller road. In addition, there were two New York attorneys of great prominence, whom I had met. The banker's own special lieutenant of the law, Mr. Clement T. Grolier, for whom I looked, was absent; but it was forthwith explained that he was offering, that morning, a resolution of some importance in the Convention of his Church, but that he would be present after lunch.

"I have asked you to come here, Mr. Paret," said the banker, "not only because I know something personally of your legal ability, but because I have been told by Mr. Scherer and Mr. Barbour that you happen to have considerable knowledge of the situation we are discussing, as well as some experience with cases involving that statute somewhat hazy to lay minds, the Sherman anti-trust law."

A smile went around the table. Mr. Watling winked at me; I nodded, but said nothing. The banker was not a man to listen to superfluous words. The keynote of his character was despatch....

The subject of the conference, like many questions bitterly debated and fought over in their time, has in the year I write these words come to be of merely academic interest. Indeed, the very situation we discussed that day has been cited in some of our modern text-books as a classic consequence of that archaic school of economics to which the name of Manchester is attached. Some half dozen or so of the railroads running through the anthracite coal region had pooled their interests,—an extremely profitable proceeding. The public paid. We deemed it quite logical that the public should pay—having been created largely for that purpose; and very naturally we resented the fact that the meddling Person who had got into the White House without asking anybody's leave,—who apparently did not believe in the infallibility of our legal Bible, the Constitution,—should maintain that the anthracite roads had formed a combination in restraint of trade, should lay down the preposterous doctrine—so subversive of the Rights of Man—that railroads should not own coal mines. Congress had passed a law to meet this contention, suit had been brought, and in the lower court the government had won.

As the day wore on our numbers increased, we were joined by other lawyers of renown, not the least of whom was Mr. Grolier himself, fresh from his triumph over religious heresy in his Church Convention. The note of the conference became tinged with exasperation, and certain gentlemen seized the opportunity to relieve their pent-up feelings on the subject of the President and his slavish advisers,—some of whom, before they came under the spell of his sorcery, had once been sound lawyers and sensible men. With the exception of the great Banker himself, who made few comments, Theodore Watling was accorded the most deference; as one of the leaders of that indomitable group of senators who had dared to stand up against popular clamour, his opinions were of great value, and his tactical advice was listened to with respect. I felt more pride than ever in my former chief, who had lost none of his charm. While in no way minimizing the seriousness of the situation, his wisdom was tempered, as always, with humour; he managed, as it were, to neutralize the acid injected into the atmosphere by other gentlemen present; he alone seemed to bear no animus against the Author of our troubles; suave and calm, good natured, he sometimes brought the company into roars of laughter and even succeeded in bringing occasional smiles to the face of the man who had summoned us—when relating some characteristic story of the queer genius whom the fates (undoubtedly as a practical joke) had made the chief magistrate of the United States of America. All geniuses have weaknesses; Mr. Wading had made a study of the President's, and more than once had lured him into an impasse. The case had been appealed to the Supreme Court, and Mr. Wading, with remarkable conciseness and penetration, reviewed the characteristics of each and every member of that tribunal, all of whom he knew intimately. They were, of course, not subject to "advice," as were some of the gentlemen who sat on our state courts; no sane and self-respecting American would presume to "approach" them. Nevertheless they were human, and it were wise to take account, in the conduct of the case, of the probable bias of each individual.

The President, overstepping his constitutional, Newtonian limits, might propose laws, Congress might acquiesce in them, but the Supreme Court, after listening to lawyers like Grolier (and he bowed to the attorney), made them: made them, he might have added, without responsibility to any man in our unique Republic that scorned kings and apotheosized lawyers. A Martian with a sense of humour witnessing a stormy session of Congress would have giggled at the thought of a few tranquil gentlemen in another room of the Capitol waiting to decide what the people's representatives meant—or whether they meant anything....

For the first time since I had known Theodore Watling, however, I saw him in the shadow of another individual; a man who, like a powerful magnet, continually drew our glances. When we spoke, we almost invariably addressed him, his rare words fell like bolts upon the consciousness. There was no apparent rift in that personality.

When, about five o'clock, the conference was ended and we were dismissed, United States Senator, railroad presidents, field-marshals of the law, the great banker fell into an eager conversation with Grolier over the Canon on Divorce, the subject of warm debate in the convention that day. Grolier, it appeared, had led his party against the theological liberals. He believed that law was static, but none knew better its plasticity; that it was infallible, but none so well as he could find a text on either side. His reputation was not of the popular, newspaper sort, but was known to connoisseurs, editors, financiers, statesmen and judges,—to those, in short, whose business it is to make themselves familiar with the instruments of power. He was the banker's chief legal adviser, the banker's rapier of tempered steel, sheathed from the vulgar view save when it flashed forth on a swift errand.

"I'm glad to be associated with you in this case, Mr. Paret," Mr. Grolier said modestly, as we emerged into the maelstrom of Wall Street. "If you can make it convenient to call at my office in the morning, we'll go over it a little. And I'll see you in a day or two in Washington, Watling. Keep your eye on the bull," he added, with a twinkle, "and don't let him break any more china than you can help. I don't know where we'd be if it weren't for you fellows."

By "you fellows," he meant Mr. Watling's distinguished associates in the Senate....

Mr. Watling and I dined together at a New York club. It was not a dinner of herbs. There was something exceedingly comfortable about that club, where the art of catering to those who had earned the right to be catered to came as near perfection as human things attain. From the great, heavily curtained dining-room the noises of the city had been carefully excluded; the dust of the Avenue, the squalour and smells of the brown stone fronts and laddered tenements of those gloomy districts lying a pistol-shot east and west. We had a vintage champagne, and afterwards a cigar of the club's special importation.

"Well," said Mr. Watling, "mow that you're a member of the royal council, what do you think of the King?"

"I've been thinking a great deal about him," I said, and indeed it was true. He had made, perhaps, his greatest impression when I had shaken his hand in parting. The manner in which he had looked at me then had puzzled me; it was as though he were seeking to divine something in me that had escaped him. "Why doesn't the government take him over?" I exclaimed.

Mr. Watling smiled.

"You mean, instead of his mines and railroads and other properties?"

"Yes. But that's your idea. Don't you remember you said something of the kind the night of the election, years ago? It occurred to me to-day, when I was looking at him."

"Yes," he agreed thoughtfully, "if some American genius could find a way to legalize that power and utilize the men who created it the worst of our problems would be solved. A man with his ability has a right to power, and none would respond more quickly or more splendidly to a call of the government than he. All this fight is waste, Hugh, damned waste of the nation's energy." Mr. Watling seldom swore. "Look at the President! There's a man of remarkable ability, too. And those two oughtn't to be fighting each other. The President's right, in a way. Yes, he is, though I've got to oppose him."

I smiled at this from Theodore Watling, though I admired him the more for it. And suddenly, oddly, I happened to remember what Krebs had said, that our troubles were not due to individuals, but to a disease that had developed in industrial society. If the day should come when such men as the President and the great banker would be working together, was it not possible, too, that the idea of Mr. Watling and the vision of Krebs might coincide? I was struck by a certain seeming similarity in their views; but Mr. Watling interrupted this train of thought by continuing to express his own.

"Well,—they're running right into a gale when they might be sailing with it," he said.

"You think we'll have more trouble?" I asked.

"More and more," he replied. "It'll be worse before it's better I'm afraid." At this moment a club servant announced his cab, and he rose. "Well, good-bye, my son," he said.

"I'll hope to see you in Washington soon. And remember there's no one thinks any more of you than I do."

I escorted him to the door, and it was with a real pang I saw him wave to me from his cab as he drove away. My affection for him was never more alive than in this hour when, for the first time in my experience, he had given real evidence of an inner anxiety and lack of confidence in the future.

Chapter Twenty-One

In spite of that unwonted note of pessimism from Mr. Watling, I went home in a day or two flushed with my new honours, and it was impossible not to be conscious of the fact that my aura of prestige was increased— tremendously increased—by the recognition I had received. A certain subtle deference in the attitude of the small minority who owed allegiance to the personage by whom I had been summoned was more satisfying than if I had been acclaimed at the station by thousands of my fellow-citizens who knew nothing of my journey and of its significance, even though it might have a concern for them. To men like Berringer, Grierson and Tallant and our lesser great lights the banker was a semi- mythical figure, and many times on the day of my return I was stopped on the street to satisfy the curiosity of my friends as to my impressions. Had he, for instance, let fall any opinions, prognostications on the political and financial situation? Dickinson and Scherer were the only other men in the city who had the honour of a personal acquaintance with him, and Scherer was away, abroad, gathering furniture and pictures for the house in New York Nancy had predicted, and which he had already begun to build! With Dickinson I lunched in private, in order to give him a detailed account of the conference. By five o'clock I was ringing the door-bell of Nancy's new mansion on Grant Avenue. It was several blocks below my own.

"Well, how does it feel to be sent for by the great sultan?" she asked, as I stood before her fire. "Of course, I have always known that ultimately he couldn't get along without you."

"Even if he has been a little late in realizing it," I retorted.

"Sit down and tell me all about him," she commanded.

"I met him once, when Ham had the yacht at Bar Harbor."

"And how did he strike you?"

"As somewhat wrapped up in himself," said Nancy.

We laughed together.

"Oh, I fell a victim," she went on. "I might have sailed off with him, if he had asked me."

"I'm surprised he didn't ask you."

"I suspect that it was not quite convenient," she said. "Women are secondary considerations to sultans, we're all very well when they haven't anything more serious to occupy them. Of course that's why they fascinate us. What did he want with you, Hugh?"

"He was evidently afraid that the government would win the coal roads suit unless I was retained."

"More laurels!" she sighed. "I suppose I ought to be proud to know you."

"That's exactly what I've been trying to impress on you all these years," I declared. "I've laid the laurels at your feet, in vain."

She sat with her head back on the cushions, surveying me.

"Your dress is very becoming," I said irrelevantly.

"I hoped it would meet your approval," she mocked.

"I've been trying to identify the shade. It's elusive—like you."

"Don't be banal.... What is the colour?"

"Poinsetta!"

"Pretty nearly," she agreed, critically.

I took the soft crepe between my fingers.

"Poet!" she smiled. "No, it isn't quite poinsetta. It's nearer the red- orange of a tree I remember one autumn, in the White Mountains, with the setting sun on it. But that wasn't what we were talking about. Laurels! Your laurels."

"My laurels," I repeated. "Such as they are, I fling them into your lap."

"Do you think they increase your value to me, Hugh?"

"I don't know," I said thickly.

She shook her head.

"No, it's you I like—not the laurels."

"But if you care for me—?" I began.

She lifted up her hands and folded them behind the knot of her hair.

"It's extraordinary how little you have changed since we were children, Hugh. You are still sixteen years old, that's why I like you. If you got to be the sultan of sultans yourself, I shouldn't like you any better, or any worse."

"And yet you have just declared that power appeals to you!"

"Power—yes. But a woman—a woman like me—wants to be first, or nothing."

"You are first," I asserted. "You always have been, if you had only realized it."

She gazed up at me dreamily.

"If you had only realized it! If you had only realized that all I wanted of you was to be yourself. It wasn't what you achieved. I didn't want you to be like Ralph or the others."

"Myself? What are you trying to say?"

"Yourself. Yes, that is what I like about you. If you hadn't been in such a hurry—if you hadn't misjudged me so. It was the power in you, the craving, the ideal in you that I cared for—not the fruits of it. The fruits would have come naturally. But you forced them, Hugh, for quicker results."

"What kind of fruits?" I asked.

"Ah," she exclaimed, "how can I tell what they might have been! You have striven and striven, you have done extraordinary things, but have they made you any happier? have you got what you want?"

I stooped down and seized her wrists from behind her head.

"I want you, Nancy," I said. "I have always wanted you. You're more wonderful to-day than you have ever been. I could find myself—with you."

She closed her eyes. A dreamy smile was on her face, and she lay unresisting, very still. In that tremendous moment, for which it seemed I had waited a lifetime, I could have taken her in my arms—and yet I did not. I could not tell why: perhaps it was because she seemed to have passed beyond me—far beyond—in realization. And she was so still!

"We have missed the way, Hugh," she whispered, at last.

"But we can find it again, if we seek it together," I urged.

"Ah, if I only could!" she said. "I could have once. But now I'm afraid—afraid of getting lost." Slowly she straightened up, her hands falling into her lap. I seized them again, I was on my knees in front of her, before the fire, and she, intent, looking down at me, into me, through me it seemed—at something beyond which yet was me.

"Hugh," she asked, "what do you believe? Anything?"

"What do I believe?"

"Yes. I don't mean any cant, cut-and-dried morality. The world is getting beyond that. But have you, in your secret soul, any religion at all? Do you ever think about it? I'm not speaking about anything orthodox, but some religion—even a tiny speck of it, a germ—harmonizing with life, with that power we feel in us we seek to express and continually violate."

"Nancy!" I exclaimed.

"Answer me—answer me truthfully," she said....

I was silent, my thoughts whirling like dust atoms in a storm.

"You have always taken things—taken what you wanted. But they haven't satisfied you, convinced you that that is all of life."

"Do you mean—that we should renounce?" I faltered.

"I don't know what I mean. I am asking, Hugh, asking. Haven't you any clew? Isn't there any voice in you, anywhere, deep down, that can tell me? give me a hint? just a little one?"

I was wracked. My passion had not left me, it seemed to be heightened, and I pressed her hands against her knees. It was incredible that my hands should be there, in hers, feeling her. Her beauty seemed as fresh, as un-wasted as the day, long since, when I despaired of her. And yet and yet against the tumult and beating of this passion striving to throb down thought, thought strove. Though I saw her as a woman, my senses and my spirit commingled and swooned together.

"This is life," I murmured, scarcely knowing what I said.

"Oh, my dear!" she cried, and her voice pierced me with pain, "are we to be lost, overpowered, engulfed, swept down its stream, to come up below drifting—wreckage? Where, then, would be your power? I'm not speaking of myself. Isn't life more than that? Isn't it in us, too,—in you? Think, Hugh. Is there no god, anywhere, but this force we feel, restlessly creating only to destroy? You must answer—you must find out."

I cannot describe the pleading passion in her voice, as though hell and heaven were wrestling in it. The woman I saw, tortured yet uplifted, did not seem to be Nancy, yet it was the woman I loved more than life itself and always had loved.

"I can't think," I answered desperately, "I can only feel—and I can't express what I feel. It's mixed, it's dim, and yet bright and shining— it's you."

"No, it's you," she said vehemently. "Yon must interpret it." Her voice sank: "Could it be God?" she asked.

"God!" I exclaimed sharply.

Her hands fell away from mine.... The silence was broken only by the crackling of the wood fire as a log turned over and fell. Never before, in all our intercourse that I could remember, had she spoken to me about religion.... With that apparent snap in continuity incomprehensible to the masculine mind-her feminine mood had changed. Elements I had never suspected, in Nancy, awe, even a hint of despair, entered into it, and when my hand found hers again, the very quality of its convulsive pressure seemed to have changed. I knew then that it was her soul I loved most; I had been swept all unwittingly to its very altar.

"I believe it is God," I said. But she continued to gaze at me, her lips parted, her eyes questioning.

"Why is it," she demanded, "that after all these centuries of certainty we should have to start out to find him again? Why is it when something happens like—like this, that we should suddenly be torn with doubts about him, when we have lived the best part of our lives without so much as thinking of him?"

"Why should you have qualms?" I said. "Isn't this enough? and doesn't it promise—all?"

"I don't know. They're not qualms—in the old sense." She smiled down at me a little tearfully. "Hugh, do you remember when we used to go to Sunday-school at Dr. Pound's church, and Mrs. Ewan taught us? I really believed something then—that Moses brought down the ten commandments of God from the mountain, all written out definitely for ever and ever. And I used to think of marriage" (I felt a sharp twinge), "of marriage as something sacred and inviolable,—something ordained by God himself. It ought to be so—oughtn't it? That is the ideal."

"Yes—but aren't you confusing—?" I began.

"I am confusing and confused. I shouldn't be—I shouldn't care if there weren't something in you, in me, in our—friendship, something I can't explain, something that shines still through the fog and the smoke in which we have lived our lives—something which, I think, we saw clearer as children. We have lost it in our hasty groping. Oh, Hugh, I couldn't bear to think that we should never find it! that it doesn't really exist! Because I seem to feel it. But can we find it this way, my dear?" Her hand tightened on mine.

"But if the force drawing us together, that has always drawn us together, is God?" I objected.

"I asked you," she said. "The time must come when you must answer, Hugh. It may be too late, but you must answer."

"I believe in taking life in my own hands," I said.

"It ought to be life," said Nancy. "It—it might have been life.... It is only when a moment, a moment like this comes that the quality of what we have lived seems so tarnished, that the atmosphere which we ourselves have helped to make is so sordid. When I think of the intrigues, and divorces, the self-indulgences,—when I think of my own marriage—" her voice caught. "How are we going to better it, Hugh, this way? Am I to get that part of you I love, and are you to get what you crave in me? Can we just seize happiness? Will it not elude us just as much as though we believed firmly in the ten commandments?"

"No," I declared obstinately.

She shook her head.

"What I'm afraid of is that the world isn't made that way—for you—for me. We're permitted to seize those other things because they're just baubles, we've both found out how worthless they are. And the worst of it is they've made me a coward, Hugh. It isn't that I couldn't do without them, I've come to depend on them in another way. It's because they give me a certain protection,—do you see? they've come to stand in the place of the real convictions we've lost. And—well, we've taken the baubles, can we reach out our hands and take—this? Won't we be punished for it, frightfully punished?"

"I don't care if we are," I said, and surprised myself.

"But I care. It's weak, it's cowardly, but it's so. And yet I want to face the situation—I'm trying to get you to face it, to realize how terrible it is."

"I only know that I want you above everything else in the world—I'll take care of you—"

I seized her arms, I drew her down to me.

"Don't!" she cried. "Oh, don't!" and struggled to her feet and stood before me panting. "You must go away now—please, Hugh. I can't bear any more—I want to think."

I released her. She sank into the chair and hid her face in her hands....

As may be imagined, the incident I have just related threw my life into a tangle that would have floored a less persistent optimist and romanticist than myself, yet I became fairly accustomed to treading what the old moralists called the devious paths of sin. In my passion I had not hesitated to lay down the doctrine that the courageous and the strong took what they wanted,—a doctrine of which I had been a consistent disciple in the professional and business realm. A logical buccaneer, superman, "master of life" would promptly have extended this doctrine to the realm of sex. Nancy was the mate for me, and Nancy and I, our development, was all that mattered, especially my development. Let every man and woman look out for his or her development, and in the end the majority of people would be happy. This was going Adam Smith one better. When it came to putting that theory into practice, however, one needed convictions: Nancy had been right when she had implied that convictions were precisely what we lacked; what our world in general lacked. We had desires, yes convictions, no. What we wanted we got not by defying the world, but by conforming to it: we were ready to defy only when our desires overcame the resistance of our synapses, and even then not until we should have exhausted every legal and conventional means.

A superman with a wife and family he had acquired before a great passion has made him a superman is in rather a predicament, especially if he be one who has achieved such superhumanity as he possesses not by challenging laws and conventions, but by getting around them. My wife and family loved me; and paradoxically I still had affection for them, or thought I had. But the superman creed is, "be yourself, realize yourself, no matter how cruel you may have to be in order to do so." One trouble with me was that remnants of the Christian element of pity still clung to me. I would be cruel if I had to, but I hoped I shouldn't have to: something would turn up, something in the nature of an intervening miracle that would make it easy for me. Perhaps Maude would take the initiative and relieve me.... Nancy had appealed for a justifying doctrine, and it was just what I didn't have and couldn't evolve. In the meanwhile it was quite in character that I should accommodate myself to a situation that might well be called anomalous.

This "accommodation" was not unaccompanied by fever. My longing to realize my love for Nancy kept me in a constant state of tension—of "nerves"; for our relationship had merely gone one step farther, we had reached a point where we acknowledged that we loved each other, and paradoxically halted there; Nancy clung to her demand for new sanctions with a tenacity that amazed and puzzled and often irritated me. And yet, when I look back upon it all, I can see that some of the difficulty lay with me: if she had her weakness—which she acknowledged—I had mine—and kept it to myself. It was part of my romantic nature not to want to break her down. Perhaps I loved the ideal better than the woman herself, though that scarcely seems possible.

We saw each other constantly. And though we had instinctively begun to be careful, I imagine there was some talk among our acquaintances. It is to be noted that the gossip never became riotous, for we had always been friends, and Nancy had a saving reputation for coldness. It seemed incredible that Maude had not discovered my secret, but if she knew of it, she gave no sign of her knowledge. Often, as I looked at her, I wished she would. I can think of no more expressive sentence in regard to her than the trite one that she pursued the even tenor of her way; and I found the very perfection of her wifehood exasperating. Our relationship would, I thought, have been more endurable if we had quarrelled. And yet we had grown as far apart, in that big house, as though we had been separated by a continent; I lived in my apartments, she in hers; she consulted me about dinner parties and invitations; for, since we had moved to Grant Avenue, we entertained and went out more than before. It seemed as though she were making every effort consistent with her integrity and self-respect to please me. Outwardly she conformed to the mould; but I had long been aware that inwardly a person had developed. It had not been a spontaneous development, but one in resistance to pressure; and was probably all the stronger for that reason. At times her will revealed itself in astonishing and unexpected flashes, as when once she announced that she was going to change Matthew's school.

"He's old enough to go to boarding-school," I said. "I'll look up a place for him."

"I don't wish him to go to boarding-school yet, Hugh," she said quietly.

"But that's just what he needs," I objected. "He ought to have the rubbing-up against other boys that boarding-school will give him. Matthew is timid, he should have learned to take care of himself. And he will make friendships that will help him in a larger school."

"I don't intend to send him," Maude said.

"But if I think it wise?"

"You ought to have begun to consider such things many years ago. You have always been too—busy to think of the children. You have left them to me. I am doing the best I can with them."

"But a man should have something to say about boys. He understands them."

"You should have thought of that before."

"They haven't been old enough."

"If you had taken your share of responsibility for them, I would listen to you."

"Maude!" I exclaimed reproachfully.

"No, Hugh," she went on, "you have been too busymaking money. You have left them tome. It is my task to see that the money they are to inherit doesn't ruin them."

"You talk as though it were a great fortune," I said.

But I did not press the matter. I had a presentiment that to press it might lead to unpleasant results.

It was this sense of not being free, of having gained everything but freedom that was at times galling in the extreme: this sense of living with a woman for whom I had long ceased to care, a woman with a baffling will concealed beneath an unruffled and serene exterior. At moments I looked at her across the table; she did not seem to have aged much: her complexion was as fresh, apparently, as the day when I had first walked with her in the garden at Elkington; her hair the same wonderful colour; perhaps she had grown a little stouter. There could be no doubt about the fact that her chin was firmer, that certain lines had come into her face indicative of what is called character. Beneath her pliability she was now all firmness; the pliability had become a mockery. It cannot be said that I went so far as to hate her for this,—when it was in my mind,—but my feelings were of a strong antipathy. And then again there were rare moments when I was inexplicably drawn to her, not by love and passion; I melted a little in pity, perhaps, when my eyes were opened and I saw the tragedy, yet I am not referring now to such feelings as these. I am speaking of the times when I beheld her as the blameless companion of the years, the mother of my children, the woman I was used to and should—by all canons I had known—have loved....

And there were the children. Days and weeks passed when I scarcely saw them, and then some little incident would happen to give me an unexpected wrench and plunge me into unhappiness. One evening I came home from a long talk with Nancy that had left us both wrought up, and I had entered the library before I heard voices. Maude was seated under the lamp at the end of the big room reading from "Don Quixote"; Matthew and Biddy were at her feet, and Moreton, less attentive, at a little distance was taking apart a mechanical toy. I would have tiptoed out, but Biddy caught sight of me.

"It's father!" she cried, getting up and flying to me.

"Oh, father, do come and listen! The story's so exciting, isn't it, Matthew?"

I looked down into the boy's eyes shining with an expression that suddenly pierced my heart with a poignant memory of myself. Matthew was far away among the mountains and castles of Spain.

"Matthew," demanded his sister, "why did he want to go fighting with all those people?"

"Because he was dotty," supplied Moreton, who had an interesting habit of picking up slang.

"It wasn't at all," cried Matthew, indignantly, interrupting Maude's rebuke of his brother.

"What was it, then?" Moreton demanded.

"You wouldn't understand if I told you," Matthew was retorting, when Maude put her hand on his lips.

"I think that's enough for to-night," she said, as she closed the book. "There are lessons to do—and father wants to read his newspaper in quiet."

This brought a protest from Biddy.

"Just a little more, mother! Can't we go into the schoolroom? We shan't disturb father there."

"I'll read to them—a few minutes," I said.

As I took the volume from her and sat down Maude shot at me a swift look of surprise. Even Matthew glanced at me curiously; and in his glance I had, as it were, a sudden revelation of the boy's perplexity concerning me. He was twelve, rather tall for his age, and the delicate modelling of his face resembled my father's. He had begun to think.. What did he think of me?

Biddy clapped her hands, and began to dance across the carpet.

"Father's going to read to us, father's going to read to us," she cried, finally clambering up on my knee and snuggling against me.

"Where is the place?" I asked.

But Maude had left the room. She had gone swiftly and silently.

"I'll find it," said Moreton.

I began to read, but I scarcely knew what I was reading, my fingers tightening over Biddy's little knee....

Presently Miss Allsop, the governess, came in. She had been sent by Maude. There was wistfulness in Biddy's voice as I kissed her good night.

"Father, if you would only read oftener!" she said, "I like it when you read—better than anyone else."....

Maude and I were alone that night. As we sat in the library after our somewhat formal, perfunctory dinner, I ventured to ask her why she had gone away when I had offered to read.

"I couldn't bear it, Hugh," she answered.

"Why?" I asked, intending to justify myself.

She got up abruptly, and left me. I did not follow her. In my heart I understood why....

Some years had passed since Ralph's prophecy had come true, and Perry and the remaining Blackwoods had been "relieved" of the Boyne Street line. The process need not be gone into in detail, being the time-honoured one employed in the Ribblevale affair of "running down" the line, or perhaps it would be better to say "showing it up." It had not justified its survival in our efficient days, it had held out—thanks to Perry—with absurd and anachronous persistence against the inevitable consolidation. Mr. Tallant's newspaper had published many complaints of the age and scarcity of the cars, etc.; and alarmed holders of securities, in whose vaults they had lain since time immemorial, began to sell.... I saw little of Perry in those days, as I have explained, but one day I met him in the Hambleton Building, and he was white.

"Your friends are doing thus, Hugh," he said.

"Doing what?"

"Undermining the reputation of a company as sound as any in this city, a company that's not overcapitalized, either. And we're giving better service right now than any of your consolidated lines."...

He was in no frame of mind to argue with; the conversation was distinctly unpleasant. I don't remember what I said sething to the effect that he was excited, that his language was extravagant. But after he had walked off and left me I told Dickinson that he ought to be given a chance, and one of our younger financiers, Murphree, went to Perry and pointed out that he had nothing to gain by obstruction; if he were only reasonable, he might come into the new corporation on the same terms with the others.

All that Murphree got for his pains was to be ordered out of the office by Perry, who declared that he was being bribed to desert the other stockholders.

"He utterly failed to see the point of view," Murphree reported in some astonishment to Dickinson.

"What else did he say?" Mr. Dickinson asked.

Murphree hesitated.

"Well—what?" the banker insisted.

"He wasn't quite himself," said Murphree, who was a comparative newcomer in the city and had a respect for the Blackwood name. "He said that that was the custom of thieves: when they were discovered, they offered to divide. He swore that he would get justice in the courts."

Mr. Dickinson smiled....

Thus Perry, through his obstinacy and inability to adapt himself to new conditions, had gradually lost both caste and money. He resigned from the Boyne Club. I was rather sorry for him. Tom naturally took the matter to heart, but he never spoke of it; I found that I was seeing less of him, though we continued to dine there at intervals, and he still came to my house to see the children. Maude continued to see Lucia. For me, the situation would have been more awkward had I been less occupied, had my relationship with Maude been a closer one. Neither did she mention Perry in those days. The income that remained to him being sufficient for him and his family to live on comfortably, he began to devote most of his time to various societies of a semipublic nature until—in the spring of which I write his activities suddenly became concentrated in the organization of a "Citizens Union," whose avowed object was to make a campaign against "graft" and political corruption the following autumn. This announcement and the call for a mass-meeting in Kingdon Hall was received by the newspapers with a good-natured ridicule, and in influential quarters it was generally hinted that this was Mr. Blackwood's method of "getting square" for having been deprived of the Boyne Street line. It was quite characteristic of Ralph Hambleton that he should go, out of curiosity, to the gathering at Kingdon Hall, and drop into my office the next morning.

"Well, Hughie, they're after you," he said with a grin.

"After me? Why not include yourself?"

He sat down and stretched his long legs and his long arms, and smiled as he gaped.

"Oh, they'll never get me," he said. And I knew, as I gazed at him, that they never would.

"What sort of things did they say?" I asked.

"Haven't you read the Pilot and the Mail and State?"

"I just glanced over them. Did they call names?"

"Call names! I should say they did. They got drunk on it, worked themselves up like dervishes. They didn't cuss you personally,—that'll come later, of course. Judd Jason got the heaviest shot, but they said he couldn't exist a minute if it wasn't for the 'respectable' crowd— capitalists, financiers, millionaires and their legal tools. Fact is, they spoke a good deal of truth, first and last, in a fool kind of way."

"Truth!" I exclaimed irritatedly.

Ralph laughed. He was evidently enjoying himself.

"Is any of it news to you, Hughie, old boy?"

"It's an outrage."

"I think it's funny," said Ralph. "We haven't had such a circus for years. Never had. Of course I shouldn't like to see you go behind the bars,—not that. But you fellows can't expect to go on forever skimming off the cream without having somebody squeal sometime. You ought to be reasonable."

"You've skimmed as much cream as anybody else."

"You've skimmed the cream, Hughie,—you and Dickinson and Scherer and Grierson and the rest,—I've only filled my jug. Well, these fellows are going to have a regular roof-raising campaign, take the lid off of everything, dump out the red-light district some of our friends are so fond of."

"Dump it where?" I asked curiously.

"Oh," answered Ralph, "they didn't say. Out into the country, anywhere."

"But that's damned foolishness," I declared.

"Didn't say it wasn't," Ralph admitted. "They talked a lot of that, too, incidentally. They're going to close the saloons and dance halls and make this city sadder than heaven. When they get through, it'll all be over but the inquest."

"What did Perry do?" I asked.

"Well, he opened the meeting,—made a nice, precise, gentlemanly speech. Greenhalge and a few young highbrows and a reformed crook named Harrod did most of the hair-raising. They're going to nominate Greenhalge for mayor; and he told 'em something about that little matter of the school board, and said he would talk more later on. If one of the ablest lawyers in the city hadn't been hired by the respectable crowd and a lot of other queer work done, the treasurer and purchasing agent would be doing time. They seemed to be interested, all right."

I turned over some papers on my desk, just to show Ralph that he hadn't succeeded in disturbing me.

"Who was in the audience? anyone you ever heard of?" I asked.

"Sure thing. Your cousin Robert Breck; and that son-in-law of his— what's his name? And some other representatives of our oldest families,- -Alec Pound. He's a reformer now, you know. They put him on the resolutions committee. Sam Ogilvy was there, he'd be classed as respectably conservative. And one of the Ewanses. I could name a few others, if you pressed me. That brother of Fowndes who looks like an up- state minister. A lot of women—Miller Gorse's sister, Mrs. Datchet, who never approved of Miller. Quite a genteel gathering, I give you my word, and all astonished and mad as hell when the speaking was over. Mrs. Datchet said she had been living in a den of iniquity and vice, and didn't know it."

"It must have been amusing," I said.

"It was," said Ralph. "It'll be more amusing later on. Oh, yes, there was another fellow who spoke I forgot to mention—that queer Dick who was in your class, Krebs, got the school board evidence, looked as if he'd come in by freight. He wasn't as popular as the rest, but he's got more sense than all of them put together."

"Why wasn't he popular?"

"Well, he didn't crack up the American people,—said they deserved all they got, that they'd have to learn to think straight and be straight before they could expect a square deal. The truth was, they secretly envied these rich men who were exploiting their city, and just as long as they envied them they hadn't any right to complain of them. He was going into this campaign to tell the truth, but to tell all sides of it, and if they wanted reform, they'd have to reform themselves first. I admired his nerve, I must say."

"He always had that," I remarked. "How did they take it?"

"Well, they didn't like it much, but I think most of them had a respect for him. I know I did. He has a whole lot of assurance, an air of knowing what he's talking about, and apparently he doesn't give a continental whether he's popular or not. Besides, Greenhalge had cracked him up to the skies for the work he'd done for the school board."

"You talk as if he'd converted you," I said.

Ralph laughed as he rose and stretched himself.

"Oh, I'm only the intelligent spectator, you ought to know that by this time, Hughie. But I thought it might interest you, since you'll have to go on the stump and refute it all. That'll be a nice job. So long."

And he departed. Of course I knew that he had been baiting me, his scent for the weaknesses of his friends being absolutely fiendish. I was angry because he had succeeded,—because he knew he had succeeded. All the morning uneasiness possessed me, and I found it difficult to concentrate on the affairs I had in hand. I felt premonitions, which I tried in vain to suppress, that the tide of the philosophy of power and might were starting to ebb: I scented vague calamities ahead, calamities I associated with Krebs; and when I went out to the Club for lunch this sense of uneasiness, instead of being dissipated, was increased. Dickinson was there, and Scherer, who had just got back from Europe; the talk fell on the Citizens Union, which Scherer belittled with an air of consequence and pompousness that struck me disagreeably, and with an eye newly critical I detected in him a certain disintegration, deterioration. Having dismissed the reformers, he began to tell of his experiences abroad, referring in one way or another to the people of consequence who had entertained him.

"Hugh," said Leonard Dickinson to me as we walked to the bank together, "Scherer will never be any good any more. Too much prosperity. And he's begun to have his nails manicured."

After I had left the bank president an uncanny fancy struck me that in Adolf Scherer I had before me a concrete example of the effect of my philosophy on the individual....

Nothing seemed to go right that spring, and yet nothing was absolutely wrong. At times I became irritated, bewildered, out of tune, and unable to understand why. The weather itself was uneasy, tepid, with long spells of hot wind and dust. I no longer seemed to find refuge in my work. I was unhappy at home. After walking for many years in confidence and security along what appeared to be a certain path, I had suddenly come out into a vague country in which it was becoming more and more difficult to recognize landmarks. I did not like to confess this; and yet I heard within me occasional whispers. Could it be that I, Hugh Paret, who had always been so positive, had made a mess of my life? There were moments when the pattern of it appeared to have fallen apart, resolved itself into pieces that refused to fit into each other.

Of course my relationship with Nancy had something to do with this....

One evening late in the spring, after dinner, Maude came into the library.

"Are you busy, Hugh?" she asked.

I put down my newspapers.

"Because," she went on, as she took a chair near the table where I was writing, "I wanted to tell you that I have decided to go to Europe, and take the children."

"To Europe!" I exclaimed. The significance of the announcement failed at once to register in my brain, but I was aware of a shock.

"Yes."

"When?" I asked.

"Right away. The end of this month."

"For the summer?"

"I haven't decided how long I shall stay."

I stared at her in bewilderment. In contrast to the agitation I felt rising within me, she was extraordinarily calm, unbelievably so.

"But where do you intend to go in Europe?"

"I shall go to London for a month or so, and after that to some quiet place in France, probably at the sea, where the children can learn French and German. After that, I have no plans."

"But—you talk as if you might stay indefinitely."

"I haven't decided," she repeated.

"But why—why are you doing this?"

I would have recalled the words as soon as I had spoken them. There was the slightest unsteadiness in her voice as she replied:—

"Is it necessary to go into that, Hugh? Wouldn't it be useless as well as a little painful? Surely, going to Europe without one's husband is not an unusual thing in these days. Let it just be understood that I want to go, that the children have arrived at an age when it will do them good."

I got up and began to walk up and down the room, while she watched me with a silent calm which was incomprehensible. In vain I summoned my faculties to meet it.

I had not thought her capable of such initiative.

"I can't see why you want to leave me," I said at last, though with a full sense of the inadequacy of the remark, and a suspicion of its hypocrisy.

"That isn't quite true," she answered. "In the first place, you don't need me. I am not of the slightest use in your life, I haven't been a factor in it for years. You ought never to have married me,—it was all a terrible mistake. I began to realize that after we had been married a few months—even when we were on our wedding trip. But I was too inexperienced—perhaps too weak to acknowledge it to myself. In the last few years I have come to see it plainly. I should have been a fool if I hadn't. I am not your wife in any real sense of the word, I cannot hold you, I cannot even interest you. It's a situation that no woman with self-respect can endure."

"Aren't those rather modern sentiments, for you, Maude?" I said.

She flushed a little, but otherwise retained her remarkable composure.

"I don't care whether they are 'modern' or not, I only know that my position has become impossible."

I walked to the other end of the room, and stood facing the carefully drawn curtains of the windows; fantastically, they seemed to represent the impasse to which my mind had come. Did she intend, ultimately, to get a divorce? I dared not ask her. The word rang horribly in my ears, though unpronounced; and I knew then that I lacked her courage, and the knowledge was part of my agony.

I turned.

"Don't you think you've overdrawn things, Maude exaggerated them? No marriages are perfect. You've let your mind dwell until it has become inflamed on matters which really don't amount to much."

"I was never saner, Hugh," she replied instantly. And indeed I was forced to confess that she looked it. That new Maude I had seen emerging of late years seemed now to have found herself; she was no longer the woman I had married,—yielding, willing to overlook, anxious to please, living in me.

"I don't influence you, or help you in any way. I never have."

"Oh, that's not true," I protested.

But she cut me short, going on inexorably:—

"I am merely your housekeeper, and rather a poor one at that, from your point of view. You ignore me. I am not blaming you for it—you are made that way. It's true that you have always supported me in luxury,—that might have been enough for another woman. It isn't enough for me—I, too, have a life to live, a soul to be responsible for. It's not for my sake so much as for the children's that I don't want it to be crushed."

"Crushed!" I repeated.

"Yes. You are stifling it. I say again that I'm not blaming you, Hugh. You are made differently from me. All you care for, really, is your career. You may think that you care, at times, for—other things, but it isn't so."

I took, involuntarily, a deep breath. Would she mention Nancy? Was it in reality Nancy who had brought about this crisis? And did Maude suspect the closeness of that relationship?

Suddenly I found myself begging her not to go; the more astonishing since, if at any time during the past winter this solution had presented itself to me as a possibility, I should eagerly have welcomed it! But should I ever have had the courage to propose a separation? I even wished to delude myself now into believing that what she suggested was in reality not a separation. I preferred to think of it as a trip.... A vision of freedom thrilled me, and yet I was wracked and torn. I had an idea that she was suffering, that the ordeal was a terrible one for her; and at that moment there crowded into my mind, melting me, incident after incident of our past.

"It seems to me that we have got along pretty well together, Maude. I have been negligent—I'll admit it. But I'll try to do better in the future. And—if you'll wait a month or so, I'll go to Europe with you, and we'll have a good time."

She looked at me sadly,—pityingly, I thought.

"No, Hugh, I've thought it all out. You really don't want me. You only say this because you are sorry for me, because you dislike to have your feelings wrung. You needn't be sorry for me, I shall be much happier away from you."

"Think it over, Maude," I pleaded. "I shall miss you and the children. I haven't paid much attention to them, either, but I am fond of them, and depend upon them, too."

She shook her head.

"It's no use, Hugh. I tell you I've thought it all out. You don't care for the children, you were never meant to have any."

"Aren't you rather severe in your judgments?"

"I don't think so," she answered. "I'm willing to admit my faults, that I am a failure so far as you are concerned. Your ideas of life and mine are far apart."

"I suppose," I exclaimed bitterly, "that you are referring to my professional practices."

A note of weariness crept into her voice. I might have known that she was near the end of her strength.

"No, I don't think it's that," she said dispassionately. "I prefer to put it down, that part of it, to a fundamental difference of ideas. I do not feel qualified to sit in judgment on that part of your life, although I'll admit that many of the things you have done, in common with the men with whom you are associated, have seemed to me unjust and inconsiderate of the rights and feelings of others. You have alienated some of your best friends. If I were to arraign you at all, it would be on the score of heartlessness. But I suppose it isn't your fault, that you haven't any heart."

"That's unfair," I put in.

"I don't wish to be unfair," she replied. "Only, since you ask me, I have to tell you that that is the way it seems to me. I don't want to introduce the question of right and wrong into this, Hugh, I'm not capable of unravelling it; I can't put myself into your life, and see things from your point of view, weigh your problems and difficulties. In the first place, you won't let me. I think I understand you, partly—but only partly. You have kept yourself shut up. But why discuss it? I have made up my mind."

The legal aspect of the matter occurred to me. What right had she to leave me? I might refuse to support her. Yet even as these thoughts came I rejected them; I knew that it was not in me to press this point. And she could always take refuge with her father; without the children, of course. But the very notion sickened me. I could not bear to think of Maude deprived of the children. I had seated myself again at the table. I put my hand to my forehead.

"Don't make it hard, Hugh," I heard her say, gently. "Believe me, it is best. I know. There won't be any talk about it,—right away, at any rate. People will think it natural that I should wish to go abroad for the summer. And later—well, the point of view about such affairs has changed. They are better understood."

She had risen. She was pale, still outwardly composed,—but I had a strange, hideous feeling that she was weeping inwardly.

"Aren't you coming back—ever?" I cried.

She did not answer at once.

"I don't know," she said, "I don't know," and left the room abruptly....

I wanted to follow her, but something withheld me. I got up and walked around the room in a state of mind that was near to agony, taking one of the neglected books out of the shelves, glancing at its meaningless print, and replacing it; I stirred the fire, opened the curtains and gazed out into the street and closed them again. I looked around me, a sudden intensity of hatred seized me for this big, silent, luxurious house; I recalled Maude's presentiment about it. Then, thinking I might still dissuade her, I went slowly up the padded stairway—to find her door locked; and a sense of the finality of her decision came over me. I knew then that I could not alter it even were I to go all the lengths of abjectness. Nor could I, I knew, have brought myself to have feigned a love I did not feel.

What was it I felt? I could not define it. Amazement, for one thing, that Maude with her traditional, Christian view of marriage should have come to such a decision. I went to my room, undressed mechanically and got into bed....

She gave no sign at the breakfast table of having made the decision of the greatest moment in our lives; she conversed as usual, asked about the news, reproved the children for being noisy; and when the children had left the table there were no tears, reminiscences, recriminations. In spite of the slight antagonism and envy of which I was conscious,—that she was thus superbly in command of the situation, that she had developed her pinions and was thus splendidly able to use them,—my admiration for her had never been greater. I made an effort to achieve the frame of mind she suggested: since she took it so calmly, why should I be tortured by the tragedy of it? Perhaps she had ceased to love me, after all! Perhaps she felt nothing but relief. At any rate, I was grateful to her, and I found a certain consolation, a sop to my pride in the reflection that the initiative must have been hers to take. I could not have deserted her.

"When do you think of leaving?" I asked.

"Two weeks from Saturday on the Olympic, if that is convenient for you." Her manner seemed one of friendly solicitude. "You will remain in the house this summer, as usual, I suppose?"

"Yes," I said.

It was a sunny, warm morning, and I went downtown in the motor almost blithely. It was the best solution after all, and I had been a fool to oppose it.... At the office, there was much business awaiting me; yet once in a while, during the day, when the tension relaxed, the recollection of what had happened flowed back into my consciousness. Maude was going!

I had telephoned Nancy, making an appointment for the afternoon. Sometimes—not too frequently—we were in the habit of going out into the country in one of her motors, a sort of landaulet, I believe, in which we were separated from the chauffeur by a glass screen. She was waiting for me when I arrived, at four; and as soon as we had shot clear of the city, "Maude is going away," I told her.

"Going away?" she repeated, struck more by the tone of my voice than by what I had said.

"She announced last night that she was going abroad indefinitely."

I had been more than anxious to see how Nancy would take the news. A flush gradually deepened in her cheeks.

"You mean that she is going to leave you?"

"It looks that way. In fact, she as much as said so."

"Why?" said Nancy.

"Well, she explained it pretty thoroughly. Apparently, it isn't a sudden decision," I replied, trying to choose my words, to speak composedly as I repeated the gist of our conversation. Nancy, with her face averted, listened in silence—a silence that continued some time after I had ceased to speak.

"She didn't—she didn't mention—?" the sentence remained unfinished.

"No," I said quickly, "she didn't. She must know, of course, but I'm sure that didn't enter into it."

Nancy's eyes as they returned to me were wet, and in them was an expression I had never seen before,—of pain, reproach, of questioning. It frightened me.

"Oh, Hugh, how little you know!" she cried.

"What do you mean?" I demanded.

"That is what has brought her to this decision—you and I."

"You mean that—that Maude loves me? That she is jealous?" I don't know how I managed to say it.

"No woman likes to think that she is a failure," murmured Nancy.

"Well, but she isn't really," I insisted. "She could have made another man happy—a better man. It was all one of those terrible mistakes our modern life seems to emphasize so."

"She is a woman," Nancy said, with what seemed a touch of vehemence. "It's useless to expect you to understand.... Do you remember what I said to you about her? How I appealed to you when you married to try to appreciate her?"

"It wasn't that I didn't appreciate her," I interrupted, surprised that Nancy should have recalled this, "she isn't the woman for me, we aren't made for each other. It was my mistake, my fault, I admit, but I don't agree with you at all, that we had anything to do with her decision. It is just the—the culmination of a long period of incompatibility. She has come to realize that she has only one life to live, and she seems happier, more composed, more herself than she has ever been since our marriage. Of course I don't mean to say it isn't painful for her.... But I am sure she isn't well, that it isn't because of our seeing one another," I concluded haltingly.

"She is finer than either of us, Hugh,—far finer."

I did not relish this statement.

"She's fine, I admit. But I can't see how under the circumstances any of us could have acted differently." And Nancy not replying, I continued: "She has made up her mind to go,—I suppose I could prevent it by taking extreme measures,—but what good would it do? Isn't it, after all, the most sensible, the only way out of a situation that has become impossible? Times have changed, Nancy, and you yourself have been the first to admit it. Marriage is no longer what it was, and people are coming to look upon it more sensibly. In order to perpetuate the institution, as it was, segregation, insulation, was the only course. Men segregated their wives, women their husbands,—the only logical method of procedure, but it limited the individual. Our mothers and fathers thought it scandalous if husband or wife paid visits alone. It wasn't done. But our modern life has changed all that. A marriage, to be a marriage, should be proof against disturbing influences, should leave the individuals free; the binding element should be love, not the force of an imposed authority. You seemed to agree to all this."

"Yes, I know," she admitted. "But I cannot think that happiness will ever grow out of unhappiness."

"But Maude will not be unhappy," I insisted. "She will be happier, far happier, now that she has taken the step."

"Oh, I wish I thought so," Nancy exclaimed. "Hugh, you always believe what you want to believe. And the children. How can you bear to part with them?"

I was torn, I had a miserable sense of inadequacy.

"I shall miss them," I said. "I have never really appreciated them. I admit I don't deserve to have them, and I am willing to give them up for you, for Maude..."

We had made one of our favourite drives among the hills on the far side of the Ashuela, and at six were back at Nancy's house. I did not go in, but walked slowly homeward up Grant Avenue. It had been a trying afternoon. I had not expected, indeed, that Nancy would have rejoiced, but her attitude, her silences, betraying, as they did, compunctions, seemed to threaten our future happiness.

Chapter Twenty-Two

One evening two or three days later I returned from the office to gaze up at my house, to realize suddenly that it would be impossible for me to live there, in those great, empty rooms, alone; and I told Maude that I would go to the Club—during her absence. I preferred to keep up the fiction that her trip would only be temporary. She forbore from contradicting me, devoting herself efficiently to the task of closing the house, making it seem, somehow, a rite,—the final rite in her capacity as housewife. The drawing-room was shrouded, and the library; the books wrapped neatly in paper; a smell of camphor pervaded the place; the cheerful schoolroom was dismantled; trunks and travelling bags appeared. The solemn butler packed my clothes, and I arranged for a room at the Club in the wing that recently had been added for the accommodation of bachelors and deserted husbands. One of the ironies of those days was that the children began to suggest again possibilities of happiness I had missed—especially Matthew. With all his gentleness, the boy seemed to have a precocious understanding of the verities, and the capacity for suffering which as a child I had possessed. But he had more self-control. Though he looked forward to the prospect of new scenes and experiences with the anticipation natural to his temperament, I thought he betrayed at moments a certain intuition as to what was going on.

"When are you coming over, father?" he asked once. "How soon will your business let you?"

He had been brought up in the belief that my business was a tyrant.

"Oh, soon, Matthew,—sometime soon," I said.

I had a feeling that he understood me, not intellectually, but emotionally. What a companion he might have been!.... Moreton and Biddy moved me less. They were more robust, more normal, less introspective and imaginative; Europe meant nothing to them, but they were frankly delighted and excited at the prospect of going on the ocean, asking dozens of questions about the great ship, impatient to embark.....

"I shan't need all that, Hugh," Maude said, when I handed her a letter of credit. "I—I intend to live quite simply, and my chief expenses will be the children's education. I am going to give them the best, of course."

"Of course," I replied. "But I want you to live over there as you have been accustomed to live here. It's not exactly generosity on my part,—I have enough, and more than enough."

She took the letter.

"Another thing—I'd rather you didn't go to New York with us, Hugh. I know you are busy—"

"Of course I'm going," I started to protest.

"No," she went on, firmly. "I'd rather you didn't. The hotel people will put me on the steamer very comfortably,—and there are other reasons why I do not wish it." I did not insist.... On the afternoon of her departure, when I came uptown, I found her pinning some roses on her jacket.

"Perry and Lucia sent them," she informed me. She maintained the friendly, impersonal manner to the very end; but my soul, as we drove to the train, was full of un-probed wounds. I had had roses put in her compartments in the car; Tom and Susan Peters were there with more roses, and little presents for the children. Their cheerfulness seemed forced, and I wondered whether they suspected that Maude's absence would be prolonged.

"Write us often, and tell us all about it, dear," said Susan, as she sat beside Maude and held her hand; Tom had Biddy on his knee. Maude was pale, but smiling and composed.

"I hope to get a little villa in France, near the sea," she said. "I'll send you a photograph of it, Susan."

"And Chickabiddy, when she comes back, will be rattling off French like a native," exclaimed Tom, giving her a hug.

"I hate French," said Biddy, and she looked at him solemnly. "I wish you were coming along, Uncle Tom."

Bells resounded through the great station. The porter warned us off. I kissed the children one by one, scarcely realizing what I was doing. I kissed Maude. She received my embrace passively.

"Good-bye, Hugh," she said.

I alighted, and stood on the platform as the train pulled out. The children crowded to the windows, but Maude did not appear.... I found myself walking with Tom and Susan past hurrying travellers and porters to the Decatur Street entrance, where my automobile stood waiting.

"I'll take you home, Susan," I said.

"We're ever so much obliged, Hugh," she answered, "but the street-cars go almost to ferry's door. We're dining there."

Her eyes were filled with tears, and she seemed taller, more ungainly than ever—older. A sudden impression of her greatness of heart was borne home to me, and I grasped the value of such rugged friendship as hers—as Tom's.

"We shouldn't know how to behave in an automobile," he said, as though to soften her refusal. And I stood watching their receding figures as they walked out into the street and hailed the huge electric car that came to a stop beyond them. Above its windows was painted "The Ashuela Traction Company," a label reminiscent of my professional activities. Then I heard the chauffeur ask:—

"Where do you wish to go, sir?"

"To the Club," I said.

My room was ready, my personal belongings, my clothes had been laid out, my photographs were on the dressing-table. I took up, mechanically, the evening newspaper, but I could not read it; I thought of Maude, of the children, memories flowed in upon me,—a flood not to be dammed.... Presently the club valet knocked at my door. He had a dinner card.

"Will you be dining here, sir?" he inquired.

I went downstairs. Fred Grierson was the only man in the dining-room.

"Hello, Hugh," he said, "come and sit down. I hear your wife's gone abroad."

"Yes," I answered, "she thought she'd try it instead of the South Shore this summer."

Perhaps I imagined that he looked at me queerly. I had made a great deal of money out of my association with Grierson, I had valued very highly being an important member of the group to which he belonged; but to- night, as I watched him eating and drinking greedily, I hated him even as I hated myself. And after dinner, when he started talking with a ridicule that was a thinly disguised bitterness about the Citizens Union and their preparations for a campaign I left him and went to bed.

Before a week had passed my painful emotions had largely subsided, and with my accustomed resiliency I had regained the feeling of self-respect so essential to my happiness. I was free. My only anxiety was for Nancy, who had gone to New York the day after my last talk with her; and it was only by telephoning to her house that I discovered when she was expected to return.... I found her sitting beside one of the open French windows of her salon, gazing across at the wooded hills beyond the Ashuela. She was serious, a little pale; more exquisite, more desirable than ever; but her manner implied the pressure of control, and her voice was not quite steady as she greeted me.

"You've been away a long time," I said.

"The dressmakers," she answered. Her colour rose a little. "I thought they'd never get through."

"But why didn't you drop me a line, let me know when you were coming?" I asked, taking a chair beside her, and laying my hand on hers. She drew it gently away.

"What's the matter?" I asked.

"I've been thinking it all over—what we're doing. It doesn't seem right, it seems terribly wrong."

"But I thought we'd gone over all that," I replied, as patiently as I could. "You're putting it on an old-fashioned, moral basis."

"But there must be same basis," she urged. "There are responsibilities, obligations—there must be!—that we can't get away from. I can't help feeling that we ought to stand by our mistakes, and by our bargains; we made a choice—it's cheating, somehow, and if we take this—what we want- -we shall be punished for it."

"But I'm willing to be punished, to suffer, as I told you. If you loved me—"

"Hugh!" she exclaimed, and I was silent. "You don't understand," she went on, a little breathlessly, "what I mean by punishment is deterioration. Do you remember once, long ago, when you came to me before I was married, I said we'd both run after false gods, and that we couldn't do without them? Well, and now this has come; it seems so wonderful to me, coming again like that after we had passed it by, after we thought it had gone forever; it's opened up visions for me that I never hoped to see again. It ought to restore us, dear—that's what I'm trying to say—to redeem us, to make us capable of being what we were meant to be. If it doesn't do that, if it isn't doing so, it's the most horrible of travesties, of mockeries. If we gain life only to have it turn into death—slow death; if we go to pieces again, utterly. For now there's hope. The more I think, the more clearly I see that we can't take any step without responsibilities. If we take this, you'll have me, and I'll have you. And if we don't save each other—"

"But we will," I said.

"Ah," she exclaimed, "if we could start new, without any past. I married Ham with my eyes open."

"You couldn't know that he would become—well, as flagrant as he is. You didn't really know what he was then."

"There's no reason why I shouldn't have anticipated it. I can't claim that I was deceived, that I thought my marriage was made in heaven. I entered into a contract, and Ham has kept his part of it fairly well. He hasn't interfered with my freedom. That isn't putting it on a high plane, but there is an obligation involved. You yourself, in your law practice, are always insisting upon the sacredness of contract as the very basis of our civilization."

Here indeed would have been a home thrust, had I been vulnerable at the time. So intent was I on overcoming her objections, that I resorted unwittingly to the modern argument I had more than once declared in court to be anathema-the argument of the new reform in reference to the common law and the constitution.

"A contract, no matter how seriously entered into at the time it was made, that later is seen to violate the principles of humanity should be void. And not only this, but you didn't consent that he should disgrace you."

Nancy winced.

"I never told you that he paid my father's debts, I never told anyone," she said, in a low voice.

"Even then," I answered after a moment, "you ought to see that it's too terrible a price to pay for your happiness. And Ham hasn't ever pretended to consider you in any way. It's certain you didn't agree that he should do—what he is doing."

"Suppose I admitted it," she said, "there remain Maude and your children. Their happiness, their future becomes my responsibility as well as yours."

"But I don't love Maude, and Maude doesn't love me. I grant it's my fault, that I did her a wrong in marrying her, but she is right in leaving me. I should be doing her a double wrong. And the children will be happy with her, they will be well brought up. I, too, have thought this out, Nancy," I insisted, "and the fact is that in our respective marriages we have been, each of us, victims of our time, of our education. We were born in a period of transition, we inherited views of life that do not fit conditions to-day. It takes courage to achieve happiness, initiative to emancipate one's self from a morality that begins to hamper and bind. To stay as we are, to refuse to take what is offered us, is to remain between wind and water. I don't mean that we should do anything—hastily. We can afford to take a reasonable time, to be dignified about it. But I have come to the conclusion that the only thing that matters in the world is a love like ours, and its fulfilment. Achievement, success, are empty and meaningless without it. And you do love me—you've admitted it."

"Oh, I don't want to talk about it," she exclaimed, desperately.

"But we have to talk about it," I persisted. "We have to thrash it out, to see it straight, as you yourself have said."

"You speak of convictions, Hugh,—new convictions, in place of the old we have discarded. But what are they? And is there no such thing as conscience—even though it be only an intuition of happiness or unhappiness? I do care for you, I do love you—"

"Then why not let that suffice?" I exclaimed, leaning towards her.

She drew back.

"But I want to respect you, too," she said.

I was shocked, too shocked to answer.

"I want to respect you," she repeated, more gently. "I don't want to think that—that what we feel for each other is—unconsecrated."

"It consecrates itself," I declared.

She shook her head.

"Surely it has its roots in everything that is fine in both of us."

"We both went wrong," said Nancy. "We both sought to wrest power and happiness from the world, to make our own laws. How can we assert that— this is not merely a continuation of it?"

"But can't we work out our beliefs together?" I demanded. "Won't you trust me, trust our love for one another?"

Her breath came and went quickly.

"Oh, you know that I want you, Hugh, as much as you want me, and more. The time may come when I can't resist you."

"Why do you resist me?" I cried, seizing her hands convulsively, and swept by a gust of passion at her confession.

"Try to understand that I am fighting for both of us!" she pleaded—an appeal that wrung me in spite of the pitch to which my feelings had been raised. "Hugh, dear, we must think it out. Don't now."

I let her hands drop....

Beyond the range of hills rising from the far side of the Ashuela was the wide valley in which was situated the Cloverdale Country Club, with its polo field, golf course and tennis courts; and in this same valley some of our wealthy citizens, such as Howard Ogilvy and Leonard Dickinson, had bought "farms," week-end playthings for spring and autumn. Hambleton Durrett had started the fashion. Capriciously, as he did everything else, he had become the owner of several hundred acres of pasture, woodland and orchard, acquired some seventy-five head of blooded stock, and proceeded to house them in model barns and milk by machinery; for several months he had bored everyone in the Boyne Club whom he could entice into conversation on the subject of the records of pedigreed cows, and spent many bibulous nights on the farm in company with those parasites who surrounded him when he was in town. Then another interest had intervened; a feminine one, of course, and his energies were transferred (so we understood) to the reconstruction and furnishing of a little residence in New York, not far from Fifth Avenue. The farm continued under the expert direction of a superintendent who was a graduate of the State Agricultural College, and a select clientele, which could afford to pay the prices, consumed the milk and cream and butter. Quite consistent with their marital relations was the fact that Nancy should have taken a fancy to the place after Ham's interest had waned. Not that she cared for the Guernseys, or Jerseys, or whatever they may have been; she evinced a sudden passion for simplicity,—occasional simplicity, at least,—for a contrast to and escape from a complicated life of luxury. She built another house for the superintendent banished him from the little farmhouse (where Ham had kept two rooms); banished along with the superintendent the stiff plush furniture, the yellow-red carpets, the easels and the melodeon, and decked it out in bright chintzes, with wall-papers to match, dainty muslin curtains, and rag- carpet rugs on the hardwood floors. The pseudo-classic porch over the doorway, which had suggested a cemetery, was removed, and a wide piazza added, furnished with wicker lounging chairs and tables, and shaded with gay awnings.

Here, to the farm, accompanied by a maid, she had been in the habit of retiring from time to time, and here she came in early July. Here, dressed in the simplest linen gowns of pink or blue or white, I found a Nancy magically restored to girlhood,—anew Nancy, betraying only traces of the old, a new Nancy in a new Eden. We had all the setting, all the illusion of that perfect ideal of domesticity, love in a cottage. Nancy and I, who all our lives had spurned simplicity, laughed over the joy we found in it: she made a high art of it, of course; we had our simple dinners, which Mrs. Olsen cooked and served in the open air; sometimes on the porch, sometimes under the great butternut tree spreading its shade over what in a more elaborate country-place, would have been called a lawn,—an uneven plot of grass of ridges and hollows that ran down to the orchard. Nancy's eyes would meet mine across the little table, and often our gaze would wander over the pastures below, lucent green in the level evening light, to the darkening woods beyond, gilt-tipped in the setting sun. There were fields of ripening yellow grain, of lusty young corn that grew almost as we watched it: the warm winds of evening were heavy with the acrid odours of fecundity. Fecundity! In that lay the elusive yet insistent charm of that country; and Nancy's, of course, was the transforming touch that made it paradise. It was thus, in the country, I suggested that we should spend the rest of our existence. What was the use of amassing money, when happiness was to be had so simply?

"How long do you think you could stand it?" she asked, as she handed me a plate of blackberries.

"Forever, with the right woman," I announced.

"How long could the woman stand it?".... She humoured, smilingly, my crystal-gazing into our future, as though she had not the heart to deprive me of the pleasure.

"I simply can't believe in it, Hugh," she said when I pressed her for an answer.

"Why not?"

"I suppose it's because I believe in continuity, I haven't the romantic temperament,—I always see the angel with the flaming sword. It isn't that I want to see him."

"But we shall redeem ourselves," I said. "It won't be curiosity and idleness. We are not just taking this thing, and expecting to give nothing for it in return."

"What can we give that is worth it?" she exclaimed, with one of her revealing flashes.

"We won't take it lightly, but seriously," I told her. "We shall find something to give, and that something will spring naturally out of our love. We'll read together, and think and plan together."

"Oh, Hugh, you are incorrigible," was all she said.

The male tendency in me was forever strained to solve her, to deduce from her conversation and conduct a body of consistent law. The effort was useless. Here was a realm, that of Nancy's soul, in which there was apparently no such thing as relevancy. In the twilight, after dinner, we often walked through the orchard to a grassy bank beside the little stream, where we would sit and watch the dying glow in the sky. After a rain its swollen waters were turbid, opaque yellow-red with the clay of the hills; at other times it ran smoothly, temperately, almost clear between the pasture grasses and wild flowers. Nancy declared that it reminded her of me. We sat there, into the lush, warm nights, and the moon shone down on us, or again through long silences we searched the bewildering, starry chart of the heavens, with the undertones of the night-chorus of the fields in our ears. Sometimes she let my head rest upon her knee; but when, throbbing at her touch, with the life-force pulsing around us, I tried to take her in my arms, to bring her lips to mine, she resisted me with an energy of will and body that I could not overcome, I dared not overcome. She acknowledged her love for me, she permitted me to come to her, she had the air of yielding but never yielded. Why, then, did she allow the words of love to pass? and how draw the line between caresses? I was maddened and disheartened by that elusive resistance in her—apparently so frail a thing!—that neither argument nor importunity could break down. Was there something lacking in me? or was it that I feared to mar or destroy the love she had. This, surely, had not been the fashion of other loves, called unlawful, the classic instances celebrated by the poets of all ages rose to mock me.

"Incurably romantic," she had called me, in calmer moments, when I was able to discuss our affair objectively. And once she declared that I had no sense of tragedy. We read "Macbeth" together, I remember, one rainy Sunday. The modern world, which was our generation, would seem to be cut off from all that preceded it as with a descending knife. It was precisely from "the sense of tragedy" that we had been emancipated: from the "agonized conscience," I should undoubtedly have said, had I been acquainted then with Mr. Santayana's later phrase. Conscience—the old kind of conscience,—and nothing inherent in the deeds themselves, made the tragedy; conscience was superstition, the fear of the wrath of the gods: conscience was the wrath of the gods. Eliminate it, and behold! there were no consequences. The gods themselves, that kind of gods, became as extinct as the deities of the Druids, the Greek fates, the terrible figures of German mythology. Yes, and as the God of Christian orthodoxy.

Had any dire calamities overtaken the modern Macbeths, of whose personal lives we happened to know something? Had not these great ones broken with impunity all the laws of traditional morality? They ground the faces of the poor, played golf and went to church with serene minds, untroubled by criticism; they appropriated, quite freely, other men's money, and some of them other men's wives, and yet they were not haggard with remorse. The gods remained silent. Christian ministers regarded these modern transgressors of ancient laws benignly and accepted their contributions. Here, indeed, were the supermen of the mad German prophet and philosopher come to life, refuting all classic tragedy. It is true that some of these supermen were occasionally swept away by disease, which in ancient days would have been regarded as a retributive scourge, but was in fact nothing but the logical working of the laws of hygiene, the result of overwork. Such, though stated more crudely, were my contentions when desire did not cloud my brain and make me incoherent. And I did not fail to remind Nancy, constantly, that this was the path on which her feet had been set; that to waver now was to perish. She smiled, yet she showed concern.

"But suppose you don't get what you want?" she objected. "What then? Suppose one doesn't become a superman? or a superwoman? What's to happen to one? Is there no god but the superman's god, which is himself? Are there no gods for those who can't be supermen? or for those who may refuse to be supermen?"

To refuse, I maintained, were a weakness of the will.

"But there are other wills," she persisted, "wills over which the superman may conceivably have no control. Suppose, for example, that you don't get me, that my will intervenes, granting it to be conceivable that your future happiness and welfare, as you insist, depend upon your getting me—which I doubt."

"You've no reason to doubt it."

"Well, granting it, then. Suppose the orthodoxies and superstitions succeed in inhibiting me. I may not be a superwoman, but my will, or my conscience, if you choose, may be stronger than yours. If you don't get what you want, you aren't happy. In other words, you fail. Where are your gods then? The trouble with you, my dear Hugh, is that you have never failed," she went on, "you've never had a good, hard fall, you've always been on the winning side, and you've never had the world against you. No wonder you don't understand the meaning and value of tragedy."

"And you?" I asked.

"No," she agreed, "nor I. Yet I have come to feel, instinctively, that somehow concealed in tragedy is the central fact of life, the true reality, that nothing is to be got by dodging it, as we have dodged it. Your superman, at least the kind of superman you portray, is petrified. Something vital in him, that should be plastic and sensitive, has turned to stone."

"Since when did you begin to feel this?" I inquired uneasily.

"Since—well, since we have been together again, in the last month or two. Something seems to warn me that if we take—what we want, we shan't get it. That's an Irish saying, I know, but it expresses my meaning. I may be little, I may be superstitious, unlike the great women of history who have dared. But it's more than mere playing safe—my instinct, I mean. You see, you are involved. I believe I shouldn't hesitate if only myself were concerned, but you are the uncertain quantity—more uncertain than you have any idea; you think you know yourself, you think you have analyzed yourself, but the truth is, Hugh, you don't know the meaning of struggle against real resistance."

I was about to protest.

"I know that you have conquered in the world of men and affairs," she hurried on, "against resistance, but it isn't the kind of resistance I mean. It doesn't differ essentially from the struggle in the animal kingdom."

I bowed. "Thank you," I said.

She laughed a little.

"Oh, I have worshipped success, too. Perhaps I still do—that isn't the point. An animal conquers his prey, he is in competition, in constant combat with others of his own kind, and perhaps he brings to bear a certain amount of intelligence in the process. Intelligence isn't the point, either. I know what I'm saying is trite, it's banal, it sounds like moralizing, and perhaps it is, but there is so much confusion to-day that I think we are in danger of losing sight of the simpler verities, and that we must suffer for it. Your super-animal, your supreme-stag subdues the other stags, but he never conquers himself, he never feels the need of it, and therefore he never comprehends what we call tragedy."

"I gather your inference," I said, smiling.

"Well," she admitted, "I haven't stated the case with the shade of delicacy it deserves, but I wanted to make my meaning clear. We have raised up a class in America, but we have lost sight, a little— considerably, I think—of the distinguishing human characteristics. The men you were eulogizing are lords of the forest, more or less, and we women, who are of their own kind, what they have made us, surrender ourselves in submission and adoration to the lordly stag in the face of all the sacraments that have been painfully inaugurated by the race for the very purpose of distinguishing us from animals. It is equivalent to saying that there is no moral law; or, if there is, nobody can define it. We deny, inferentially, a human realm as distinguished from the animal, and in the denial it seems to me we are cutting ourselves off from what is essential human development. We are reverting to the animal. I have lost and you have lost—not entirely, perhaps, but still to a considerable extent—the bloom of that fervour, of that idealism, we may call it, that both of us possessed when we were in our teens. We had occasional visions. We didn't know what they meant, or how to set about their accomplishment, but they were not, at least, mere selfish aspirations; they implied, unconsciously no doubt, an element of service, and certainly our ideal of marriage had something fine in it."

"Isn't it for a higher ideal of marriage that we are searching?" I asked.

"If that is so," Nancy objected, "then all the other elements of our lives are sadly out of tune with it. Even the most felicitous union of the sexes demands sacrifice, an adjustment of wills, and these are the very things we balk at; and the trouble with our entire class in this country is that we won't acknowledge any responsibility, there's no sacrifice in our eminence, we have no sense of the whole."

"Where did you get all these ideas?" I demanded.

She laughed.

"Well," she admitted, "I've been thrashing around a little; and I've read some of the moderns, you know. Do you remember my telling you I didn't agree with them? and now this thing has come on me like a judgment. I've caught their mania for liberty, for self-realization—whatever they call it—but their remedies are vague, they fail to convince me that individuals achieve any quality by just taking what they want, regardless of others."....

I was unable to meet this argument, and the result was that when I was away from her I too began to "thrash around" among the books in a vain search for a radical with a convincing and satisfying philosophy. Thus we fly to literature in crises of the heart! There was no lack of writers who sought to deal—and deal triumphantly with the very situation in which I was immersed. I marked many passages, to read them over to Nancy, who was interested, but who accused me of being willing to embrace any philosophy, ancient or modern, that ran with the stream of my desires. It is worth recording that the truth of this struck home. On my way back to the city I reflected that, in spite of my protests against

Maude's going—protests wholly sentimental and impelled by the desire to avoid giving pain on the spot—I had approved of her departure because I didn't want her. On the other hand I had to acknowledge if I hadn't wanted Nancy, or rather, if I had become tired of her, I should have been willing to endorse her scruples.... It was not a comforting thought.

One morning when I was absently opening the mail I found at my office I picked up a letter from Theodore Watling, written from a seaside resort in Maine, the contents of which surprised and touched me, troubled me, and compelled me to face a situation with which I was wholly unprepared to cope. He announced that this was to be his last term in the Senate. He did not name the trouble his physician had discovered, but he had been warned that he must retire from active life. "The specialist whom I saw in New York," he went on, "wished me to resign at once, but when I pointed out to him how unfair this would be to my friends in the state, to my party as a whole—especially in these serious and unsettled times— he agreed that I might with proper care serve out the remainder of my term. I have felt it my duty to write to Barbour and Dickinson and one or two others in order that they might be prepared and that no time may be lost in choosing my successor. It is true that the revolt within the party has never gained much headway in our state, but in these days it is difficult to tell when and where a conflagration may break out, or how far it will go. I have ventured to recommend to them the man who seems to me the best equipped to carry on the work I have been trying to do here—in short, my dear Hugh, yourself. The Senate, as you know, is not a bed of roses just now for those who think as we do; but I have the less hesitancy in making the recommendation because I believe you are not one to shun a fight for the convictions we hold in common, and because you would regard, with me, the election of a senator with the new views as a very real calamity. If sound business men and lawyers should be eliminated from the Senate, I could not contemplate with any peace of mind what might happen to the country. In thus urging you, I know you will believe me when I say that my affection and judgment are equally involved, for it would be a matter of greater pride than I can express to have you follow me here as you have followed me at home. And I beg of you seriously to consider it.... I understand that Maude and the children are abroad. Remember me to them affectionately when you write. If you can find it convenient to come here, to Maine, to discuss the matter, you may be sure of a welcome. In any case, I expect to be in Washington in September for a meeting of our special committee. Sincerely and affectionately yours, Theodore Watling."

It was characteristic of him that the tone of the letter should be uniformly cheerful, that he should say nothing whatever of the blow this must be to his ambitions and hopes; and my agitation at the new and disturbing prospect thus opened up for me was momentarily swept away by feelings of affection and sorrow. A sharp realization came to me of how much I admired and loved this man, and this was followed by a pang at the thought of the disappointment my refusal would give him. Complications I did not wish to examine were then in the back of my mind; and while I still sat holding the letter in my hand the telephone rang, and a message came from Leonard Dickinson begging me to call at the bank at once.

Miller Gorse was there, and Tallant, waving a palm-leaf while sitting under the electric fan. They were all very grave, and they began to talk about the suddenness of Mr. Watling's illness and to speculate upon its nature. Leonard Dickinson was the most moved of the three; but they were all distressed, and showed it—even Tallant, whom I had never credited with any feelings; they spoke about the loss to the state. At length Gorse took a cigar from his pocket and lighted it; the smoke, impelled by the fan, drifted over the panelled partition into the bank.

"I suppose Mr. Watling mentioned to you what he wrote to us," he said.

"Yes," I admitted.

"Well," he asked, "what do you think of it?"

"I attribute it to Mr. Watling's friendship," I replied.

"No," said Gorse, in his businesslike manner, "Watling's right, there's no one else." Considering the number of inhabitants of our state, this remark had its humorous aspect.

"That's true," Dickinson put in, "there's no one else available who understands the situation as you do, Hugh, no one else we can trust as we trust you. I had a wire from Mr. Barbour this morning—he agrees. We'll miss you here, but now that Watling will be gone we'll need you there. And he's right—it's something we've got to decide on right away, and get started on soon, we can't afford to wobble and run any chances of a revolt."

"It isn't everybody the senatorship comes to on a platter—especially at your age," said Tallant.

"To tell you the truth," I answered, addressing Dickinson, "I'm not prepared to talk about it now. I appreciate the honour, but I'm not at all sure I'm the right man. And I've been considerably upset by this news of Mr. Watling."

"Naturally you would be," said the banker, sympathetically, "and we share your feelings. I don't know of any man for whom I have a greater affection than I have for Theodore Wading. We shouldn't have mentioned it now, Hugh, if Watling hadn't started the thing himself, if it weren't important to know where we stand right away. We can't afford to lose the seat. Take your time, but remember you're the man we depend upon."

Gorse nodded. I was aware, all the time Dickinson was speaking, of being surrounded by the strange, disquieting gaze of the counsel for the Railroad....

I went back to my office to spend an uneasy morning. My sorrow for Mr. Watling was genuine, but nevertheless I found myself compelled to consider an honour no man lightly refuses. Had it presented itself at any other time, had it been due to a happier situation than that brought about by the illness of a man whom I loved and admired, I should have thought the prospect dazzling indeed, part and parcel of my amazing luck. But now—now I was in an emotional state that distorted the factors of life, all those things I hitherto had valued; even such a prize as this I weighed in terms of one supreme desire: how would the acceptance of the senatorship affect the accomplishment of this desire? That was the question. I began making rapid calculations: the actual election would take place in the legislature a year from the following January; provided I were able to overcome Nancy's resistance—which I was determined to do- -nothing in the way of divorce proceedings could be thought of for more than a year; and I feared delay. On the other hand, if we waited until after I had been duly elected to get my divorce and marry Nancy my chances of reelection would be small. What did I care for the senatorship anyway—if I had her? and I wanted her now, as soon as I could get her. She—a life with her represented new values, new values I did not define, that made all I had striven for in the past of little worth. This was a bauble compared with the companionship of the woman I loved, the woman intended for me, who would give me peace of mind and soul and develop those truer aspirations that had long been thwarted and starved for lack of her. Gradually, as she regained the ascendency over my mind she ordinarily held—and from which she had been temporarily displaced by the arrival of Mr. Watling's letter and the talk in the bank—I became impatient and irritated by the intrusion. But what answer should I give to Dickinson and Gorse? what excuse for declining such an offer? I decided, as may be imagined, to wait, to temporize.

The irony of circumstances—of what might have been—prevented now my laying this trophy at Nancy's feet, for I knew I had only to mention the matter to be certain of losing her.

Chapter Twenty-Three

I had bought a small automobile, which I ran myself, and it was my custom to arrive at the farm every evening about five o'clock. But as I look back upon those days they seem to have lost succession, to be fused together, as it were, into one indeterminable period by the intense pressure of emotion; unsatisfied emotion,—and the state of physical and mental disorganization set up by it is in the retrospect not a little terrifying. The world grew more and more distorted, its affairs were neglected, things upon which I had set high values became as nothing. And even if I could summon back something of the sequence of our intercourse, it would be a mere repetition—growing on my part more irrational and insistent—of what I have already related. There were long, troubled, and futile silences when we sat together on the porch or in the woods and fields; when I wondered whether it were weakness or strength that caused Nancy to hold out against my importunities: the fears she professed of retribution, the benumbing effects of the conventional years, or the deep-rooted remnants of a Calvinism which—as she proclaimed—had lost definite expression to persist as an intuition. I recall something she said when she turned to me after one of these silences.

"Do you know how I feel sometimes? as though you and I had wandered together into a strange country, and lost our way. We have lost our way, Hugh—it's all so clandestine, so feverish, so unnatural, so unrelated to life, this existence we're leading. I believe it would be better if it were a mere case of physical passion. I can't help it," she went on, when I had exclaimed against this, "we are too—too complicated, you are too complicated. It's because we want the morning stars, don't you see?" She wound her fingers tightly around mine. "We not only want this, but all of life besides—you wouldn't be satisfied with anything less. Oh, I know it. That's your temperament, you were made that way, and I shouldn't be satisfied if you weren't. The time would come when you would blame me I don't mean vulgarly—and I couldn't stand that. If you weren't that way, if that weren't your nature, I mean, I should have given way long ago."

I made some sort of desperate protest.

"No, if I didn't know you so well I believe I should have given in long ago. I'm not thinking of you alone, but of myself, too. I'm afraid I shouldn't be happy, that I should begin to think—and then I couldn't stop. The plain truth, as I've told you over and over again, is that I'm not big enough." She continued smiling at me, a smile on which I could not bear to look. "I was wrong not to have gone away," I heard her say. "I will go away."

I was, at the time, too profoundly discouraged to answer....

One evening after an exhausting talk we sat, inert, on the grass hummock beside the stream. Heavy clouds had gathered in the sky, the light had deepened to amethyst, the valley was still, swooning with expectancy, louder and louder the thunder rolled from behind the distant hills, and presently a veil descended to hide them from our view. Great drops began to fall, unheeded.

"We must go in," said Nancy, at length.

I followed her across the field and through the orchard. From the porch we stood gazing out at the whitening rain that blotted all save the nearer landscape, and the smell of wet, midsummer grasses will always be associated with the poignancy of that moment.... At dinner, between the intervals of silence, our talk was of trivial things. We made a mere pretence of eating, and I remember having my attention arrested by the sight of a strange, pitying expression on the face of Mrs. Olsen, who waited on us. Before that the woman had been to me a mere ministering automaton. But she must have had ideas and opinions, this transported Swedish peasant.... Presently, having cleared the table, she retired.... The twilight deepened to dusk, to darkness. The storm, having spent the intensity of its passion in those first moments of heavy downpour and wind, had relaxed to a gentle rain that pattered on the roof, and from the stream came recurringly the dirge of the frogs. All I could see of Nancy was the dim outline of her head and shoulders: she seemed fantastically to be escaping me, to be fading, to be going; in sudden desperation I dropped on my knees beside her, and I felt her hands straying with a light yet agonized touch, over my head.

"Do you think I haven't suffered, too? that I don't suffer?" I heard her ask.

Some betraying note for which I had hitherto waited in vain must have pierced to my consciousness, yet the quiver of joy and the swift, convulsive movement that followed it seemed one. Her strong, lithe body was straining in my arms, her lips returning my kisses.... Clinging to her hands, I strove to summon my faculties of realization; and I began to speak in broken, endearing sentences.

"It's stronger than we are—stronger than anything else in the world," she said.

"But you're not sorry?" I asked.

"I don't want to think—I don't care," she replied. "I only know that I love you. I wonder if you will ever know how much!"

The moments lengthened into hours, and she gently reminded me that it was late. The lights in the little farmhouses near by had long been extinguished. I pleaded to linger; I wanted her, more of her, all of her with a fierce desire that drowned rational thought, and I feared that something might still come between us, and cheat me of her.

"No, no," she cried, with fear in her voice. "We shall have to think it out very carefully—what we must do. We can't afford to make any mistakes."

"We'll talk it all over to-morrow," I said.

With a last, reluctant embrace I finally left her, walked blindly to where the motor car was standing, and started the engine. I looked back. Outlined in the light of the doorway I saw her figure in what seemed an attitude of supplication....

I drove cityward through the rain, mechanically taking the familiar turns in the road, barely missing a man in a buggy at a four-corners. He shouted after me, but the world to which he belonged didn't exist. I lived again those moments that had followed Nancy's surrender, seeking to recall and fix in my mind every word that had escaped from her lips—the trivial things that to lovers are so fraught with meaning. I lived it all over again, as I say, but the reflection of it, though intensely emotional, differed from the reality in that now I was somewhat able to regard the thing, to regard myself, objectively; to define certain feelings that had flitted in filmy fashion through my consciousness, delicate shadows I recognized at the time as related to sadness. When she had so amazingly yielded, the thought for which my mind had been vaguely groping was that the woman who lay there in my arms, obscured by the darkness, was not Nancy at all! It was as if this one precious woman I had so desperately pursued had, in the capture, lost her identity, had mysteriously become just woman, in all her significance, yes, and helplessness. The particular had merged (inevitably, I might have known) into the general: the temporary had become the lasting, with a chain of consequences vaguely implied that even in my joy gave me pause. For the first time in my life I had a glimpse of what marriage might mean,—marriage in a greater sense than I had ever conceived it, a sort of cosmic sense, implying obligations transcending promises and contracts, calling for greatness of soul of a kind I had not hitherto imagined. Was there in me a grain of doubt of my ability to respond to such a high call? I began to perceive that such a union as we contemplated involved more obligations than one not opposed to traditional views of morality. I fortified myself, however,—if indeed I really needed fortification in a mood prevailingly triumphant and exalted,—with the thought that this love was different, the real thing, the love of maturity steeped in the ideals of youth. Here was a love for which I must be prepared to renounce other things on which I set a high value; prepared, in case the world, for some reason, should not look upon us with kindliness. It was curious that such reflections as these should have been delayed until after the achievement of my absorbing desire, more curious that they should have followed so closely on the heels of it. The affair had shifted suddenly from a basis of adventure, of uncertainty; to one of fact, of commitment; I am exaggerating my concern in order to define it; I was able to persuade myself without much difficulty that these little, cloudy currents in the stream of my joy were due to a natural reaction from the tremendous strain of the past weeks, mere morbid fancies.

When at length I reached my room at the Club I sat looking out at the rain falling on the shining pavements under the arc-lights. Though waves of heat caused by some sudden recollection or impatient longing still ran through my body, a saner joy of anticipation was succeeding emotional tumult, and I reflected that Nancy had been right in insisting that we walk circumspectly in spite of passion. After all, I had outwitted circumstance, I had gained the prize, I could afford to wait a little. We should talk it over to-morrow,—no, to-day. The luminous face of the city hall clock reminded me that midnight was long past....

I awoke with the consciousness of a new joy, suddenly to identify it with Nancy. She was mine! I kept repeating it as I dressed; summoning her, not as she had lain in my arms in the darkness—though the intoxicating sweetness of that pervaded me—but as she had been before the completeness of her surrender, dainty, surrounded by things expressing an elusive, uniquely feminine personality. I could afford to smile at the weather, at the obsidian sky, at the rain still falling persistently; and yet, as I ate my breakfast, I felt a certain impatience to verify what I knew was a certainty, and hurried to the telephone booth. I resented the instrument, its possibilities of betrayal, her voice sounded so matter- of-fact as she bade me good morning and deplored the rain.

"I'll be out as soon as I can get away," I said. "I have a meeting at three, but it should be over at four." And then I added irresistibly: "Nancy, you're not sorry? You—you still—?"

"Yes, don't be foolish," I heard her reply, and this time the telephone did not completely disguise the note for which I strained. I said something more, but the circuit was closed....

I shall not attempt to recount the details of our intercourse during the week that followed. There were moments of stress and strain when it seemed to me that we could not wait, moments that strengthened Nancy's resolution to leave immediately for the East: there were other, calmer periods when the wisdom of her going appealed to me, since our ultimate union would be hastened thereby. We overcame by degrees the distastefulness of the discussion of ways and means.... We spent an unforgettable Sunday among the distant high hills, beside a little lake of our own discovery, its glinting waters sapphire and chrysoprase. A grassy wood road, at the inviting entrance to which we left the automobile, led down through an undergrowth of laurel to a pebbly shore, and there we lunched; there we lingered through the long summer afternoon, Nancy with her back against a tree, I with my head in her lap gazing up at filmy clouds drifting imperceptibly across the sky, listening to the droning notes of the bees, notes that sometimes rose in a sharp crescendo, and again were suddenly hushed. The smell of the wood-mould mingled with the fainter scents of wild flowers. She had brought along a volume by a modern poet: the verses, as Nancy read them, moved me,—they were filled with a new faith to which my being responded, the faith of the forth-farer; not the faith of the anchor, but of the sail. I repeated some of the lines as indications of a creed to which I had long been trying to convert her, though lacking the expression. She had let the book fall on the grass. I remember how she smiled down at me with the wisdom of the ages in her eyes, seeking my hand with a gesture that was almost maternal.

"You and the poets," she said, "you never grow up. I suppose that's the reason why we love you—and these wonderful visions of freedom you have. Anyway, it's nice to dream, to recreate the world as one would like to have it."

"But that's what you and I are doing," I insisted.

"We think we're doing it—or rather you think so," she replied. "And sometimes, I admit that you almost persuade me to think so. Never quite. What disturbs me," she continued, "is to find you and the poets founding your new freedom on new justifications, discarding the old law only to make a new one,—as though we could ever get away from necessities, escape from disagreeable things, except in dreams. And then, this delusion of believing that we are masters of our own destiny—" She paused and pressed my fingers.

"There you go-back to predestination!" I exclaimed.

"I don't go back to anything, or forward to anything," she exclaimed. "Women are elemental, but I don't expect you to understand it. Laws and codes are foreign to us, philosophies and dreams may dazzle us for the moment, but what we feel underneath and what we yield to are the primal forces, the great necessities; when we refuse joys it's because we know these forces by a sort of instinct, when we're overcome it's with a full knowledge that there's a price. You've talked a great deal, Hugh, about carving out our future. I listened to you, but I resisted you. It wasn't the morality that was taught me as a child that made me resist, it was something deeper than that, more fundamental, something I feel but can't yet perceive, and yet shall perceive some day. It isn't that I'm clinging to the hard and fast rules because I fail to see any others, it isn't that I believe that all people should stick together whether they are happily married or not, but—I must say it even now—I have a feeling I can't define that divorce isn't for us. I'm not talking about right and wrong in the ordinary sense—it's just what I feel. I've ceased to think."

"Nancy!" I reproached her.

"I can't help it—I don't want to be morbid. Do you remember my asking you about God?—the first day this began? and whether you had a god? Well, that's the trouble with us all to-day, we haven't any God, we're wanderers, drifters. And now it's just life that's got hold of us, my dear, and swept us away together. That's our justification—if we needed one—it's been too strong for us." She leaned back against the tree and closed her eyes. "We're like chips in the torrent of it, Hugh."....

It was not until the shadow of the forest had crept far across the lake and the darkening waters were still that we rose reluctantly to put the dishes in the tea basket and start on our homeward journey. The tawny fires of the sunset were dying down behind us, the mist stealing, ghostlike, into the valleys below; in the sky a little moon curled like a freshly cut silver shaving, that presently turned to gold, the white star above it to fire.

Where the valleys widened we came to silent, decorous little towns and villages where yellow-lit windows gleaming through the trees suggested refuge and peace, while we were wanderers in the night. It was Nancy's mood; and now, in the evening's chill, it recurred to me poignantly. In one of these villages we passed a church, its doors flung open; the congregation was singing a familiar hymn. I slowed down the car; I felt her shoulder pressing against my own, and reached out my hand and found hers.

"Are you warm enough?" I asked....

We spoke but little on that drive, we had learned the futility of words to express the greater joys and sorrows, the love that is compounded of these.

It was late when we turned in between the white dates and made our way up the little driveway to the farmhouse. I bade her good night on the steps of the porch.

"You do love me, don't you?" she whispered, clinging to me with a sudden, straining passion. "You will love me, always no matter what happens?"

"Why, of course, Nancy," I answered.

"I want to hear you say it, 'I love you, I shall love you always.'"

I repeated it fervently....

"No matter what happens?"

"No matter what happens. As if I could help it, Nancy! Why are you so sad to-night?"

"Ah, Hugh, it makes me sad—I can't tell why. It is so great, it is so terrible, and yet it's so sweet and beautiful."

She took my face in her hands and pressed a kiss against my forehead....

The next day was dark. At two o'clock in the afternoon the electric light was still burning over my desk when the telephone rang and I heard Nancy's voice.

"Is that you, Hugh?"

"Yes."

"I have to go East this afternoon."

"Why?" I asked. Her agitation had communicated itself to me. "I thought you weren't going until Thursday. What's the matter?"

"I've just had a telegram," she said. "Ham's been hurt—I don't know how badly—he was thrown from a polo pony this morning at Narragansett, in practice, and they're taking him to Boston to a private hospital. The telegram's from Johnny Shephard. I'll be at the house in town at four."

Filled with forebodings I tried in vain to suppress I dropped the work I was doing and got up and paced the room, pausing now and again to gaze out of the window at the wet roofs and the grey skies. I was aghast at the idea of her going to Ham now even though he were hurt badly hurt; and yet I tried to think it was natural, that it was fine of her to respond to such a call. And she couldn't very well refuse his summons. But it was not the news of her husband's accident that inspired the greater fear, which was quelled and soothed only to rise again when I recalled the note I had heard in her voice, a note eloquent of tragedy—of tragedy she had foreseen. At length, unable to remain where I was any longer, I descended to the street and walked uptown in the rain. The Durrett house was closed, the blinds of its many windows drawn, but Nancy was watching for me and opened the door. So used had I grown to seeing her in the simple linen dresses she had worn in the country, a costume associated with exclusive possession, that the sight of her travelling suit and hat renewed in me an agony of apprehension. The unforeseen event seemed to have transformed her once more. Her veil was drawn up, her face was pale, in her eyes were traces of tears.

"You're going?" I asked, as I took her hands.

"Hugh, I have to go."

She led me through the dark, shrouded drawing room into the little salon where the windows were open on the silent city-garden. I took her in my arms; she did not resist, as I half expected, but clung to me with what seemed desperation.

"I have to go, dear—you won't make it too hard for me! It's only— ordinary decency, and there's no one else to go to him."

She drew me to the sofa, her eyes beseeching me.

"Listen, dear, I want you to see it as I see it. I know that you will, that you do. I should never be able to forgive myself if I stayed away now, I—neither of us could ever be happy about it. You do see, don't you?" she implored.

"Yes," I admitted agitatedly.

Her grasp on my hand tightened.

"I knew you would. But it makes me happier to hear you say it."

We sat for a moment in helpless silence, gazing at one another. Slowly her eyes had filled.

"Have you heard anything more?" I managed to ask.

She drew a telegram from her bag, as though the movement were a relief.

"This is from the doctor in Boston—his name is Magruder. They have got Ham there, it seems. A horse kicked him in the head, after he fell,—he had just recovered consciousness."

I took the telegram. The wordy seemed meaningless, all save those of the last sentence. "The situation is serious, but by no means hopeless." Nancy had not spoken of that. The ignorant cruelty of its convention! The man must have known what Hambleton Durrett was! Nancy read my thoughts, and took the paper from my hand.

"Hugh, dear, if it's hard for you, try to understand that it's terrible for me to think that he has any claim at all. I realize now, as I never did before, how wicked it was in me to marry him. I hate him, I can't bear the thought of going near him."

She fell into wild weeping. I tried to comfort her, who could not comfort myself; I don't remember my inadequate words. We were overwhelmed, obliterated by the sense of calamity.... It was she who checked herself at last by an effort that was almost hysterical.

"I mustn't yield to it!" she said. "It's time to leave and the train goes at six. No, you mustn't come to the station, Hugh—I don't think I could stand it. I'll send you a telegram." She rose. "You must go now —you must."

"You'll come back to me?" I demanded thickly, as I held her.

"Hugh, I am yours, now and always. How can you doubt it?"

At last I released her, when she had begged me again. And I found myself a little later walking past the familiar, empty houses of those streets....

The front pages of the evening newspapers announced the accident to Hambleton Durrett, and added that Mrs. Durrett, who had been lingering in the city, had gone to her husband's bedside. The morning papers contained more of biography and ancestry, but had little to add to the bulletin; and there was no lack of speculation at the Club and elsewhere as to Ham's ability to rally from such a shock. I could not bear to listen to these comments: they were violently distasteful to me. The unforeseen accident and Nancy's sudden departure had thrown my life completely out of gear: I could not attend to business, I dared not go away lest the news from Nancy be delayed. I spent the hours in an exhausting mental state that alternated between hope and fear, a state of unmitigated, intense desire, of balked realization, sometimes heightening into that sheer terror I had felt when I had detected over the telephone that note in her voice that seemed of despair. Had she had a presentiment, all along, that something would occur to separate us? As I went back over the hours we had passed together since she had acknowledged her love, in spite of myself the conviction grew on me that she had never believed in the reality of our future. Indeed, she had expressed her disbelief in words. Had she been looking all along for a sign—a sign of wrath? And would she accept this accident of Ham's as such?

Retrospection left me trembling and almost sick.

It was not until the second morning after her departure that I received a telegram giving the name of her Boston hotel, and saying that there was to be a consultation that day, and as soon as it had taken place she would write. Such consolation as I could gather from it was derived from four words at the end,—she missed me dreadfully. Some tremor of pity for her entered into my consciousness, without mitigating greatly the wildness of my resentment, of my forebodings.

I could bear no longer the city, the Club, the office, the daily contact with my associates and clients. Six hours distant, near Rossiter, was a small resort in the mountains of which I had heard. I telegraphed Nancy to address me there, notified the office, packed my bag, and waited impatiently for midday, when I boarded the train. At seven I reached a little station where a stage was waiting to take me to Callender's Mill.

It was not until morning that I beheld my retreat, when little wisps of vapour were straying over the surface of the lake, and the steep green slopes that rose out of the water on the western side were still in shadow. The hotel, a much overgrown and altered farm-house, stood, surrounded by great trees, in an ancient clearing that sloped gently to the water's edge, where an old-fashioned, octagonal summerhouse overlooked a landing for rowboats. The resort, indeed, was a survival of simpler times....

In spite of the thirty-odd guests, people of very moderate incomes who knew the place and had come here year after year, I was as much alone as if I had been the only sojourner. The place was so remote, so peaceful in contrast to the city I had left, which had become intolerable. And at night, during hours of wakefulness, the music of the waters falling over the dam was soothing. I used to walk down there and sit on the stones of the ruined mill; or climb to the crests on the far side of the pond to gaze for hours westward where the green billows of the Alleghenies lost themselves in the haze. I had discovered a new country; here, when our trials should be over, I would bring Nancy, and I found distraction in choosing sites for a bungalow. In my soul hope flowered with little watering. Uncertain news was good news. After two days of an impatience all but intolerable, her first letter arrived, I learned that the specialists had not been able to make a diagnosis, and I began to take heart again. At times, she said, Ham was delirious and difficult to manage; at other times he sank into a condition of coma; and again he seemed to know her and Ralph, who had come up from Southampton, where he had been spending the summer. One doctor thought that Ham's remarkable vitality would pull him through, in spite of what his life had been. The shock—as might have been surmised—had affected the brain.... The letters that followed contained no additional news; she did not dwell on the depressing reactions inevitable from the situation in which she found herself—one so much worse than mine; she expressed a continual longing for me; and yet I had trouble to convince myself that they did not lack the note of reassurance for which I strained as I eagerly scanned them— of reassurance that she had no intention of permitting her husband's condition to interfere with that ultimate happiness on which it seemed my existence depended. I tried to account for the absence of this note by reflecting that the letters were of necessity brief, hurriedly scratched off at odd moments; and a natural delicacy would prevent her from referring to our future at such a time. They recorded no change in Ham's condition save that the periods of coma had ceased. The doctors were silent, awaiting the arrival in this country of a certain New York specialist who was abroad. She spent most of her days at the hospital, returning to the hotel at night exhausted: the people she knew in the various resorts around Boston had been most kind, sending her flowers, and calling when in town to inquire. At length came the news that the New York doctor was home again; and coming to Boston. In that letter was a sentence which rang like a cry in my ears: "Oh, Hugh, I think these doctors know now what the trouble is, I think I know. They are only waiting for Dr. Jameson to confirm it."

It was always an effort for me to control my impatience after the first rattling was heard in the morning of the stage that brought the mail, and I avoided the waiting group in front of the honeycombed partition of boxes beside the "office." On the particular morning of which I am now writing the proprietor himself handed me a letter of ominous thickness which I took with me down to the borders of the lake before tearing open the flap. In spite of the calmness and restraint of the first lines, because of them, I felt creeping over me an unnerving sensation I knew for dread....

"Hugh, the New York doctor has been here. It is as I have feared for some weeks, but I couldn't tell you until I was sure. Ham is not exactly insane, but he is childish. Sometimes I think that is even worse. I have had a talk with Dr. Jameson, who has simply confirmed the opinion which the other physicians have gradually been forming. The accident has precipitated a kind of mental degeneration, but his health, otherwise, will not be greatly affected.

"Jameson was kind, but very frank, for which I was grateful. He did not hesitate to say that it would have been better if the accident had been fatal. Ham won't be helpless, physically. Of course he won't be able to play polo, or take much active exercise. If he were to be helpless, I could feel that I might be of some use, at least of more use. He knows his friends. Some of them have been here to see him, and he talks quite rationally with them, with Ralph, with me, only once in a while he says something silly. It seems odd to write that he is not responsible, since he never has been,—his condition is so queer that I am at a loss to describe it. The other morning, before I arrived from the hotel and when the nurse was downstairs, he left the hospital, and we found him several blocks along Commonwealth Avenue, seated on a bench, without a hat—he was annoyed that he had forgotten it, and quite sensible otherwise. We began by taking him out every morning in an automobile. To-day he had a walk with Ralph, and insisted on going into a club here, to which they both belong. Two or three men were there whom they knew, and he talked to them about his fall from the pony and told them just how it happened.

"At such times only a close observer can tell from his manner that everything is not right.

"Ralph, who always could manage him, prevented his taking anything to drink. He depends upon Ralph, and it will be harder for me when he is not with us. His attitude towards me is just about what it has always been. I try to amuse him by reading the newspapers and with games; we have a chess-board. At times he seems grateful, and then he will suddenly grow tired and hard to control. Once or twice I have had to call in Dr. Magruder, who owns the hospital.

"It has been terribly hard for me to write all this, but I had to do it, in order that you might understand the situation completely. Hugh dear, I simply can't leave him. This has been becoming clearer and clearer to me all these weeks, but it breaks my heart to have to write it. I have struggled against it, I have lain awake nights trying to find justification for going to you, but it is stronger than I. I am afraid of it—I suppose that's the truth. Even in those unforgettable days at the farm I was afraid of it, although I did not know what it was to be. Call it what you like, say that I am weak. I am willing to acknowledge that it is weakness. I wish no credit for it, it gives me no glow, the thought of it makes my heart sick. I'm not big enough I suppose that's the real truth. I once might have been; but I'm not now,—the years of the life I chose have made a coward of me. It's not a question of morals or duty it's simply that I can't take the thing for which my soul craves. It's too late. If I believed in prayer I'd pray that you might pity and forgive me. I really can't expect you to understand what I can't myself explain. Oh, I need pity—and I pity you, my dear. I can only hope that you will not suffer as I shall, that you will find relief away to work out your life. But I will not change my decision, I cannot change it. Don't come on, don't attempt to see me now. I can't stand any more than I am standing, I should lose my mind."

Here the letter was blotted, and some words scratched out. I was unable to reconstruct them.

"Ralph and I," she proceeded irrelevantly, "have got Ham to agree to go to Buzzard's Bay, and we have taken a house near Wareham. Write and tell me that you forgive and pity me. I love you even more, if such a thing is possible, than I have ever loved you. This is my only comfort and compensation, that I have had and have been able to feel such a love, and I know I shall always feel it.—Nancy." The first effect of this letter was a paralyzing one. I was unable to realize or believe the thing that had happened to me, and I sat stupidly holding the sheet in my hand until I heard voices along the path, and then I fled instinctively, like an animal, to hide my injury from any persons I might meet. I wandered down the shore of the lake, striking at length into the woods, seeking some inviolable shelter; nor was I conscious of physical effort until I found myself panting near the crest of the ridge where there was a pasture, which some ancient glacier had strewn with great boulders. Beside one of these I sank. Heralded by the deep tones of bells, two steers appeared above the shoulder of a hill and stood staring at me with bovine curiosity, and fell to grazing again. A fleet of white clouds, like ships pressed with sail, hurried across the sky as though racing for some determined port; and the shadows they cast along the hillsides accentuated the high brightness of the day, emphasized the vivid and hateful beauty of the landscape. My numbness began to be penetrated by shooting pains, and I grasped little by little the fulness of my calamity, until I was in the state of wild rebellion of one whom life for the first time has foiled in a supreme desire. There was no fate about this thing, it was just an absurd accident. The operation of the laws of nature had sent a man to the ground: another combination of circumstances would have killed him, still another, and he would have arisen unhurt. But because of this particular combination my happiness was ruined, and Nancy's! She had not expected me to understand. Well, I didn't understand, I had no pity, in that hour I felt a resentment almost amounting to hate; I could see only unreasoning superstition in the woman I wanted above everything in the world. Women of other days had indeed renounced great loves: the thing was not unheard of. But that this should happen in these times—and to me! It was unthinkable that Nancy of all women shouldn't be emancipated from the thralls of religious inhibition! And if it wasn't "conscience," what was it?

Was it, as she said, weakness, lack of courage to take life when it was offered her?.... I was suddenly filled with the fever of composing arguments to change a decision that appeared to me to be the result of a monstrous caprice and delusion; writing them out, as they occurred to me, in snatches on the backs of envelopes—her envelopes. Then I proceeded to make the draft of a letter, the effort required for composition easing me until the draft was finished; when I started for the hotel, climbing fences, leaping streams, making my way across rock faces and through woods; halting now and then as some reenforcing argument occurred to me to write it into my draft at the proper place until the sheets were interlined and blurred and almost illegible. It was already three o'clock when I reached my room, and the mail left at four. I began to copy and revise my scrawl, glancing from time to time at my watch, which I had laid on the table. Hurriedly washing my face and brushing my hair, I arrived downstairs just as the stage was leaving....

After the letter had gone still other arguments I might have added began to occur to me, and I regretted that I had not softened some of the things I wrote and made others more emphatic. In places argument had degenerated into abject entreaty. Never had my desire been so importunate as now, when I was in continual terror of losing her. Nor could I see how I was to live without her, life lacking a motive being incomprehensible: yet the fire of optimism in me, though died down to ashes, would not be extinguished. At moments it flared up into what almost amounted to a conviction that she could not resist my appeal. I had threatened to go to her, and more than once I started packing....

Three days later I received a brief note in which she managed to convey to me, though tenderly and compassionately, that her decision was unalterable. If I came on, she would refuse to see me. I took the afternoon stage and went back to the city, to plunge into affairs again; but for weeks my torture was so acute that it gives me pain to recall it, to dwell upon it to-day.... And yet, amazing as it may seem, there came a time when hope began to dawn again out of my despair. Perhaps my life had not been utterly shattered, after all: perhaps Ham Durrett would get well: such things happened, and Nancy would no longer have an excuse for continuing to refuse me. Little by little my anger at what I had now become convinced was her weakness cooled, and—though paradoxically I had continued to love her in spite of the torture for which she was responsible, in spite of the resentment I felt, I melted toward her. True to my habit of reliance on miracles, I tried to reconcile myself to a period of waiting.

Nevertheless I was faintly aware—consequent upon if not as a result of this tremendous experience—of some change within me. It was not only that I felt at times a novel sense of uneasiness at being a prey to accidents, subject to ravages of feeling; the unity of mind that had hitherto enabled me to press forward continuously toward a concrete goal showed signs of breaking up:—the goal had lost its desirability. I seemed oddly to be relapsing into the states of questioning that had characterized my earlier years. Perhaps it would be an exaggeration to say that I actually began to speculate on the possible existence of a realm where the soul might find a refuge from the buffetings of life, from which the philosophy of prosperity was powerless to save it....

Chapter Twenty-Four

It was impossible, of course, that my friends should have failed to perceive the state of disorganization I was in, and some of them at least must have guessed its cause. Dickinson, on his return from Maine, at once begged me to go away. I rather congratulated myself that Tom had chosen these months for a long-delayed vacation in Canada. His passion for fishing still persisted.

In spite of the fact I have noted, that I had lost a certain zest for results, to keep busy seemed to be the only way to relieve my mind of an otherwise intolerable pressure: and I worked sometimes far into the evening. In the background of my thoughts lay the necessity of coming to a decision on the question of the senatorship; several times Dickinson and Gorse had spoken of it, and I was beginning to get letters from influential men in other parts of the state. They seemed to take it for granted that there was no question of my refusing. The time came when I had grown able to consider the matter with a degree of calmness. What struck me first, when I began to debate upon it, was that the senatorship offered a new and possibly higher field for my energies, while at the same time the office would be a logical continuation of a signal legal career. I was now unable to deny that I no longer felt any exhilaration at the prospect of future legal conquests similar to those of the past; but once in the Senate, I might regain something of that intense conviction of fighting for a just and sound cause with which Theodore Wading had once animated me: fighting there, in the Capitol at Washington, would be different; no stigma of personal gain attached to it; it offered a nearer approach to the ideal I had once more begun to seek, held out hopes of a renewal of my unity of mind. Mr. Watling had declared that there was something to fight for; I had even glimpsed that something, but I had to confess that for some years I had not been consciously fighting for it. I needed something to fight for.

There was the necessity, however, of renewing my calculations. If Hambleton Durrett should recover, even during the ensuing year, and if Nancy relented it would not be possible for us to be divorced and married for some time. I still clung tenaciously to the belief that there were no relationships wholly unaffected by worldly triumphs, and as Senator I should have strengthened my position. It did not strike me—even after all my experience—that such a course as I now contemplated had a parallel in the one that I had pursued in regard to her when I was young.

It seemed fitting that Theodore Watling should be the first to know of my decision. I went to Washington to meet him. It pained me to see him looking more worn, but he was still as cheerful, as mentally vigorous as ever, and I perceived that he did not wish to dwell upon his illness. I did venture to expostulate with him on the risk he must be running in serving out his term. We were sitting in the dining room of his house.

"We've only one life to live, Hugh," he answered, smiling at me, "and we might as well get all out of it we can. A few years more or less doesn't make much difference—and I ought to be satisfied. I'd resign now, to please my wife, to please my friends, but we can't trust this governor to appoint a safe man. How little we suspected when we elected him that he'd become infected. You never can tell, in these days, can you?"

It was the note of devotion to his cause that I had come to hear: I felt it renewing me, as I had hoped. The threat of disease, the louder clamourings of the leaders of the mob had not sufficed to dismay him— though he admitted more concern over these. My sympathy and affection were mingled with the admiration he never failed to inspire.

"But you, Hugh," he said concernedly, "you're not looking very well, my son. You must manage to take a good rest before coming here—before the campaign you'll have to go through. We can't afford to have anything happen to you—you're too young."

I wondered whether he had heard anything.... He spoke to me again about the work to be done, the work he looked to me to carry on.

"We'll have to watch for our opportunity," he said, "and when it comes we can handle this new movement not by crushing it, but by guiding it. I've come to the conclusion that there is a true instinct in it, that there are certain things we have done which have been mistakes, and which we can't do any more. But as for this theory that all wisdom resides in the people, it's buncombe. What we have to do is to work out a practical programme."

His confidence in me had not diminished. It helped to restore confidence in myself.

The weather was cool and bracing for September, and as we drove in a motor through the beautiful avenues of the city he pointed out a house for me on one of the circles, one of those distinguished residences, instances of a nascent good taste, that are helping to redeem the polyglot aspect of our national capital. Mr. Watling spoke—rather tactfully, I thought—of Maude and the children, and ventured the surmise that they would be returning in a few months. I interpreted this, indeed, as in rather the nature of a kindly hint that such a procedure would be wise in view of the larger life now dawning for me, but I made no comment.... He even sympathized with Nancy Durrett.

"She did the right thing, Hugh," he said, with the admirable casual manner he possessed of treating subjects which he knew to be delicate. "Nancy's a fine woman. Poor devil!" This in reference to Ham....

Mr. Watling reassured me on the subject of his own trouble, maintaining that he had many years left if he took care. He drove me to the station. I travelled homeward somewhat lifted out of myself by this visit to him; with some feeling of spaciousness derived from Washington itself, with its dignified Presidential Mansion among the trees, its granite shaft drawing the eye upward, with its winged Capitol serene upon the hill. Should we deliver these heirlooms to the mob? Surely Democracy meant more than that!

All this time I had been receiving, at intervals, letters from Maude and the children. Maude's were the letters of a friend, and I found it easy to convince myself that their tone was genuine, that the separation had brought contentment to her; and those independent and self-sufficient elements in her character I admired now rather than deplored. At Etretat, which she found much to her taste, she was living quietly, but making friends with some American and English, and one French family of the same name, Buffon, as the great naturalist. The father was a retired silk manufacturer; they now resided in Paris, and had been very kind in helping her to get an apartment in that city for the winter. She had chosen one on the Avenue Kleber, not far from the Arc. It is interesting, after her arraignment of me, that she should have taken such pains to record their daily life for my benefit in her clear, conscientious handwriting. I beheld Biddy, her dresses tucked above slim little knees, playing in the sand on the beach, her hair flying in the wind and lighted by the sun which gave sparkle to the sea. I saw Maude herself in her beach chair, a book lying in her lap, its pages whipped by the breeze. And there was Moreton, who must be proving something of a handful, since he had fought with the French boys on the beach and thrown a "rock" through the windows of the Buffon family. I remember one of his letters—made perfect after much correcting and scratching,—in which he denounced both France and the French, and appealed to me to come over at once to take him home. Maude had enclosed it without comment. This letter had not been written under duress, as most of his were.

Matthew's letters—he wrote faithfully once a week—I kept in a little pile by themselves and sometimes reread them. I wondered whether it were because of the fact that I was his father—though a most inadequate one— that I thought them somewhat unusual. He had learned French—Maude wrote—with remarkable ease. I was particularly struck in these letters with the boy's power of observation, with his facile use of language, with the vivid simplicity of his descriptions of the life around him, of his experiences at school. The letters were thoughtful—not dashed off in a hurry; they gave evidence in every line of the delicacy of feeling that was, I think, his most appealing quality, and I put them down with the impression strong on me that he, too, longed to return home, but would not say so. There was a certain pathos in this youthful restraint that never failed to touch me, even in those times when I had been most obsessed with love and passion.... The curious effect of these letters was that of knowing more than they expressed. He missed me, he wished to know when I was coming over. And I was sometimes at a loss whether to be grateful to Maude or troubled because she had as yet given him no hint of our separation. What effect would it have on him when it should be revealed to him?.... It was through Matthew I began to apprehend certain elements in Maude I had both failed to note and appreciate; her little mannerisms that jarred, her habits of thought that exasperated, were forgotten, and I was forced to confess that there was something fine in the achievement of this attitude of hers that was without ill will or resentment, that tacitly acknowledged my continued rights and interest in the children. It puzzled and troubled me.

The Citizens Union began its campaign early that autumn, long before the Hons. Jonathan Parks and Timothy MacGuire—Republican and Democratic candidates for Mayor—thought of going on the stump. For several weeks the meetings were held in the small halls and club rooms of various societies and orders in obscure portions of the city.

The forces of "privilege and corruption" were not much alarmed. Perry Blackwood accused the newspapers of having agreed to a "conspiracy of silence"; but, as Judah B.

Tallant remarked, it was the business of the press to give the public what it wanted, and the public as yet hadn't shown much interest in the struggle being waged in its behalf. When the meetings began to fill up it would be time to report them in the columns of the Era. Meanwhile, however, the city had been quietly visited by an enterprising representative of a New York periodical of the new type that developed with the opening years of the century—one making a specialty of passionate "muck-raking." And since the people of America love nothing better than being startled, Yardley's Weekly had acquired a circulation truly fabulous. The emissary of the paper had attended several of the Citizens meetings; interviewed, it seemed, many persons: the result was a revelation to make the blood of politicians, capitalists and corporation lawyers run cold. I remember very well the day it appeared on our news stands, and the heated denunciations it evoked at the Boyne Club. Ralph Hambleton was the only one who took it calmly, who seemed to derive a certain enjoyment from the affair. Had he been a less privileged person, they would have put him in chancery. Leonard Dickinson asserted that Yardley's should be sued for libel.

"There's just one objection to that," said Ralph.

"What?" asked the banker.

"It isn't libel."

"I defy them to prove it," Dickinson snapped. "It's a d—d outrage! There isn't a city or village in the country that hasn't exactly the same conditions. There isn't any other way to run a city—"

"That's what Mr. Krebs says," Ralph replied, "that the people ought to put Judd Jason officially in charge. He tells 'em that Jason is probably a more efficient man than Democracy will be able to evolve in a coon's age, that we ought to take him over, instead of letting the capitalists have him."

"Did Krebs say that?" Dickinson demanded.

"You can't have read the article very thoroughly, Leonard," Ralph commented. "I'm afraid you only picked out the part of it that compliments you. This fellow seems to have been struck by Krebs, says he's a coming man, that he's making original contributions to the people's cause. Quite a tribute. You ought to read it."

Dickinson, who had finished his lunch, got up and left the table after lighting his cigar. Ralph's look followed him amusedly.

"I'm afraid it's time to cash in and be good," he observed.

"We'll get that fellow Krebs yet," said Grierson, wrathfully. Miller Gorse alone made no remarks, but in spite of his silence he emanated an animosity against reform and reformers that seemed to charge the very atmosphere, and would have repressed any man but Ralph....

I sat in my room at the Club that night and reread the article, and if its author could have looked into my soul and observed the emotions he had set up, he would, no doubt, have experienced a grim satisfaction. For I, too, had come in for a share of the comment. Portions of the matter referring to me stuck in my brain like tar, such as the reference to my father, to the honoured traditions of the Parets and the Brecks which I had deliberately repudiated. I had less excuse than many others. The part I had played in various reprehensible transactions such as the Riverside Franchise and the dummy telephone company affair was dwelt upon, and I was dismissed with the laconic comment that I was a graduate of Harvard....

My associates and myself were referred to collectively as a "gang," with the name of our city prefixed; we were linked up with and compared to the gangs of other cities—the terminology used to describe us being that of the police reporter. We "operated," like burglars; we "looted": only, it was intimated in one place, "second-story men" were angels compared to us, who had never seen the inside of a penitentiary. Here we were, all arraigned before the bar of public opinion, the relentless Dickinson, the surfeited Scherer, the rapacious Grierson, the salacious Tallant. I have forgotten what Miller Gorse was called; nothing so classic as a Minotaur; Judd Jason was a hairy spider who spread his net and lurked in darkness for his victims. Every adjective was called upon to do its duty.... Even Theodore Watling did not escape, but it was intimated that he would be dealt with in another connection in a future number.

The article had a crude and terrifying power, and the pain it aroused, following almost immediately upon the suffering caused by my separation from Nancy, was cumulative in character and effect, seeming actively to reenforce the unwelcome conviction I had been striving to suppress, that the world, which had long seemed so acquiescent in conforming itself to my desires, was turning against me.

Though my hunger for Nancy was still gnawing, I had begun to fear that I should never get her now; and the fact that she would not even write to me seemed to confirm this.

Then there was Matthew—I could not bear to think that he would ever read that article.

In vain I tried that night to belittle to myself its contentions and probable results, to summon up the heart to fight; in vain I sought to reconstruct the point of view, to gain something of that renewed hope and power, of devotion to a cause I had carried away from Washington after my talk with Theodore Watling. He, though stricken, had not wavered in his faith. Why should I?

Whether or not as the result of the article in Yardley's, which had been read more or less widely in the city, the campaign of the Citizens Union gained ground, and people began to fill the little halls to hear Krebs, who was a candidate for district attorney. Evidently he was entertaining and rousing them, for his reputation spread, and some of the larger halls were hired. Dickinson and Gorse became alarmed, and one morning the banker turned up at the Club while I was eating my breakfast.

"Look here, Hugh," he said, "we may as well face the fact that we've got a fight ahead of us,—we'll have to start some sort of a back-fire right away."

"You think Greenhalge has a chance of being elected?" I asked.

"I'm not afraid of Greenhalge, but of this fellow Krebs. We can't afford to have him district attorney, to let a demagogue like him get a start. The men the Republicans and Democrats have nominated are worse than useless. Parks is no good, and neither is MacGuire. If only we could have foreseen this thing we might have had better candidates put up—but there's no use crying over spilt milk. You'll have to go on the stump, Hugh—that's all there is to it. You can answer him, and the newspapers will print your speeches in full. Besides it will help you when it comes to the senatorship."

The mood of extreme dejection that had followed the appearance of the article in Yardley's did not last. I had acquired aggressiveness: an aggressiveness, however, differing in quality from the feeling I once would have had,—for this arose from resentment, not from belief. It was impossible to live in the atmosphere created by the men with whom I associated—especially at such a time—without imbibing something of the emotions animating them,—even though I had been free from these emotions myself. I, too, had begun to be filled with a desire for revenge; and when this desire was upon me I did not have in my mind a pack of reformers, or even the writer of the article in Yardley's. I thought of Hermann Krebs. He was my persecutor; it seemed to me that he always had been....

"Well, I'll make speeches if you like," I said to Dickinson.

"I'm glad," he replied. "We're all agreed, Gorse and the rest of us, that you ought to. We've got to get some ginger into this fight, and a good deal more money, I'm afraid.

Jason sends word we'll need more. By the way, Hugh, I wish you'd drop around and talk to Jason and get his idea of how the land lies."

I went, this time in the company of Judah B. Tallant. Naturally we didn't expect to see Mr. Jason perturbed, nor was he. He seemed to be in an odd, rather exultant mood—if he can be imagined as exultant. We were not long in finding out what pleased him—nothing less than the fact that Mr. Krebs had proposed him for mayor!

"D—d if I wouldn't make a good one, too," he said. "D—d if I wouldn't show 'em what a real mayor is!"

"I guess there's no danger of your ever being mayor, Judd," Tallant observed, with a somewhat uneasy jocularity.

"I guess there isn't, Judah," replied the boss, quickly, but with a peculiar violet flash in his eyes. "They won't ever make you mayor, either, if I can help it. And I've a notion I can. I'd rather see Krebs mayor."

"You don't think he meant to propose you seriously," Tallant exclaimed.

"I'm not a d—d fool," said the boss. "But I'll say this, that he half meant it. Krebs has a head-piece on him, and I tell you if any of this reform dope is worth anything his is. There's some sense in what he's talking, and if all the voters was like him you might get a man like me for mayor. But they're not, and I guess they never will be."

"Sure," said Mr. Jason. "The people are dotty—there ain't one in ten thousand understands what he's driving at when he gets off things like that. They take it on the level."

Tallant reflected.

"By gum, I believe you're right," he said. "You think they will blow up?" he added.

"Krebs is the whole show, I tell you. They wouldn't be anywhere without him. The yaps that listen to him don't understand him, but somehow he gets under their skins. Have you seen him lately?"

"Never saw him," replied Tallant.

"Well, if you had, you'd know he was a sick man."

"Sick!" I exclaimed. "How do you know?"

"It's my business to know things," said Judd Jason, and added to Tallant, "that your reporters don't find out."

"What's the matter with him?" Tallant demanded. A slight exultation in his tone did not escape me.

"You've got me there," said Jason, "but I have it pretty straight. Any one of your reporters will tell you that he looks sick."....

The Era took Mr. Jason's advice and began to publish those portions of Krebs's speeches that were seemingly detrimental to his own cause. Other conservative newspapers followed suit....

Both Tallant and I were surprised to hear these sentiments out of the mouth of Mr. Jason.

"You don't think that crowd's going to win, do you?" asked the owner of the Era, a trifle uneasily.

"Win!" exclaimed the boss contemptuously. "They'll blow up, and you'll never hear of 'em. I'm not saying we won't need a little—powder," he added—which was one of the matters we had come to talk about. He gave us likewise a very accurate idea of the state of the campaign, mentioning certain things that ought to be done. "You ought to print some of Krebs's speeches, Judah, like what he said about me. They're talking it all around that you're afraid to."

"Print things like his proposal to make you mayor!"

The information that I was to enter the lists against Krebs was received with satisfaction and approval by those of our friends who were called in to assist at a council of war in the directors' room of the Corn National Bank. I was flattered by the confidence these men seemed to have in my ability. All were in a state of anger against the reformers; none of them seriously alarmed as to the actual outcome of the campaign,— especially when I had given them the opinion of Mr. Jason. What disturbed them was the possible effect upon the future of the spread of heretical, socialistic doctrines, and it was decided to organize a publicity bureau, independently of the two dominant political parties, to be in charge of a certain New York journalist who made a business of such affairs, who was to be paid a sum commensurate with the emergency. He was to have carte blanche, even in the editorial columns of our newspapers. He was also to flood the city with "literature." We had fought many wars before this, and we planned our campaign precisely as though we were dealing with one of those rebellions in the realm of finance of which I have given an instance. But now the war chest of our opponents was negligible; and we were comforted by the thought that, however disagreeable the affair might be while it lasted, in the long run capital was invincible.

Before setting to work to prepare my speeches it was necessary to make an attempt to familiarize myself with the seemingly unprecedented line of argument Krebs had evolved—apparently as disconcerting to his friends as to his opponents. It occurred to me, since I did not care to attend Krebs's meetings, to ask my confidential stenographer, Miss McCoy, to go to Turner's Hall and take down one of his speeches verbatim. Miss McCoy had never intruded on me her own views, and I took for granted that they coincided with my own.

"I'd like to get an accurate record of what he is saying," I told her. "Do you mind going?"

"No, I'll be glad to go, Mr. Paret," she said quietly.

"He's doing more harm than we thought," I remarked, after a moment. "I've known him for a good many years. He's clever. He's sowing seeds of discontent, starting trouble that will be very serious unless it is headed off."

Miss McCoy made no comment....

Before noon the next day she brought in the speech, neatly typewritten, and laid it on my desk. Looking up and catching her eye just as she was about to withdraw, I was suddenly impelled to ask:—

"Well, what did you think of it?"

She actually flushed, for the first time in my dealings with her betraying a feeling which I am sure she deemed most unprofessional.

"I liked it, Mr. Paret," she replied simply, and I knew that she had understated. It was quite apparent that Krebs had captivated her. I tried not to betray my annoyance.

"Was there a good audience?" I asked,

"Yes," she said.

"How many do you think?"

She hesitated.

"It isn't a very large hall, you know. I should say it would hold about eight hundred people."

"And—it was full?"—I persisted.

"Oh, yes, there were numbers of people standing."

I thought I detected in her tone-although it was not apologetic—a desire to spare my feelings. She hesitated a moment more, and then left the room, closing the door softly behind her...

Presently I took up the pages and began to read. The language was simple and direct, an appeal to common sense, yet the words strangely seemed charged with an emotional power that I found myself resisting. When at length I laid down the sheets I wondered whether it were imagination, or the uncomfortable result of memories of conversations I had had with him.

I was, however, confronted with the task of refuting his arguments: but with exasperating ingenuity, he seemed to have taken the wind out of our sails. It is difficult to answer a man who denies the cardinal principle of American democracy,—that a good mayor or a governor may be made out of a dog-catcher. He called this the Cincinnatus theory: that any American, because he was an American, was fit for any job in the gift of state or city or government, from sheriff to Ambassador to Great Britain. Krebs substituted for this fallacy what may be called the doctrine of potentiality. If we inaugurated and developed a system of democratic education, based on scientific principles, and caught the dog-catcher, young enough, he might become a statesman or thinker or scientist and make his contribution to the welfare and progress of the nation: again, he might not; but he would have had his chance, he would not be in a position to complain.

Here was a doctrine, I immediately perceived, which it would be suicidal to attempt to refute. It ought, indeed, to have been my line. With a growing distaste I began to realize that all there was left for me was to flatter a populace that Krebs, paradoxically, belaboured. Never in the history of American "uplift" had an electorate been in this manner wooed! upbraided for expediency, a proneness to demand immediate results, an unwillingness to think, yes, and an inability to think straight. Such an electorate deserved to be led around by the nose by the Jasons and Dickinsons, the Gorses and the Griersons and the Parets.

Yes, he had mentioned me. That gave me a queer sensation. How is one to handle an opponent who praises one with a delightful irony? We, the Dickinsons, Griersons, Parets, Jasons, etc., had this virtue at least, and it was by no means the least of the virtues,—that we did think. We had a plan, a theory of government, and we carried it out. He was inclined to believe that morality consisted largely, if not wholly, in clear thinking, and not in the precepts of the Sunday-school. That was the trouble with the so-called "reform" campaigns, they were conducted on lines of Sunday-school morality; the people worked themselves up into a sort of revivalist frenzy, an emotional state which, if the truth were told, was thoroughly immoral, unreasonable and hypocritical: like all frenzies, as a matter of course it died down after the campaign was over. Moreover, the American people had shown that they were unwilling to make any sacrifices for the permanent betterment of conditions, and as soon as their incomes began to fall off they turned again to the bosses and capitalists like an abject flock of sheep.

He went on to explain that he wasn't referring now to that part of the electorate known as the labour element, the men who worked with their hands in mills, factories, etc. They had their faults, yet they possessed at least the virtue of solidarity, a willingness to undergo sacrifices in order to advance the standard of conditions; they too had a tenacity of purpose and a plan, such as it was, which the small business men, the clerks lacked....

We must wake up to the fact that we shouldn't get Utopia by turning out Mr. Jason and the highly efficient gentlemen who hired and financed him. It wasn't so simple as that. Utopia was not an achievement after all, but an undertaking, a state of mind, the continued overcoming of resistance by a progressive education and effort. And all this talk of political and financial "wickedness" was rubbish; the wickedness they complained of did not reside merely in individuals it was a social disorder, or rather an order that no longer suited social conditions. If the so-called good citizens would take the trouble to educate themselves, to think instead of allowing their thinking to be done for them they would see that the "evils" which had been published broadcast were merely the symptoms of that disease which had come upon the social body through their collective neglect and indifference. They held up their hands in horror at the spectacle of a commercial, licensed prostitution, they shunned the prostitute and the criminal; but there was none of us, if honest, who would not exclaim when he saw them, "there, but for the Grace of God, go I!" What we still called "sin" was largely the result of lack of opportunity, and the active principle of society as at present organized tended more and more to restrict opportunity. Lack of opportunity, lack of proper nutrition,—these made sinners by the wholesale; made, too, nine-tenths of the inefficient of whom we self- righteously complained. We had a national philosophy that measured prosperity in dollars and cents, included in this measurement the profits of liquor dealers who were responsible for most of our idiots. So long as we set our hearts on that kind of prosperity, so long as we failed to grasp the simple and practical fact that the greatest assets of a nation are healthy and sane and educated, clear-thinking human beings, just so long was prostitution logical, Riverside Franchises, traction deals, Judd Jasons, and the respectable gentlemen who continued to fill their coffers out of the public purse inevitable.

The speaker turned his attention to the "respectable gentlemen" with the full coffers, amongst whom I was by implication included. We had simply succeeded under the rules to which society tacitly agreed. That was our sin. He ventured to say that there were few men in the hall who at the bottom of their hearts did not envy and even honour our success. He, for one, did not deem these "respectable gentlemen" utterly reprehensible; he was sufficiently emancipated to be sorry for us. He suspected that we were not wholly happy in being winners in such a game,—he even believed that we could wish as much as any others to change the game and the prizes. What we represented was valuable energy misdirected and misplaced, and in a reorganized community he would not abolish us, but transform us: transform, at least, the individuals of our type, who were the builders gone wrong under the influence of an outworn philosophy. We might be made to serve the city and the state with the same effectiveness that we had served ourselves.

If the best among the scientists, among the university professors and physicians were willing to labour—and they were—for the advancement of humanity, for the very love of the work and service without disproportionate emoluments, without the accumulation of a wealth difficult to spend, why surely these big business men had been moulded in infancy from no different clay! All were Americans. Instance after instance might be cited of business men and lawyers of ability making sacrifices, giving up their personal affairs in order to take places of honour in the government in which the salary was comparatively small, proving that even these were open to inducements other than merely mercenary ones.

It was unfortunate, he went on, but true, that the vast majority of people of voting age in the United States to-day who thought they had been educated were under the obligation to reeducate themselves. He suggested, whimsically, a vacation school for Congress and all legislative bodies as a starter. Until the fact of the utter inadequacy of the old education were faced, there was little or no hope of solving the problems that harassed us. One thing was certain—that they couldn't be solved by a rule-of-thumb morality. Coincident with the appearance of these new and mighty problems, perhaps in response to them, a new and saner view of life itself was being developed by the world's thinkers, new sciences were being evolved, correlated sciences; a psychology making a truer analysis of human motives, impulses, of human possibilities; an economics and a theory of government that took account of this psychology, and of the vast changes applied science had made in production and distribution. We lived in a new world, which we sought to ignore; and the new education, the new viewpoint was in truth nothing but religion made practical. It had never been thought practical before. The motive that compelled men to work for humanity in science, in medicine, in art—yes, and in business, if we took the right view of it, was the religious motive. The application of religion was to-day extending from the individual to society. No religion that did not fill the needs of both was a true religion.

This meant the development of a new culture, one to be founded on the American tradition of equality of opportunity. But culture was not a weed that grew overnight; it was a leaven that spread slowly and painfully, first inoculating a few who suffered and often died for it, that it might gradually affect the many. The spread of culture implied the recognition of leadership: democratic leadership, but still leadership. Leadership, and the wisdom it implied, did not reside in the people, but in the leaders who sprang from the people and interpreted their needs and longings.... He went on to discuss a part of the programme of the Citizens Union....

What struck me, as I laid down the typewritten sheets, was the extraordinary resemblance between the philosophies of Hermann Krebs and Theodore Watling. Only—Krebs's philosophy was the bigger, held the greater vision of the two; I had reluctantly and rather bitterly to admit it. The appeal of it had even reached and stirred me, whose task was to refute it! Here indeed was something to fight for—perhaps to die for, as he had said: and as I sat there in my office gazing out of the window I found myself repeating certain phrases he had used—the phrase about leadership, for instance. It was a tremendous conception of Democracy, that of acquiescence to developed leadership made responsible; a conception I was compelled to confess transcended Mr. Watling's, loyal as I was to him.... I began to reflect how novel all this was in a political speech—although what I have quoted was in the nature of a preamble. It was a sermon, an educational sermon. Well, that is what sermons always had been,—and even now pretended to be,—educational and stirring, appealing to the emotions through the intellect. It didn't read like the Socialism he used to preach, it had the ring of religion. He had called it religion.

With an effort of the will I turned from this ironical and dangerous vision of a Hugh Paret who might have been enlisted in an inspiring struggle, of a modern yet unregenerate Saul kicking against the pricks, condemned to go forth breathing fire against a doctrine that made a true appeal; against the man I believed I hated just because he had made this appeal. In the act of summoning my counter-arguments I was interrupted by the entrance of Grierson. He was calling on a matter of business, but began to talk about the extracts from Krebs's speech he had read in the Mail and State.

"What in hell is this fellow driving at, Paret?" he demanded. "It sounds to me like the ranting of a lunatic dervish. If he thinks so much of us, and the way we run the town, what's he squawking about?"

I looked at Grierson, and conceived an intense aversion for him. I wondered how I had ever been able to stand him, to work with him. I saw him in a sudden flash as a cunning, cruel bird of prey, a gorged, drab vulture with beady eyes, a resemblance so extraordinary that I wondered I had never remarked it before. For he had the hooked vulture nose, while the pink baldness of his head was relieved by a few scanty tufts of hair.

"The people seem to like what he's got to say," I observed.

"It beats me," said Grierson. "They don't understand a quarter of it— I've been talking to some of 'em. It's their d—d curiosity, I guess. You know how they'll stand for hours around a street fakir."

"It's more than that," I retorted.

Grierson regarded me piercingly.

"Well, we'll put a crimp in him, all right," he said, with a laugh.

I was in an unenviable state of mind when he left me. I had an impulse to send for Miss McCoy and ask her if she had understood what Krebs was "driving at," but for reasons that must be fairly obvious I refrained. I read over again that part of Krebs's speech which dealt with the immediate programme of the Citizens Union. After paying a tribute to Greenhalge as a man of common sense and dependability who would make a good mayor, he went on to explain the principle of the new charter they hoped ultimately to get, which should put the management of the city in the hands of one man, an expert employed by a commission; an expert whose duty it would be to conduct the affairs of the city on a business basis, precisely as those of any efficient corporation were conducted. This plan had already been adopted, with encouraging results, in several smaller cities of the country. He explained in some detail, with statistics, the waste and inefficiency and dishonesty in various departments under the present system, dwelling particularly upon the deplorable state of affairs in the city hospital.

I need not dwell upon this portion of his remarks. Since then text-books and serious periodicals have dealt with these matters thoroughly. They are now familiar to all thinking Americans.

Chapter Twenty-Five

My entrance into the campaign was accompanied by a blare of publicity, and during that fortnight I never picked up a morning or evening newspaper without reading, on the first page, some such headline as "Crowds flock to hear Paret." As a matter of fact, the crowds did flock; but I never quite knew as I looked down from platforms on seas of faces how much of the flocking was spontaneous. Much of it was so, since the struggle had then become sufficiently dramatic to appeal to the larger public imagination that is but occasionally waked; on the other hand, the magic of advertising cannot be underestimated; nor must the existence be ignored of an organized corps of shepherds under the vigilant direction of Mr. Judd Jason, whose duty it was to see that none of our meetings was lacking in numbers and enthusiasm. There was always a demonstrative gathering overflowing the sidewalk in front of the entrance, swaying and cheering in the light of the street lamps, and on the floor within an ample scattering of suspiciously bleary-eyed voters to start the stamping and applauding. In spite of these known facts, the impression of popularity, of repudiation of reform by a large majority of level-headed inhabitants had reassuring and reenforcing effects.

Astute citizens, spectators of the fray—if indeed there were any—might have remarked an unique and significant feature of that campaign: that the usual recriminations between the two great parties were lacking. Mr. Parks, the Republican candidate, did not denounce Mr. MacGuire, the Democratic candidate. Republican and Democratic speakers alike expended their breath in lashing Mr. Krebs and the Citizens Union.

It is difficult to record the fluctuations of my spirit. When I was in the halls, speaking or waiting to speak, I reacted to that phenomenon known as mob psychology, I became self-confident, even exhilarated; and in those earlier speeches I managed, I think, to strike the note for which I strove—the judicial note, suitable to a lawyer of weight and prominence, of deprecation rather than denunciation. I sought to embody and voice a fine and calm sanity at a time when everyone else seemed in danger of losing their heads, and to a large extent achieved it. I had known Mr. Krebs for more than twenty years, and while I did not care to criticise a fellow-member of the bar, I would go so far as to say that he was visionary, that the changes he proposed in government would, if adopted, have grave and far-reaching results: we could not, for instance, support in idleness those who refused to do their share of the work of the world. Mr. Krebs was well-meaning. I refrained from dwelling too long upon him, passing to Mr. Greenhalge, also well-meaning, but a man of mediocre ability who would make a mess of the government of a city which would one day rival New York and Chicago. (Loud cheers.) And I pointed out that Mr. Perry Blackwood had been unable to manage the affairs of the Boyne Street road. Such men, well-intentioned though they might be, were hindrances to progress. This led me naturally to a discussion of the Riverside Franchise and the Traction Consolidation. I was one of those whose honesty and good faith had been arraigned, but I would not stoop to refute the accusations. I dwelt upon the benefits to the city, uniform service, electricity and large comfortable cars instead of rattletrap conveyances, and the development of a large and growing population in the Riverside neighbourhood: the continual extension of lines to suburban districts that enabled hard-worked men to live out of the smoke: I called attention to the system of transfers, the distance a passenger might be conveyed, and conveyed quickly, for the sum of five cents. I spoke of our capitalists as men more sinned against than sinning. Their money was always at the service of enterprises tending to the development of our metropolis.

When I was not in the meetings, however, and especially when in my room at night, I was continually trying to fight off a sense of loneliness that seemed to threaten to overwhelm me. I wanted to be alone, and yet I feared to be. I was aware, in spite of their congratulations on my efforts, of a growing dislike for my associates; and in the appalling emptiness of the moments when my depression was greatest I was forced to the realization that I had no disinterested friend—not one—in whom I could confide. Nancy had failed me; I had scarcely seen Tom Peters that winter, and it was out of the question to go to him. For the third time in my life, and in the greatest crisis of all, I was feeling the need of Something, of some sustaining and impelling Power that must be presented humanly, possessing sympathy and understanding and love.... I think I had a glimpse just a pathetic glimpse—of what the Church might be of human solidarity, comfort and support, of human tolerance, if stripped of the superstition of an ancient science. My tortures weren't of the flesh, but of the mind. My mind was the sheep which had gone astray. Was there no such thing, could there be no such thing as a human association that might at the same time be a divine organism, a fold and a refuge for the lost and divided minds? The source of all this trouble was social....

Then toward the end of that last campaign week, madness suddenly came upon me. I know now how near the breaking point I was, but the immediate cause of my "flying to pieces"—to use a vivid expression—was a speech made by Guptill, one of the Citizens Union candidates for alderman, a young man of a radical type not uncommon in these days, though new to my experience: an educated man in the ultra-radical sense, yet lacking poise and perspective, with a certain brilliance and assurance. He was a journalist, a correspondent of some Eastern newspapers and periodicals. In this speech, which was reported to me—for it did not get into the newspapers—I was the particular object of his attack. Men of my kind, and not the Judd Jasons (for whom there was some excuse) were the least dispensable tools of the capitalists, the greatest menace to civilization. We were absolutely lacking in principle, we were ready at any time to besmirch our profession by legalizing steals; we fouled our nests with dirty fees. Not all that he said was vituperation, for he knew something of the modern theory of the law that legal radicals had begun to proclaim, and even to teach in some tolerant universities.

The next night, in the middle of a prepared speech I was delivering to a large crowd in Kingdom Hall there had been jeers from a group in a corner at some assertion I made. Guptill's accusations had been festering in my mind. The faces of the people grew blurred as I felt anger boiling, rising within me; suddenly my control gave way, and I launched forth into a denunciation of Greenhalge, Krebs, Guptill and even of Perry Blackwood that must have been without license or bounds. I can recall only fragments of my remarks: Greenhalge wanted to be mayor, and was willing to put the stigma of slander on his native city in order to gain his ambition; Krebs had made a failure of his profession, of everything save in bringing shame on the place of his adoption; and on the single occasion heretofore when he had been before the public, in the School Board fiasco, the officials indicted on his supposed evidence had triumphantly been vindicated—, Guptill was gaining money and notoriety out of his spleen; Perry Blackwood was acting out of spite.... I returned to Krebs, declaring that he would be the boss of the city if that ticket were elected, demanding whether they wished for a boss an agitator itching for power and recognition....

I was conscious at the moment only of a wild relief and joy in letting myself go, feelings heightened by the clapping and cheers with which my characterizations were received. The fact that the cheers were mingled with hisses merely served to drive me on. At length, when I had returned to Krebs, the hisses were redoubled, angering me the more because of the evidence they gave of friends of his in my audiences. Perhaps I had made some of these friends for him! A voice shouted out above the uproar:—

"I know about Krebs. He's a d—d sight better man than you." And this started a struggle in a corner of the hall.... I managed, somehow, when the commotion had subsided, to regain my poise, and ended by uttering the conviction that the common sense of the community would repudiate the Citizens Union and all it stood for....

But that night, as I lay awake listening to the street noises and staring at the glint from a street lamp on the brass knob of my bedstead, I knew that I had failed. I had committed the supreme violation of the self that leads inevitably to its final dissolution.... Even the exuberant headlines of the newspapers handed me by the club servant in the morning brought but little relief.

On the Saturday morning before the Tuesday of election there was a conference in the directors' room of the Corn National. The city reeked with smoke and acrid, stale gas, the electric lights were turned on to dispel the November gloom. It was not a cheerful conference, nor a confident one. For the first time in a collective experience the men gathered there were confronted with a situation which they doubted their ability to control, a situation for which there was no precedent. They had to reckon with a new and unsolvable equation in politics and finance,—the independent voter. There was an element of desperation in the discussion. Recriminations passed. Dickinson implied that Gorse with all his knowledge of political affairs ought to have foreseen that something like this was sure to happen, should have managed better the conventions of both great parties. The railroad counsel retorted that it had been as much Dickinson's fault as his. Grierson expressed a regret that I had broken out against the reformers; it had reacted, he said,— and this was just enough to sting me to retaliate that things had been done in the campaign, chiefly through his initiative, that were not only unwise, but might land some of us in the penitentiary if Krebs were elected.

"Well," Grierson exclaimed, "whether he's elected or not, I wouldn't give much now for your chances of getting to the Senate. We can't afford to fly in the face of the dear public."

A tense silence followed this remark. In the street below the rumble of the traffic came to us muffled by the heavy plate-glass windows. I saw Tallant glance at Gorse and Dickinson, and I knew the matter had been decided between themselves, that they had been merely withholding it from me until after election. I was besmirched, for the present at least.

"I think you will do me the justice, gentlemen," I remember saying slowly, with the excessive and rather ridiculous formality of a man who is near the end of his tether, "that the idea of representing you in the Senate was yours, not mine. You begged me to take the appointment against my wishes and my judgment. I had no desire to go to Washington then, I have less to-day. I have come to the conclusion that my usefulness to you is at an end."

I got to my feet. I beheld Miller Gorse sitting impassive, with his encompassing stare, the strongest man of them all. A change of firmaments would not move him. But Dickinson had risen and put his hand on my shoulder. It was the first time I had ever seen him white.

"Hold on, Hugh," he exclaimed, "I guess we're all a little cantankerous today. This confounded campaign has got on our nerves, and we say things we don't mean. You mustn't think we're not grateful for the services you've rendered us. We're all in the same boat, and there isn't a man who's been on our side of this fight who could take a political office at this time. We've got to face that fact, and I know you have the sense to see it, too. I, for one, won't be satisfied until I see you in the Senate. It's where you belong, and you deserve to be there. You understand what the public is, how it blows hot and cold, and in a few years they'll be howling to get us back, if these demagogues win.

"Sure," chimed in Grierson, who was frightened, "that's right, Hugh. I didn't mean anything. Nobody appreciates you more than I do, old man."

Tallant, too, added something, and Berringer,—I've forgotten what. I was tired, too tired to meet their advances halfway. I said that I had a speech to get ready for that night, and other affairs to attend to, and left them grouped together like crestfallen conspirators—all save Miller Gorse, whose pervasive gaze seemed to follow me after I had closed the door.

An elevator took me down to the lobby of the Corn Bank Building. I paused for a moment, aimlessly regarding the streams of humanity hurrying in and out, streaking the white marble floor with the wet filth of the streets. Someone spoke my name. It was Bitter, Judd Jason's "legal" tool, and I permitted myself to be dragged out of the eddies into a quiet corner by the cigar stand.

"Say, I guess we've got Krebs's goat all right, this time," he told me confidentially, in a voice a little above a whisper; "he was busy with the shirt-waist girls last year, you remember, when they were striking. Well, one of 'em, one of the strike leaders, has taken to easy street; she's agreed to send him a letter to-night to come 'round to her room after his meeting, to say that she's sick and wants to see him. He'll go, all right. We'll have some fun, we'll be ready for him. Do you get me? So long. The old man's waiting for me."

It may seem odd that this piece of information did not produce an immediately revolting effect. I knew that similar practices had been tried on Krebs, but this was the first time I had heard of a definite plan, and from a man like Bitter. As I made my way out of the building I had, indeed, a nauseated feeling; Jason's "lawyer" was a dirty little man, smelling of stale cigars, with a blue-black, unshaven face. In spite of the shocking nature of his confidence, he had actually not succeeded in deflecting the current of my thoughts; these were still running over the scene in the directors' room. I had listened to him passively while he had held my buttonhole, and he had detained me but an instant.

When I reached the street I was wondering whether Gorse and Dickinson and the others, Grierson especially, could possibly have entertained the belief that I would turn traitor? I told myself that I had no intention of this. How could I turn traitor? and what would be the object? revenge? The nauseated feeling grew more acute.... Reaching my office, I shut the door, sat down at my desk, summoned my will, and began to jot down random notes for the part of my speech I was to give the newspapers, notes that were mere silly fragments of arguments I had once thought effective. I could no more concentrate on them than I could have written a poem. Gradually, like the smoke that settled down on our city until we lived in darkness at midday, the horror of what Bitter had told me began to pervade my mind, until I was in a state of terror.

Had I, Hugh Paret, fallen to this, that I could stand by consenting to an act which was worse than assassination? Was any cause worth it? Could any cause survive it? But my attempts at reasoning might be likened to the strainings of a wayfarer lost on a mountain side to pick his way in the gathering dusk. I had just that desperate feeling of being lost, and with it went an acute sense of an imminent danger; the ground, no longer firm under my feet, had become a sliding shale sloping toward an unseen precipice. Perhaps, like the wayfarer, my fears were the sharper for the memory of the beauty of the morning on that same mountain, when, filled with vigour, I had gazed on it from the plain below and beheld the sun breaking through the mists....

The necessity of taking some action to avert what I now realized as an infamy pressed upon me, yet in conflict with the pressure of this necessity there persisted that old rebellion, that bitterness which had been growing all these years against the man who, above all others, seemed to me to represent the forces setting at nought my achievements, bringing me to this pass....

I thought of appealing to Leonard Dickinson, who surely, if he knew of it, would not permit this thing to be done; and he was the only man with the possible exception of Miller Gorse who might be able to restrain Judd Jason. But I delayed until after the luncheon hour, when I called up the bank on the telephone, to discover that it was closed. I had forgotten that the day was Saturday. I was prepared to say that I would withdraw from the campaign, warn Krebs myself if this kind of tactics were not suppressed. But I could not get the banker. Then I began to have doubts of Dickinson's power in the matter. Judd Jason had never been tractable, by any means; he had always maintained a considerable independence of the financial powers, and to-day not only financial control, but the dominance of Jason himself was at stake. He would fight for it to the last ditch, and make use of any means. No, it was of no use to appeal to him. What then? Well, there was a reaction, or an attempt at one. Krebs had not been born yesterday, he had avoided the wiles of the politicians heretofore, he wouldn't be fool enough to be taken in now. I told myself that if I were not in a state bordering on a nervous breakdown, I should laugh at such morbid fears, I steadied myself sufficiently to dictate the extract from my speech that was to be published. I was to make addresses at two halls, alternating with Parks, the mayoralty candidate. At four o'clock I went back to my room in the Club to try to get some rest....

Seddon's Hall, the place of my first meeting, was jammed that Saturday night. I went through my speech automatically, as in a dream, the habit of long years asserting itself. And yet—so I was told afterwards—my delivery was not mechanical, and I actually achieved more emphasis, gave a greater impression of conviction than at any time since the night I had lost my control and violently denounced the reformers. By some astonishing subconscious process I had regained my manner, but the applause came to me as from a distance. Not only was my mind not there; it did not seem to be anywhere. I was dazed, nor did I feel—save once— a fleeting surge of contempt for the mob below me with their silly faces upturned to mine. There may have been intelligent expressions among them, but they failed to catch my eye.

I remember being stopped by Grierson as I was going out of the side entrance. He took my hand and squeezed it, and there was on his face an odd, surprised look.

"That was the best yet, Hugh," he said.

I went on past him. Looking back on that evening now, it would almost seem as though the volition of another possessed me, not my own: seemingly, I had every intention of going on to the National Theatre, in which Parks had just spoken, and as I descended the narrow stairway and emerged on the side street I caught sight of my chauffeur awaiting me by the curb.

"I'm not going to that other meeting," I found myself saying. "I'm pretty tired."

"Shall I drive you back to the Club, sir?" he inquired.

"No—I'll walk back. Wait a moment." I entered the ear, turned on the light and scribbled a hasty note to Andrews, the chairman of the meeting at the National, telling him that I was too tired to speak again that night, and to ask one of the younger men there to take my place. Then I got out of the car and gave the note to the chauffeur.

"You're all right, sir?" he asked, with a note of anxiety in his voice. He had been with me a long time.

I reassured him. He started the car, and I watched it absently as it gathered speed and turned the corner. I began to walk, slowly at first, then more and more rapidly until I had gained a breathless pace; in ten minutes I was in West Street, standing in front of the Templar's Hall where the meeting of the Citizens Union west in progress. Now that I had arrived there, doubt and uncertainty assailed me. I had come as it were in spite of myself, thrust onward by an impulse I did not understand, which did not seem to be mine. What was I going to do? The proceeding suddenly appeared to me as ridiculous, tinged with the weirdness of somnambulism. I revolted, walked away, got as far as the corner and stood beside a lamp post, pretending to be waiting for a car. The street lights were reflected in perpendicular, wavy-yellow ribbons on the wet asphalt, and I stood staring with foolish intentness at this phenomenon, wondering how a painter would get the effect in oils. Again I was walking back towards the hall, combating the acknowledgment to myself that I had a plan, a plan that I did not for a moment believe I would carry out. I was shivering.

I climbed the steps. The wide vestibule was empty except for two men who stopped a low-toned conversation to look at me. I wondered whether they recognized me; that I might be recognized was an alarming possibility which had not occurred to me.

"Who is speaking?" I asked.

"Mr. Krebs," answered the taller man of the two.

The hum of applause came from behind the swinging doors. I pushed them open cautiously, passing suddenly out of the cold into the reeking, heated atmosphere of a building packed with human beings. The space behind the rear seats was filled with men standing, and those nearest glanced around with annoyance at the interruption of my entrance. I made my way along the wall, finally reaching a side aisle, whence I could get sight of the platform and the speaker.

I heard his words distinctly, but at first lacked the faculty of stringing them together, or rather of extracting their collective sense. The phrases indeed were set ringing through my mind, I found myself repeating them without any reference to their meaning; I had reached the peculiar pitch of excitement that counterfeits abnormal calm, and all sense of strangeness at being there in that meeting had passed away. I began to wonder how I might warn Krebs, and presently decided to send him a note when he should have finished speaking—but I couldn't make up my mind whether to put my name to the note or not. Of course I needn't have entered the hall at all: I might have sent in my note at the side door.

I must have wished to see Krebs, to hear him speak; to observe, perhaps, the effect on the audience. In spite of my inability to take in what he was saying, I was able to regard him objectively,—objectively, in a restricted sense. I noticed that he had grown even thinner; the flesh had fallen away from under his cheek-bones, and there were sharp, deep, almost perpendicular lines on either side of his mouth. He was emaciated, that was the word. Once in a while he thrust his hand through his dry, ashy hair which was of a tone with the paleness of his face. Such was his only gesture.

He spoke quietly, leaning with one elbow against the side of his reading stand. The occasional pulsations of applause were almost immediately hushed, as though the people feared to lose even a word that should fall from his dry lips. What was it he was talking about? I tried to concentrate my attention, with only partial success. He was explaining the new theory of city government that did not attempt to evade, but dealt frankly with the human needs of to-day, and sought to meet those needs in a positive way... What had happened to me, though I did not realize it, was that I had gradually come under the influence of a tragic spell not attributable to the words I heard, existing independently of them, pervading the spacious hall, weaving into unity dissentient minds. And then, with what seemed a retarded rather than sudden awareness, I knew that he had stopped speaking. Once more he ran his hand through his hair, he was seemingly groping for words that would not come. I was pierced by a strange agony—the amazing source of which, seemed to be a smile on the face of Hermann Krebs, an ineffable smile illuminating the place like a flash of light, in which suffering and tragedy, comradeship and loving kindness—all were mingled. He stood for a moment with that smile on his face—swayed, and would have fallen had it not been for the quickness of a man on the platform behind him, and into whose arms he sank.

In an instant people had risen in their seats, men were hurrying down the aisles, while a peculiar human murmur or wail persisted like an undertone beneath the confusion of noises, striking the very note of my own feelings. Above the heads of those about me I saw Krebs being carried off the platform.... The chairman motioned for silence and inquired if there were a physician in the audience, and then all began to talk at once. The man who stood beside me clutched my arm.

"I hope he isn't dead! Say, did you see that smile? My God, I'll never forget it!"

The exclamation poignantly voiced the esteem in which Krebs was held. As I was thrust along out of the hall by the ebb of the crowd still other expressions of this esteem came to me in fragments, expressions of sorrow and dismay, of a loyalty I had not imagined. Mingled with these were occasional remarks of skeptics shaken, in human fashion, by the suggestion of the inevitable end that never fails to sober and terrify humanity.

"I guess he was a bigger man than we thought. There was a lot of sense in what he had to say."

"There sure was," the companion of this speaker answered.

They spoke of him in the past tense. I was seized and obsessed by the fear that I should never see him again, and at the same moment I realized sharply that this was the one thing I wanted—to see him. I pushed through the people, gained the street, and fairly ran down the alley that led to the side entrance of the hall, where a small group was gathered under the light that hung above the doorway. There stood on the step, a little above the others, a young man in a grey flannel shirt, evidently a mechanic. I addressed him.

"What does the doctor say?"

Before replying he surveyed me with surprise and, I think, with instinctive suspicion of my clothes and bearing.

"What can he say?" he retorted.

"You mean—?" I began.

"I mean Mr. Krebs oughtn't never to have gone into this campaign," he answered, relenting a trifle, perhaps at the tone of my voice. "He knew it, too, and some of us fellows tried to stop him. But we couldn't do nothing with him," he added dejectedly.

"What is—the trouble?" I asked.

"They tell me it's his heart. He wouldn't talk about it."

"When I think of what he done for our union!" exclaimed a thick-set man, plainly a steel worker. "He's just wore himself out, fighting that crooked gang." He stared with sudden aggressiveness at me. "Haven't I seen you some-wheres?" he demanded.

A denial was on my lips when the sharp, sinister strokes of a bell were heard coming nearer.

"It's the ambulance," said the man on the step.

Glancing up the alley beyond the figures of two policemen who had arrived and were holding the people back, I saw the hood of the conveyance as it came to a halt, and immediately a hospital doctor and two assistants carrying a stretcher hurried towards us, and we made way for them to enter. After a brief interval, they were heard coming slowly down the steps inside. By the white, cruel light of the arc I saw Krebs lying motionless.... I laid hold of one of the men who had been on the platform. He did not resent the act, he seemed to anticipate my question.

"He's conscious. The doctors expect him to rally when he gets to the hospital."

I walked back to the Club to discover that several inquiries had been made about me. Reporters had been there, Republican Headquarters had telephoned to know if I were ill. Leaving word that I was not to be disturbed under any circumstances, I went to my room, and spent most of the night in distracted thought. When at last morning came I breakfasted early, searching the newspapers for accounts of the occurrence at Templar's Hall; and the fact that these were neither conspicuous nor circumstantial was in the nature of a triumph of self-control on the part of editors and reporters. News, however sensational, had severely to be condensed in the interest of a cause, and at this critical stage of the campaign to make a tragic hero of Hermann Krebs would have been the height of folly. There were a couple of paragraphs giving the gist of his speech, and a statement at the end that he had been taken ill and conveyed to the Presbyterian Hospital....

The hospital itself loomed up before me that Sunday morning as I approached it along Ballantyne Street, a diluted sunshine washing the extended, businesslike facade of grimy, yellow brick. We were proud of that hospital in the city, and many of our foremost citizens had contributed large sums of money to the building, scarcely ten years old. It had been one of Maude's interests. I was ushered into the reception room, where presently came the physician in charge, a Dr. Castle, one of those quiet-mannered, modern young medical men who bear on their persons the very stamp of efficiency, of the dignity of a scientific profession. His greeting implied that he knew all about me, his presence seemed to increase the agitation I tried not to betray, and must have betrayed.

"Can I do anything for you, Mr. Paret?" he asked.

"I have come to inquire about Mr. Krebs, who was brought here last night, I believe."

I was aware for an instant of his penetrating, professional glance, the only indication of the surprise he must have felt that Hermann Krebs, of all men, should be the object of my solicitude.

"Why, we sent him home this morning. Nineteen twenty six Fowler Street. He wanted to go, and there was no use in his staying."

"He will recover?" I asked.

The physician shook his head, gazing at me through his glasses.

"He may live a month, Mr. Paret, he may die to-morrow. He ought never to have gone into this campaign, he knew he had this trouble. Hepburn warned him three months ago, and there's no man who knows more about the heart than Hepburn."

"Then there's no hope?" I asked.

"Absolutely none. It's a great pity." He added, after a moment, "Mr. Krebs was a remarkable man."

"Nineteen twenty-six Fowler Street?" I repeated.

"Yes."

I held out my hand mechanically, and he pressed it, and went with me to the door.

"Nineteen twenty-six Fowler Street," he repeated...

The mean and sordid aspect of Fowler Street emphasized and seemed to typify my despair, the pungent coal smoke stifled my lungs even as it stifled my spirit. Ugly factories, which were little more than sweatshops, wore an empty, menacing, "Sunday" look, and the faint November sunlight glistened on dirty pavements where children were making a semblance of play. Monotonous rows of red houses succeeded one another, some pushed forward, others thrust back behind little plots of stamped earth. Into one of these I turned. It seemed a little cleaner, better kept, less sordid than the others. I pulled the bell, and presently the door was opened by a woman whose arms were bare to the elbow. She wore a blue-checked calico apron that came to her throat, but the apron was clean, and her firm though furrowed face gave evidences of recent housewifely exertions. Her eyes had the strange look of the cheerfulness that is intimately acquainted with sorrow. She did not seem surprised at seeing me.

"I have come to ask about Mr. Krebs," I told her.

"Oh, yes," she said, "there's been so many here this morning already. It's wonderful how people love him, all kinds of people. No, sir, he don't seem to be in any pain. Two gentlemen are up there now in his room, I mean."

She wiped her arms, which still bore traces of soap-suds, and then, with a gesture natural and unashamed, lifted the corner of her apron to her eyes.

"Do you think I could see him—for a moment?" I asked. "I've known him for a long time."

"Why, I don't know," she said, "I guess so. The doctor said he could see some, and he wants to see his friends. That's not strange—he always did. I'll ask. Will you tell me your name?"

I took out a card. She held it without glancing at it, and invited me in.

I waited, unnerved and feverish, pulsing, in the dark and narrow hall beside the flimsy rack where several coats and hats were hung. Once before I had visited Krebs in that lodging-house in Cambridge long ago with something of the same feelings. But now they were greatly intensified. Now he was dying....

The woman was descending.

"He says he wants to see you, sir," she said rather breathlessly, and I followed her. In the semi-darkness of the stairs I passed the three men who had been with Krebs, and when I reached the open door of his room he was alone. I hesitated just a second, swept by the heat wave that follows sudden shyness, embarrassment, a sense of folly it is too late to avert.

Krebs was propped up with pillows.

"Well, this is good of you," he said, and reached out his hand across the spread. I took it, and sat down beside the shiny oak bedstead, in a chair covered with tobacco-colored plush.

"You feel better?" I asked.

"Oh, I feel all right," he answered, with a smile. "It's queer, but I do."

My eye fell upon the long line of sectional book-cases that lined one side of the room. "Why, you've got quite a library here," I observed.

"Yes, I've managed to get together some good books. But there is so much to read nowadays, so much that is really good and new, a man has the hopeless feeling he can never catch up with it all. A thousand writers and students are making contributions today where fifty years ago there was one."

"I've been following your speeches, after a fashion,—I wish I might have been able to read more of them. Your argument interested me. It's new, unlike the ordinary propaganda of—"

"Of agitators," he supplied, with a smile.

"Of agitators," I agreed, and tried to return his smile. "An agitator who appears to suggest the foundations of a constructive programme and who isn't afraid to criticise the man with a vote as well as the capitalist is an unusual phenomenon."

"Oh, when we realize that we've only got a little time left in which to tell what we think to be the truth, it doesn't require a great deal of courage, Paret. I didn't begin to see this thing until a little while ago. I was only a crude, hot-headed revolutionist. God knows I'm crude enough still. But I began to have a glimmering of what all these new fellows in the universities are driving at." He waved his hand towards the book-cases. "Driving at collectively, I mean. And there are attempts, worthy attempts, to coordinate and synthesize the sciences. What I have been saying is not strictly original. I took it on the stump, that's all. I didn't expect it to have much effect in this campaign, but it was an opportunity to sow a few seeds, to start a sense of personal dissatisfaction in the minds of a few voters. What is it Browning says? It's in Bishop Blougram, I believe. 'When the fight begins within himself, a man's worth something.' It's an intellectual fight, of course."

His words were spoken quietly, but I realized suddenly that the mysterious force which had drawn me to him now, against my will, was an intellectual rather than apparently sentimental one, an intellectual force seeming to comprise within it all other human attractions. And yet I felt a sudden contrition.

"See here, Krebs," I said, "I didn't come here to bother you about these matters, to tire you. I mustn't stay. I'll call in again to see how you are—from time to time."

"But you're not tiring me," he protested, stretching forth a thin, detaining hand. "I don't want to rot, I want to live and think as long as I can. To tell you the truth, Paret, I've been wishing to talk to you—I'm glad you came in."

"You've been wishing to talk to me?" I said.

"Yes, but I didn't expect you'd come in. I hope you won't mind my saying so, under the circumstances, but I've always rather liked you, admired you, even back in the Cambridge days. After that I used to blame you for going out and taking what you wanted, and I had to live a good many years before I began to see that it's better for a man to take what he wants than to take nothing at all. I took what I wanted, every man worth his salt does. There's your great banker friend in New York whom I used to think was the arch-fiend. He took what he wanted, and he took a good deal, but it happened to be good for him. And by piling up his corporations, Ossa on Pelion, he is paving the way for a logical economic evolution. How can a man in our time find out what he does want unless he takes something and gives it a trial?"

"Until he begins to feel that it disagrees with him," I said. "But then," I added involuntarily, "then it may be too late to try something else, and he may not know what to try." This remark of mine might have surprised me had it not been for the feeling—now grown definite—that Krebs had something to give me, something to pass on to me, of all men. Indeed, he had hinted as much, when he acknowledged a wish to talk to me. "What seems so strange," I said, as I looked at him lying back on his pillows, "is your faith that we shall be able to bring order out of all this chaos—your belief in Democracy."

"Democracy's an adventure," he replied, "the great adventure of mankind. I think the trouble in many minds lies in the fact that they persist in regarding it as something to be made safe. All that can be done is to try to make it as safe as possible. But no adventure is safe—life itself is an adventure, and neither is that safe. It's a hazard, as you and I have found out. The moment we try to make life safe we lose all there is in it worth while."

I thought a moment.

"Yes, that's so," I agreed. On the table beside the bed in company with two or three other volumes, lay a Bible. He seemed to notice that my eye fell upon it.

"Do you remember the story of the Prodigal Son?" he asked. "Well, that's the parable of democracy, of self-government in the individual and in society. In order to arrive at salvation, Paret, most of us have to take our journey into a far country."

"A far country!" I exclaimed. The words struck a reminiscent chord.

"We have to leave what seem the safe things, we have to wander and suffer in order to realize that the only true safety lies in development. We have first to cast off the leading strings of authority. It's a delusion that we can insure ourselves by remaining within its walls—we have to risk our lives and our souls. It is discouraging when we look around us to-day, and in a way the pessimists are right when they say we don't see democracy. We see only what may be called the first stage of it; for democracy is still in a far country eating the husks of individualism, materialism. What we see is not true freedom, but freedom run to riot, men struggling for themselves, spending on themselves the fruits of their inheritance; we see a government intent on one object alone—exploitation of this inheritance in order to achieve what it calls prosperity. And God is far away."

"And—we shall turn?" I asked.

"We shall turn or perish. I believe that we shall turn." He fixed his eyes on my face. "What is it," he asked, "that brought you here to me, to-day?"

I was silent.

"The motive, Paret—the motive that sends us all wandering into is divine, is inherited from God himself. And the same motive, after our eyes shall have been opened, after we shall have seen and known the tragedy and misery of life, after we shall have made the mistakes and committed the sins and experienced the emptiness—the same motive will lead us back again. That, too, is an adventure, the greatest adventure of all. Because, when we go back we shall not find the same God—or rather we shall recognize him in ourselves. Autonomy is godliness, knowledge is godliness. We went away cringing, superstitious, we saw everywhere omens and evidences of his wrath in the earth and sea and sky, we burned candles and sacrificed animals in the vain hope of averting scourges and other calamities. But when we come back it will be with a knowledge of his ways, gained at a price,—the price he, too, must have paid—and we shall be able to stand up and look him in the face, and all our childish superstitions and optimisms shall have been burned away."

Some faith indeed had given him strength to renounce those things in life I had held dear, driven him on to fight until his exhausted body failed him, and even now that he was physically helpless sustained him. I did not ask myself, then, the nature of this faith. In its presence it could no more be questioned than the light. It was light; I felt bathed in it. Now it was soft, suffused: but I remembered how the night before in the hall, just before he had fallen, it had flashed forth in a smile and illumined my soul with an ecstasy that yet was anguish....

"We shall get back," I said at length. My remark was not a question—it had escaped from me almost unawares.

"The joy is in the journey," he answered. "The secret is in the search."

"But for me?" I exclaimed.

"We've all been lost, Paret. It would seem as though we have to be."

"And yet you are—saved," I said, hesitating over the word.

"It is true that I am content, even happy," he asserted, "in spite of my wish to live. If there is any secret, it lies, I think, in the struggle for an open mind, in the keeping alive of a desire to know more and more. That desire, strangely enough, hasn't lost its strength. We don't know whether there is a future life, but if there is, I think it must be a continuation of this." He paused. "I told you I was glad you came in— I've been thinking of you, and I saw you in the hall last night. You ask what there is for you—I'll tell you,—the new generation."

"The new generation."

"That's the task of every man and woman who wakes up. I've come to see how little can be done for the great majority of those who have reached our age. It's hard—but it's true. Superstition, sentiment, the habit of wrong thinking or of not thinking at all have struck in too deep, the habit of unreasoning acceptance of authority is too paralyzing. Some may be stung back into life, spurred on to find out what the world really is, but not many. The hope lies in those who are coming after us—we must do for them what wasn't done for us. We really didn't have much of a chance, Paret. What did our instructors at Harvard know about the age that was dawning? what did anybody know? You can educate yourself—or rather reeducate yourself. All this"—and he waved his hand towards his bookshelves—"all this has sprung up since you and I were at Cambridge; if we don't try to become familiar with it, if we fail to grasp the point of view from which it's written, there's little hope for us. Go away from all this and get straightened out, make yourself acquainted with the modern trend in literature and criticism, with modern history, find out what's being done in the field of education, read the modern sciences, especially biology, and psychology and sociology, and try to get a glimpse of the fundamental human needs underlying such phenomena as the labour and woman's movements. God knows I've just begun to get my glimpse, and I've floundered around ever since I left college.... I don't mean to say we can ever see the whole, but we can get a clew, an idea, and pass it on to our children. You have children, haven't you?"

"Yes," I said....

He said nothing—he seemed to be looking out of the window.

"Then the scientific point of view in your opinion hasn't done away with religion?" I asked presently.

"The scientific point of view is the religious point of view," he said earnestly, "because it's the only self-respecting point of view. I can't believe that God intended to make a creature who would not ultimately weigh his beliefs with his reason instead of accepting them blindly. That's immoral, if you like—especially in these days."

"And are there, then, no 'over-beliefs'?" I said, remembering the expression in something I had read.

"That seems to me a relic of the method of ancient science, which was upside down,—a mere confusion with faith. Faith and belief are two different things; faith is the emotion, the steam, if you like, that drives us on in our search for truth. Theories, at a stretch, might be identified with 'over-beliefs' but when it comes to confusing our theories with facts, instead of recognizing them as theories, when it comes to living by 'over-beliefs' that have no basis in reason and observed facts,—that is fatal. It's just the trouble with so much of our electorate to-day—unreasoning acceptance without thought."

"Then," I said, "you admit of no other faculty than reason?"

"I confess that I don't. A great many insights that we seem to get from what we call intuition I think are due to the reason, which is unconsciously at work. If there were another faculty that equalled or transcended reason, it seems to me it would be a very dangerous thing for the world's progress. We'd come to rely on it rather than on ourselves the trouble with the world is that it has been relying on it. Reason is the mind—it leaps to the stars without realizing always how it gets there. It is through reason we get the self-reliance that redeems us."

"But you!" I exclaimed. "You rely on something else besides reason?"

"Yes, it is true," he explained gently, "but that Thing Other-than- Ourselves we feel stirring in us is power, and that power, or the Source of it, seems to have given us our reason for guidance—if it were not so we shouldn't have a semblance of freedom. For there is neither virtue nor development in finding the path if we are guided. We do rely on that power for movement—and in the moments when it is withdrawn we are helpless. Both the power and the reason are God's."

"But the Church," I was moved by some untraced thought to ask, "you believe there is a future for the Church?"

"A church of all those who disseminate truth, foster open-mindedness, serve humanity and radiate faith," he replied—but as though he were speaking to himself, not to me....

A few moments later there was a knock at the door, and the woman of the house entered to say that Dr. Hepburn had arrived. I rose and shook Krebs's hand: sheer inability to express my emotion drove me to commonplaces.

"I'll come in soon again, if I may," I told him.

"Do, Paret," he said, "it's done me good to talk to you—more good than you imagine."

I was unable to answer him, but I glanced back from the doorway to see him smiling after me. On my way down the stairs I bumped into the doctor as he ascended. The dingy brown parlour was filled with men, standing in groups and talking in subdued voices. I hurried into the street, and on the sidewalk stopped face to face with Perry Blackwood.

"Hugh!" he exclaimed. "What are you doing here?"

"I came to inquire for Krebs," I answered. "I've seen him."

"You—you've been talking to him?" Perry demanded.

I nodded. He stared at me for a moment with an astonishment to which I was wholly indifferent. He did not seem to know just how to act.

"Well, it was decent of you, Hugh, I must say. How does he seem?"

"Not at all like—like what you'd expect, in his manner."

"No," agreed Perry agitatedly, "no, he wouldn't. My God, we've lost a big man in him."

"I think we have," I said.

He stared at me again, gave me his hand awkwardly, and went into the house. It was not until I had walked the length of the block that I began to realize what a shock my presence there must have been to him, with his head full of the contrast between this visit and my former attitude. Could it be that it was only the night before I had made a speech against him and his associates? It is interesting that my mind rejected all sense of anomaly and inconsistency. Krebs possessed me; I must have been in reality extremely agitated, but this sense of being possessed seemed a quiet one. An amazing thing had happened—and yet I was not amazed. The Krebs I had seen was the man I had known for many years, the man I had ridiculed, despised and oppressed, but it seemed to me then that he had been my friend and intimate all my life: more than that, I had an odd feeling he had always been a part of me, and that now had begun to take place a merging of personality. Nor could I feel that he was a dying man. He would live on....

I could not as yet sort and appraise, reduce to order the possessions he had wished to turn over to me.

It was noon, and people were walking past me in the watery, diluted sunlight, men in black coats and top hats and women in bizarre, complicated costumes bright with colour. I had reached the more respectable portion of the city, where the churches were emptying. These very people, whom not long ago I would have acknowledged as my own kind, now seemed mildly animated automatons, wax figures. The day was like hundreds of Sundays I had known, the city familiar, yet passing strange. I walked like a ghost through it....

Chapter Twenty-Six

Accompanied by young Dr. Strafford, I went to California. My physical illness had been brief. Dr. Brooke had taken matters in his own hands and ordered an absolute rest, after dwelling at some length on the vicious pace set by modern business and the lack of consideration and knowledge shown by men of affairs for their bodies. There was a limit to the wrack and strain which the human organism could stand. He must of course have suspected the presence of disturbing and disintegrating factors, but he confined himself to telling me that only an exceptional constitution had saved me from a serious illness; he must in a way have comprehended why I did not wish to go abroad, and have my family join me on the Riviera, as Tom Peters proposed. California had been my choice, and Dr. Brooke recommended the climate of Santa Barbara.

High up on the Montecito hills I found a villa beside the gateway of one of the deep canons that furrow the mountain side, and day after day I lay in a chair on the sunny terrace, with a continually recurring amazement at the brilliancy of my surroundings. In the early morning I looked down on a feathery mist hiding the world, a mist presently to be shot with silver and sapphire-blue, dissolved by slow enchantment until there lay revealed the plain and the shimmering ocean with its distant islands trembling in the haze. At sunset my eyes sought the mountains, mountains unreal, like glorified scenery of grand opera, with violet shadows in the wooded canon clefts, and crags of pink tourmaline and ruby against the skies. All day long in the tempered heat flowers blazed around me, insects hummed, lizards darted in and out of the terrace wall, birds flashed among the checkered shadows of the live oaks. That grove of gnarled oaks summoned up before me visions of some classic villa poised above Grecian seas, shining amidst dark foliage, the refuge of forgotten kings. Below me, on the slope, the spaced orange trees were heavy with golden fruit.

After a while, as I grew stronger, I was driven down and allowed to walk on the wide beach that stretched in front of the gay houses facing the sea. Cormorants dived under the long rollers that came crashing in from the Pacific; gulls wheeled and screamed in the soft wind; alert little birds darted here and there with incredible swiftness, leaving tiny footprints across the ribs and furrows of the wet sand. Far to the southward a dark barrier of mountains rose out of the sea. Sometimes I sat with my back against the dunes watching the drag of the outgoing water rolling the pebbles after it, making a gleaming floor for the light to dance.

At first I could not bear to recall the events that had preceded and followed my visit to Krebs that Sunday morning. My illness had begun that night; on the Monday Tom Peters had come to the Club and insisted upon my being taken to his house.... When I had recovered sufficiently there had been rather a pathetic renewal of our friendship. Perry came to see me. Their attitude was one of apprehension not unmixed with wonder; and though they, knew of the existence of a mental crisis, suspected, in all probability, some of the causes of it, they refrained carefully from all comments, contenting themselves with telling me when I was well enough that Krebs had died quite suddenly that Sunday afternoon; that his death—occurring at such a crucial moment—had been sufficient to turn the tide of the election and make Edgar Greenhalge mayor. Thousands who had failed to understand Hermann Krebs, but whom he had nevertheless stirred and troubled, suddenly awoke to the fact that he had had elements of greatness....

My feelings in those first days at Santa Barbara may be likened, indeed, to those of a man who has passed through a terrible accident that has deprived him of sight or hearing, and which he wishes to forget. What I was most conscious of then was an aching sense of loss—an ache that by degrees became a throbbing pain as life flowed back into me, re-inflaming once more my being with protest and passion, arousing me to revolt against the fate that had overtaken me. I even began at moments to feel a fierce desire to go back and take up again the fight from which I had been so strangely removed—removed by the agency of things still obscure. I might get Nancy yet, beat down her resistance, overcome her, if only I could be near her and see her. But even in the midst of these surges of passion I was conscious of the birth of a new force I did not understand, and which I resented, that had arisen to give battle to my passions and desires. This struggle was not mentally reflected as a debate between right and wrong, as to whether I should or should not be justified in taking Nancy if I could get her: it seemed as though some new and small yet dogged intruder had forced an entrance into me, an insignificant pigmy who did not hesitate to bar the pathway of the reviving giant of my desires. These contests sapped my strength. It seemed as though in my isolation I loved Nancy, I missed her more than ever, and the flavour she gave to life.

Then Hermann Krebs began to press himself on me. I use the word as expressive of those early resentful feelings,—I rather pictured him then as the personification of an hostile element in the universe that had brought about my miseries and accomplished my downfall; I attributed the disagreeable thwarting of my impulses to his agency; I did not wish to think of him, for he stood somehow for a vague future I feared to contemplate. Yet the illusion of his presence, once begun, continued to grow upon me, and I find myself utterly unable to describe that struggle in which he seemed to be fighting as against myself for my confidence; that process whereby he gradually grew as real to me as though he still lived—until I could almost hear his voice and see his smile. At moments I resisted wildly, as though my survival depended on it; at other moments he seemed to bring me peace. One day I recalled as vividly as though it were taking place again that last time I had been with him; I seemed once more to be listening to the calm yet earnest talk ranging over so many topics, politics and government, economics and science and religion. I did not yet grasp the synthesis he had made of them all, but I saw them now all focussed in him elements he had drawn from human lives and human experiences. I think it was then I first felt the quickenings of a new life to be born in travail and pain.... Wearied, yet exalted, I sank down on a stone bench and gazed out at the little island of Santa Cruz afloat on the shimmering sea.

I have mentioned my inability to depict the terrible struggle that went on in my soul. It seems strange that Nietzsche—that most ruthless of philosophers to the romantic mind!—should express it for me. "The genius of the heart, from contact with which every man goes away richer, not 'blessed' and overcome,....but richer himself, fresher to himself than before, opened up, breathed upon and sounded by a thawing wind; more uncertain, perhaps, more delicate, more bruised; but full of hopes which as yet lack names, full of a new will and striving, full of a new unwillingness and counterstriving."....

Such was my experience with Hermann Krebs. How keenly I remember that new unwillingness and counter-striving! In spite of the years it has not wholly died down, even to-day....

Almost coincident with these quickenings of which I have spoken was the consciousness of a hunger stronger than the craving for bread and meat, and I began to meditate on my ignorance, on the utter inadequacy and insufficiency of my early education, on my neglect of the new learning during the years that had passed since I left Harvard. And I remembered Krebs's words—that we must "reeducate ourselves." What did I know? A system of law, inherited from another social order, that was utterly unable to cope with the complexities and miseries and injustices of a modern industrial world. I had spent my days in mastering an inadequate and archaic code—why? in order that I might learn how to evade it? This in itself condemned it. What did I know of life? of the shining universe that surrounded me? What did I know of the insect and the flower, of the laws that moved the planets and made incandescent the suns? of the human body, of the human soul and its instincts? Was this knowledge acquired at such cost of labour and life and love by my fellow-men of so little worth to me that I could ignore it? declare that it had no significance for me? no bearing on my life and conduct? If I were to rise and go forward—and I now felt something like a continued impulse, in spite of relaxations and revolts—I must master this knowledge, it must be my guide, form the basis of my creed. I—who never had had a creed, never felt the need of one! For lack of one I had been rudely jolted out of the frail shell I had thought so secure, and stood, as it were, naked and shivering to the storms, staring at a world that was no function of me, after all. My problem, indeed, was how to become a function of it....

I resolved upon a course of reading, but it was a question what books to get. Krebs could have told me, if he had lived. I even thought once of writing Perry Blackwood to ask him to make a list of the volumes in Krebs's little library; but I was ashamed to do this.

Dr. Strafford still remained with me. Not many years out of the medical school, he had inspired me with a liking for him and a respect for his profession, and when he informed me one day that he could no longer conscientiously accept the sum I was paying him, I begged him to stay on. He was a big and wholesome young man, companionable, yet quiet and unobtrusive, watchful without appearing to be so, with the innate as well as the cultivated knowledge of psychology characteristic of the best modern physicians. When

I grew better I came to feel that he had given his whole mind to the study of my case, though he never betrayed it in his conversation.

"Strafford," I said to him one morning with such an air of unconcern as I could muster, "I've an idea I'd like to read a little science. Could you recommend a work on biology?"

I chose biology because I thought he would know something about it.

"Popular biology, Mr. Paret?"

"Well, not too popular," I smiled. "I think it would do me good to use my mind, to chew on something. Besides, you can help me over the tough places."

He returned that afternoon with two books.

"I've been rather fortunate in getting these," he said. "One is fairly elementary. They had it at the library. And the other—" he paused delicately, "I didn't know whether you might be interested in the latest speculations on the subject."

"Speculations?" I repeated.

"Well, the philosophy of it." He almost achieved a blush under his tan. He held out the second book on the philosophy of the organism. "It's the work of a German scientist who stands rather high. I read it last winter, and it interested me. I got it from a clergyman I know who is spending the winter in Santa Barbara."

"A clergyman!"

Strafford laughed. "An 'advanced' clergyman," he explained. "Oh, a lot of them are reading science now. I think it's pretty decent of them."

I looked at Strafford, who towered six feet three, and it suddenly struck me that he might be one of the forerunners of a type our universities were about to turn out. I wondered what he believed. Of one thing I was sure, that he was not in the medical profession to make money. That was a faith in itself.

I began with the elementary work.

"You'd better borrow a Century Dictionary," I said.

"That's easy," he said, and actually achieved it, with the clergyman's aid.

The absorption in which I fought my way through those books may prove interesting to future generations, who, at Sunday-school age, when the fable of Adam and Eve was painfully being drummed into me (without any mention of its application), will be learning to think straight, acquiring easily in early youth what I failed to learn until after forty. And think of all the trouble and tragedy that will have been averted. It is true that I had read some biology at Cambridge, which I had promptly forgotten; it had not been especially emphasized by my instructors as related to life—certainly not as related to religion: such incidents as that of Adam and Eve occupied the religious field exclusively. I had been compelled to commit to memory, temporarily, the matter in those books; but what I now began to perceive was that the matter was secondary compared to the view point of science—and this had been utterly neglected. As I read, I experienced all the excitement of an old- fashioned romance, but of a romance of such significance as to touch the very springs of existence; and above all I was impressed with the integrity of the scientific method—an integrity commensurate with the dignity of man—that scorned to quibble to make out a case, to affirm something that could not be proved.

Little by little I became familiar with the principles of embryonic evolution, ontogeny, and of biological evolution, phylogeny; realized, for the first time, my own history and that of the ancestors from whom I had developed and descended. I, this marvellously complicated being, torn by desires and despairs, was the result of the union of two microscopic cells. "All living things come from the egg," such had been Harvey's dictum. The result was like the tonic of a cold douche. I began to feel cleansed and purified, as though something sticky-sweet which all my life had clung to me had been washed away. Yet a question arose, an insistent question that forever presses itself on the mind of man; how could these apparently chemical and mechanical processes, which the author of the book contented himself with recording, account for me? The spermia darts for the egg, and pierces it; personal history begins. But what mysterious shaping force is it that repeats in the individual the history of the race, supervises the orderly division of the cells, by degrees directs the symmetry, sets aside the skeleton and digestive tract and supervises the structure?

I took up the second book, that on the philosophy of the organism, to read in its preface that a much-to-be-honoured British nobleman had established a foundation of lectures in a Scotch University for forwarding the study of a Natural Theology. The term possessed me. Unlike the old theology woven of myths and a fanciful philosophy of the decadent period of Greece, natural theology was founded on science itself, and scientists were among those who sought to develop it. Here was a synthesis that made a powerful appeal, one of the many signs and portents of a new era of which I was dimly becoming cognizant; and now that I looked for signs, I found them everywhere, in my young Doctor, in Krebs, in references in the texts; indications of a new order beginning to make itself felt in a muddled, chaotic human world, which might—which must have a parallel with the order that revealed itself in the egg! Might not both, physical and social, be due to the influence of the same invisible, experimenting, creating Hand?

My thoughts lingered lovingly on this theology so well named "natural," on its conscientiousness, its refusal to affirm what it did not prove, on its lack of dogmatic dictums and infallible revelations; yet it gave me the vision of a new sanction whereby man might order his life, a sanction from which was eliminated fear and superstition and romantic hope, a sanction whose doctrines—unlike those of the sentimental theology—did not fly in the face of human instincts and needs. Nor was it a theology devoid of inspiration and poetry, though poetry might be called its complement. With all that was beautiful and true in the myths dear to mankind it did not conflict, annulling only the vicious dogmatism of literal interpretation. In this connection I remembered something that Krebs had said—in our talk about poetry and art,—that these were emotion, religion expressed by the tools reason had evolved. Music, he had declared, came nearest to the cry of the human soul....

That theology cleared for faith an open road, made of faith a reasonable thing, yet did not rob it of a sense of high adventure; cleansed it of the taints of thrift and selfish concern. In this reaffirmation of vitalism there might be a future, yes, an individual future, yet it was far from the smug conception of salvation. Here was a faith conferred by the freedom of truth; a faith that lost and regained itself in life; it was dynamic in its operation; for, as Lessing said, the searching after truth, and not its possession, gives happiness to man. In the words of an American scientist, taken from his book on Heredity, "The evolutionary idea has forced man to consider the probable future of his own race on earth and to take measures to control that future, a matter he had previously left largely to fate."

Here indeed was another sign of the times, to find in a strictly scientific work a sentence truly religious! As I continued to read these works, I found them suffused with religion, religion of a kind and quality I had not imagined. The birthright of the spirit of man was freedom, freedom to experiment, to determine, to create—to create himself, to create society in the image of God! Spiritual creation the function of cooperative man through the coming ages, the task that was to make him divine. Here indeed was the germ of a new sanction, of a new motive, of a new religion that strangely harmonized with the concepts of the old—once the dynamic power of these was revealed.

I had been thinking of my family—of my family in terms of Matthew—and yet with a growing yearning that embraced them all. I had not informed Maude of my illness, and I had managed to warn Tom Peters not to do so. I had simply written her that after the campaign I had gone for a rest to California; yet in her letters to me, after this information had reached her, I detected a restrained anxiety and affection that troubled me. Sequences of words curiously convey meanings and implications that transcend their literal sense, true thoughts and feelings are difficult to disguise even in written speech. Could it be possible after all that had happened that Maude still loved me? I continually put the thought away from me, but continually it returned to haunt me. Suppose Maude could not help loving me, in spite of my weaknesses and faults, even as I loved Nancy in spite of hers? Love is no logical thing.

It was Matthew I wanted, Matthew of whom I thought, and trivial, long- forgotten incidents of the past kept recurring to me constantly. I still received his weekly letters; but he did not ask why, since I had taken a vacation, I had not come over to them. He represented the medium, the link between Maude and me that no estrangement, no separation could break.

All this new vision of mine was for him, for the coming generation, the soil in which it must be sown, the Americans of the future. And who so well as Matthew, sensitive yet brave, would respond to it? I wished not only to give him what I had begun to grasp, to study with him, to be his companion and friend, but to spare him, if possible, some of my own mistakes and sufferings and punishments. But could I go back? Happy coincidences of desires and convictions had been so characteristic of that other self I had been struggling to cast off: I had so easily been persuaded, when I had had a chance of getting Nancy, that it was the right thing to do! And now, in my loneliness, was I not growing just as eager to be convinced that it was my duty to go back to the family which in the hour of self-sufficiency I had cast off? I had believed in divorce then—why not now? Well, I still believed in it. I had thought of a union with Nancy as something that would bring about the "self-realization that springs from the gratification of a great passion,"—an appealing phrase I had read somewhere. But, it was at least a favourable symptom that I was willing now to confess that the "self-realization" had been a secondary and sentimental consideration, a rosy, self-created halo to give a moral and religious sanction to my desire. Was I not trying to do that very thing now? It tortured me to think so; I strove to achieve a detached consideration of the problem,—to arrive at length at a thought that seemed illuminating: that the it "wrongness" or "rightness," utility and happiness of all such unions depend upon whether or not they become a part of the woof and warp of the social fabric; in other words, whether the gratification of any particular love by divorce and remarriage does or does not tend to destroy a portion of that fabric. Nancy certainly would have been justified in divorce. It did not seem in the retrospect that I would have been: surely not if, after I had married Nancy, I had developed this view of life that seemed to me to be the true view. I should have been powerless to act upon it. But the chances were I should not have developed it, since it would seem that any salvation for me at least must come precisely through suffering, through not getting what I wanted. Was this equivocating?

My mistake had been in marrying Maude instead of Nancy—a mistake largely due to my saturation with a false idea of life. Would not the attempt to cut loose from the consequences of that mistake in my individual case have been futile? But there was a remedy for it—the remedy Krebs had suggested: I might still prevent my children from making such a mistake, I might help to create in them what I might have been, and thus find a solution for myself. My errors would then assume a value.

But the question tortured me: would Maude wish it? Would it be fair to her if she did not? By my long neglect I had forfeited the right to go. And would she agree with my point of view if she did permit me to stay? I had less concern on this score, a feeling that that development of hers, which once had irritated me, was in the same direction as my own....

I have still strangely to record moments when, in spite of the aspirations I had achieved, of the redeeming vision I had gained, at the thought of returning to her I revolted. At such times recollections came into my mind of those characteristics in her that had seemed most responsible for my alienation.... That demon I had fed so mightily still lived. By what right—he seemed to ask—had I nourished him all these years if now I meant to starve him? Thus sometimes he defied me, took on Protean guises, blustered, insinuated, cajoled, managed to make me believe that to starve him would be to starve myself, to sap all there was of power in me. Let me try and see if I could do it! Again he whispered, to what purpose had I gained my liberty, if now I renounced it? I could not live in fetters, even though the fetters should be self- imposed. I was lonely now, but I would get over that, and life lay before me still.

Fierce and tenacious, steel in the cruelty of his desires, fearful in the havoc he had wrought, could he be subdued? Foiled, he tore and rent me....

One morning I rode up through the shady canon, fragrant with bay, to the open slopes stained smoky-blue by the wild lilac, where the twisted madrona grows. As I sat gazing down on tiny headlands jutting out into a vast ocean my paralyzing indecision came to an end. I turned my horse down the trail again. I had seen at last that life was bigger than I, bigger than Maude, bigger than our individual wishes and desires. I felt as though heavy shackles had been struck from me. As I neared the house I spied my young doctor in the garden path, his hands in his pockets watching a humming-bird poised over the poppies. He greeted me with a look that was not wholly surprise at my early return, that seemed to have in it something of gladness.

"Strafford," I said, "I've made up my mind to go to Europe."

"I have been thinking for some time, Mr. Paret," he replied, "that a sea- voyage is just what you need to set you on your feet."

I started eastward the next morning, arriving in New York in time to catch one of the big liners sailing for Havre. On my way across the continent I decided to send a cable to Maude at Paris, since it were only fair to give her an opportunity to reflect upon the manner in which she would meet the situation. Save for an impatience which at moments I restrained with difficulty, the moods that succeeded one another as I journeyed did not differ greatly from those I had experienced in the past month. I was alternately exalted and depressed; I hoped and doubted and feared; my courage, my confidence rose and fell. And yet I was aware of the nascence within me of an element that gave me a stability I had hitherto lacked: I had made my decision, and I felt the stronger for it.

It was early in March. The annual rush of my countrymen and women for foreign shores had not as yet begun, the huge steamer was far from crowded. The faint throbbing of her engines as she glided out on the North River tide found its echo within me as I leaned on the heavy rail and watched the towers of the city receding in the mist; they became blurred and ghostlike, fantastic in the grey distance, sad, appealing with a strange beauty and power. Once the sight of them, sunlit, standing forth sharply against the high blue of American skies, had stirred in me that passion for wealth and power of which they were so marvellously and uniquely the embodiment. I recalled the bright day of my home-coming with Maude, when she too had felt that passion drawing me away from her, after the briefest of possessions.... Well, I had had it, the power. I had stormed and gained entrance to the citadel itself. I might have lived here in New York, secure, defiant of a veering public opinion that envied while it strove to sting. Why was I flinging it all away? Was this a sudden resolution of mine, forced by events, precipitated by a failure to achieve what of all things on earth I had most desired? or was it the inevitable result of the development of the Hugh Paret of earlier days, who was not meant for that kind of power?

The vibration of the monster ship increased to a strong, electric pulsation, the water hummed along her sides, she felt the swell of the open sea. A fine rain began to fall that hid the land—yes, and the life I was leaving. I made my way across the glistening deck to the saloon where, my newspapers and periodicals neglected, I sat all the morning beside a window gazing out at the limited, vignetted zone of waters around the ship. We were headed for the Old World. The wind rose, the rain became pelting, mingling with the spume of the whitecaps racing madly past: within were warmth and luxury, electric lights, open fires, easy chairs, and men and women reading, conversing as unconcernedly as though the perils of the deep had ceased to be. In all this I found an impelling interest; the naive capacity in me for wonder, so long dormant, had been marvellously opened up once more. I no longer thought of myself as the important man of affairs; and when in the progress of the voyage I was accosted by two or three men I had met and by others who had heard of me it was only to feel amazement at the remoteness I now felt from a world whose realities were stocks and bonds, railroads and corporations and the detested new politics so inimical to the smooth conduct of "business."

It all sounded like a language I had forgotten.

It was not until near the end of the passage that we ran out of the storm. A morning came when I went on deck to survey spaces of a blue and white sea swept by the white March sunlight; to discern at length against the horizon toward which we sped a cloud of the filmiest and most delicate texture and design. Suddenly I divined that the cloud was France! Little by little, as I watched, it took on substance. I made out headlands and cliffs, and then we were coasting beside them. That night I should be in Paris with Maude. My bag was packed, my steamer trunk closed. I strayed about the decks, in and out of the saloons, wondering at the indifference of other passengers who sat reading in steamer-chairs or wrote last letters to be posted at Havre. I was filled with impatience, anticipation, yes, with anxiety concerning the adventure that was now so imminent; with wavering doubts. Had I done the wisest thing after all? I had the familiar experience that often comes just before reunion after absence of recalling intimate and forgotten impressions of those whom I was about to see again the tones of their voices, little gestures....

How would they receive me?

The great ship had slowed down and was entering the harbour, carefully threading her way amongst smaller craft, the passengers lining the rails and gazing at the animated scene, at the quaint and cheerful French city bathed in sunlight.... I had reached the dock and was making my way through the hurrying and shifting groups toward the steamer train when I saw Maude. She was standing a little aside, scanning the faces that passed her.

I remember how she looked at me, expectantly, yet timidly, almost fearfully. I kissed her.

"You've come to meet me!" I exclaimed stupidly. "How are the children?"

"They're very well, Hugh. They wanted to come, too, but I thought it better not."

Her restraint struck me as extraordinary; and while I was thankful for the relief it brought to a situation which might have been awkward, I was conscious of resenting it a little. I was impressed and puzzled. As I walked along the platform beside her she seemed almost a stranger: I had difficulty in realizing that she was my wife, the mother of my children. Her eyes were clear, more serious than I recalled them, and her physical as well as her moral tone seemed to have improved. Her cheeks glowed with health, and she wore a becoming suit of dark blue.

"Did you have a good trip, Hugh?" she asked.

"Splendid," I said, forgetting the storm. We took our seats in an empty compartment. Was she glad to see me? She had come all the way from Paris to meet me! All the embarrassment seemed to be on my side. Was this composure a controlled one or had she indeed attained to the self- sufficiency her manner and presence implied? Such were the questions running through my head.

"You've really liked Paris?" I asked.

"Yes, Hugh, and it's been very good for us all. Of course the boys like America better, but they've learned many things they wouldn't have learned at home; they both speak French, and Biddy too. Even I have improved."

"I'm sure of it," I said.

She flushed.

"And what else have you been doing?"

"Oh, going to galleries. Matthew often goes with me. I think he quite appreciates the pictures. Sometimes I take him to the theatre, too, the Francais. Both boys ride in the Bois with a riding master. It's been rather a restricted life for them, but it won't have hurt them. It's good discipline. We have little excursions in an automobile on fine days to Versailles and other places of interest around Paris, and Matthew and I have learned a lot of history. I have a professor of literature from the Sorbonne come in three times a week to give me lessons."

"I didn't know you cared for literature."

"I didn't know it either." She smiled. "Matthew loves it. Monsieur Despard declares he has quite a gift for language."

Maude had already begun Matthew's education!

"You see a few people?" I inquired.

"A few. And they have been very kind to us. The Buffons, whom I met at Etretat, and some of their friends, mostly educated French people."

The little railway carriage in which we sat rocked with speed as we flew through the French landscape. I caught glimpses of solid, Norman farm buildings, of towers and keeps and delicate steeples, and quaint towns; of bare poplars swaying before the March gusts, of green fields ablaze in the afternoon sun. I took it all in distractedly. Here was Maude beside me, but a Maude I had difficulty in recognizing, whom I did not understand: who talked of a life she had built up for herself and that seemed to satisfy her; one with which I had nothing to do. I could not tell how she regarded my re-intrusion. As she continued to talk, a feeling that was almost desperation grew upon me. I had things to say to her, things that every moment of this sort of intercourse was making more difficult. And I felt, if I did not say them now, that perhaps I never should: that now or never was the appropriate time, and to delay would be to drift into an impossible situation wherein the chance of an understanding would be remote.

There was a pause. How little I had anticipated the courage it would take to do this thing! My blood was hammering.

"Maude," I said abruptly, "I suppose you're wondering why I came over here."

She sat gazing at me, very still, but there came into her eyes a frightened look that almost unnerved me. She seemed to wish to speak, to be unable to. Passively, she let my hand rest on hers.

"I've been thinking a great deal during the last few months," I went on unsteadily. "And I've changed a good many of my ideas—that is, I've got new ones, about things I never thought of before. I want to say, first, that I do not put forth any claim to come back into your life. I know I have forfeited any claim. I've neglected you, and I've neglected the children. Our marriage has been on a false basis from the start, and I've been to blame for it. There is more to be said about the chances for a successful marriage in these days, but I'm not going to dwell on that now, or attempt to shoulder off my shortcomings on my bringing up, on the civilization in which we have lived. You've tried to do your share, and the failure hasn't been your fault. I want to tell you first of all that I recognize your right to live your life from now on, independently of me, if you so desire. You ought to have the children—" I hesitated a moment. It was the hardest thing I had to say. "I've never troubled myself about them, I've never taken on any responsibility in regard to their bringing up."

"Hugh!" she cried.

"Wait—I've got more to tell you, that you ought to know. I shouldn't be here to-day if Nancy Durrett had consented to—to get a divorce and marry me. We had agreed to that when this accident happened to Ham, and she went back to him. I have to tell you that I still love her—I can't say how much, or define my feelings toward her now. I've given up all idea of her. I don't think I'd marry her now, even if I had the chance, and you should decide to live away from me. I don't know. I'm not so sure of myself as I once was. The fact is, Maude, circumstances have been too much for me. I've been beaten. And I'm not at all certain that it wasn't a cowardly thing for me to come back to you at all."

I felt her hand trembling under mine, but I had not the courage to look at her. I heard her call my name again a little cry, the very poignancy of pity and distress. It almost unnerved me.

"I knew that you loved her, Hugh," she said. "It was only—only a little while after you married me that I found it out. I guessed it—women do guess such things—long before you realized it yourself. You ought to have married her instead of me. You would have been happier with her."

I did not answer.

"I, too, have thought a great deal," she went on, after a moment. "I began earlier than you, I had to." I looked up suddenly and saw her smiling at me, faintly, through her tears. "But I've been thinking more, and learning more since I've been over here. I've come to see that that our failure hasn't been as much your fault as I once thought, as much as you yourself declare. You have done me a wrong, and you've done the children a wrong. Oh, it is frightful to think how little I knew when I married you, but even then I felt instinctively that you didn't love me as I deserved to be loved. And when we came back from Europe I knew that I couldn't satisfy you, I couldn't look upon life as you saw it, no matter how hard I tried. I did try, but it wasn't any use. You'll never know how much I've suffered all these years.

"I have been happier here, away from you, with the children; I've had a chance to be myself. It isn't that I'm—much. It isn't that I don't need guidance and counsel and—sympathy. I've missed those, but you've never given them to me, and I've been learning more and more to do without them. I don't know why marriage should suddenly have become such a mockery and failure in our time, but I know that it is, that ours hasn't been such an exception as I once thought. I've come to believe that divorce is often justified."

"It is justified so far as you are concerned, Maude," I replied. "It is not justified for me. I have forfeited, as I say, any rights over you. I have been the aggressor and transgressor from the start. You have been a good wife and a good mother, you have been faithful, I have had absolutely nothing to complain of."

"Sometimes I think I might have tried harder," she said. "At least I might have understood better. I was stupid. But everything went wrong. And I saw you growing away from me all the time, Hugh, growing away from the friends who were fond of you, as though you were fading in the distance. It wasn't wholly because—because of Nancy that I left you. That gave me an excuse—an excuse for myself. Long before that I realized my helplessness, I knew that whatever I might have done was past doing."

"Yes, I know," I assented.

We sat in silence for a while. The train was skirting an ancient town set on a hill, crowned with a castle and a Gothic church whose windows were afire in the setting sun.

"Maude," I said, "I have not come to plead, to appeal to your pity as against your judgment and reason. I can say this much, that if I do not love you, as the word is generally understood, I have a new respect for you, and a new affection, and I think that these will grow. I have no doubt that there are some fortunate people who achieve the kind of mutual love for which it is human to yearn, whose passion is naturally transmuted into a feeling that may be even finer, but I am inclined to think, even in such a case, that some effort and unselfishness are necessary. At any rate, that has been denied to us, and we can never know it from our own experience. We can only hope that there is such a thing,—yes, and believe in it and work for it."

"Work for it, Hugh?" she repeated.

"For others—for our children. I have been thinking about the children a great deal in the last few months especially about Matthew."

"You always loved him best," she said.

"Yes," I admitted. "I don't know why it should be so. And in spite of it, I have neglected him, neglected them, failed to appreciate them all. I did not deserve them. I have reproached myself, I have suffered for it, not as much as I deserved. I came to realize that the children were a bond between us, that their existence meant something greater than either of us. But at the same time I recognized that I had lost my right over them, that it was you who had proved yourself worthy.... It was through the children that I came to think differently, to feel differently toward you. I have come to you to ask your forgiveness."

"Oh, Hugh!" she cried.

"Wait," I said.... "I have come to you, through them. I want to say again that I should not be here if I had obtained my desires. Yet there is more to it than that. I think I have reached a stage where I am able to say that I am glad I didn't obtain them. I see now that this coming to you was something I have wanted to do all along, but it was the cowardly thing to do, after I had failed, for it was not as though I had conquered the desires, the desires conquered me. At any rate, I couldn't come to you to encumber you, to be a drag upon you. I felt that I must have something to offer you. I've got a plan, Maude, for my life, for our lives. I don't know whether I can make a success of it, and you are entitled to decline to take the risk. I don't fool myself that it will be all plain sailing, that there won't be difficulties and discouragements. But I'll promise to try."

"What is it?" she asked, in a low voice. "I—I think I know."

"Perhaps you have guessed it. I am willing to try to devote what is left of my life to you and to them. And I need your help. I acknowledge it. Let us try to make more possible for them the life we have missed."

"The life we have missed!" she said.

"Yes. My mistakes, my failures, have brought us to the edge of a precipice. We must prevent, if we can, those mistakes and failures for them. The remedy for unhappy marriages, for all mistaken, selfish and artificial relationships in life is a preventive one. My plan is that we try to educate ourselves together, take advantage of the accruing knowledge that is helping men and women to cope with the problems, to think straight. We can then teach our children to think straight, to avoid the pitfalls into which we have fallen."

I paused. Maude did not reply. Her face was turned away from me, towards the red glow of the setting sun above the hills.

"You have been doing this all along, you have had the vision, the true vision, while I lacked it, Maude. I offer to help you. But if you think it is impossible for us to live together, if you believe my feeling toward you is not enough, if you don't think I can do what I propose, or if you have ceased to care for me—"

She turned to me with a swift movement, her eyes filled with tears.

"Oh, Hugh, don't say any more. I can't stand it. How little you know, for all your thinking. I love you, I always have loved you. I grew to be ashamed of it, but I'm not any longer. I haven't any pride any more, and I never want to have it again."

"You're willing to take me as I am,—to try?" I said.

"Yes," she answered, "I'm willing to try." She smiled at me. "And I have more faith than you, Hugh. I think we'll succeed."....

At nine o'clock that night, when we came out through the gates of the big, noisy station, the children were awaiting us. They had changed, they had grown. Biddy kissed me shyly, and stood staring up at me.

"We'll take you out to-morrow and show you how we can ride," said Moreton.

Matthew smiled. He stood very close to me, with his hand through my arm.

"You're going to stay, father?" he asked.

"I'm going to stay, Matthew," I answered, "until we all go back to America."....

About the Publisher

As part of our mission to publish great works of literary fiction and nonfiction, Sheba Blake Publishing Corp. is extremely dedicated to bringing to the forefront the amazing works of long dead and truly talented authors.

instagram.com/shebablake

twitter.com/shebablake

facebook.com/shebablakepublishing

Printed in June 2023
by Rotomail Italia S.p.A., Vignate (MI) - Italy